MW00655237

DEAD
MONEY

DEAD MONEY

A NOVEL

JAKOB KERR

BANTAM BOOKS
New York

Copyright © 2025 by Jakob Kerr

Published in the United States by Bantam Books,
an imprint of Random House, a division of
Penguin Random House LLC, New York.

BANTAM & B colophon are registered trademarks
of Penguin Random House LLC.

LIBRARY OF CONGRESS CATALOGING-IN-PUBLICATION DATA
Names: Kerr, Jakob, author.
Title: Dead money : a novel / Jakob Kerr.
Description: First edition. | New York : Bantam Books, 2025.
Identifiers: LCCN 2024033539 (print) | LCCN 2024033540 (ebook) |
ISBN 9780593726709 (hardcover) | ISBN 9780593726716 (ebook)
Subjects: LCGFT: Novels. | Detective and mystery fiction.
Classification: LCC PS3611.E763555 D43 2025 (print) |
LCC PS3611.E763555 (ebook) | DDC 813/.6—dc23/eng/20240724
LC record available at https://lccn.loc.gov/2024033539
LC ebook record available at https://lccn.loc.gov/2024033540

Printed in the United States of America on acid-free paper

randomhousebooks.com

1st Printing

First Edition

Book design by Alexis Flynn

For Meghan, Teddy, and Sam

DEAD
MONEY

PROLOGUE

Tony found the body on a Tuesday.

The shift began like any other. Tony rolled his custodial station across the carpet, wheels echoing in the deserted office.

Standing desks lurked to either side, chairs abandoned. Whiteboards sat clustered with unfinished ideas, Post-its scattered in rainbows of paper buckshot. The conference rooms were shadowed and vacant.

The designer sofas were unoccupied.

The craft beer taps were covered.

The ping-pong tables were pingless.

The arcade games were unplugged, the movie theater shuttered, the alternative-milk frothers cleaned and dormant.

Even the ball pit was empty.

Tony was surrounded by black Apple monitors. Their quiet faces stared back at him, eerie and reflective in the soft darkness.

It was 2:36 A.M.

During the day, Tony imagined Journy's headquarters abuzz with energy, an idealistic thrum of twenty-something tech workers.

But now the building was a mausoleum. There was something distinctly ominous about the quiet of an office at night. The silence felt heavier in a place that was normally full of life.

Mind blank, body on autopilot, Tony stepped to the next workstation and executed his straightforward list of tasks.

One, push the chair under the desk.

Two, clean up leftover food. Empty mason jars of kombucha, crumbs of Journy's house-made vegan cookies.

Three, and most important: Don't touch anything else.

Tony moved to the desk and grabbed a plate. Its porcelain was smeared with the remnants of chicken parm. Tony shook it into the trash can on his station. He dropped the plate and utensils into a plastic tub. Then he glanced at the rest of the desk.

The gargantuan monitor was caked with dust, edges festooned with nonsensical stickers. A heap of papers was strewn across the composite work surface. Even the chair (a fuselage of webbed plastic that cost $2800—Tony had looked it up) was askew, one of its many adjustment knobs dangling from the socket.

The scene was crying out for Tony's custodial services—even a single squeeze of the spray bottle would work wonders.

But Tony didn't give it a second look. Methodically, he moved back to his cart and rolled on to the next.

One-forty-one down. One-seventy to go.

Journy's facilities team was adamant about the rules for Tony and his colleagues. Push in the chair. Clean up the food. Otherwise, don't touch a thing.

Nothing.

Don't touch any papers on the desks, even if wadded up—they could be vital technological specs.

Don't adjust a chair's settings when you move it back into place—software engineers are *incredibly* specific about their ergonomics.

And under no circumstances, never, ever, even *think* about touching a keyboard.

Not that Tony cared. He'd worked in every type of office there was. Most of them had peculiarities. If anything, Journy's rules just made the job easier.

When Tony had started working Journy's offices, he'd assumed it was the same as the rest of the startups. Slick app, cartoony logo, rich white kid at the top.

But Tony had learned that Journy was a little different from the others. It was flush with cash—even by San Francisco standards. Tony had worked in a lot of nice tech offices, but Journy took the opulence to another level.

More surprising was the way that Journy had seeped into Tony's everyday landscape. He saw the company's green go-karts and bikes all over the Bay Area—even out by his sister's place in Fremont. Their ads were inescapable: on BART, on TV, on the Web. And Tony had never met Journy's CEO, but he saw the guy's face everywhere. Magazine covers, local news, and, of course, pasted all over this very office.

None of that really mattered to Tony's job, of course. But he wondered if the company would stick around longer than some of the others.

One-sixty-two down. One-forty-nine to go.

Journy's headquarters were organized in the open-plan style that had become default in San Francisco. It was an airy, post-industrial warehouse space. Workstations were placed in long, orderly rows. The layout was all right angles and straight lines, easy to navigate. Tony took a familiar path as he rolled through the desks, completing his tasks at an unhurried pace.

Empty a beer glass.

Scrape kale chips off a desk.

Push in the chair.

Next.

After the desks Tony moved to the kitchen on his floor. He took a rag over the broad recycled-glass counters, swiping it between the gleaming taps, past the bowls of fresh fruit, over the Italian espresso machine. He dusted the enormous pantry shelves, bins full of gourmet snacks with whimsical, Journy-branded names: "Go Your Own Way Granola," "Off the Beaten Trail Mix."

Tony checked his watch: 3:25 A.M. Time to move.

Tony pushed his station down a wide hallway, heading toward his final task of the night. Journy's offices were organized around an atrium that ran vertically through the center of the building. Tony moved along one edge of the atrium, glancing over the waist-high glass that ran alongside. From here he could look down into the central courtyard.

During daylight hours the courtyard was the hub of Journy's headquarters: a broad plaza filled with tables, plants, artwork, and the steady buzz of optimistic conversation.

Now, like the rest of the building, the atrium slumbered. A full moon filtered through the retractable glass ceiling, bathing the courtyard in an ethereal glow. Tony looked for his colleagues on the lower floors but saw no one.

Tony moved to a back corner of the building, pushing his station toward a single, inconspicuous elevator. The elevator was plain and unmarked, as though it'd been purposefully tucked out of the way. The only sign of its important destination was the portrait that hung next to it.

Trevor Canon's face stared back at Tony in the dark.

Canon was the CEO and founder of Journy. If the magazine covers were to be believed, he was the visionary force behind the hottest startup on the planet. Every single piece of the company fell under Canon's domain, from the desks and taps that Tony had just spent two hours cleaning out to the green bicycles that now dotted his sister's neighborhood. All of it traced back to one man. Even the ping-pong balls, Tony thought.

Canon's portrait expression was stoic, his black hair cut short. His skin was pale and ghostly, calling attention to his bright blue eyes. They beamed out from the portrait with a strange intensity.

Tony found himself staring at the portrait for longer than he intended; he'd always found it unsettling. Canon's eyes felt like Tony's only companion in the deserted office, their cold, iridescent blue cutting like ice through the surrounding darkness.

Tony checked his watch. It was 3:30 exactly.

He pressed the call button. After a moment the doors opened and

Tony rolled his station inside, grabbing a badge that dangled at his waist. The badge was part of Tony's additional security protocol. It only activated the elevator for a narrow sliver of time: 3:30 A.M. to 3:35 A.M.

Tony swiped the badge over a black card reader. It flashed green and beeped, the *ping* echoing in the quiet office.

The doors closed. The elevator rose smoothly.

It brought Tony to the most secluded part of Journy's headquarters. The sixth floor was a cube-shaped barnacle of steel and glass affixed to one quadrant of the building's roof. It housed Trevor Canon's private office and a small foyer. Outside lay a lavish roof deck replete with hot tub, wet bar, fire pit, and propane grill. Tony heard that Canon referred to it as his "sanctuary."

The doors opened and Tony stepped into the sanctuary's modest foyer. The ceiling was painted in bright Journy green. The floor was polished hardwood. To Tony's right, floor-to-ceiling glass treated him to a dazzling view of downtown San Francisco, a tableau of shadowed light clouded in the fog.

Straight ahead, Canon's office was guarded by a tall door of privacy glass. Through the frost Tony saw light glowing in Canon's office; a sliver of yellow spilled out from the door's edges.

Tony's orders for cleaning Trevor Canon's private sanctuary were explicit. If the light in Canon's office was off, Tony was free to execute a short checklist of tasks.

But Canon pulled the occasional all-nighter. Under absolutely no condition was Tony to disturb him. If Tony saw light in Canon's office, his orders were ironclad: Get back on the elevator and leave.

In practice this happened rarely. Tony had only seen it twice during his time on the job.

Tonight made three.

Tony's body began an automatic pivot back to the elevator. Time to make himself scarce.

But as he turned his eyes fell downward, catching on the thin band of light under Canon's door.

That was when he saw it.

Blood.

A narrow serpentine trail of red seeped across the foyer floor. It traced over the light wooden planks like a dark Nile through the floodplains.

Tony's eyes followed the blood trail as it led back to Canon's office door, disappearing underneath.

His immediate thought was a simple one.

Fuck.

His flight instinct cried out: Leave. Get back on the elevator. Pretend he hadn't seen a thing.

But he didn't move. He breathed in the silence, staring at the blood on the floor. His mind unspooled the consequences.

What did the blood lead back to?

What if Canon was hurt, and Tony didn't help him?

Tony had badged the elevator. They'd know he was in Canon's sanctuary. They'd see the blood trail. It was impossible to miss. They'd know that he ignored it.

Leaving his custodial station behind him, Tony clenched his jaw and crept forward. With each step, his anxiety settled deeper in his gut. There was no sound from Canon's office.

Tony reached for the door handle and gave a tug: It was unlocked. Carefully, one inch at a time, he pushed the door open.

Trevor Canon's body was splayed across the floor.

Canon was flat on his back. His arms were flailed in a graceless pose, feet facing Tony, head tumbled to one side.

Tony grimaced, but he forced himself ahead. He followed the blood trail as it led up to Canon's face.

Canon's bright blue eyes stared back at him, empty and lifeless. And pierced between them lay a single round bullet hole, red as ruby and filled with blood.

CHAPTER 1

Twenty-two days after Trevor Canon's death

In Mackenzie Clyde's experience, there were exactly two ways of dealing with a rich asshole.

The first method was universal. It applied across the full spectrum of the rich asshole genus: CEOs, athletes, actors and influencers, micro-dick hedge funders, god complex surgeons, trust-funded Ivy Leaguers.

Flattery.

The key, Mackenzie knew, was subtlety. You had to flatter the asshole without them realizing they were being flattered. Only total idiots enjoy being pandered to.

Flattery of any kind didn't come easily to Mackenzie. But out of professional necessity, she'd developed it as a weapon in her arsenal.

The second method of dealing with a rich asshole was far from universal.

It was a carefully tailored technique that Mackenzie had developed out of geographic, as well as professional, necessity. Mackenzie found it uniquely suited to a very particular strain of rich asshole: the young, entitled, uber-wealthy tech bros of modern San Francisco.

It was this second method that Mackenzie reflected on as she followed a hostess across the shiny wooden floor of the Battery. The Battery was a private social club in San Francisco, archetypal for the tech industry: expensive, exclusive, and utterly lacking in self-awareness. Mackenzie loathed it.

She took long strides into the Battery's bar area, an oozy space stuffed with polished concrete and reclaimed wood, the booths all tufted leather Chesterfields. She ignored the eyes that flitted in her direction. Most of them, she knew, were compelled by simple anomaly: the instinctive curiosity that comes from something incongruous to the typical environment.

Not that it made the stares any more welcome. But after several decades, she'd learned to live with them. Mackenzie was a very tall woman.

Kevin Reiter waited in a corner booth, staring at his phone. The hostess pointed him out and slunk away, leaving Mackenzie solo for her approach.

"Hello, Kevin."

Kevin looked up, squinting with confusion. "Who are you?"

"Mackenzie Clyde."

Kevin blinked at her. "You're very tall."

"Taller than you." Mackenzie tossed her bag into the empty side of the booth. She plopped down next to it.

Kevin frowned. "I'm supposed to meet Rebecca."

Mackenzie settled into her seat. "Rebecca's not coming."

"What do you mean, she's not coming?"

"They sent me instead."

"Does Rebecca know about this?"

"Yep."

"So you work with her at Hammersmith Venture?"

"I do."

Kevin's eyes narrowed. "Are you a partner?"

Mackenzie tilted her head to one side. "Not exactly."

"Another lawyer, then." Kevin shook his head. "I've told you guys a million times: I didn't go with HV so I could get Legal shoved down my throat."

"I'm not a lawyer." Mackenzie paused. "Well, not *really*."

Kevin sniffed. "Look, I don't do surprises."

"Check your email," Mackenzie said. "You'll have something from Roger."

Kevin hesitated at the name. "He sent me," Mackenzie said, waving a hand. "The email explains."

Kevin opened his phone while Mackenzie glanced at a menu. A server approached in a uniform. It had suspenders. "Drinks?"

"Manhattan." Kevin spoke, eyes still on his phone. "The Duniway. Up. Rocks glass. Light vermouth. Keep the twist on the rim. Don't let it touch the Duniway."

"Very good." The server turned to Mackenzie. "And for you?"

She handed him the menu. "Glass of white."

"Any preferences?"

"Anything that doesn't come in a box."

The server smiled and glided away.

Kevin finished with his phone. "Roger says you're taking this off Rebecca's desk."

"I am."

"But that's all he says. He didn't give a reason."

Mackenzie shrugged. "Roger's not big on explaining himself."

Kevin shifted in his seat, scowling. He wore a tight black V-neck, the type that comes free with a CrossFit membership. Mackenzie didn't recognize the logo on the chest pocket: an arrow pointing up and to the right, bisected by another half-line of equal width.

"Why are you replacing Rebecca? I worked with her for months."

"Yeah," Mackenzie replied. "That's the problem."

"What is?"

"It's been *months*. Three of them, to be exact. And this lawsuit still hasn't been resolved."

Kevin bristled. "That's not my fault."

"No?"

"Fuck no." Kevin's brow fell. "Go talk to my neighbors. They're the problem here."

Kevin Reiter was the prototypical Peter Pan, an overgrown man-child set loose in the consequence-free playground of San Francisco. He was founder of a fintech company that'd just closed its Series B, making him worth a few hundred million on paper.

Kevin was also emblematic of the latest iteration of tech bro, one that fused the new age faux-optimism of Silicon Valley with the unapologetic, old money privilege of Wall Street. Ten years prior Kevin would've been safely ensconced in the buffoonery of an investment bank. But now the capital had moved west, and the money hounds like Kevin had followed the scent, tails wagging behind them.

Hammersmith Venture, Mackenzie's firm, had invested $72 million in Kevin Reiter's company. Roger Hammersmith, Mackenzie's boss, had personally overseen the investment. And because the gravitational laws of corporate physics require that shit always slides downhill, Mackenzie now found herself at the Battery, tasked with talking reality into a man who'd grown accustomed to creating his own.

The server arrived with their drinks. Mackenzie took a long sip of her white wine, enjoying the familiar acidity as it washed down her throat. She stared at the twist of lemon perched on the edge of Kevin's glass.

"What does 'not really' mean?" Kevin asked.

"Excuse me?"

Kevin tasted his Manhattan. "I asked if you were a lawyer. You said 'not really.'"

"I went to law school. I'm a member of the Bar. I joined the legal department at Hammersmith Venture." Mackenzie took another sip. "But no, I'm not a lawyer."

"Then what are you?"

"Someone who finds things. Solves problems." Mackenzie paused. "Like this one."

"So you're a fixer."

Mackenzie gave a thin smile. "This isn't HBO." She dug into her bag and emerged with a business card, passing it to Kevin. He read the text aloud.

"Mackenzie Clyde. Director of investigations." The embossed text reflected in the Battery's calibrated light.

Mackenzie nodded. "That's right."

Kevin frowned. "I still don't know what that means."

It means nothing, Mackenzie thought. Her title had been vague for the five years she'd been in the role. Both she and Roger Hammersmith preferred it that way.

"When one of Hammersmith Venture's portfolio companies becomes entangled in a particularly thorny knot, I find a way to untie it." Mackenzie stared across the table. "Like I said: I solve problems."

"So Roger put you on this because he thinks it needs to be solved."

"Roger put me on this because it needs to *end*. Roger is bullish on your company. That's why he's so concerned about the specter of this nasty lawsuit. It's bad for you, bad for your company, bad for our firm." Mackenzie sipped her wine. "Roger sent me here to do my job: Make it all go away."

Kevin made a low snort. "And how do you expect to do that?"

"A settlement."

"No." Kevin's entire face fell; he dropped his glass heavily on the table. "I told Rebecca a thousand times: I'm not settling."

Mackenzie raised a hand. "Listen—" But Kevin cut her off.

"My neighbors are a bunch of whiny NIMBYs. They don't *want* to settle. They want to bleed me dry."

"Stop—"

Kevin jabbed a finger on the table. "I want to *countersue*. I want to take them to fucking court."

"*Stop*," Mackenzie said.

She took a breath and quelled her rising irritation. Stick to the game plan, she thought. "I've talked to Rebecca. I've talked to the neighbors. I know all the huffing and puffing. But that's exactly why I'm here. I've put something together that will make everyone happy."

Kevin's scowl lightened, but only slightly. "I don't know."

"Listen, Kevin, let's zoom out for a second." Mackenzie reclined against the tufted upholstery of the booth. "Your company's growing like a weed. You just closed the Series B."

Kevin shrugged. "So?"

"It was a monster round. Some of the biggest VCs out there. Including us."

"I guess."

"You're also on the verge of a huge partnership. I won't say the name of the bank, but . . ."

Kevin's eyebrows raised. "How did you hear that?"

"Roger trusts me," Mackenzie said. "The deal's going to be big. Lots of press, right?"

Another shrug. "So?"

"So you've got much bigger shit going on than your neighbors. Stuff that *actually* matters. This thing is small potatoes. It's beneath you."

She could see Kevin's posture begin to thaw. His shoulders receded toward his seat by a fraction of an inch. "Your neighbors aren't worth it, Kevin. Don't think of it as settling. Think of it as eliminating a distraction, moving on to all the things that are bigger than them."

Kevin returned to his Manhattan. "You have something prepared?"

Mackenzie nodded. "Your neighbors have already agreed. All you have to do is sign."

"Give me the broad strokes."

Finally, Mackenzie thought. She took another slug of wine and unlocked her phone. "I can do better," she said. "I'll send you the agreement now."

Kevin checked his phone while Mackenzie continued. "Here are the main points. First, you can keep the solarium in your backyard."

Kevin looked up. "Damn right I can. I paid six-four for that fucking house. I'm not taking anything down."

Mackenzie groaned inwardly at the offhand *six-four*, which in San Francisco parlance stood for $6.4 million. Only in California and Manhattan could such a vast sum of money be dismissed into such a casual term.

She pressed forward. "To be fair, the solarium wasn't there when you bought it. You built it."

"So?"

"So, this is San Francisco. Your backyard is the size of a Texas plunge pool. The solarium's only twenty feet from your neighbors' windows."

"What's your point?"

"It's understandable why they'd want it demolished."

"I don't give a shit," Kevin said. "You said the solarium stays. What else?"

"So the solarium stays, but what happens *inside* the solarium has to change."

Kevin shook his head. "No."

"Then you have to install shades."

"Not gonna happen."

Mackenzie leaned in and lowered her voice. "Kevin, it's a *solarium*. All the walls are glass. Your neighbors can see right in."

"So?"

"So you gotta stop jerking off in it."

Kevin didn't blanch. He stared right back at Mackenzie, unembarrassed. "It's my property. When I'm on it, I can do whatever I want."

"It's your property, but your neighbors still have to see it. Imagine sitting down for dessert and seeing *that*."

"They don't have to look."

Mackenzie felt her momentum stalling, but kept her voice level. "It's happening right outside their window."

Kevin leaned forward. "I've been telling Rebecca for months: That's their problem, not mine."

"Okay."

"I've read your firm's investment agreement. There's no morality clause."

"So?"

"So you can't make me sign anything."

"It's a good settlement. The terms are fair."

"I don't care."

"Roger's not going to like this."

"I don't *care*," Kevin repeated, voice acidic. "Roger's not my boss."

Mackenzie flattened her gaze. "This is really how you want to play it?"

Kevin leaned back and crossed his arms. "This is *my* company. I started it. I make the decisions." He dumped his phone on the table. "And I'm not signing this. I'm not signing *shit*."

"Fine," Mackenzie said.

It all felt so inevitable. Flattery had gone as far as it could—not that Mackenzie was surprised. From the moment she entered the Battery, Mackenzie had expected she'd need to employ the second method for dealing with a rich asshole, the one best suited for the Kevin Reiters of the world.

Verbal blunt force trauma.

Hit them hard. Hit them square.

Mackenzie leaned forward and stared at Kevin.

"I have to admit," she said. "You've surprised me."

Kevin frowned. "What do you mean?"

Mackenzie kept her expression impassive. "I knew you were disgusting," she said. "The details of the lawsuit made that obvious. But I didn't think you'd be this stupid."

Kevin's features locked with confusion. "What did you just say?"

Kevin Reiter was used to being stroked with the same breathless reverence provided to all of San Francisco's startup founders. At the helm of his fintech rocket ship, Kevin was a modern-day rainmaker. Adjacency to him and his company presented the opportunity for esteem, status, and gobs of money.

So Kevin was accustomed to being *sold*. Let me work for you, wear our product, donate money to our cause, let us put you on the cover of our magazine, come on our podcast.

Kevin went through his day-to-day without being disagreed with, let alone confronted. Certainly not as brazenly as Mackenzie just had.

Which was precisely why she did it.

"You're willing to make an enemy out of Roger Hammersmith," Mackenzie continued. "Over a *solarium*. That's as stupid as it gets."

Kevin frowned, raising a hand. "Hold on—

Mackenzie steamrolled him. "Your product isn't special," she said. "I can think of two others just like it. The only thing that makes you different is that our firm, the best in the industry, gave you a dump truck full of cash. You're built on Hammersmith Venture's money. Sure, maybe you started your company. But we *made* it. And we can unmake it just as easily."

"No." Kevin blinked at Mackenzie, squirming in his seat. "You can't. I told you: I read the investment agreement."

Mackenzie smirked. She reached into her bag, pulling out a document. She tossed it across the table.

Kevin stared at it. "What's this?"

"An affidavit," Mackenzie said. "From a guy named Justin Zhen. He designed your solarium."

Kevin's mouth tightened. His voice dropped an octave. "Zhen left the country," Kevin said. "Moved to Bali."

"Jakarta, actually. I tracked him down." Mackenzie pointed at the document. "Zhen says you *specifically asked* him about the solarium's sight lines. You wanted to make sure your neighbors would be able to see in."

Kevin was still; he stared at the folder like it was radioactive. "Zhen's under NDA."

"I paid him to break it," Mackenzie said. "With enough resources, anything's possible. You'll learn all about that if you go against us."

Mackenzie saw panic breaking through Kevin's natural self-assurance. His shoulders drooped, hands clasped on the table. Mackenzie downed the last of her wine, letting him stew.

"Zhen's a fucking snake," Kevin muttered.

Mackenzie leaned forward. "His affidavit shows your intent, which exposes you to a whole new world of criminal liability. I'll make sure it comes out in discovery. So keep throwing your tantrum, Kevin, and you won't just lose the lawsuit—you'll lose everything."

Kevin's eyes widened. "But that's—"

"I say the word," Mackenzie continued, brandishing her phone, "and Roger pulls our investment. All seventy-two million. Feel free to sue us about the morality clause. See how far you get against Roger's battalion of law firms. Or . . ."

Mackenzie paused and leaned back. "You grow up and end this. Right here. Right now."

Kevin's eyes lost focus, face falling. He's trying to calculate a way out, Mackenzie thought. She pressed on. "Like you said: It's your company. *You* make the decisions. So what'll it be?"

Kevin's lips thinned. "Why are you doing this? You're my biggest investor. You're supposed to *work* for me, not blackmail me."

Mackenzie straightened in the booth. She dragged her bag to her hip.

"First, Roger invested in you—not me. I don't work for you. I work for him. Second, I'm doing this because it's my job. Your neighbors are reasonable people, Kevin."

Mackenzie dropped her phone on the table, gesturing to it. "Sign the settlement. The lawsuit goes away. Your neighbors will be happy. Roger will be happy. You keep his money. Everybody wins. All you have to do is be an adult."

Kevin shifted in his seat. He reached for his Manhattan and slowly emptied it, making her wait.

"Fine," Kevin said. "I'll sign the fucking settlement."

"Great." Mackenzie stared at him. "Well?"

"You want me to sign it *now*?"

"DocuSign's in your inbox."

Kevin scoffed. "Fuck it." He opened his phone and swiped. "There, I signed. It's done."

Mackenzie glanced down at her phone. A confirmation pinged. "Fantastic."

Mackenzie tapped her phone to summon a Journy Car, then slid past the table. Hoisting her bag onto her shoulder, Mackenzie rose from the booth, unfolding to her full height.

Mackenzie was six foot two. She stared down at Kevin, towering over him.

"Goodbye, Kevin."

"That's it?" Kevin said.

"We'll bill you."

"Wait—you're *charging me* for this?"

Mackenzie didn't reply. She turned and strode out of the Battery. She didn't look back.

CHAPTER 2

Twenty-two days after Trevor Canon's death

Mackenzie was four minutes into her ride home when Roger Hammersmith called. She answered on the first ring.

"The settlement came through." The voice of Mackenzie's boss echoed through her iPhone. "How'd you get him to sign?"

"Trade secret," Mackenzie said.

Hammersmith grunted. "Kevin's always been a tool, even before he was rich. What'd it take?"

Mackenzie relaxed in the back seat. "No different than the others. Dig for the right information. Find the levers. Where to push, where to pull."

Hammersmith's tone changed. "I have something else. When can you be here?"

It was nearing eight P.M. Mackenzie still hadn't eaten dinner. Her Journy Car was only a few blocks from her house.

She didn't hesitate. "Ten minutes."

Hammersmith hung up. In Mackenzie's experience, Hammersmith never spent a second more on the phone than he wanted to.

Roger Hammersmith was the founder and president of Hammersmith Venture, the tech industry's most prestigious venture capital firm. Few men in Silicon Valley wielded more influence. Hammersmith had been in venture capital since the nineties, and he ruled over his firm with a gilded fist.

Mackenzie had carved out a unique role that reported directly to Hammersmith. So his schedule was her schedule. She leaned forward and told the Journy driver her change in plan.

Mackenzie had been at Hammersmith Venture for eight years. She'd taken a position in the firm's legal department after graduating top of her class from Georgetown Law. At the time, Mackenzie had been excited. The firm's investment portfolio included the biggest names in tech.

Her initial years at HV, however, had been an uninspiring grind. She organized documents. She argued simplistic points. She catered to the juvenile whims of the startups in HV's portfolio. Mackenzie had considered leaving the firm more times than she could count.

And then she'd made the discovery that had changed her life.

As her Journy Car pulled up to Hammersmith's office building, Mackenzie realized that was nearly five years ago to the day.

Hammersmith Venture's headquarters were housed in the Embarcadero Center, a cluster of glowering, sharp-edged towers that hung over the edges of the Financial District.

Roger Hammersmith's office was an expansive suite full of masculine leather furniture and walnut wainscoting. Displayed photographs showed Hammersmith posing with dignitaries and celebrities. A color print of Hammersmith on his personal helicopter, the *Hammer Angel,* above the Cristo statue in Rio. Nearby, a black-and-white of Hammersmith with the current president, the type of photo reserved for those who had cobbled together an eight-figure PAC.

The defining feature of Hammersmith's office was what lay beyond it: a stunning panoramic view that captured the full sweep of the San Francisco Bay, from the prideful arches of the Golden Gate to the bucolic hills of Marin. Mackenzie had been in Hammersmith's office hundreds of times, but the view still had a way of shocking her senses. One instant she was burrowing through a bland warren of corporate hallways; the next she was perched on the edge of the universe, thrust into the eyes of god.

Roger Hammersmith couldn't care less about the view. Not once had Mackenzie seen her boss even glance out the windows behind his desk. As always, he stood with his back to them, head down, eyes glued to a tablet.

Luxury is wasted on the rich, Mackenzie thought.

"Have a seat," Hammersmith said, not looking up. Mackenzie eased onto a five-figure leather sofa. "Let's talk about Trevor Canon."

Mackenzie felt a jolt in her blood. "Okay."

"I assume you're aware that he's dead."

"Of course."

Everyone was aware, especially at Hammersmith Venture. Trevor Canon was the founder of Journy. Not only was Journy the biggest, buzziest startup on the planet, it was also the crown jewel of HV's investment portfolio.

Canon had been murdered in his office three weeks prior. The media had devoured the story in a gluttonous scrum of headlines. News networks formed a base camp outside Journy's offices, providing round-the-clock coverage. Canon's murder consumed social media. For a week, it was the only thing anyone talked about.

But then the story stagnated. The police made no charges, announced no suspects. The news cycle moved on. The press tents disappeared as quickly as they'd arrived. Mackenzie kept close tabs on the coverage, but these days there was little for her to read.

Hammersmith dropped the tablet on his desk and moved away from the window, taking a seat on a sofa opposite Mackenzie's. He stared across a continent-sized coffee table. "Tell me what you know."

Mackenzie gazed up at the ceiling. "Trevor Canon was killed at Journy's headquarters in SoMa. Murdered in his private office." Mackenzie paused, as though recalling a detail. "It was at night, after work. I think reports said around eleven or twelve? So Canon was working late, alone."

Hammersmith nodded. "How was he killed?"

"Shot in the head," Mackenzie said. "Single bullet."

Roger Hammersmith was fifty-eight years old, with a round, cherubic face and wide brown eyes set behind glasses. His hair was gray and disheveled, and his naturally wide frame disguised an ample gut. He dressed poorly and expensively: ill-fitting pants that billowed as he walked, like two sails attached to their masts, along with a mismatched cashmere and button-down. Mackenzie caught the Pebble Beach logo embroidered on his sweater. Hammersmith had always been proof of an old Silicon Valley axiom: The worse a man dressed, the richer he was.

Hammersmith exuded an effortless authority that complemented his disarming appearance. His rounded features appeared as though constantly on the verge of laughter. When he did laugh, he got his money's worth: a loud, rich guffaw that filled any room. It gave him a Yogi Bear quality that ingratiated him with founders. But Mackenzie had learned that Hammersmith's chummy persona only made him more formidable. She could rarely decipher what he was actually thinking. Underneath the big laugh and mismatched wardrobe, Hammersmith was shrewd and—when it came to business—utterly pitiless.

"Single bullet," Hammersmith agreed, nodding. "To the head."

Mackenzie caught herself fidgeting: twisting her wrist in her lap, flexing her right fingers involuntarily. She forced herself to be still. Be patient, she thought.

Hammersmith continued. "Some of the circumstances surrounding Canon's death are . . . complex. That'd be the case for anyone in Trevor's position. But for him, particularly so."

Hammersmith looked away, lips pressing together. "It's a tragic thing, truly. Deeply, deeply tragic." Hammersmith lost focus, his eyes glazing as he stared at the floor.

Mackenzie's instinct told her to stay quiet. There was a long pause before Hammersmith continued.

"The first few days were a circus, but since then the investigation has gone into lockdown. Outside a small circle, nobody knows anything."

But you're in that circle, Mackenzie thought. That's why we're here.

"What else do you know about Trevor Canon?" Hammersmith asked. "Besides the fact that he's been killed."

"Journy was the storybook startup," Mackenzie said. "Canon started the company eight years ago, scaled the crap out of it before anyone could blink. Overnight he became the primary lust object on Sand Hill Road. Raised a ton of money, scaled it more. Pretty soon Journy became a household name. Magazine covers, TV commercials, offices on every continent. Canon went to Sun Valley, Davos, the whole deal. Now you even see grandmas buzzing around town in the green Journy golf carts."

"What about Canon himself? Not the company—the man. Did you know him?"

Mackenzie shook her head. "All I know is what I've heard. Type of stuff you get after a few drinks."

"Such as?"

"The usual. Canon was a brilliant visionary but extremely difficult. Charismatic but relentless. In other words, a colossal asshole."

Hammersmith laughed, a loud *HA!* that reverberated across the office.

Mackenzie continued. "Canon wasn't popular. He was exacting. Demanding. Totally irrational in his expectations." Mackenzie shrugged. "But that's tech. His company was a rocket ship. People will climb across an entire rainbow of shit if they think there's a pot of gold at the end of it."

Hammersmith chuckled again. "An IPO."

"Tale as old as time. People were happy to put up with Canon because there was a pile of cash waiting for them if they did."

"Do you know anyone at Journy?"

"One person." Mackenzie paused. "But we haven't been in touch for years."

Hammersmith shifted position on the sofa. "The investigation is entering a new phase," he said. "The police, predictably, have gotten nowhere. The crime scene is clean. Everyone at Journy's lawyered up. Weeks have gone by with no progress. So the SFPD is out. New blood's taking over."

Mackenzie remained still. "Who?"

"The FBI," Hammersmith said. "And us."

Mackenzie felt a tingle in the back of her neck. "The FBI is taking over the investigation?"

Hammersmith nodded. "The Feds have decided they better get involved."

"How do they have jurisdiction?"

"They don't." Hammersmith chuckled. "They'll claim national security or some other nonsense, but it doesn't matter." Hammersmith scowled, eyes darkening behind his glasses. "The SFPD have been incompetent. The lead detective was just put on leave—turns out he's a drunk. Whole thing is an embarrassment. So now the FBI's coming in."

"And so are we."

"That's right."

Mackenzie asked the question she knew Hammersmith was waiting for. "Where do we come in?"

"You're aware, obviously, of our position in Trevor Canon. In Journy."

"I am." *Position* was an understatement. Hammersmith Venture had injected Journy with the largest venture capital investment in history.

"I oversaw Journy personally," Roger said. "A rarity, as you know."

There were several hundred companies in Hammersmith Venture's portfolio. Roger didn't personally keep tabs on most of them. That's what he paid others to do. But Journy was different.

Hammersmith continued. "Trevor demanded that I directly manage the firm's relationship." Hammersmith gave a half-shrug. "But I was happy to do it."

"Why?"

"When you invest in a company of Journy's size, you're not betting on the company. You're betting on the founder. From the first time we met, I was inspired by Trevor's vision. After we invested, he and I became very close. We spoke daily, strategized for hours, traveled together."

Hammersmith leaned back. "Journy was capable of ascending to the same level as Palisade, Spyder, StoryBoard. There have been plenty of pretenders. Journy was the real deal. I made sure Trevor knew that."

"Is that why you invested so heavily?"

"Yes." There was a nearly imperceptible hesitation. "Among other reasons." Hammersmith smiled thinly, voice clipped. "Soti was lurking."

Indira Soti's venture capital firm was the only one truly competitive with Hammersmith. Soti was Hammersmith's greatest rival.

"Soti pitched Trevor on a huge investment package. Over five billion. Biggest in history." Hammersmith crossed one leg over the other, pointing an eighteen-hundred-dollar loafer in Mackenzie's direction. "Trevor was tempted. So I had to trump it."

Mackenzie recalled the exact number that Hammersmith had ultimately invested into Journy: $5.2 billion. It had been the biggest venture capital investment ever, in any company, any industry. Hammersmith called it the Journy Fund.

"We have over five billion invested in Trevor Canon's company," Mackenzie said.

"That's right."

"And now Canon's dead."

"That's right."

Mackenzie stared across the table. "What a clusterfuck."

Hammersmith gave a rueful smile. "Amen."

"Sorry. That shouldn't have been my first reaction."

"You're not wrong."

"Still." Roger was the opposite of sentimental. But Mackenzie sensed she had veered off script. "I'm very sorry, Roger. When Trevor died you must have been devastated."

Hammersmith sighed. "It's been hard. And the fact that Trevor was *murdered*, in cold blood, in his own office . . . that's made it harder. Obviously we have a significant financial interest, but . . ." Hammersmith looked away. "Trevor and I were kindred spirits. Very close."

"I'm sorry," Mackenzie said again.

"Thank you."

Mackenzie waited an appropriate amount of time. "Now that Trevor's gone, what happens to the five billion that HV invested in Journy?"

"Fair question," Hammersmith said. "And it's why I said you weren't wrong, a moment ago."

Hammersmith stood from the sofa, circling around its back. He leaned over, hands near the cushions.

"Normally, in a situation like this, Trevor's shares of the company would be divvied up and distributed to all the remaining shareholders."

"So some of Trevor's shares would go to us."

"A plurality of them, yes. When we invested in Journy we became the company's biggest shareholder—after Trevor himself, of course. Trevor owned thirty-three percent of Journy. We're not far behind."

Mackenzie did the math in her head. At Journy's latest valuation, that meant Trevor's stock was worth over $20 billion. And now, that $20 billion would go to all the other Journy shareholders. Including Hammersmith Venture.

"So if Trevor is gone," she said, "and his shares go to all the *other* shareholders, that would mean . . ."

"Hammersmith Venture would have the controlling interest in Journy."

"So we'd be in charge of the company."

"Yes," Hammersmith said. "We'd appoint a new CEO, determine the next course of action. Take Trevor's vision for Journy—*our* vision for Journy—and execute it on his behalf. That's what should happen."

Mackenzie blinked. "I'm sensing there's a problem."

"Before he died," Hammersmith said, "Trevor did something strange. He amended his will."

"Trevor had a will?"

"He had to. Regulators require it for someone in his position."

"What did it say?"

Hammersmith squeezed a cushion between meaty fingers. "It was boilerplate. Until just before he died, when he added a new section."

Mackenzie played along to Hammersmith's rhythm. "What was the new section?"

"The lawyers call it a 'dead money' provision. It said that in the event Trevor was killed, all of his assets would be frozen."

"Frozen? Until when?"

"Until someone is tried for his murder."

Mackenzie said nothing for a long moment. "You're kidding."

Hammersmith's expression was hard to read. "I wish I was."

"So . . . Trevor knew someone was planning to kill him," Mackenzie said.

"Apparently."

"But . . ." Mackenzie brought a hand to her forehead. "He didn't say anything about it to you?"

Hammersmith shook his head. "We hadn't spoken in a while. We'd both been traveling." When Trevor died Hammersmith had been in Jackson Hole at an annual retreat for the uber-rich. "Trevor thought he was in danger. For what reason, I'm not sure."

"So what happens to his assets? What happens to his shares in Journy?"

"It's all frozen," Hammersmith said.

"All of it?"

Hammersmith smirked. "That's what the lawyers say."

"*All* of Trevor's shares?"

"Correct."

"But that's . . . twenty *billion* dollars' worth. Not to mention the five billion we already put in. And all of it's just . . . sitting there, where nobody can touch it?"

Hammersmith nodded. "That's why they call it dead money."

"That's ridiculous."

Hammersmith smiled thinly. "I would call it a clusterfuck." Hammersmith moved back around the sofa, retaking his place.

"Thanks to the dead money provision, none of Trevor's shares can be settled. The company can't do anything without a controlling interest. Nothing can happen when nobody's in control. The company, investors, shareholders—we're all in limbo."

"Until someone is tried for Trevor's murder," Mackenzie said.

"Now you understand the full import of the investigation. Obviously, the priority is bringing Trevor's killer to justice . . ."

Mackenzie said it so Hammersmith wouldn't have to. "But there's also twenty billion dollars on the line."

Hammersmith nodded. "The future of Journy is at stake."

And the five billion we poured into it, Mackenzie thought.

"Now I understand," she said, "why you were frustrated by the SFPD."

"That's putting it mildly," Hammersmith said. "But yes. I pushed for the FBI to take over the investigation. And I demanded that Hammersmith Venture be attached as an advisor."

Now, finally, they were getting to the questions Mackenzie had been waiting to ask. But she knew Hammersmith liked to play his cards methodically, at his own pace. It was one of the many indirect ways he wielded his authority. No shortcuts.

"What are we doing, exactly?" Mackenzie asked. "It's a murder investigation."

"Hammersmith Venture is operating in an advisory capacity. We will 'assist with all aspects of the investigation.'"

"We're 'advisors.'"

"Yes. The SFPD failed because they don't understand our world. Trevor was killed in his office. Journy is worth billions. Trevor *knew* that someone was after him. It's obvious that his murder was connected to his work. But the SFPD detectives had no experience with technology companies. They didn't know what questions to ask. Most of them could barely operate an iPhone."

Hammersmith harrumphed, adjusting his glasses. "The staff at Journy didn't feel compelled to speak to SFPD because they knew it was pointless: They and the detectives didn't speak the same language."

Mackenzie suppressed an eye roll and kept quiet.

"I persuaded the Justice Department that an external perspective was necessary. People who understand tech. People who are good at finding out information."

"People like us," Mackenzie said.

"People like *you*," Hammersmith said.

Mackenzie felt her eyes widen. "Me?"

"You're going to represent us in the investigation."

A sudden blast of heat radiated through her gut. "You want *me* to be the advisor? Work with the FBI?"

"You figured that out a while ago." Hammersmith blinked at her behind his glasses. "Don't play coy. It's beneath you."

Mackenzie stammered. "Sure, once you brought up Canon's murder I figured I'd be involved. But this . . ."

"Don't you want the assignment?"

"Of course I want it."

"Then what's the problem?"

Mackenzie took a deep breath. "What's it entail?"

"It's straightforward," Hammersmith said. "Make sure the FBI doesn't fuck this up. Show them how to navigate the world of a tech startup. Convince the people at Journy to talk. Tell the FBI what questions to ask. Unlock our money." Hammersmith appraised Mackenzie from across the coffee table. "Represent the firm. Represent *me*."

Mackenzie hesitated. "On a federal homicide investigation."

Hammersmith remained uncharacteristically stone-faced. "Yes."

"But I'm not a detective."

"You're an investigator."

"I'm not familiar with police work. I don't know how they do things."

"That's a mark in your favor."

Mackenzie tried to clear any incredulity from her features. "What about the FBI?"

"What about them?" Hammersmith's eyes were steel. "You know this world. I have far more confidence in you than I do in the federal government."

"It's not my type of work."

"It is precisely your type of work," Hammersmith said. "Investigation is synthesis. That's your strong suit. Dig for information. Find the levers."

"That's different," Mackenzie said.

"I fail to see how."

"Getting a dumbass like Kevin Reiter to sign a settlement is one thing. But a federal homicide investigation? With billions of dollars on the line?" Mackenzie shook her head again. "You can't pretend this isn't different."

Hammersmith uncrossed his legs and edged to the front of the sofa. He placed a hand on each knee. "This isn't a pep talk, Mackenzie."

"I get—"

Hammersmith spoke over her. "We had everything invested in Trevor Canon. Not just financially, but personally." Hammersmith paused. "Do you understand?"

Mackenzie answered quickly. "I do."

Hammersmith's tone sharpened. "The terms of our arrangement were clear. When I give assignments, you take them. No questions asked."

Careful, Mackenzie reminded herself. Don't push too far. "I know," she said. "I remember."

"Do you?"

Mackenzie let the question hang in the air for a beat. "Of course."

Hammersmith fixed Mackenzie with a dead-eyed gaze; the Yogi Bear bemusement was somewhere far away. "Everything is on the line here. Not just the money, but our arrangement. Our future together."

Mackenzie straightened in her seat, and adopted what she hoped was a confident expression. "I understand," she said. "I can do it."

"Good." Hammersmith stood. Mackenzie sensed an air of conversational finality that compelled her to do the same.

"You'll report everything you learn directly to me," he said. "Everything you learn from Canon's colleagues, everything you learn from the FBI. *Everything.* Only to me. Understood?"

Mackenzie nodded. "Understood."

Hammersmith moved toward his desk, giving Mackenzie a pat on the shoulder. "Go get some sleep. You start tomorrow morning."

CHAPTER 3

Twenty-two days after Trevor Canon's death

Mackenzie strode through the darkness of North Beach, adrenaline jumping through her bloodstream. Thirty minutes had passed since she left Hammersmith's office, but her pulse still pounded with her steps.

Mackenzie had spent the past several weeks hovering between expectation and doubt. She'd thought it likely that Hammersmith would involve himself in Canon's murder investigation. And if Hammersmith involved himself, then it was likely he'd involve Mackenzie, too.

On its face, the idea had seemed preposterous. Mackenzie inserted into the biggest incident in the recent history of the tech industry? But her logic was sound. She was Roger's investigator, reported directly to him. She had taken huge risks to earn the position and earn his trust. Roger had too much at stake with Canon *not* to involve himself, in some way. The pieces fit.

For several weeks, Mackenzie had waited. Expectant, but realistic. She'd get a sign from Roger, one way or the other.

Now she had it.

One conversation and a pat on the shoulder—that was all it took for Mackenzie to be thrust into the highest profile murder in the country.

Her mind reeled with the implications. She took a certain satisfaction in being right; but now came the hard part. As she walked through the quiet, foggy streets of her neighborhood, Mackenzie's heartbeat pounded in her eardrums. Everything she'd worked for, carefully planned for, was finally coming to fruition.

She was in. This was the type of opportunity she'd been waiting for.

But that wasn't what spiked her adrenaline.

What set her mind racing was something else. A simple fact, clear as a single cloud in a bluebird sky. Mackenzie knew, with a deep, instinctual certainty, that she was entering the most treacherous period of her life.

Her Journy Car had dropped her at her favorite Thai place. Now she walked home, the night deepening around her. Pad kee mao swung from her hand in a plastic bag.

Mackenzie's walk-up was on Green, three long San Francisco blocks from the boisterous sidewalks that drew tourists to North Beach. As she turned onto her street, Mackenzie's world plunged into silence.

It was nearly ten; there was nobody around. The only sound was the soft pad of her flats as they hit the sidewalk. The air was cool and wet with marine humidity. Her strides were long and purposeful. Mackenzie walked another block, her apartment now a football field away. She crossed an empty intersection.

It was then that Mackenzie sensed she was being watched.

Mackenzie's height had bred in her a unique awareness of the sensation. She'd been stared at—whether purposefully or inadvertently—for most of her life. Relatives, teachers, classmates, co-workers, competitors. She knew exactly how the gaze of another person felt. It was a dull, instinctual heat that rose in the back of her neck.

A heat she felt now.

She didn't break stride. Casually, she turned her neck and pretended to adjust the position of her bag, shifting the noodles to her opposite hand. She got a quick wide-angle view of the street behind her.

Nobody was there.

No figures in windows. No bikes or cars lurking. No Journy scooters. The street was deserted.

She took a deep breath and kept walking. Her apartment was one long block away.

But the heat was still there. The sensation was unmistakable. She had known it her whole life.

Somebody, somewhere, had eyes on her.

A dull, stiff pain bloomed suddenly in her right hand, accompanied by a stray question that drifted across her subconscious.

Is it him?

A wave of rationalization pushed the thought away. It was only anticipation, she told herself. She'd just gotten the Canon assignment and already her mind was imagining dark things, preparing itself for the weeks to come.

But still.

A small bodega rested on Mackenzie's corner, a classic San Francisco corner store with overpriced booze and unhealthy snacks. Mackenzie rarely stopped there; her apartment was only half a block away. But instinct told her to step inside the bodega for a moment, rather than go straight to her building.

She popped through the glass door, standing just inside the threshold. A bell chimed.

A clerk stood before a wall of liquor bottles. He glanced up from his phone.

"I'm just waiting for a car," Mackenzie explained.

The clerk shrugged and returned to his screen.

Mackenzie stood behind a rack of room-temperature Red Bull. She angled her body so it was semi-hidden from the street while affording her a view of the intersection. She stood and waited.

Nobody came.

A white Prius rolled through the intersection, barely stopping before it turned south. It was followed shortly after by a black Tesla.

Each car had a familiar, bright green Journy sign illuminated in its windshield, drivers en route to their next pickup or drop-off.

Another minute ticked by. An Amazon Prime truck chugged past, revving its engine up the hill.

Mackenzie waited another two minutes. Nobody else came.

She waited another five. Still nobody.

The heat in the back of her neck subsided, replaced by a growing sense of embarrassment.

After ten minutes, the bodega clerk gave Mackenzie the side-eye. She put a hand to her carton of noodles—they were getting cold.

She sighed, feeling ridiculous, and exited back to the street.

Nobody was there. The street was just as empty as when she'd left it.

Mackenzie shook her head. She prided herself on following a strict code of analytical rationality. But only one hour into the Canon job and it was already tweaking her out. There was a reasonable explanation for the heat she'd felt. It was her adrenaline playing tricks, her mind tensing for the difficulty of the task that lay ahead.

She walked up the street to her building, forcing an unhurried gait. She calmly punched in the entrance code on the building security panel. She heard the familiar *click* of the heavy glass-and-oak door as it opened. Motions smooth and relaxed, Mackenzie stepped inside. She glanced back at the street behind her.

Nobody was there.

Mackenzie grabbed her junk mail and trudged up the three flights of stairs. Carefully, she unlocked the deadbolt and entered her apartment. It was a classic San Francisco one-bedroom, long and narrow. The floors creaked as Mackenzie padded down her hallway. She passed a tiny kitchen and miniature bathroom before reaching the living room at the end of the hall. Like the rest of the apartment it was undersized, with French doors demarcating a small "bedroom" that barely fit a queen. But the ceilings were high, and a giant, street-facing bay window brought in southern light. Mackenzie stepped to it now, glancing down to Green below.

The street was quiet. She watched for a moment, then turned away.

Mackenzie threw the noodles in the microwave and hopped in

the shower. She ate dinner in her typical position: standing against the ancient white tiles of her kitchen counter, leaning over her open MacBook. Twenty minutes later she shut her laptop and turned off the lights. She moved to the bay window and closed the curtains.

She knew nobody had been following her. There had been no eyes on her. The specter of murder had scrambled her circuits.

Her rational mind scolded her: She'd need to stay levelheaded if she was going to get through the coming days.

Logic. Reason. Rationality.

Mackenzie brushed her teeth and went to bed. She slept like shit.

CHAPTER 4

Twenty-three days after Trevor Canon's death

Mackenzie's Journy Car sat moored in the slog of morning traffic. The lanes around her were stuffed with an unmoving armada of Priuses, Camrys, Sonatas, and Fusions, each backseat filled with a passenger exactly like her: face angled downward, mind buried in their phone.

Her screen lit up with an incoming call: Hammersmith.

"Are you on your way to the Journy offices?"

"Stuck on Gough as we speak," Mackenzie said.

Hammersmith grunted. "The FBI assigned a lead agent to the investigation. He'll meet you there."

"What do we know about him?"

"He doesn't have much of a track record. Name is Jameson Danner. He's young. He's with the Bureau's Criminal Investigative Division but hasn't been there long."

Mackenzie frowned in the back of the Journy Car. "Okay."

"Another thing: Journy's assigned a liaison to the investigation.

A main point of contact to get you what you need. You'll meet them this morning."

"Great," Mackenzie said. "Who is it?"

"Eleanor Eden."

Mackenzie paused. "Oh."

"Why 'oh'?"

"Well," Mackenzie said. "I know Eleanor."

"You do?"

"A little."

"Last night you said you didn't know anyone at Journy." Hammersmith's tone was curious, rather than accusatory.

"I said I knew *one* person at Journy," Mackenzie said. "But that we hadn't been in touch for years."

"And that person is Eleanor Eden."

"Yes."

Eleanor Eden was the chief operating officer at Journy, having spent the last six years as Trevor Canon's top lieutenant. She also carried a high profile. A decade prior she'd written a bestselling book, *A Seat at the Table,* that made her famous in business circles. Eleanor's story became a cultural touchstone for women across the corporate landscape.

In more recent years Eden had also become the target of criticism. Trevor Canon rarely gave interviews. Eleanor, in his stead, became the face of Journy's many controversies: regulatory clashes with local governments, accusations of a "bro-y" workplace culture, fatal accidents with Journy vehicles.

Depending who was asked, Eleanor Eden was either one of the most admired or most loathed leaders in tech. Within the past year, two magazines had put her on their cover. *Fortune* had named her the Most Powerful Woman in Tech. *Blender* had dubbed her "Trevor Canon's Hatchet Woman."

"How do you know Eleanor?" Hammersmith asked.

"We used to date," Mackenzie said.

"Oh. I—"

Hammersmith stopped mid-sentence. Mackenzie smiled into the silence. Hammersmith's natural instincts as an older white male had readied a reaction. Mackenzie knew the questions that lay unspoken on the tip of his tongue: *I thought you were straight? I didn't know you were gay?* Only years of HR training had stopped him.

"I . . . wasn't aware of that," Hammersmith said finally.

"It was just a month or so," Mackenzie replied. "It's been years since we talked."

"Okay." Another pause. "Thank you for that information."

Mackenzie stifled a laugh at Hammersmith's sudden formality. "So I meet with Agent Danner, and then together we'll meet with Eleanor Eden."

"Yes. Remember: full report, only to me. All the details. If you hear it, see it, smell it, I want to know."

Journy's headquarters were identical to every tech company Mackenzie had ever visited. Vast open atrium, brimming with light and the hum of arriving workers. Shimmering glass-paneled walls and minimalist wooden furniture. Tasteful scattering of plant life. Small espresso bar tucked in a corner.

There was one notable exception. At the front entrance, a massive semicircular driveway had been carved off the street to accommodate a continuous flow of Journy "urban transport vehicles." Journy Cars rotated through a wide loading zone. Parallel ran a separate, purpose-built track for Journy UTVs: electric scooters (Scoots), pedal-assist bikes (Glides), and square, covered golf carts (Buggies).

Cars pulled up, doors opened, Glides chimed, Scoots zipped around corners, Buggies buzzed in and out of designated parking spaces. Every UTV was painted in the bright traffic-light green of Journy's corporate branding. In the center of it all rested a towering metal sculpture of Journy's logo: an italicized, uppercase *J*, again in the company green.

A security checkpoint sat just inside the huge glass entry doors. Mackenzie received a Journy green visitor badge, then passed through turnstiles and walked into the atrium.

The morning sun drifted through a retractable glass roof, draping the atrium with a golden, sparkly optimism. Journy's marketing slogan was stenciled in big block letters on the far wall: IT'S NOT THE DESTINATION—IT'S THE JOURNY. A coffee grinder churned in the espresso corner.

If the death of their founder had cast a pall over Journy, it didn't feel that way in the company's headquarters. Clusters of employees chattered as they flowed into the cafeteria. Two women, each clad in a ludicrously wide-brimmed hat, laughed at something on a phone. A heavily tattooed guy whipped past Mackenzie on a Razor scooter, his black T-shirt reading CREATIVES ARE THE NEW ATHLETES.

Everyone appeared unaware that, only a few weeks earlier, their boss had been shot in the head, just steps from where they now sipped their free macchiatos.

Mackenzie scanned for Agent Danner and spotted him waiting in the exact center of the atrium. She groaned.

Dressed in a charcoal suit, white shirt, and thick black tie, Jameson Danner appeared comically out of place amid the flows of skinny denim and Allbirds. He stood upright, stiff as a rod, feet set apart. One hand was at his side and the other was holding his iPhone, which had his full attention. He resembled a dad who'd insisted on tagging along with his teenagers to a concert.

Mackenzie, by contrast, wore the same "San Francisco Formal" outfit she wore every day: white shirt, black jeans, and flats. Always flats.

Mackenzie sighed and walked toward Danner. He was white, of medium height, with dark hair and dark brows. His eyes were muddled green and positioned slightly too close together. Combined with his angular jaw and clean cheeks, it gave his face a cartoonish Playmobil effect.

Mackenzie reached out a hand as she approached. "Hi. Mackenzie Clyde."

Danner looked up and blinked at her. They shook.

"Special Agent Jameson Danner," he said. "FBI."

"Nice to meet you," Mackenzie said.

Danner only nodded in reply. Face-to-face, Mackenzie realized he was younger than she.

There was an awkward pause. Mackenzie felt a regrettable need to fill it. "I'm from Hammersmith Venture," she added.

"The venture capital firm," Danner said. He carefully enunciated his words.

"Yep," Mackenzie said. "Sounds like we'll be meeting with Eleanor Eden."

"That's right." Danner filed his phone into a pocket. "How long have you been with your firm?"

"Eight years. How long have you been with the Bureau?"

"Six," Danner said. His cadence was stiff; Mackenzie noticed that he didn't like it when she called it the Bureau.

Danner continued. "Have you ever been involved in an investigation before?"

From his tone, Mackenzie suspected he'd already decided the answer. "I've spent the last five years running investigations for HV."

"Didn't know VC firms did investigatory work."

"Most don't." Mackenzie shrugged. "But Hammersmith has a lot of money invested in a lot of companies. We like to do our homework."

Danner looked at her, his features flat. "*This* kind of investigation—a violent crime. I'm assuming you haven't been involved with many of those before."

"No," Mackenzie said.

"Do you have experience on any criminal investigations—even non-violent ones?"

"Nope."

"You ever worked with law enforcement? FBI, police?"

"Not directly."

"I understand you're a lawyer," Danner said.

"By training, yes."

"No experience with criminal law?"

"Not since law school."

Danner looked away, falling quiet. There was no sign of Eleanor Eden, but a man's voice cut in. "Hi there."

Mackenzie and Danner turned to face a bald, bearded man. He wore a black T-shirt, the Journy logo embossed in the ever-present green. "You must be the folks here to see Eleanor."

"Special Agent Jameson Danner, FBI." Danner stuck out his arm.

The bearded man returned the shake, then turned to Mackenzie. "And you're from HV," he said. Mackenzie nodded, introducing herself.

"I'm Hector," he said. "Chief people officer here at Journy. Eleanor's stuck in something; she asked me to show you around while you're waiting."

"That works," Danner said.

Hector began walking. "Follow me."

Hector guided them through the main levels of Journy's offices. There were glass-walled conference rooms named after famous roads and highways. There were banks of open-plan desks, each littered with five figures in technical equipment. There were colorful posters advertising a performance by Journy's a cappella group. There were oversized geometric sofas in the familiar green. There were posters emblazoned with inspiring quotes like YOU MISS 100% OF THE SHOTS YOU DON'T TAKE. —WAYNE GRETZKY. There were snack bars and a gleaming cafeteria. Kombucha fountains, bulk bins. A massage station, a movie theater. A yoga room. A ball pit.

The usual, Mackenzie thought.

The tour ended on the third floor, at a quiet spot near the back side of the building. "Chief people officer" was a classic tech company title, a needlessly huggy twist on "head of human resources." Mackenzie knew that Hector's responsibilities as chief people officer extended well beyond HR. Apparently Agent Danner knew the same.

"Your remit," Danner said, looking at Hector, "includes facilities security, is that correct?"

Hector nodded. "That's right."

Danner peered at him. "I'd like to ask about your security protocols."

Hector had been expecting the question. "Sure," he said. "But I've been instructed by our head of Legal not to answer anything that's not about security."

Danner seemed unfazed. "On the night of the murder, was there any security personnel here at the building?"

"Two people at the front checkpoint, where you walked in today. SFPD's already talked to them."

"I read the report," Danner said. "The front desk didn't see anyone until custodial staff, little after one A.M."

"That's right," Hector said. "Nobody else came or went through the front."

"Does the front desk security also patrol the rest of the office?"

Hector nodded. "Every hour or so."

"Did they see anyone working late?"

"No," Hector said. "Dinner service ends at eight. Office was empty after that."

Danner twisted his neck, looking around. "Besides the front entrance, what are other ways into the building?"

"There's only one other entrance, at the back. It's directly below us, on the ground floor. You come in from the alley behind the building."

"Is the back entrance used often?"

Hector shook his head. "Most employees take Journy transportation to work, and the front entrance has the big loading zone."

"But anyone can use the back entrance?"

Hector pulled on a bright green badge that was clipped to his belt. "Anyone with one of these, yeah."

Danner thought for a moment. "Did Trevor Canon ever use it?"

"All the time," Hector said. "It leads right to the elevator that goes up to his office."

"Show me," Danner said. Throughout his questions he'd ignored Mackenzie. She remained quiet, off to one side.

Hector led them to a nondescript elevator. "This part of the building doesn't get much traffic," he said. "Only reason to come over here is to take the elevator up to Trevor's office, or down to the back exit."

Mackenzie studied a portrait on the wall. Trevor Canon, hair cut short, stared out at them with a challenging, unsmiling gaze. Canon's eyes pierced into Mackenzie's, glowing and unnaturally blue. Mackenzie wondered if they'd been digitally enhanced.

"There's a different portrait," Hector said, "next to this elevator on every floor."

Mackenzie made a face. "Really?"

Hector tried to hide a smile. "Really."

"Shouldn't they be taken down at this point?"

Hector's smile fell. "Felt right to wait, at least awhile. But now . . ." He sighed. "Nobody knows what to do."

As they stepped into the elevator, Hector turned to Danner. "Up or down?"

"Up first," Danner said. "I want to see Canon's office."

Hector swiped his green badge on a scanner and hit the round six button. The elevator glided upward.

"Do you have to badge every time you use this elevator?" Danner asked.

"Yes," Hector said. "Elevator won't move otherwise."

"Will any employee badge do?"

"I know what you're asking," Hector said. "Trevor was sensitive about his office being perceived like a castle tower. He wanted to give an impression of accessibility: Drop in and see the boss. So yes, in theory, any employee could take this elevator up to Trevor's office if they badged in."

"In theory," Mackenzie said.

"Right. In practice, Trevor wasn't here much."

The doors opened and they stepped onto the sixth floor.

"I assume," Danner said, "that if Canon was rarely here, then security personnel didn't come up during their patrols."

Hector shook his head. "Didn't need to. Trevor wasn't often here at night."

They stood in a small foyer with *Mad Men* couches and fiddle-leaf figs. It was all glass and steel and clean lines, with a sparkling view of the downtown skyline. Mackenzie spied an outdoor lounge, its broad pergola crawling with pink bougainvillea.

Mackenzie glanced at Danner. "Looks like a Soho House."

Danner gave no indication he heard her. He moved through the waiting area into Canon's office itself. Mackenzie followed.

She stopped in the threshold. Directly ahead, an ugly, wine-dark stain covered the wood near Canon's desk.

Blood.

Mackenzie felt her stomach tighten.

"We had the space professionally cleaned," Hector said. "But it's been hard to get that out."

Danner seemed unperturbed. He stepped over the stain in his

black dress shoes, moving deeper into the office. Mackenzie followed him in.

There was little to see. Beyond the bloodstain the office had been thoroughly cleaned. The furniture was straightened, surfaces dusted.

There was no monitor, no laptop, no phone. All relevant technology had been removed from Canon's office almost immediately, Mackenzie assumed. Active privacy glass gave the space a soft, gossamer darkness, contrasting against the bright San Francisco morning. The office felt oddly still to Mackenzie—monastic, even.

"A few days after the . . ." Hector coughed. "After Trevor's body was discovered, SFPD told us we could clean everything. Said they'd gotten all the evidence they'd need."

"I'm not looking for evidence," Danner said. "Just want to get a visual." He pointed at Canon's desk, which was bare. "Any luck tracking Canon's laptop?"

Hector shook his head. "Still nothing."

Mackenzie chimed in. "Canon's laptop is missing?"

"Mm-hmm," said Danner. He pulled out his phone.

"Are we sure it was taken?" Mackenzie asked. "How do we know it was up here?"

"The killer left the charging cord plugged in," Danner said. "Laptop wasn't at Canon's house or anywhere else. Whoever shot Canon took it."

Mackenzie looked at Hector. "Wouldn't Canon's laptop have remote management? Security protocols, for that kind of thing?"

"Absolutely," Hector said. "Whoever has Trevor's laptop won't be able to do anything with it. It's locked up."

"Then why can't you track it?" Danner asked.

"Because it's powered off. We can't track it until it's turned on."

Danner frowned. "So somebody has Canon's laptop, but hasn't turned it on, or tried to do anything with it?"

Hector nodded. "We assume they know it has the security protocols all over it."

"Then why take it in the first place?" Mackenzie asked.

Hector shrugged. "No idea." He glanced down at the bloodstain again, grimacing. "I'm going to hang in the waiting room, if you don't need me."

Danner waved a hand. "Do what you need to do."

Mackenzie watched as Danner examined the positioning of Canon's furniture. He studied the bloodstain on the floor, then stared at his phone for a moment. He was comparing against photos, Mackenzie realized.

Mackenzie pointed to the bloodstain. "Trevor's head was here, right?" she said.

"Mm-hmm," Danner said.

"What position?"

"On his back." Danner didn't look at her, immersed in his phone.

"What about the gun?"

"Dead end."

"How do you know?" Mackenzie asked.

Danner didn't look up. "Based on the casings and the bullet recovered from Canon's head, the gun was an older model Glock 19. Bestselling pistol in America. Standard issue for law enforcement."

Eyes still on the floor, Danner opened his suit jacket to reveal a shoulder holster and the dull black of his pistol. Mackenzie was impressed by the concealment; she hadn't noticed the gun until then.

"They're everywhere," Danner said. "Unless we find the specific gun itself, it's a dead end."

Mackenzie studied a bookshelf behind Canon's desk. It contained the usual founder favorites: Friedman, Isaacson, *The Innovator's Dilemma*. Mackenzie spied a hardback of Eleanor's book, *A Seat at the Table*. The shelf above held a series of framed photographs. One showed Canon surrounded by early Journy employees, gathered under a large banner that read ONE MILLION RIDERS. All green T-shirts and smiles.

Another photo showed Canon standing next to a tall Korean American man that Mackenzie recognized as Stanley Yoo, Journy's chief technology officer. Yoo and Canon were arm in arm, smiling broadly, with some kind of electric lighting behind them. Each wore elaborate eye makeup, neon purple.

The last photo was a selfie in black and white: Canon and his girlfriend, Cassiopeia Moreau, mugging for the camera.

Mackenzie turned back to Danner. He was still studying his phone.

"Are you looking at photos from the scene? The SFPD file?"

"Mm-hmm."

"How much is in it?"

"Fair amount." Danner was barely paying attention.

"Can you share it with me?"

"Most of it's useless."

"I'd still like to look."

"I'll need to clear it with the office."

Mackenzie rolled her eyes. "Fine."

Danner stood abruptly. He moved past Mackenzie, out of Canon's office, and back into the foyer. He looked at Hector, voice authoritative. "We're good here. Let's head downstairs."

The back entrance of Journy's headquarters was as barren as the front entrance was bustling. The elevator dropped them in a small ground-floor entryway. There were no plants, no posters. Mackenzie spied a tunnel-like passageway off one side. She assumed it led to the atrium, but she couldn't hear or see anything from the rest of the building.

"Like I told you," Hector said, "not many people use this entrance."

Danner looked up at the ceiling. He pointed to an old metal plate attached to a corner. "Were cameras there?"

Hector nodded. "We used to have a whole system in place, but we removed it in the spring."

"Why?"

Hector rubbed a hand over his head. "I still don't know for sure. Trevor said all the cameras were manufactured in China and lost his shit."

"China?" Danner took notes on his phone. "Not Russia?"

Mackenzie frowned as Hector continued. "China," he repeated. "Trevor screamed at my security team. It was a mess."

Mackenzie interjected. "He was worried about China?"

"I guess so," Hector said. "Never mentioned the cameras, for years. Then in the spring he suddenly flew off the handle." He paused, thinking. "To be honest, he'd gotten more touchy about *everything* over the last few months. Almost paranoid."

Danner looked up from his phone. "Paranoid how?"

Hector gave a sheepish smile. "I should probably have a lawyer around before I say any more."

"Don't worry about it. Show us the alley."

Hector led them through a pair of utilitarian double doors and into Prince Alley. The alley was desolate, lined with garage doors and back entrances to neighboring warehouses. In the distance Mackenzie spied a frozen stampede of cars trying to jam onto I-80. The hum of the freeway echoed in the background.

Danner pointed at a badge scanner attached to the exterior wall, near the double doors. "This is where you badge in for the back."

Hector nodded, swiping his green key card. They heard a click as the doors unlatched.

"My understanding," Danner said, "is that the badges are anonymized. When you just swiped, the system didn't log 'Hector Ibarra' as the person who entered."

"Close," Hector said. "The *scanners* are anonymized. Badges are still tied to individual employees. If a badge is lost, we can deactivate it remotely. But you're essentially correct. When you *swipe* your badge anywhere around the building, you're anonymous."

"Why?" Danner asked. "Isn't it common to log employee entrances?"

"Not out here," Mackenzie said. "Tech people are used to coming and going as they please. If they get their work done, they say it shouldn't matter how long they're actually at the office."

"That's right," Hector said.

Danner sniffed. He pulled out his phone. "No cameras. Anonymous entry and exit. Doesn't seem very secure."

"We're a tech company," Hector said, "not Fort Knox."

Mackenzie thought of something. "Even if the badge-ins are anonymous, they're still logged, right?"

"Right. Entries into the building are all logged in the system, with time stamps and dates. Just without any names attached."

Mackenzie raised her eyebrows. "Can we look at those logs? For the day Trevor died?"

Hector looked confused. He glanced at Danner. "They should be in the SFPD file. We gave them all the entry logs for the day Trevor was killed."

Danner stared at his phone. "I've seen them."

Mackenzie looked at Danner. "And? Did someone badge into this back entrance on the night Canon was killed?"

Danner nodded. "Yep."

"What? When?"

"Eleven-eighteen P.M."

Mackenzie felt her eyes pop. "But that's right around Canon's time of death. Isn't it?"

Danner's voice was cool. "Just a few minutes before, yes."

Mackenzie shook her head with disbelief. "So . . . that had to be the killer, then. Right?"

Danner finally raised his eyes from his phone. "That would seem logical. The killer came in through here at 11:18. They badged the back elevator, took it directly up to Canon's office. They shot Canon, grabbed the laptop, and exited back this way."

A red tide of resentment swelled in Mackenzie's chest. "You already put all that together?"

Danner shrugged. "It lines up."

"So when were you planning to share it with me?"

Danner didn't reply, and for a long, thick moment the alley was silent. Mackenzie and Danner stared at each other.

Hector's phone pinged, the friendly, high-pitched chime breaking the quiet.

"Eleanor's assistant," he said, glancing at his screen. "She's ready for you."

They returned to the third floor. Hector pointed them toward a conference room on the opposite side of the building. They made their goodbyes.

Danner and Mackenzie walked along the edge of the atrium, Mackenzie's strides long and angry. She grinded her teeth. Several Journy employees passed them; Mackenzie watched as each gave an extra look at Danner in his suit.

Mackenzie attempted to calm herself. She kept her voice low. "Were you going to tell me?"

Danner stared straight ahead. "I'm not sure what you mean."

"During that whole song and dance with Hector, you already knew about the badge-in at 11:18 P.M. You already knew how the killer got in."

"So?"

"So it seems like important information for, you know, a fucking murder investigation. Information that might be helpful for me."

"It's all in the SFPD file."

Mackenzie didn't attempt to hide her irritation. "The file you called 'useless.' And that you haven't shared with me."

Danner kept his eyes forward. "Like I told you: soon as I clear it with the office."

Mackenzie scoffed. "I bet."

They turned a corner and moved off the main walkway. Mackenzie saw their destination: a bank of glass-walled conference rooms that ran along the south edge of the atrium.

Fine, Mackenzie thought. Danner wants to freeze me out, he can go ahead. He thinks I'm an amateur.

What Danner didn't realize was that Mackenzie was okay with that. In fact, it suited her perfectly.

They walked the rest of the way in silence.

CHAPTER 5

Mackenzie moved into the low block and pivoted, her back to the hoop. She felt her defender brace against her torso, fighting for leverage.

Mackenzie squatted and shoved back against the smaller girl's force. She raised an arm. Rachel, Reno Valley's point guard, lobbed the ball into Mackenzie's outstretched hand.

Mackenzie feinted right, then spun back to the left, whipping her left elbow into the key. It smashed into her defender's shoulder. The girl tumbled to the floor.

Mackenzie stood over her and calmly finished the layup.

"Two points, Clyde. Two points."

The gymnasium filled with light applause.

Mackenzie glanced at the scoreboard as she trotted back down the court. The fourth quarter had just begun, but everyone in the gym knew the outcome was already decided.

As a junior, Mackenzie was one of the best players in the conference—and she'd only been playing basketball for two years.

Mackenzie entered high school at six foot one. She'd never had a taste for organized sports, but Reno Valley's coach convinced her to join the team.

The experience had been a revelation. In every other venue, Mackenzie's height brought her unwanted attention. In classrooms, in hallways, in her job at the Dairy Queen, Mackenzie's life was a series of raised eyebrows and predictable questions. How tall are you? And how *old* are you? Even Mackenzie's favorite teachers couldn't help but double take when they saw her.

But on the basketball court, her frame was something to be utilized, rather than questioned. The game became her refuge; she threw herself into it. After just two years, Mackenzie was the best player on Reno Valley. She settled into the center of the key, watching as Haverford's point guard called a play.

To Mackenzie's surprise, basketball had grown into more than escapism. She loved the dull ache that blossomed in her muscles after every practice. She loved that when she stepped on the court, she thought of nothing else. The sweat of competition cleared her mind.

She even loved the dingy gymnasiums in towns like Haverford, Nevada. She loved the roll-out bleachers dotted with hopeful parents and students. She loved the inevitable silence that settled over them when they realized that Mackenzie was the best player on the court. And she loved making that clear, mercilessly, one shot, one rebound, one block at a time.

When the Haverford point guard drove to the hoop, Mackenzie was ready. She slid laterally across the key, long legs gulping the space. The point guard launched a floater, but Mackenzie was simply too tall. It was an easy block. A calm voice in her mind told her to block it softly—tip the ball to a teammate to retain possession.

But the latent competitor in Mackenzie, the one that seemed to ignite spontaneously every time she stepped on the court, told her something else.

Mackenzie swung her arm and swatted the shot out of the air. The ball skied out of bounds, bouncing against the bleachers with a satisfying *thunk.*

Mackenzie didn't celebrate. She stared blankly into space, wiping the sweat off her brow, enjoying the sting that radiated through her hand.

Then she heard the voice.

"Jessica, I *told* you: Don't take it straight at the Giraffe."

It was Haverford's coach. He stood on the sideline in a too-tight red polo with HAVERFORD BASKETBALL stenciled on the chest. He was young for a high school coach, maybe thirty, with gelled hair and an abominable goatee.

He'd been yelling all game, but Mackenzie had tuned him out. Her ears had become inured to opposing coaches and fans.

Until now.

Mackenzie's attention caught on the word. *Giraffe*. He'd said it earlier, too. Sometime in the third quarter.

Coach Goatee implored the Haverford point guard. "Go *around* the Giraffe, not over her." Mackenzie ignored the snickers from the Haverford bench.

The teams traded possessions. Mackenzie drained a jump shot, building Reno Valley's lead.

Haverford's coach threw his hands up with disgust. "Tisha! Tisha!" Goatee thrust his hands toward Mackenzie. "When the Giraffe gets the ball, you have to double her."

Now the snickers were louder. They came not just from the Haverford bench, but from the bleachers as well. Mackenzie felt a prickling sensation in her shoulders.

Ignore it, she told herself.

Two minutes later Mackenzie inbounded the ball on the sideline. The Haverford coach was standing just feet away. Mackenzie could smell a waft of Walgreens cologne.

Goatee barked again. "When the Giraffe is inbounding, double one of her teammates! Go, come on!" Mackenzie's defender scrambled away. "That's it, go! Leave the Giraffe!"

The snickers evolved into full-blown laughter. In the bleachers, Haverford students roared in appreciation of Goatee's comedic genius.

The laughs were unavoidable. For a moment, the gym filled with them.

Ignore it, she told herself. Mackenzie found a teammate and in-bounded the ball.

The game plodded forward. The familiar, resigned silence settled over the Haverford crowd. Coach Goatee gesticulated wildly from the sideline as the game slipped away.

Mackenzie went after a loose ball as it bounced toward the Haverford bench. She dove across the sideline, snatching the ball and flinging it over her head, back onto the court.

Mackenzie landed hard on the wooden floor. A flash of pain shot through her shoulder. She groaned, rolling to one side.

Goatee was standing nearby. Through the haze of her pain, Mackenzie watched the Haverford coach glance down at her. Then he leapt into action.

"The Giraffe is down!" Goatee yelled to his players. "Go, go, go! She's a wounded animal!"

A fresh wave of laughter rose from the Haverford crowd and crashed over Mackenzie.

She felt something stir in her mind. It was a familiar feeling, deep and lingering. The basketball court had been one place where she'd always been able to keep it at bay—until now. It bloomed in her gut like a black rose.

They're all staring at me, she realized. I'm the Giraffe.

In Mackenzie's mind the entire gym had fallen into darkness and only she was illuminated. A tall, gangly pile of limbs in a spotlight on the floor.

Mackenzie stared at the Haverford coach as he waved at his players. "Go, go, go!" he shouted. She watched the sweat reflect off the shine of his goatee. Saw the spittle escape his mouth as he yelled the word again: *Giraffe!*

The shame in Mackenzie's gut evaporated. It was replaced by an overwhelming wave of something else.

Fury.

Mackenzie jumped up from the floor. She stood to her full height, just ten feet away from the Haverford coach. She stared at him. "Hey. Asshole!"

Goatee snapped to face Mackenzie. "What did you just say?"

Her body prepared to move. I'm going to hit him, she thought.

Suddenly she lurched backward. Someone had grabbed her from behind, pulling at her waist. She heard a plaintive voice in her ear.

"Stop."

It was Whitney, her coach.

Mackenzie struggled for a moment, but Whitney held firm. She pulled Mackenzie toward the Reno Valley bench.

"Come on, Mackenzie. He's not worth it. Forget him. He's *not worth it*."

Slowly, Mackenzie felt her rage begin to cool, the red wave ebbing from her mind. She allowed Whitney to pull her backward. Goatee turned away, refocusing on the court.

Whitney and Mackenzie reached the Reno Valley bench. Whitney turned Mackenzie around and faced her, raising her hands to Mackenzie's shoulders. Her voice was quiet.

"Let it go," Whitney said. "Okay?"

Mackenzie dropped her head in embarrassment, breaking Whitney's eye contact. She stared at the floor. "Okay."

"You played your ass off," Whitney said. "The guy's a slapdick, but he doesn't *matter*. Got it?"

"Got it."

"Look at me." Mackenzie raised her head, and Whitney stared at her, eyes square and serious. "You're better than him, better than anyone else in this gym. In an hour you'll forget all about him."

"I know," Mackenzie said, meaning it. "You're right."

"Good. Take a seat. You're done for the night."

Mackenzie dropped to the bench. The game moved on. As her blood cooled, her rational mind regained control. Mackenzie realized the obvious: Whitney had saved her.

Hitting the Haverford coach would've earned her a suspension. Maybe worse. You've got to be smarter than that, Mackenzie told herself.

The clock ran out. Mackenzie's teammates trotted off the court and huddled up. Several gave her an encouraging slap on the back.

"Their coach is a fucking loser," Rachel said.

"You kicked ass tonight," said another.

Mackenzie smiled, mind clear. "Thanks."

Whitney looked around the huddle. "Good game. Now go line up and let's get the hell out of here." Mackenzie joined her teammates in laughter.

The teams lined up and high-fived as they passed each other. The gym was quiet. The last vestiges of Haverford fans trickled out of the bleachers.

"Good game," Mackenzie said to each girl.

"Good game," each girl responded. None of them gave Mackenzie a second look.

Coaches went last, at the back of the line. Goatee was waiting. He shook hands with Mackenzie's teammates, grinning broadly. The bulldog persona had disappeared; now the Haverford coach was all bright eyes and ingratiating comments.

"Hey, great game. Good shooting. You got a solid team here. Hope to see you again in the playoffs."

Mackenzie reached the end of the line. She and the Haverford coach were about equal height; their eyes met as they approached each other. Mackenzie saw sweat running through the gel in his hair, wetlands seeping at the armpits of his red polo.

The Haverford coach called Mackenzie by her number. "Hey, fifty-five. Tell you what, you're a hell of a competitor."

Goatee gave Mackenzie a winning smile. "Leave it all out there on the court, right? What do you say?" He extended a hand.

Giraffe, Mackenzie thought.

Then she balled her fist as hard as she could, reached down, and punched him in the nuts.

CHAPTER 6

Twenty-three days after Trevor Canon's death

Eleanor Eden met them in the conference room doorway.

"Apologies," she said. "Things have been a mess here." She waved Mackenzie and Danner inside. "Come in, come in."

Eleanor Eden's hair was thin and wavy brown, face oval, white skin fair but not pale, eyes blue but not memorably so. She was dressed in Martha Stewart–meets–tech: a billowy gray sweater draped over jeans and black Nikes.

Even accounting for the stress of her job, she looked unwell. There were dark rings under her eyes, her skin red with fatigue. Her hair was stringy and tied back in a messy ponytail. A solar flare of rash had broken out on one cheek. She moved methodically, as though lacking the energy for anything more. To Mackenzie, she looked like a woman carrying the weight of the world on her shoulders.

Or just the fate of a seventy-billion-dollar company, Mackenzie thought. And the livelihoods of its thousands of employees.

Danner extended a stiff hand. "Special Agent Jameson Danner, FBI."

Eleanor gave him a weary smile and shook. "Nice to meet you, Agent Danner. Eleanor Eden, COO of Journy. Please sit down, get comfortable."

Eleanor had converted a conference room into a makeshift office. Two whiteboards. A square, counter-height table in the middle, white stools around the edges. Oversized windows with a view back to the atrium. Late morning sun poured through the atrium's retractable roof and suffused the conference room with a utopian glow.

Eleanor occupied one side of the square table. Mackenzie and Danner moved toward the opposite, but Eleanor ushered them closer.

"Over here," she said, gesturing to an adjacent edge. "Table's too damn big, I hate when people sit across from me. Feels like dining in Downton Abbey."

Mackenzie chose a stool. Danner carefully unbuttoned his jacket and did the same. He took out his phone.

"Mackenzie," Eleanor said, "it's good to see you."

Mackenzie felt a flush in her cheeks, a carousel of memories flashing through her mind. She hoped it didn't show. "Good to see you, too," Mackenzie said. "Though I'm sorry it's under these circumstances."

Danner looked up from his phone, glancing between the two women. His brow furrowed. "You two already know each other?"

"Yes," Eleanor said simply. "We dated."

"Oh." Danner's features relaxed.

Eleanor gave a small smile. "It was very brief, and very long ago."

"Huh." As though to signal his disinterest, Danner returned his attention to his phone.

Mackenzie looked at Eleanor. "I can't imagine what it's been like. Everyone at Hammersmith Venture sends their condolences."

"The folks at HV have been very kind," Eleanor said. "They've bombarded us with flowers."

Danner slid his phone back into his pocket. "Okay," he said, as though the two women hadn't already begun a conversation. "Let's begin."

"Yes," Eleanor said, with a hint of authority. Her posture was relaxed, gaze steady. Despite her obvious exhaustion, Eleanor's natural self-assurance reminded Mackenzie of Hammersmith.

"Agent Danner," Eleanor said, "I'd like to express how gratified I am that the FBI is taking over the investigation. I have great respect for the police: My aunt was a cop in Indiana for thirty-two years. But the SFPD was an embarrassment."

"I'm aware," Danner said.

"Trevor's killer," Eleanor continued, "is still running free. Meanwhile, our company is suffering. Trevor's death was a traumatic event. Especially considering it happened here, in this building."

"I understand," Danner said, nodding.

Eleanor's voice hardened. "There are two thousand employees at Journy, and I'm responsible for them. I need to bring them closure."

"That's what I'm here for," Danner said. He delivered the words like a Boy Scout.

"Excellent." Eleanor grabbed a legal pad and a thin-point Sharpie from the conference table. "You tell me what you need and I'll get it for you. Where do you want to start?"

"Canon's laptop," Danner said. "Hector Ibarra said you can't track it until it's powered on."

Eleanor gave a half-nod. "Whoever stole it has been smart enough to keep it off."

"If Canon's laptop turns on, we need to be notified. Immediately."

"You'll know the instant it happens," Eleanor said. "What's next?"

"Employee interviews."

Eleanor nodded. "I thought you'd want to start there."

"My understanding," Danner said, "is that nobody at Journy spoke to SFPD."

"Correct." Eleanor leaned against the back of her stool. She crossed one leg over the other. "After Trevor was killed, we gave SFPD everything we could. Hector's entire team was dedicated to helping them." Eleanor smirked. "Didn't take long to realize that was a mistake."

Danner's expression remained impassive. "Why?"

"Our efforts weren't reciprocated. Forensics found nothing. Then they disappeared for a week." Eleanor shook her head softly. "Said they wouldn't treat Trevor's homicide as any different than the others on their docket. I was shocked at the bureaucracy."

"City departments are understaffed," Danner said. "It's not the best and the brightest."

"Maybe I've watched too much *Law & Order*. Did you know that in big cities, the majority of murders go unsolved?"

Danner's voice was officious. "This is America, Miss Eden. People get away with murder every day."

Mackenzie almost choked. She coughed to hide it.

Danner continued. "That's why the FBI has stepped in. We get results."

"I sincerely hope so," Eleanor said. She waved a hand. "Once we learned that one of the SFPD detectives was an alcoholic, we resolved not to give them anything else. In the end, nobody spoke to them." Eleanor looked at Danner. "Now that you're here, of course, that will change."

"Good," Danner said. "I'll start the interviews as quickly as possible."

"Just tell me where you want to begin."

"With the people Canon trusted most," Danner said. "Who was on Canon's senior staff?"

"It's easier to show you."

Eleanor stood and moved to a whiteboard, grabbing a dry-erase pen from an attached tray. Mackenzie noted it was bright green. The color was becoming inescapable.

Eleanor wrote Trevor's name near the top of the board. "Trevor was the top. Directly under him was the executive team, including me."

Under Trevor's name Eleanor left a gap and then wrote out *EXECS* followed by five names:

ELEANOR
HC
CASS
STAN
B

Eleanor's handwriting was friendly and rounded, with oversized loops that reminded Mackenzie of a schoolteacher's. "You'll want to start with the execs. We were Trevor's direct reports. Effectively, we ran—run, I suppose now—Journy."

"Did Canon work closely with anyone else at the company?" Danner asked.

Eleanor shook her head. "Not really," she said. "He delegated almost everything to us."

Danner nodded. "Then I'll need to speak to everyone on the executive team as soon as possible."

"We have a meeting this afternoon," Eleanor said. "We can introduce you and go from there."

Danner studied the list of names. "It'd be helpful if you could remind me who's who. I don't recognize your shorthand."

"Of course." Still holding the green pen, Eleanor gestured at her name. "COO," she said. "I run everything in the company that isn't directly touching the technical product. Customer service, finance, HR, more."

Then Eleanor pointed at HC. "Hugo Chamberlain," she said. "Chief product officer. Oversees everything related to product experience and design."

Mackenzie sensed Danner trying to hide his confusion. "That means every time you open the Journy app," she said to him, "Hugo Chamberlain's team is in control of how it looks, how it works, everything you click on. All of that."

Danner nodded. "Let's keep going."

You're welcome, thought Mackenzie.

Eleanor pointed to Cass. "Cassiopeia Moreau, chief marketing officer. Oversees everything related to marketing and . . ." Eleanor cleared her throat. "Journy's 'brand expression.'"

"Moreau was also Trevor Canon's girlfriend," Danner said. "Is that correct?"

"That's right," Eleanor said. Her mouth curled into an odd shape, but she moved on, pointing to Stan. "Stanley Yoo. CTO, chief technology officer. Oversees all the engineering, all the code."

Danner pointed to the last name on the list. "And what about B?"

"Brady Fitzgerald," Eleanor said. "Journy's original co-founder, with Trevor. Now he's our CIO."

"Chief information officer?" Danner asked.

Eleanor hesitated. "Not quite. Brady is Journy's chief innovation officer."

Mackenzie was unable to stop herself: A tiny snicker escaped her lips. Danner snapped his eyes to hers. "Why the laugh?"

"In tech," Mackenzie said, "chief innovation officer is a bullshit title. A company like Journy gives it to someone they can't get rid of but don't want anywhere important. It's like being put out to pasture."

Danner looked back to Eleanor. "Is that true of Brady?"

Eleanor returned to her stool. "Mackenzie's characterization is . . . not inaccurate."

Danner didn't reply; he typed something on his phone. "If we're going to start with the executive team," Danner said, "then I'd like to ask you some questions while we're here."

"I assumed you would," Eleanor said.

Danner paused. There was an awkward moment where he and Eleanor each waited for the other to speak.

"Go ahead," Eleanor said.

"Do we need to wait for a lawyer?"

"No." Eleanor waved a hand. "Like I said, I'll give you anything you need."

"Okay." Danner glanced at his phone. "You worked with Canon for six years, is that correct?"

"That's right."

"How did you and Canon originally meet?"

"I assume you know that I spent many years at Spyder, working for Tobias." Danner nodded. "I thought I would be at Spyder for my entire career. But then I wrote *A Seat at the Table* and, well . . ." Eleanor gave an embarrassed smile. "It did much better than I expected. Zoe and I had our second child right after it was published."

"Zoe," Danner interjected. "Your ex-wife."

"Yes," Eleanor said. "So I left Spyder and focused on family for a while. Lecture circuit, some consulting. I was still doing that when I met Trevor at a dinner party." Eleanor laughed. "His recruiting pitch was relentless. Started the full-court press before appetizers and didn't let up for a full year. Finally I put an end to it and came to work for him."

"A year?" Danner said. "You were hard to persuade."

"Journy was still very small back then. And I was hesitant to jump into something that I knew would be all-consuming."

"What convinced you?"

Eleanor shrugged. "Trevor did. His energy, his perspective . . . he reminded me of Tobias, back in Spyder's early days. Trevor's passion for Journy was contagious. And his ideas had real potential. I knew I could help make them into reality."

Danner typed on his phone, fingers flying over his screen.

"During your six years with Canon," Danner said, "you were his chief lieutenant."

"Yes. We spoke all the time. Even on holidays, weekends." Eleanor chuckled. "Zoe joked that Trevor was the de facto third member of our marriage. Not as funny after the divorce, I guess."

Mackenzie smiled, but Danner didn't laugh. "It's fair to say you knew Canon as well as anyone."

"Sure."

"Did you notice any changes in Canon recently? Any differences in behavior?"

Eleanor's eyes dropped to the table. "I think everybody did. Trevor had . . . changed. It'd gotten worse."

"What had gotten worse?"

"His paranoia," Eleanor said.

"Ibarra mentioned the same thing," Danner said. "Canon demanded he remove all the cameras."

"Yes, the cameras were one example. Though Trevor was *always* paranoid, to a degree. Every founder has a healthy dose of paranoia."

"Why?"

"There are no original ideas in the tech industry, Agent Danner. Everything is a copy, an amalgamation. It doesn't matter how original your idea is: All that matters is how well you execute it. Founders live in constant fear of someone stealing their idea and doing it *better* than they could."

"And that's what set Canon off about the cameras? He was worried about spying?"

"That's what I thought." Eleanor sighed. "But looking back, the cameras were part of a broader pattern. Trevor's behavior had grown strange over the past few months."

"How? Had he become more demanding?"

Eleanor gave a soft smile. "Trevor was always demanding. He was always, frankly, difficult to work for. This went beyond his typical. He was acting . . . not himself."

Danner leaned in. "How so?"

Eleanor looked upward, as though conjuring something from memory. "Trevor began to disappear from the office for long stretches. He was gone all the time. And he wouldn't tell anyone where he was going."

"How long was that happening?"

"Three or four months, at least. He'd be unreachable for hours, even days at a time."

"He wouldn't tell anybody where he was?"

"Like you say, I knew him as well as anyone. And he didn't tell me."

Danner continued to type on his phone. "What else?"

"Well, there's the will, obviously."

"Yes," Danner said. He looked up from his phone, eyes searching. Mackenzie watched him closely. "We should talk about the will. Canon added the new section."

"The dead money," Eleanor said. "Froze all his assets in the event he was murdered."

"It's an unusual thing for a person to add to a will," Danner said. "It strikes me as an escalation of the behavior you've been describing."

"I'd agree."

"It appears that Canon wasn't just paranoid. He was frightened for his life."

Eleanor nodded. "For good reason, it turns out."

"He never said anything about it to you? Never gave any indication that he was fearing for his safety?"

Eleanor shook her head. "With him out of the office so much, I didn't see him as often as I normally did."

Danner took a note on his phone. "This dead money provision," he said. "When did you learn that Canon had put it in his will?"

"After he died," Eleanor said. "Like everyone else."

"When after he died?"

"I don't remember exactly. The lawyers told all of us on the executive team at the same time. They were explaining what a mess it was going to create for Journy."

"What about other employees?" Danner asked. "Would anyone else have known about the change?"

Eleanor shook her head again. "The lawyers said Trevor's will was private. If he didn't want to tell anybody he'd amended it, he didn't have to."

To her surprise, Danner looked at Mackenzie. "What about your boss?"

"Roger?" Mackenzie asked. "What about him?"

"Did he know Canon had changed his will?"

"He didn't know anything about it. If he had, he would've shit a brick."

"The dead money provision," Eleanor said, "hurts Roger worst of all. Without it, he'd have billions more in Journy shares. And controlling interest in the company."

Danner's face was rigid. He looked back at Eleanor. "Without the dead money provision," he said, "my understanding is that Canon's assets would be distributed among *all* the existing shareholders. Not just Hammersmith."

"That's right."

"Including you and the executive team."

"Including us, yes," Eleanor said. "Though not anywhere near the level of Roger and his firm."

"Still, if Canon's will were distributed normally, everyone on the executive team would come into a lot of Journy shares."

Danner's angle was clear, but Eleanor didn't seem perturbed by it. "That's correct."

"What was the value of those shares?"

Eleanor paused, calculating. "About a hundred million dollars per person."

Danner let the implication hang in the air. After Canon's death, each member of the executive team would have netted one hundred million dollars in Journy shares—until Canon put in the dead money clause and gummed it all up.

Now Mackenzie understood Danner's questions about timing. If nobody at Journy knew Canon had amended his will, they all would've assumed that killing Canon would earn them a massive windfall.

There's your motive, Mackenzie thought.

Danner's tone changed subtly. "I imagine you worked a lot of late nights."

"We all did."

"What about the night that Canon died? Did you work late?"

"No. I left around six."

"And did you see Canon before you left?"

Again, Danner's angle was transparent. "No," Eleanor said. "He'd been gone most of the day." She gave a weary chuckle. "If you want my alibi, Agent Danner, all you have to do is ask."

Danner remained stoic. "Where were you on the night of Canon's murder?"

"I was at a gala," Eleanor said.

"A gala?" Danner blinked. "For what?"

As Mackenzie expected, Eleanor turned in her direction. "Mackenzie can tell you. She was there."

Mackenzie nodded. "It was the big *Fortune* magazine gala, over at the W Hotel."

"You were both there?" Danner asked.

Mackenzie nodded again. "Eleanor was being honored. She was named this year's Most Powerful Woman in Tech."

Danner furrowed his brow. "They have a gala for that?"

"Every year," Mackenzie said. "Band, canapés, white tablecloths. Gala stuff."

"Tiny food and big egos," Eleanor said dismissively. "It was all quite ridiculous."

"How many people were there?" Danner asked.

"Probably a couple hundred," Eleanor said.

"And you were there all night?"

Eleanor smiled. "I was the guest of honor, Agent Danner. I was expected to stay late."

"How late is late?"

"One or one-thirty. I took a Journy home. I can send my receipts, if it's helpful." Eleanor shrugged. "And there were photographers. I'm sure *Fortune* put the photos on their website. Gaia, my assistant, can send you the link."

"Have her do that," Danner said, and Eleanor took another note on her legal pad. Danner glanced at Mackenzie. "Why were you at the gala?"

"Work," Mackenzie said. "Our firm sent a bunch of people to show support."

Danner kept typing. "But how did Eleanor know you were there?"

"It was very glamorous." Eleanor smirked. "We ran into each other in the bathroom line."

There was a knock on the conference room door; a purple-haired Zoomer stuck her head in.

"Sorry to interrupt," she said. "Eleanor, you've got the call with Genevieve's school in a few."

Eleanor's face fell. "Right. I'd forgotten." She sighed, rubbing a hand through her thinning hair. "Thank you, Gaia." Gaia withdrew, door closing behind her.

Eleanor turned to Danner. "I'm happy to continue this later, Agent Danner."

"I've got what I need for now." Danner tucked his phone into a suit pocket. "We'll talk more at the executive meeting."

Eleanor consulted the list on her legal pad. "I'll make sure Gaia sends over the material you asked for." She looked up. "As we set up interviews, are there others you want to add to the list?"

Danner tilted his head. "Others?"

"Yes." Seeing Danner's blank look, Eleanor continued. "Other people of interest: competitors, former employees, spurned investors. SFPD asked me to compile a list."

"Oh," Danner said flatly. "Did any of them work closely with Canon?"

Eleanor paused. "Well . . . no."

"Then don't bother," said Danner. "I won't need it." He carefully pivoted off his stool. Mackenzie did the same.

Eleanor frowned with surprise. "You won't need it?"

"No," Danner said. "Nobody on that list killed Canon."

Eleanor blinked, surprise deepening. Mackenzie froze next to her stool. "How can you know that?" Eleanor asked.

Danner's voice was matter-of-fact. "Because I know exactly how Canon was murdered. And I'm close to knowing who did it."

There was a stunned silence in the conference room. "I have to ask you to elaborate," Eleanor said.

Danner gave another casual shrug. Mackenzie was growing to detest the tic. "According to the logs you gave SFPD, someone badged in at the back entrance at 11:18 P.M. Just minutes before Canon's time of death."

"And you think that was the killer?" Eleanor asked.

"Had to be," Danner said. "The office cleared out after dinner service. Nobody came through the front. And the back entrance leads right to Canon's office elevator."

"I understand," Eleanor said. "But over a thousand people work in this building. All of them have badges."

Danner's posture remained rigid, charcoal suit still crisp. "The killer didn't just have a badge. They knew they'd be anonymous, even after badging in. They knew they could take the back elevator straight to Canon's office without being seen. They knew there wouldn't be cameras. And they knew they could exit right back out the same path."

"They had to know our office well," Eleanor said.

"Extremely well," Danner agreed. "Especially a part of the office that's rarely used."

Danner's voice was as calm as a morning lake. Mackenzie wanted to throw a rock in it. "That doesn't narrow it down," she said. "Any longtime employee would know the headquarters."

"There's more," Danner replied. "Ibarra said that Canon was

rarely in his office, especially at night. But the killer *knew* Canon would be there the night he was killed."

"Oh, god," Eleanor said. She groaned, resting her forehead on her hands. "And Trevor had been so secretive . . ."

Danner nodded. "You said Canon didn't work closely with many people. And lately he'd gone missing for long, unexplained stretches. But on the night he was murdered, someone knew *exactly when and where* to find him. It means the killer was in Canon's inner circle, was trusted enough to have access to his whereabouts."

Mackenzie gritted her teeth. She wanted badly to find a hole in Danner's logic, to interrupt his one-man parade of deductive brilliance. But as her mind spun through Danner's arguments, she was forced to admit: His logic was sound.

Eleanor looked up from her hands, voice strained. "When the SFPD asked me to compile people of interest, part of me was relieved. It meant the killer could be from outside Journy: an old enemy, a competitor. I didn't want to think about the other possibility." Eleanor's eyes grew heavy, and for an instant Mackenzie worried she might cry.

"I empathize," Danner said, his tone so flat that it was clear he didn't. "But the deductions are clear. The killer had a badge, knew the building, knew how to come and go, and knew exactly where to find Canon."

Danner pushed in his stool and buttoned his suit. "Add it all up," he said, "and there's only one conclusion: Trevor Canon was murdered by someone he trusted."

CHAPTER 7

Twenty-three days after Trevor Canon's death

Mackenzie waited.

She stayed quiet as she and Danner made their way to the Hangar, Journy's extravagant cafeteria.

Neither of them spoke as they put together their poke bowls. Mackenzie stewed as she thrust piles of sushi rice into Heath ceramic.

Mackenzie said nothing as they poured drinks from the endless wall of taps. She chose something called a pomelo sparkler.

Mackenzie kept silent as she and Danner took seats in a corner of the Hangar. She watched Danner unfold a linen napkin—Journy green—and tuck it into his collar, covering his tie.

She waited until Danner picked up his chopsticks and snagged a piece of tuna.

Then she let it out.

"What the fuck was that?"

Danner paused, chopsticks millimeters from his lips. "What was what?"

"Let's not," Mackenzie replied. "You know what I'm talking about."

Danner stuck the tuna into his mouth, expression placid. "I'm afraid I don't."

Danner's posture remained upright, shoulders square, angular jaw chewing the fish. He held his chopsticks casually in his right hand.

Mackenzie hated him in that moment. She hated his suit. Hated the scrupulous way he chewed his tuna. Hated his clean, boyish cheeks and boxy shoulders. Hated the officious tone he'd used to dismiss her all morning long.

"You knew," Mackenzie said. "Before you even stepped foot in this office, you knew that Canon was killed by someone close to him."

Danner deftly lifted another piece of tuna. "So?"

"So we've spent all morning together," Mackenzie said. "Hector. Canon's office, the elevators, the back alley. Eleanor. But you said nothing to me."

"I was under no obligation to."

"Then why did you tell Eleanor?"

Danner's eyebrows descended a fraction of an inch. "Eden is Journy's liaison to the investigation. I decided there was value in sharing progress with her."

"But no value in telling me."

"No."

"You made me look like an ass. Like I was completely out of the loop."

Danner finally stopped eating. He removed his napkin from his collar and placed his chopsticks on the table in a tight parallel.

"I don't care if you looked like an ass," he said. "I care about doing my job. You got Ibarra's tour, same as I did. You heard Eden tell us that Canon had a small inner circle. Are you pissed because I made the obvious deduction? Or pissed because *you* didn't?"

Mackenzie grabbed her fork, leaving her chopsticks unused. She speared a piece of tuna and took a bite. It was delicious. For some reason this only furthered her irritation.

"You're freezing me out," she said. Danner didn't reply, so she continued. "I had to *pull* the badge thing out of you. You're dragging your feet on sending me SFPD files. Hell, you've barely spoken to me since we met."

"Freezing you out." Danner chuckled lightly. Mackenzie realized it was the first time she'd seen him smile. "You're not supposed to be *in* to begin with."

"I'm your advisor on this," Mackenzie said. "That was part of the deal when the Bureau got the investigation."

"'Advisor,'" Danner scoffed. Mackenzie noted traces of tension in his jaw. "This little role that Hammersmith conjured up for you, 'advisor'—it doesn't exist. You don't get to toss one of your lackeys into an FBI homicide investigation. I don't care how much money you have."

"I can help you," Mackenzie said.

"How? By whining because I didn't tell you something?" Skepticism washed over Danner's face. "This isn't a buddy cop movie. This is a federal homicide case under the Criminal Investigative Division of the FBI. Serious as it gets. We don't partner with amateurs. Especially not a VC lawyer with zero criminal training."

"I don't pretend to know how to conduct a criminal investigation," Mackenzie said. "That's not why I'm here."

"Then why *are* you here?"

"Because I know the tech world. If Canon was killed by someone in his inner circle, in his very own office, then the murder has to be connected to his work. To Journy, to the industry. I can help you navigate it."

"Don't need it," Danner said. He waved a hand, gesturing at the extravagance around them. "All this nonsense, the weird titles and the roof deck and the fancy lunches . . ." Danner shook his head. "None of it matters. What matters is I've got a body three weeks cold and a killer to find."

"I can still help you," Mackenzie said. She kept her voice calm. "I don't care about the green logo and the ball pits, either. But this industry is insular. Everyone's connected, and everyone's trying to exploit those connections to get rich. I understand how these people think. I can help you figure out why one of them would want to kill Canon."

"I've already got motive," Danner said. "The dead money. None of the execs knew Canon had changed his will. Everyone thought killing him meant they'd get some of his shares. Nine figures' worth."

Danner replaced the linen napkin over his tie, picked up his chopsticks, and resumed eating.

"From here," Danner said, "I focus on opportunity. Who had the opportunity to be here, at Journy's headquarters, at 11:18 P.M. on the night Canon was killed? Who can't prove they were somewhere else?"

"So you want to check alibis."

Danner nodded, chewing. "An alibi is a simple thing: It either holds up or it doesn't."

"But to check alibis," Mackenzie said, "you'll need to talk to people. Interview them."

"I started with Eleanor Eden. Now I'll move on to the rest of the executive team." Danner glanced at his watch. "We're meeting with them in twenty minutes."

Mackenzie hadn't noticed Danner's watch until then—for most of the day it'd been tucked under his sleeve. It was a gold Patek Philippe, easily worth six figures.

Mackenzie had developed a keen sense of the wealth of people she encountered. But she hadn't gotten a whiff of money from Danner. His suit was nice, but American. As were his shoes. But there was no denying the watch.

Mackenzie refocused. "The interviews are where I can help you," she said. "People in this industry are different. There's a language they use. A silent hierarchy that's always in play. If you don't understand it, it can be hard to navigate."

"I know how to interview someone."

"How can you be sure the executives will even talk to you? None of them spoke to SFPD."

Danner gave a thin smile. "I'm not SFPD. The tech industry likes to act like it's god's gift, but people here aren't immune from FBI authority. If the Department of Justice comes knocking, they'll answer."

Mackenzie kept her voice light. "It won't be that simple. A lot of people out here don't give a shit about the government—FBI, DOJ, or otherwise. You'd be surprised how many of them think the government is totally immaterial. Obsolete. They think they're above it."

"And you know how to talk to people like that?"

"Unfortunately, it's part of my job," Mackenzie said. "I can speak their language, even if I find it obnoxious."

Danner finished his lunch. He removed the napkin from his collar, folded it with origami precision, and placed it on the table. Then he rested his chopsticks on top, perfectly parallel.

"Maybe that is your job." Danner leaned back in his chair, tone pedantic as he opened his phone. "But I know what I'm doing. In a few minutes we'll have all the executives in one room. Maybe some will answer questions on the spot. Otherwise I'll set up the formal interviews and go from there."

Mackenzie stayed quiet, studying Danner as she finished her lunch. He's young, Mackenzie thought. And he's smart, but he's not wise.

The wise thing for Danner would have been to string Mackenzie along. He could've easily placated her. Given her just enough information to keep her feeling important, but not enough responsibility to actually get in his way.

But he's got too much pride, Mackenzie thought. Pride, or insecurity. Two sides of the same coin. When a person actually knows what they're doing, they don't have to express it out loud. Danner was acting. He was out of his depth. Playing a role.

Just like her.

Mackenzie broke the silence, straining to remove any acidity from her tone. "You're right, you know."

Danner glanced up from his phone, eyes meeting Mackenzie's. "About what?"

"It being someone Canon trusted. Think of his laptop. Whoever stole it has been smart enough not to power it on. They know exactly how the tracking works. The killer knows Canon, and Journy, inside and out."

Danner pressed his lips together. "Fair point."

Mackenzie continued. "I'm sorry I snapped at you. But I didn't choose to be here. I've got a boss, just like you. And I'm trying to do the job he gave me. I think I can help you, but the last thing I want is to be a pain in the ass."

Danner stared at her over the top of his phone. "Okay."

"All I ask," Mackenzie said, "is that you keep me in the loop. This is a huge opportunity for me. As long as you keep me informed, keep me inside the investigation, I promise I won't get in your way."

Danner dropped his phone to the table. "That's fine," he said. "But you need to understand that this is a dangerous situation."

"I get it."

"When I give this to the DOJ lawyers, it needs to be airtight. If you do something against procedure, even accidentally, it could torpedo the case. And if that happens, my director and the assistant U.S. attorney will have my ass." Danner shifted in his seat. "You can come along on the interviews, ask questions, make observations. But you need to defer to me. Follow my lead, one hundred percent."

"No problem."

Danner nodded. "Then we're on the same page."

Equilibrium, Mackenzie thought. Only achieved by pretending to be deferential, but it suited her purposes. For now.

Mackenzie's phone vibrated. She glanced at the screen: Hammersmith.

She grabbed her phone and moved away from the table. She found an empty spot out of Danner's earshot.

Mackenzie answered. "Roger."

Hammersmith spoke quickly. "What'd you learn this morning?"

Mackenzie filled him in. She went through her initial encounter with Danner, the tour with Hector, the meeting with Eleanor. She went into detail on Danner's deductions. The only piece she left out was their lunchtime argument.

"Danner thinks it was an employee," Hammersmith said.

"An employee in Canon's inner circle," Mackenzie said. "Someone who had a badge, knew the office well, knew where Canon would be that night."

"Seems logical."

"It's hard to argue with."

Mackenzie could hear Hammersmith thinking. "Then Danner will begin interviews soon."

"He already asked Eleanor some questions." Mackenzie glanced at the time on her phone. "In a few minutes we have a meeting scheduled with the rest of the executive team. Danner thinks he'll set up interviews all at once."

Hammersmith chuckled. "He thinks it's going to be that easy?"

Mackenzie smiled into the phone. "Eleanor was willing to answer questions without a lawyer. I think that's given Danner the wrong impression."

"He really thinks he can just round up all the Journy executives like that? One fell swoop?"

"Danner's not short on confidence."

"That's not surprising," Hammersmith said. "This morning I learned a bit more about Agent Danner."

"Oh?"

"Graduated from Yale, went into Quantico soon after. He's been with the FBI for six years, but he's only been with CID for fifteen months."

"Barely over a year?" Mackenzie was surprised. "Where in the Bureau was he before that?"

"Not sure," Hammersmith said. "I'm trying to track that down."

"He looks pretty young."

"He's only thirty."

Mackenzie had been right. Danner was several years younger than she was. "If he's that young, and that inexperienced on CID, how the hell did he land an investigation this high profile?"

"Now we get to the good part." Hammersmith sounded amused. "Did Agent Danner tell you his full name?"

"Jameson Danner."

"Jameson is his middle name. His *full* name is Osiris Jameson Danner, Jr."

Mackenzie stared to the far side of the Hangar. "As in Osiris Danner the senator?"

"As in Ozzie Danner, Senate minority leader." Hammersmith paused for effect. "Agent Danner is his eldest son."

Ozzie Danner was a longtime senator and former ambassador to a country Mackenzie couldn't recall. Agent Danner's father was one of the most powerful men in the country. Mackenzie's mind flashed to the Patek Philippe.

"It explains Agent Danner's rapid ascent through the FBI," Hammersmith said. "And how he landed the primary role on the Canon investigation."

"It would also explain his confidence," Mackenzie said. "And . . . the rest of his personality."

Hammersmith chuckled again. "I know Ozzie Danner. Arrogant prick. Would you say it's genetic?"

Mackenzie paused. "Agent Danner doesn't just have a stick up his ass. He's got the whole tree."

"HA!" Hammersmith released one of his bellowing laughs. "Well, be careful. Ozzie Danner may be a prick, but he's smart. His son could be the same."

"He's not stupid," Mackenzie said. "He's already made more progress in a few hours than SFPD did in weeks."

"Sounds that way. Text me after the meeting with the executive staff."

"Will do."

Mackenzie re-pocketed her phone.

Danner was half-jogging toward her, weaving between tables. He was wearing an odd expression—his normally placid features had turned dark, mouth curled tight. For a fleeting moment Mackenzie wondered if Danner had somehow overheard her conversation.

"What's going on?" Mackenzie asked.

Danner kept his voice low and glanced to either side before speaking. "Consider this me keeping you in the loop. I just got off the phone with Hector Ibarra."

"Okay."

There was an unusual intensity to Danner's voice. "I asked Ibarra to look into the badge system. Give it another review. His team found something they hadn't noticed before."

"What?"

"Around the same time Canon changed his will, he also altered the badge protocol. He went into the system and changed who could take the elevator up to his office."

"Hector told us that any Journy employee could get up to Canon's office. Part of the whole open-door policy."

Danner shook his head. "Not anymore. A week before he died, Canon restricted access. He did it quietly—didn't tell anyone."

"Restricted it how?"

"He changed the protocols so that only a few people at Journy could activate his elevator: the members of the executive team."

Mackenzie stared at him. "He did this a week before he died?"

Danner nodded. "Day before he changed his will."

"So the night Canon was killed, executive badges were the only ones that worked on Canon's elevator. That means . . ."

Danner finished the thought. "It wasn't just someone he trusted. Canon was killed by one of his own executives."

CHAPTER 8

Seventeen years before Trevor Canon's death

The room where Mackenzie's fate would be decided was a regular classroom.

The air was thick, thermostat overheated to fight the December cold. Old fluorescents banked the ceiling. Carpet thin and greige. Cheery academic detritus—maps, graphs, posters, bulletin boards—covered the walls.

The disciplinary committee had moved all the desks and chairs to the edges of the room. They'd brought in a long folding table to add an air of procedural formality. The three members of the committee sat behind the table in a neat row. They studied Mackenzie, blank-faced.

On the left was Mr. Boyd. He wore a green Christmas sweater with red Santa heads and block letters that read HO HO HO. Mackenzie didn't know much about Mr. Boyd. Based on the sweater, she wasn't optimistic.

In the middle sat Reno Valley's principal. Mr. Osborne didn't like to think of himself as a typical high school administrator. He had a trendy haircut. He carried around a guitar and occasionally hopped on a student's skateboard in the parking lot. Today, though, Osborne was all business. White shirt, yellow Reno Valley Roughriders tie, mouth a straight line.

On the right sat Miss Langley. Langley taught English and ran the school's drama program. Delving into their bottomless well of teenage cruelty, Reno Valley's students had dubbed Miss Langley with a regrettably accurate nickname: Plastic Face. Langley had some work done in her decade at Reno Valley. It hadn't escaped the attention of her students.

Plastic Face was the one who had brought Mackenzie into this mess. Now she stared at Mackenzie from behind the folding table, lips pursed, fluorescents bouncing off her cheeks with unnatural iridescence.

Mackenzie stood alone in the center of the room, sweating in her hoodie.

"It's five after," Principal Osborne said. "Mackenzie, do you want us to wait another few minutes for your mom?"

Mackenzie shook her head. "She won't be able to make it. Work."

Osborne gave a sad smile. "Anyone else you'd like us to wait for? Typically students have a parent or guardian present for disciplinary proceedings."

"I don't have anyone else."

Osborne paused. "We have a written summary of the decision we've reached. You can take it home and go over it with your mom. Okay?"

"Okay."

Osborne set the folder aside and steepled his hands on the table. Boyd and Langley stayed quiet.

"Mackenzie, the disciplinary committee has reviewed your situation. Yesterday, we had a similar hearing with Jason. We've reached a decision."

Mackenzie held her breath. Let's get this over with, she thought.

"This committee," Osborne said, "finds that your conduct on the mythology essay was a violation of our academic code."

Mackenzie blinked with surprise. "What?"

Osborne continued. "The disciplinary committee has decided you'll be suspended from school for three days."

Mackenzie tried to keep her voice level. "You're suspending *me*?"

"In addition," Osborne said, "adherence to the academic code is a prerequisite for extracurricular activities. You're also suspended from the Reno Valley girls' basketball team for two months."

"What?!"

"Lastly," Osborne said, "you will complete a new version of the Greek mythology project. Miss Langley has been kind enough to create a second prompt for you."

Mackenzie felt a rush of heat in her temples. "Wait a second. You're kicking me off the basketball team?"

"Your suspension isn't indefinite," Osborne said. "It ends in March."

"That's the whole regular season. You can't do this."

"Assuming there are no further violations of the academic code, you'll be able to return for the playoffs."

Mackenzie's entire body tensed. The possibility of a punishment this severe had never crossed her mind. "There won't *be* a playoffs without me," she said. "You're basically kicking me off the team."

There was a trace of sympathy in Osborne's eyes. "I'm sorry, Mackenzie. But our decision is final."

"But I didn't even cheat. I didn't *do* anything."

Plastic Face Langley chimed in, blue eyes staring at Mackenzie from behind her mask.

"You and Jason Masterson submitted the exact same essay," Langley said. Her voice was soft and high. "Word for word. Obviously that wasn't a coincidence."

"I told you what happened," Mackenzie said. Desperation flooded her. "I gave Jason my essay so he could look at it. I never thought he'd be stupid enough to copy the whole thing."

Jason Masterson was the star forward on the Reno Valley boys' basketball team, and his dad was among the richest men in Reno. Combined, these factors made Jason the most popular guy in school. He was also dumb as a bag of dirt.

Three weeks prior, Jason had approached Mackenzie before practice. He'd given her a big shiny grin and asked if Mackenzie had finished the Greek mythology project.

Mackenzie, entranced by Jason's mountainous cheekbones and the rare glow of attention from the most popular guy at school, had replied yes, of course—she'd completed her essay days ago. When Jason asked if he could read it, "for inspiration," Mackenzie had given it to him without hesitation. It was the first time Jason had ever spoken to her, let alone asked her for something.

Two days later she was stunned when Miss Langley asked why she and Jason Masterson had turned in the exact same essay. Word for word.

"Jason," Miss Langley said, "has given us a different version of events."

"What did he say?"

"He says he wrote the essay first, then let *you* borrow it."

Mackenzie gave a derisive laugh. "You're kidding, right?" None of the three members of the disciplinary committee moved. "You think I would copy off an essay by *Jason Masterson*?"

"That's what he says." Miss Langley's features didn't move when she spoke, other than a slight tremor of her lips. "He was very insistent."

"But that's bullshit," Mackenzie said.

"Hey," Osborne interjected. "Language."

"Look at our grades. I'm on the honor roll. I've worked my ass off for three years. Jason barely shows up for class. He's a moron."

Osborne's brow fell. "You can't say that about a fellow student."

"I'm sorry, but it's *true*." Mackenzie was incredulous. "You can't kick me off the team. You know Jason could never write an essay like that. He thinks mythology is when a bartender makes a cocktail."

"That's enough." Osborne's features tightened. Boyd and Langley maintained their impassive expressions. "Mackenzie, this was an individual assignment. Even if you gave Jason your essay, that's still a violation of the code. And this isn't your first offense—there was the incident last year, with the Haverford coach."

Mackenzie's entire body felt hot. She knew it was stupid to give her essay to Jason. It was like giving someone else the answers to a test. But the punishment here didn't fit the crime. And there was something else.

"You said you met with Jason yesterday," Mackenzie said.

Osborne nodded. "We did."

"Did he get the same punishment as me?"

Osborne hesitated; only for a microsecond, but Mackenzie saw it. "Jason will face appropriate consequences."

"Like what?"

Osborne shook his head. "That's private, Mackenzie."

"You didn't give him the same punishment as me."

"That's not what I said."

"Not out loud," Mackenzie said. "But essentially."

Osborne shook his head again. "Our hearing with Jason stays between us and his family."

His family, Mackenzie thought. Interesting. Then she remembered something else, and her anger pushed the thought away.

"I know you didn't suspend him from basketball," Mackenzie said. "He played last night. Against North Mill."

Osborne ignored her. He lifted the yellow folder from the table. "We've communicated our decision to Coach Whitney," he said. "You can return to school in four days, and return to basketball in March." He held out the folder.

Mackenzie didn't move. "You didn't suspend Jason from basketball, but you suspended me," she said. "Why?"

"This hearing is over, Mackenzie."

"He's the one who cheated."

"You're lucky I didn't fail you," Miss Langley said, her voice pitched. "You should be *thanking* Principal Osborne. He convinced me to give you a new prompt for the essay."

"I don't *give a shit* about the essay," Mackenzie said. Langley blanched, and Boyd shook his head sadly. Mackenzie knew she was losing control, but then she thought of Jason's family.

Mike Masterson was the president of Nevada Trust, biggest bank in the state. He was also a Reno Valley alum, and a massive donor to the school's extracurricular programs.

"Jason's dad is one of the richest guys in Reno," Mackenzie continued. "He's the reason Jason didn't get kicked off the team."

Osborne hesitated again. "We're not doing this," he said. "You're only making it worse for yourself."

"What did Mike Masterson say?" Mackenzie crossed her arms, staring at Osborne. "Did he threaten you? Bribe you?"

"Take the folder and leave," Osborne said. "Or I'm calling the security guard."

"This is *bullshit*. What, so my mom works, and because she's not here and Mike Masterson was, I get the shit end of the stick? That's the 'justice' of the disciplinary committee?"

Osborne's features locked with anger. He thrust the yellow folder outward in his hand. "Take it and leave. *Now*."

Mackenzie stomped forward, snatching the folder. She tried to think of something clever to say as she exited, but rage clouded her words. All she could manage was two.

"Fuck this."

Mackenzie wrenched the door open and left.

She moved through the hallways in a daze, mind pounding as she reached her car. She kept it together for the short drive through the Reno suburbs.

It wasn't until she pulled into her townhome that Mackenzie began to process the implications. She thought about her basketball gear stuffed in the trunk of her used Saturn. Shoes. Favorite practice shorts. A handful of yellow and crimson T-shirts. She'd have no reason to wear any of it anytime soon. Maybe never again.

Mackenzie's tears burst out all at once, waterfalling onto the steering wheel. She parked and turned off the engine. She stayed in her seat, tears pouring out of her, forehead resting against the top of the wheel. She cried so hard that she didn't notice her mother's car parked a few spots away.

Mackenzie raised her head just as her mom appeared at the front door. Janine Clyde hurried into the parking lot, face etched with worry. She rushed to the driver's window as Mackenzie lowered it.

"What happened?" said her mother.

Mackenzie choked down a sob. "You're here," she said dumbly.

"I caught an earlier flight, just got home." She leaned in, putting a hand on Mackenzie's shoulder. "I saw you from the kitchen. What happened?"

Mackenzie handed her mom the yellow folder. Janine opened it, reading. She raised a hand to her forehead.

"Oh shit," she said. "The disciplinary hearing was today. Kenz, I'm so sorry I missed it."

"It's fine," Mackenzie said. "You had work."

Her mother kept reading, eyes widening as she read the rest of the document. "Oh no."

A second wave of tears burst from Mackenzie as she watched her mom's reaction. "They're kicking me off the team." Mackenzie blubbered the words, her face a mess. "They're kicking me off basketball."

"What about Jason?"

"Nothing!" Mackenzie gasped between sobs.

"He's still on the boys' team?"

"Yes!"

Her mother's face hardened. "Go inside and get your jacket. Then come with me."

Fifteen minutes later Mackenzie and Janine walked through Reno's downtown, a cluster of overbearing casinos and dusty office buildings that straddled either side of the Truckee River. The December sun hung fat and low, squatting over the western horizon, and the day was fading. Mackenzie zipped her jacket to the top.

Janine was armed with an eight-dollar chardonnay and two paper cups she'd acquired from a gas station en route. The two of them made an odd pair, doppelgängers in many ways: same dark, thin hair; same pinched features; same arched brows above brown eyes. The primary difference between them was that Mackenzie stood eight inches taller than her mom. Janine often joked she was the older, shrunken version of her daughter.

Mackenzie's mom led them around a corner and came to a stop. "Here we are."

They stood at the edge of a large concrete plaza adjacent to the river. In the center stood a reasonably impressive Christmas tree, maybe three stories high, recently erected for the holidays. It was lit with a not-quite-tasteful explosion of red and white lights that blinked in the darkening gray of the winter afternoon. Next to the tree the city had set up a makeshift ice-skating rink.

"Welcome to Rockefeller Center," her mom said. "Reno style."

"Do they set this up every year?"

"I think so."

"Why haven't we been before?"

Janine chuckled. "Because we're not Christmas people. Are we?"

Mackenzie shook her head. "Definitely not." She stared at the tree for a moment, watching the lights blink. "But this isn't so bad."

Mackenzie's mom followed her gaze. "No," she agreed. She picked up her pace. "Follow me."

Janine led Mackenzie to a group of raised benches that overlooked the skating rink. They chose one in a far corner and sat down side by side. On the ice an assortment of tweens and college students coasted around the rink in long loops, holding hands and showing off.

Janine unscrewed the chardonnay and poured two large cups, handing one to Mackenzie.

"Have at it," she said.

Mackenzie had tried wine once or twice, but she'd never come close to a full glass. "Really?"

Her mother nodded. "Now's the time." She took a long slug from her own cup.

Mackenzie tipped it back. The wine tasted harsh on her tongue and burned down her throat. But as it settled into her stomach Mackenzie felt a humming warmth in her blood.

The two of them sat in the quiet cold, drinking shitty chardonnay and watching skaters on the ice. Mackenzie felt a pleasant looseness creep into her consciousness.

She wasn't sure how her mother would react to the hearing. Janine had always driven hard on academic achievement. Giving Jason Masterson her essay had been stupid.

But Janine Clyde rarely got angry. She was a deeply practical person. Mackenzie sometimes wondered where she'd gotten her temper from. She assumed it came from her father. A man she'd never met, a man she'd never meet.

"Do you know," Janine said, "what the hardest part of being a parent is?"

She kept her gaze on the ice; Mackenzie followed her example.

Mackenzie thought of her manager at the Dairy Queen. "Kendra says it's the lack of sleep."

Her mother laughed. "Piece of cake, in comparison." Janine sighed. "The hardest part of being a parent is knowing how much to protect your child from the truth of the world. How much should you insulate them? When do you expose them? And how?"

Mackenzie stayed quiet, letting her mother continue.

"I've always let you figure things out for yourself. Probably too much so. I haven't been around as much as I should."

"You've been working," Mackenzie said.

"Maybe, but it's still true." Janine took a long sip of her wine. "The world can be a cruel, ugly place. And then you bring a new life into it, something pure and innocent, and all you want to do is shelter them in a little nest. But you know you can't. You know that at some point you'll have to let them discover the world for what it really is. For their own good."

"I'm not sure I understand."

"The world is full of rich assholes like Jason Masterson," Janine said. Her voice was calm—the same tone she'd used when teaching Mackenzie how to drive, or how to apply mascara.

"Jason will coast through life on his dad's money, regardless of how smart or hardworking he is. It doesn't matter if he cheated and you didn't. It doesn't matter if he's dumber than you. Jason will stay on the team because his dad has enough money to make that happen."

"But that's so unfair," Mackenzie said.

"I know," her mother agreed. "I wish I could tell you that someday Jason will face consequences for copying your essay. That justice will come for him—somehow, some way. If you were younger, that's probably what I'd tell you. Keep you in the nest a little longer."

Janine put her paper cup on the bench, rubbing her hands together for warmth. "But you're old enough to know the truth. Fair, just, equal—that's not the world we live in. As long as there are fathers like Mike Masterson, there will be sons like Jason. Things like cause and effect, basic consequences . . . they don't apply in the same way."

Mackenzie didn't reply. She stared at the ice rink, letting the wine warm her blood.

Janine looked over at her. "Have you figured it out yet?"

"Figured what out?"

"What Mike Masterson told the disciplinary committee. How he kept Jason's place on the basketball team."

Mackenzie shrugged. "Mike Masterson sponsors the boys' team. I assume he threatened Osborne, told him he'd cut off the money."

"Good guess," Janine said. "But think about what's going on at the school right now. Think about what they're building."

"The theater." It'd been under construction since summer. Osborne had been promoting it all year. It was going to be one of the best in the state.

"Guess which bank," Janine said, "is financing construction of the new theater?"

Mackenzie smirked. "Mike Masterson's. Nevada Trust."

"And which teacher would have the most to gain from a new theater?"

"Goddammit." Plastic Face didn't just teach English—she also ran Reno Valley's drama department. "Mike Masterson didn't threaten Principal Osborne. It was Langley."

Janine leaned against the bench, eyes returning to the rink. "Langley originally raised the disciplinary issue, right?"

Mackenzie nodded. "So she had the most sway."

Mackenzie felt a heat rising in her chest, matching the warmth of the wine. Miss Langley's beady blue eyes flashed in her memory: two cold, alien dots blinking in the overgrown doll face.

"That's such bullshit," Mackenzie said. "She can't do that."

Janine grabbed the wine bottle and refilled Mackenzie's cup. "The Mastersons and us," Janine said, "we're not playing the same game."

"What's the game?"

"Money," Janine said. She took a deep breath. "Everything in our society, from the smallest thing to the biggest thing, is driven by money. How long you live, how well you live, who you're friends with, what you eat, where you can go, how you get there . . . all the way down to the smaller stuff, like whether your idiot son gets kicked off the team. All of it, every single thing, is driven by money."

"That's depressing," Mackenzie said.

"I used to think so. But then I accepted it. That's why I work so much. And that's why I made the deal with you." Janine gave an affectionate pat to Mackenzie's leg. "I'll get you as far ahead as I can. The rest is up to you."

When Mackenzie was thirteen, Janine made her a promise: Get straight As, and Mackenzie could attend college anywhere she was accepted. Her mother would make the money work. Mackenzie had already applied for early admission at a handful of schools.

The sun dropped behind the buildings on the western edge of the plaza. There was no colorful sunset, no blast of pinks and blues. The sky simply fell into a dull gray. Looking around, Mackenzie felt choked by gray. The stone of the plaza, the concrete of the casinos. She was suddenly grateful for the tawdry red and white lights of the Christmas tree.

"I want to get out of here," Mackenzie said. "I never want to deal with Jason Masterson or his jackass dad ever again. Or Miss Langley. Or Osborne."

"Then write the makeup essay," Janine said. Mackenzie groaned. "You want to get out of here? I don't blame you. You're smart enough. Work your ass off, you can go wherever you want."

Mackenzie thought about Jason Masterson, about his father, about Miss Langley. She thought about the feeling she had every time she stepped on the basketball court. Through the haze of cheap chardonnay, Mackenzie felt something crystallize in her mind. A vision, clear and cold as the Truckee River.

"I don't want to be in this position ever again," Mackenzie said. "If money's the game, I want to win. Get enough that I can control my own destiny. Live my own life. The way I want."

Her mother stared at her, eyes heavy with thought. "Then hard work will only be the start. You're also going to need something else. Luck."

"Luck?"

Mackenzie's mom nodded. "If you want the kind of money that lets you control your own life, if you never want to take shit from the Mike Mastersons of the world . . ." She shifted on the bench. "Hard work isn't enough. Our society likes to pretend it is, but everybody knows it's a lie. Look at Jason Masterson. He hasn't spent a minute working his whole damn life."

Janine scoffed. "Hell, neither has his dad. Mike inherited his position at Nevada Trust. One asshole gets rich a hundred years ago and the money just trickles down for generations. Money begets money. It was all chance."

"Then what can I do?" Mackenzie said. "Hope I get lucky?"

Janine kept her gaze on Mackenzie. "You work yourself into the right places. You get connected to the right people. Eventually, you'll be met with an opportunity. Something that transcends your day-to-day, supersedes anything that's come before. A chance at something truly big. Big enough to change your life, get you to the place you want to be."

She paused. "The Jason Mastersons of the world get those kind of opportunities all the time. But people like us . . . You might only get once chance. You won't know it's coming until it's right in front of you. You'll have to watch out for it for your entire life. Every day. If you get yourself in the right position, meet the right people, then one day it'll just . . . appear. You'll see it. The opportunity will come. And here's the important part."

Janine leaned forward and clasped Mackenzie's shoulder, her eyes steady. "When that chance comes, Mackenzie, you have to seize it. Whatever it takes. Grab it with both hands, hard as you can. And don't let go."

CHAPTER 9

Twenty-three days after Trevor Canon's death

Agent Danner barreled through Journy's headquarters, striding past rows of standing desks and headphoned engineers. Mackenzie followed, two steps behind.

Reaching the conference room, Danner shoved open the door and stormed in, Mackenzie at his shoulder.

The conference room was empty.

They stood inside the threshold. Danner surveyed the broad wooden table and dozen empty chairs. "Is this the right room?"

Mackenzie stepped back through the door and checked a small tablet on the wall. It read CHAMPS-ÉLYSÉES // EXECUTIVE STAFF MEETING.

"We're in the right place," she said.

Danner checked his watch. "Guess we're the first to arrive." He chose a chair facing the door. Mackenzie took a seat across from him.

Minutes passed. Danner didn't check his phone or his watch. He didn't fidget. He simply sat in the leather swivel chair and stared at the door.

Mackenzie took in their surroundings. An enormous monitor was mounted to the far wall. The screen was on, Journy green letters gliding across a white background. WELCOME! PRESS PLAY TO LEARN MORE ABOUT OUR JOURNY.

Nobody's coming, Mackenzie thought.

"Are we sure," Danner said, "that Eden's assistant told everyone the right time and place?"

"It was on the tablet," Mackenzie said. "All the info was correct."

Another minute passed. Mackenzie spied a remote control in the center of the table. She snagged it and pressed the play button.

"What are you doing?" Danner asked.

"If we're gonna wait," Mackenzie said, "we might as well be entertained."

The wall monitor transitioned into video: a fast-cut montage of Journy bikes, scooters, and golf carts zipping across cities around the world. Smiling passengers of ambiguous ethnicity hopped in and out of Journy Cars, their drivers giving friendly waves. A Journy Buggy puttered across the outline of the Eiffel Tower. Two Glides coasted down the boardwalk in South Beach.

A voiceover kicked in. It was deep, and male, and very familiar. "Journy is the fastest-growing startup in history. But we're more than just a way to get around. We're an urban mobility platform that's revolutionizing transportation in over a hundred thousand cities worldwide." Mackenzie suppressed a gag.

"What is this?" Danner said.

"Recruiting video," Mackenzie said. "Standard thing they show high-level candidates, outside vendors."

"Is that Morgan Freeman's voice?"

"Yep."

The voiceover continued. "Let's look back at some of the great moments in Journy history."

Another montage. A caption at the bottom read JOURNY RAISES THE BIGGEST PRIVATE INVESTMENT EVER. A cut-up of news anchors reporting snippets of the same storyline: "Journy, the transportation startup based in San Francisco, announced today that it has closed the 'Journy Fund': five *billion* dollars from Hammersmith Venture."

Danner's right hand rested on the conference table, fingers drumming. Mackenzie checked the time. Eight minutes in.

Then Trevor Canon appeared onscreen.

He was holding a microphone on a well-lit stage. His black hair was cut short. He was dressed in black jeans, black T-shirt, black unbranded sneakers. The green *J* logo hovered behind him on a wall-sized screen. Below Canon lay the orderly shadows of the audience, silhouettes against the stage lights.

Another caption floated into the picture: TREVOR ANNOUNCES THE JOURNY FUND TO THE TEAM.

"This is a historic moment for Journy," Canon said onscreen. "For our company. And for the world."

Canon paced across the stage. His voice was thin, slightly nasal, but Canon overcame it with a feral, almost manic energy. His face was alight with enthusiasm, arms taut, shoulders coiled. He stared out at the Journy employees assembled before him, polar blue eyes glinting in the lights above.

"We've grown 10x in the last year. We're gonna be the biggest startup to ever come out of Silicon Valley. We aren't just a rocket ship—we're *light speed*."

A wild cheer from the crowd.

Canon's voice grew louder as he spoke. "Soon, Journy Scoots, Glides, and Buggies will be on every street, in every neighborhood, in every city, in every country, in the entire fucking *world*!"

Another wild cheer.

Mackenzie found it jarring to see Canon onscreen, radiating with life. He wasn't a naturally gifted speaker. But what Canon lacked in organic charisma he made up for with the sheer, unbridled confidence of a man who was very young, very white, and very, very rich.

The camera cut to the audience, capturing the reactions of captivated Journy employees. Mackenzie spotted a familiar face in the front row: the broad, round shape of Roger Hammersmith. He gazed up through his glasses, smiling wide, enraptured.

Canon continued. "This news is so big that I had to share it with you before anybody else." Canon grinned like a wolf, his teeth thin and piano white. "We've just raised the biggest private investment in *history*. Five *billion* dollars, from Hammersmith Venture!"

The audience exploded into pandemonium. It looked like an *Oprah* episode. Canon stood onstage with his arms raised above his head, basking in the reaction.

"Turn it off." Danner's voice cut over the sound of the video.

"Huh?"

"Turn it off." Danner was grinding his jaw, still watching the door.

Mackenzie hit the power button and the screen went blank. She looked at her phone. Twelve minutes in. "I'm not sure they're coming."

"They'll be here."

The minutes passed in silence. Mackenzie rotated her wrist, stretching the ligaments in her hand. Nobody walked through the door. With each minute Danner's jaw locked deeper into itself, like a piece of clay hardening in the sun.

Seventeen minutes in, the door opened. Danner straightened in his seat.

But it was only the neon purple hair of Gaia, Eleanor's assistant, that popped into the doorway. Her face fell as she saw Danner and Mackenzie waiting. "Nobody else is here?"

Danner's voice was thin. "No."

"Crap," Gaia said. "Eleanor is on her way, but . . ." Gaia pulled her phone out of her pocket. "Hang on." She withdrew.

Danner spoke, his voice icy. "I'm sure you're loving this."

Mackenzie glanced over at him. "Excuse me?"

Danner waved at the empty table. "Nobody's here. Not even the executive assistant stuck around."

"I don't like wasting my time any more than you do."

Danner didn't reply.

Six more minutes passed before the door opened again. This time Gaia was followed by Eleanor. She looked even more tired than she had two hours prior. Her ponytail had loosened, her eyes glazed with the dull sheen of exhaustion.

"Agent Danner, I'm incredibly sorry," Eleanor said. She looked around the empty conference room, shaking her head. "I got stuck on a call. I would've come sooner if I had known . . ."

Danner's voice was flat. "Where are the other executives?"

"I'm not sure." Eleanor put a hand to her forehead. "This is quite embarrassing. Everyone knew we had the meeting today. I specifically told them the FBI would be here." She glanced over at Gaia, who typed rapidly on her iPhone. "Are you trying to find them?"

"I'm talking to their assistants now," Gaia said, eyes fixed to her screen. She typed while the room sat in silence. "It looks like Hugo actually declined the meeting invite."

"Hugo Chamberlain," Danner said.

Gaia nodded. "His assistant says he has another appointment."

"Another appointment," Danner repeated.

Eleanor fell into a chair. Gaia remained standing. "Hugo has another appointment," Eleanor said, "more important than finding Trevor's killer?"

Gaia stared at her phone. "I'm just repeating what I'm being told."

"Keep going," said Danner.

"So . . . Brady," Gaia said. "His assistant doesn't know where he is. She can't find him."

"He's not in the office?" Danner asked.

"Uh, no," Gaia said.

Eleanor rubbed her temples with her fingers. "What about Cassiopeia?"

"Cassiopeia is . . ." Gaia consulted her phone. "She's out, too. She's taking a mindfulness day."

Mackenzie barely covered a laugh.

"That's three," Danner said. "What about Stanley Yoo?"

Gaia broke contact from her phone, eyes flitting to Eleanor. "Uh . . . well . . ."

"We'll talk about Stanley in a minute," Eleanor said. She gave Gaia a tired smile. "Thank you, Gaia." Gaia puffed her cheeks uncomfortably and left the conference room.

"Agent Danner," Eleanor said, pivoting to face him, "I had no idea my colleagues would be so unreliable." She pulled out her phone. "I'd like to try again tomorrow. I'll reschedule the meeting."

Danner was still as a gargoyle. "It wouldn't go any different than today."

He's not wrong, Mackenzie thought.

"I understand your frustration," Eleanor said. "Gaia has sent you all their information. Maybe you'd prefer to go to them?"

"I have a different idea," Danner said. "Call the other executives right now. Tell them their boss was murdered a few weeks ago, the FBI is here, and they need to get their asses in."

Eleanor sighed. "Agent Danner, I would if I could."

"Why can't you?" An edge crept into Danner's tone. "You're the COO."

"So what?"

"Tell everyone on the executive team that if they don't come in, they're fired."

Eleanor chuckled. "I wish I had that authority. They all reported to Trevor. And now, thanks to his will, nobody's in charge."

Mackenzie turned to Danner. "We have their contact info," she said. "Brady, Cassiopeia, Hugo, Stanley. Let's go to them. It's a pain in the ass, but we can start tomorrow and go down the line."

"It'll take too long," Danner said. "They'll delay. Bring in the lawyers."

"Then we'll get subpoenas," Mackenzie said. "I'm sure a judge would grant them."

Danner shook his head. "No subpoenas. Our timeline has accelerated. We need to move faster."

Eleanor chimed in from across the table. "Accelerated? How?"

Danner paused. "We have new information," he said. "Ibarra called me."

"I missed a call from him in my rush over here," Eleanor said. "What did he say?"

"His team reviewed the badge system and found something," Danner said. "Canon changed the protocol for his office."

"How so?"

"Canon restricted access so that only a select few could badge up to his office. The members of the executive team."

Eleanor stared at Danner, blinking rapidly. She rubbed her eyes, trying to wipe away her fatigue. "But that doesn't make any sense." She shook her head slightly. "Our executive badges look the same as anyone else's."

"But the system can read them differently," Danner said. "Ibarra says it's possible to use badges to limit certain people to certain areas. Slice the badge system by seniority, or even by individual people."

"And Trevor did that for his office elevator," Eleanor said.

"You seem surprised," Danner said.

"I am," Eleanor said. "I never thought he'd have a reason to care about something like that. He is—was—the CEO. He had much bigger fish to fry."

"Well, Canon found reason to care. Hector said the protocol change was very clear. Execs only."

Eleanor leaned forward, elbows on the table. "Why would Trevor do that?"

"It was the day before he changed his will," Danner said. "Canon restricted access to his office, and then he put in the dead money clause. Clearly, he was frightened of something. Scared for his life."

Eleanor let out a low groan. "But if this is true, that means . . ."

Danner nodded, impassive as ever. "Someone on the executive team killed Canon."

"That's not possible."

"It's not just possible but logical."

"It can't be."

"We've established that the killer knew the building, knew where Canon would be, and had his trust. An executive makes perfect sense."

Eleanor brought her hands to her chin, eyes falling. Mackenzie saw tears forming near the corners. "This is a nightmare."

Mackenzie looked at Eleanor. "I'm sorry," Mackenzie said. "I know this must be hard."

"Just a few hours ago," Eleanor said, "I thought Trevor's killer might have been a business enemy. Or even something personal, outside of work. I never imagined it would be a colleague, let alone a fellow executive." Eleanor shook her head. "Journy is our entire lives. All of us had a ton invested in Trevor—not just financially, but personally."

"I understand it's difficult to process," Danner said, officious as ever. "But now you understand why it's urgent I interview the other executives."

"Well, on that note . . ." Eleanor shifted in her in seat. "There's something else I need to tell you. At first, I didn't think it really mattered, but now . . ."

"What?" Danner asked.

"Stanley Yoo, our CTO. He's . . ." Eleanor grimaced with embarrassment. "Well, I guess he's missing."

Danner lurched forward in his seat. "Yoo is missing?"

Eleanor nodded, eyes clouding. "I assumed it was just Stan being Stan, but . . ." She refocused on Danner. "Stan went to Hawaii for a while. He was supposed to be back in the office several days ago, but nobody's seen him."

"Nobody's had contact with him?"

Eleanor shook her head. "No phone calls, emails, texts, nothing. His assistant knocked on the door to his loft. No answer."

Danner whipped his phone out of his pocket and began typing. "When did he leave?"

"Right after Trevor died, I think."

"You think?"

"I can't say for sure. I haven't seen him in person since before Trevor was killed."

Danner stared at her. "You can't be serious."

"Look," Eleanor said, raising her palms, "Trevor always let Stan work remotely. He traveled a ton, came and went from HQ as he pleased. When Stan told me he was going to Hawaii for a few weeks, I didn't think twice."

"You didn't find that suspicious?"

Eleanor's mouth tightened. "You have to understand the context. Stan likes to drop off the grid. Sometimes he'd do it for a week at a time, going deep on a project."

"But now it's been far more than a week. And his boss was just murdered."

"Yes, but that's part of the context. Trevor was much more than Stan's boss. They were like brothers. When Stan said he was leaving to clear his head, take some time, I empathized." Eleanor sighed. "Obviously, given this new information, I understand that was naïve."

Danner pecked furiously at his phone. "When did Yoo say he'd be back in the office?"

"He said he'd be gone a few weeks," Eleanor said. "So he should've been back by now."

"Wouldn't his laptop have the same security protocols as Canon's? Remote management?"

"Yes," Eleanor said. "But we can't track it. Hector's team has tried. Either Stan isn't using his laptop, or . . ."

"He knows how to disable the tracking," Danner said. His mouth was a tight line of frustration. "So nobody has communicated with Yoo since Canon died."

"I talked to him the day Trevor was found," Eleanor said. "But since then, no. Not that I know of." Her shoulders slumped, expression stricken. "You don't think . . ."

"It's not useful to speculate," Danner said. He finished typing on his phone and replaced it in his suit jacket. "If anyone hears from him, contact me. Immediately."

"Of course," Eleanor said.

"My colleagues will spin up a search. We have the resources to find him."

Eleanor's phone buzzed on the table. She picked it up and made a face. "I'm sorry, Agent Danner, but I have to run."

"We're done, anyway," Danner said.

Eleanor stood. "I know you think it pointless, but I'm going to reschedule this meeting for tomorrow. I'm sorry again. I'll do whatever I can to help you get interviews with the other execs."

"Fine," Danner said. "And as casually as you can, spread word that if Yoo resurfaces, you need to be notified immediately."

"Of course," Eleanor said.

She made her exit, leaving Danner and Mackenzie alone in the conference room.

"Go ahead and say it," Danner said.

"Say what?"

Danner rose from his seat. "'I told you so.'"

Mackenzie stood to join Danner, facing him. She was perhaps an inch taller than him. "Why would I say that?"

"You said tech people would blow me off, that they didn't give a shit about law enforcement. Looks like you were right."

Mackenzie smirked. "You think I'm happy about it?"

Danner spoke through his teeth. "You're going to tell me you're not?"

"Oh my god." Mackenzie rolled her eyes. "All I care about is doing my job. Which, believe it or not, is trying to *help you.* Like I've tried to tell you a million times." Mackenzie gestured at the emptiness of the conference room. "I don't like this any more than you do. It's been a huge waste of time."

"We can agree on that," Danner said. He looked away and took a breath. "And tomorrow will be more of the same."

"So let's go to them instead. We have their addresses."

Danner shook his head. "They'll stonewall us. Delay. Make us wait for lawyers."

"They'll stonewall *you,*" Mackenzie said. "Because you're a federal agent. I'm not."

"So?"

"So I have an idea." Mackenzie grabbed her phone. She found Gaia's email with the contact info for all the Journy executives. She pressed one of the numbers, her phone dialing.

"What are you doing?" Danner asked.

Mackenzie placed her phone on the table and put it on speaker. "Calling Cassiopeia Moreau's assistant," she said.

A woman's voice answered. "Hello?"

"Hi!" Mackenzie ratcheted her voice to maximum brightness. "This is Mackenzie Clyde, with Hammersmith Venture. We're looking to get in touch with Cassiopeia."

"Hi," the assistant said, hesitating. "Sorry, can you repeat the name?"

"Mackenzie Clyde. From Hammersmith Venture."

"Oh. HV. Right, of course." A brief pause. "What can I do for you?"

"Roger heard that Cassiopeia has been working on a new project. He asked me to set up a meeting with her to learn more."

"Oh." Mackenzie and Danner heard typing in the background. "Um, so you want a meeting with Cass?"

"Yes, Roger asked me to see her in person."

A brief pause. "Cass's calendar is pretty full."

"I understand," Mackenzie said. "But I've been tasked with building out HV's portfolio in the coaching space. Roger is very keen."

"Okay," the assistant said again. "Hang on, let me see if she has anything available." More typing.

Mackenzie put the phone on mute. Danner stood at her shoulder. "She's texting Cassiopeia right now," Mackenzie said.

"Gatekeeping," Danner said. "What does 'building out HV's portfolio in the coaching space' mean?"

"Based on her social media, Cassiopeia's been working on a side project. I'm suggesting that Hammersmith is interested in funding her new venture."

"Is that true?"

"Of course not." Mackenzie unmuted and returned to the phone. "Roger wants to move fast. The sooner we can meet the better."

"Roger," the assistant murmured as she typed. "You know what? Cass actually had something open up tomorrow morning. Nine A.M. Would that work for you?"

"Perfect!" Mackenzie said.

"Cass has been working from home lately," the assistant said. "Going into the Journy offices has just been so hard . . ."

Mackenzie picked up the hint. "I'm happy to come to her."

"Terrific." More typing. "If this is your cell, I'll text you the address."

"Yep. Sounds great."

Mackenzie ended the call and turned to Danner. "We're in."

Danner frowned slightly. "I'll come with you?"

"Yep."

"How will she react when she learns I'm a federal agent?"

"We'll figure it out tomorrow," Mackenzie said. "I've got some ideas."

"You seem very confident."

Mackenzie gave Danner a thin smile. "Cassiopeia Moreau is no different than anyone else in tech. They might not respect a badge, or the government, or even the requests of their own COO. But there is one thing they respect. They'll follow it every time."

"And what's that?"

"Money."

CHAPTER 10

Twenty-three days after Trevor Canon's death

Mackenzie took a Journy Car straight to her doorstep. She'd decided to chalk the previous night up to simple adrenaline. She'd just been put on a murder investigation. Her street had been spooky. It wasn't preposterous for her to imagine things.

Still: Delivery sounded appealing. As she pushed into her building, Mackenzie ordered a salad on her phone.

She climbed the three flights of stairs and entered her apartment. She locked the deadbolt behind her and kicked off her flats, padding down the long hallway to the living room. She stood in the center of her bay window, taking in the full view of Green Street below her, and dialed Roger Hammersmith.

"What's the latest?"

"We had the meeting with the executive team," Mackenzie said. "None of them showed."

Hammersmith snorted. "How'd Danner take it?"

It was characteristically chilly for August; Mackenzie turned up the thermostat. "Like a bird shit on his blazer."

"HA!" Hammersmith guffawed into the phone.

"There's more." Mackenzie told Hammersmith about Canon's alteration of the badge protocols.

"Trevor could change the badge system?" Hammersmith sounded as surprised as Eleanor had been.

"Eleanor says he could, but she never thought he'd have reason to care," Mackenzie said. "Now, though, when you combine it with the dead money clause . . ."

Hammersmith's voice grew somber. "Trevor was afraid. Afraid enough to restrict access to his office. Afraid enough to change his will."

"Looks that way."

"An executive killed Trevor."

"Yes."

"That's very troubling." Hammersmith waited a beat. "At the same time, this is major progress for the investigation."

"Danner certainly thinks so. Despite the executive no-show, he's quite proud of himself."

Hammersmith sniffed into the phone. "How the hell did SFPD miss the access protocols for Trevor's office?"

Mackenzie shrugged to herself in her living room. "They're not officious little shits. Danner asked Hector to re-review everything about the badge system. Guess it paid off."

"Hmmm." Hammersmith paused, and Mackenzie drifted back to the bay window. Curtains open, she let her eyes fall to the pavement below, where a cyclist labored up the incline of Green Street. Mackenzie shook her head as she watched him pedal. The things people do to run from the void, she thought.

"I've got something else," Mackenzie said. She told Hammersmith about Stanley Yoo.

Hammersmith sounded irritated. "Nobody knows where Yoo is?"

"No. Eleanor says that Yoo was prone to going off grid for long stretches, working remotely."

Hammersmith's tone darkened. "Not right after his boss was murdered. They have no way of finding him? Eleanor has no idea where he is?"

"No."

Hammersmith grunted with frustration. "How long has it been?"

"Eleanor hasn't spoken to Yoo since Trevor's body was found."

Hammersmith fell silent; Mackenzie could almost hear him thinking over the static.

"Stan and Trevor were very close," Hammersmith said. "They were more than just colleagues."

"Eleanor said he and Trevor were like brothers."

"Yoo came to the pitch meetings when they were raising money. Trevor once told me that Stan was the most brilliant mind he'd ever encountered." His voice deadened. "Who disappears right after their brother gets murdered?"

"Maybe Yoo needed the time away," Mackenzie said, "to clear his head."

"Or maybe he was running."

"You think Yoo was involved in Trevor's death?"

"Occam's razor," Hammersmith said. "Especially since we know an executive murdered Trevor. What does Danner say about it?"

"He's angry. Ramping up an FBI search. Eleanor felt bad, she realized maybe she'd been naïve. Danner didn't have much sympathy."

"I can't blame him." Hammersmith paused. His voice grew urgent. "Push Danner on this, Mackenzie. Find Yoo."

"I will."

"This is now the top priority. I've got Indira Soti out there rattling founders, pointing at the chaos at Journy. He's trying to undermine confidence in our firm. This is progress. But we need to move faster."

"I understand. Danner's not being the most forthcoming with information, but I'll push him."

"What do you mean?"

Mackenzie told Hammersmith about their lunchtime argument.

"He can't pull that shit," Hammersmith said.

"I tried to convince him it wasn't in his best interests."

"He doesn't need to be convinced. It was part of my agreement with the Department of Justice. As advisors we get to be fully informed." Hammersmith grunted. "I'll talk to someone. Is there anything else?"

"That's it."

Hammersmith hung up.

Mackenzie grabbed her laptop and fell onto her couch, pulling up a Spyder search of Trevor Canon. The video in the Journy conference room had whet her appetite. Perhaps it was macabre, but Mackenzie wanted to see more.

Trevor Canon had possessed the same traits as plenty of founders in San Francisco. The difference was a matter of amplitude. Trevor reveled in dancing on the line where a trait becomes a flaw.

Founders were bold. Trevor was ludicrously brash. Founders were aggressive. Trevor was a panzer. He relished confrontation with anyone he could find.

Mackenzie found herself drawn to one interview in particular. Trevor made a series of outrageous claims about Journy's trajectory. When the interviewer pushed back with gentle skepticism, Canon replied with a story: In the first stage of Journy, seventeen different venture capitalists had passed on the opportunity to invest in him. He recited the names of every single one. He said, "We've faced plenty of skeptics before. And you know what? All of them have been dead wrong." Then he gave an impish grin. "I'll add your name to the list."

Mackenzie was interrupted by a *ping* from her phone: Her salad was arriving. She left her apartment, still in socks, and descended to the front door.

The driver was waiting outside, holding an embarrassingly large paper bag. Mackenzie opened the door and grabbed it. The driver departed as Mackenzie turned back to her foyer.

She stopped.

She froze in the doorway, eye caught on the near intersection. A car was parallel parking on the opposite side of Green Street. Its windshield had a clear view of Mackenzie's front door.

The car was a black Tesla. With a small, glowing Journy logo illuminating a corner of the windshield.

Exactly like the one she'd seen rolling down her street last night.

The car wedged itself into the parking space. The headlights flicked dark, and the green *J* in the windshield lost its glow.

Mackenzie slunk backward and leaned against the doorjamb, trying to limit the Tesla's viewing angle while maintaining her own. For
a few breaths she stood that way, waiting to see who would emerge
from the driver's door.

Nobody did.

Mackenzie waited for a full minute, then two, but there was no
sign of motion.

The doors remained closed. No interior lights illuminated. The
Tesla stared back at her like a panther in the dimming light, menacing and still.

The windshield was dark, but Mackenzie thought she detected
movement from within. The shifting outline of a man, possibly. A
very large man. The salad hung from her right hand, but a sudden,
bone-deep pain in her wrist forced her to shift the bag to her left.

Mackenzie shut the door and backpedaled into her foyer. She
bounded up the stairs, long legs taking two at a time, then dashed
into her apartment and slammed the deadbolt shut behind her. She
stood for a minute in her hallway, panting.

Don't be an idiot, she told herself. It's a black Tesla. This city is
stuffed with them.

And it's a Journy Car. There's an epidemic of Journy Cars in San
Francisco. They clog up the city like a coronary.

It's probably a coincidence. A Journy driver waiting for his fare.
Or taking a break. Be rational.

But then her rational mind conjured up a rejoinder of its own.

Two black Teslas. On her quiet street. On consecutive nights.
Each around the same time, with the same neon Journy logo, in the
same exact placement.

Mackenzie tossed the salad on her sofa and returned to the bay
window. She crept up to the glass at a sharp angle, hiding her body,
and peeked onto the street.

The Tesla was still there. It hadn't moved.

She twisted her wrist reflexively, trying to shake off the soreness.
The Tesla had parked with a clear view of her building's front door.
And, Mackenzie realized, a clear view of the window where she now
stood.

Someone was watching her.

Mackenzie stepped back from the window and flung the curtains closed.

She wasn't seeing ghosts. She was being entirely rational. When combined with her intuition, Mackenzie felt as much certainty as she could.

Someone was watching her.

Now came the important question: Why?

And what to do about it?

Her stomach grumbled. Mackenzie checked the deadbolt on her door, then she moved to the kitchen, placing the salad on the counter. She grabbed a loose fork from a drawer and bent over her dinner, mind lost in thought.

If someone was watching her, what should she do? Should she tell someone? Who? Roger was a definite no.

Danner? The thought was unpleasant. What would she even say? I've seen a black Tesla in my neighborhood two nights in a row? She'd sound hysterical. Danner was already disrespecting her—she didn't want to give him the satisfaction.

By the last bite of romaine Mackenzie had decided there wasn't much she could do about the Tesla. Not for now. She knew it was there. She knew it was watching. As long as that was *all* it did, she could wait to tell someone. If things escalated, she'd act.

Mackenzie checked the deadbolt one more time before bed. She brushed her teeth and fell into her sheets, keeping one hand near her phone.

She slept like shit.

CHAPTER 11

Twenty-four days after Trevor Canon's death

The next morning the Tesla was gone, replaced by a red Mini Cooper. There was no way to know when it'd left.

When Mackenzie emerged from her building, Danner was already waiting on the curb. He drove a forgettable government-issue sedan, nickel silver, a shrug manifested into automotive form. Mackenzie opened the passenger door and slid in.

"What happened to the Crown Vics?" Mackenzie said.

Danner sniffed. "Wrong department." He shifted gear and pulled onto Green.

Hammersmith had said he was going to talk to the DOJ. Mackenzie wondered how quickly that would trickle down to Danner. She only had to wait a block to find out.

"So," Danner said, eyes still on the road. "I owe you an apology."

Mackenzie twisted to face him. "Oh?"

"Yesterday I treated you like a pain in the ass," Danner said. "But you're here to help. I'll be more appreciative of that, going forward."

Danner looked over at Mackenzie. His features were still flat, but his voice sounded genuine. "I'm sorry."

Mackenzie was surprised. She moved her eyes back to the road. "Thanks, I guess."

They fell quiet as Danner weaved the sedan through morning traffic.

"What changed," Mackenzie asked, "between yesterday and today?"

Danner kept his eyes forward. "I had time to think about it. All you're asking is to be in the loop. And you do have knowledge that could be useful." Danner gestured to the road ahead. "You're the reason we even got this meeting."

"True."

"This is still an uncomfortable arrangement," Danner said. "And this is still a very dangerous investigation. But you've already shown you can be an asset."

And one of your bosses lit into your ass, Mackenzie thought. "Okay," she said. "Thanks, then."

"I sent over the SFPD files you asked for."

"I appreciate it."

Danner gave a slight nod. The Embarcadero came into sight and traffic congealed. Mackenzie looked out the window and counted all the Journy vehicles. Two Journy Cars ahead, one behind. Two Buggies side by side, sharing a lane. A Scoot buzzing along the sidewalk, its rider wearing AirPods. The green *J* logo was everywhere. Trevor Canon wasn't a prince, but there was no denying what he built.

"I also assume," Danner said, breaking the momentary silence, "that by now you know who my father is."

"Didn't at first," Mackenzie said. "Took me a bit."

"Everyone figures it out eventually."

Mackenzie kept her focus out the window. "You told me your name was Jameson."

"That's what I've always gone by."

"You didn't want to go by Osiris Danner, Jr.?"

Danner glanced over at her. "Would you?"

Mackenzie nodded. "Fair enough."

"This investigation," Danner continued, "has billions in pressure attached to it. Pressure to close it and get Canon's money flowing again. That pressure goes to my bosses, and from my bosses to me. My father being who he is, the scrutiny that comes with my name . . . it doesn't help."

"Sounds like a lot to have on your shoulders," Mackenzie said.

"It is."

"Still doesn't justify you being a dickhead yesterday."

"No," Danner said. "No, it doesn't."

They moved southeast, passing the brick walls of the baseball stadium. Instinct told Mackenzie not to trust Danner's overnight transformation. But if it made him easier to work with, Mackenzie wouldn't complain.

And even if Danner had resolved to be more open with her, she wasn't under any obligation to reciprocate.

"The scrutiny on this case," Mackenzie said. "That's why you don't want to subpoena anyone."

Danner hesitated, drumming his fingers on the wheel. "Yes."

"You're worried it would look bad."

"I know that sounds petty. But perception matters. These aren't international drug kingpins. They're tech workers. I should be able to get questions in without a subpoena. If I can't, it calls into question why I was put on the case to begin with."

"I can understand that."

"And it *is* too slow," Danner said. "I meant that."

They crossed a bridge into the shiny, flavorless modernism of Mission Bay. Danner sped south toward Potrero Hill. Mackenzie shifted in her seat, cracking her window. A crisp breeze filtered into the sedan.

"Yesterday you said that Cassiopeia Moreau is working on a side project," Danner said. "She thinks Hammersmith might invest."

Mackenzie nodded. "Cassiopeia is starting a coaching incubator."

Danner scoffed. "What's a 'coaching incubator'?"

Mackenzie smiled. "You're not familiar with coaching?"

"I assume we're not talking sports."

"No." Mackenzie shook her head. "Coaches help corporate types learn how to be better leaders. They guide clients on how to navigate corporate issues. Self-advocate. Deal with internal politics. Climb the ladder."

Danner raised his eyebrows. "People pay for that?"

"Exorbitantly. Cassiopeia is starting her own brand. Organizing a network of coaches under her umbrella, with whatever training system she's come up with."

"Like a consulting firm," Danner said. "McKinsey."

"Basically." Mackenzie smiled. "Though I wouldn't make that comparison in front of her."

Danner shook his head again but stayed quiet.

"We should talk about how to approach this," Mackenzie said. "We could try to imply you're with my firm, or—"

Danner cut her off. "We can't mislead her. If she asks, I'll have to be clear about who I am and why I'm there."

"Okay."

"If Moreau says anything important, it can't be compromised by bad procedure," said Danner. "The lawyers would kill me."

"Fine. But how do you know she'll answer questions?"

"I don't. But I'll be there in person, with a chance to persuade her. Better than trying to set meetings I know she won't show for."

"And what if she still refuses to answer, kicks us both out?"

"Then I'll go to a judge."

Danner guided the car up the north face of Potrero Hill. Mackenzie had looked up Cassiopeia's house online. Trevor Canon had bought the property two years prior for $9 million, all cash. Tech founders would sooner use Windows than be saddled with something as banal as a mortgage. The Sotheby's listing had been a bingo board of Bay Area luxury real estate descriptors: floating staircase, full-floor suite, EV charging, outdoor shower, mature eucalyptus, al fresco terrace, louvered pergola.

They waited to pass a garbage truck. "That's how you know we're in a rich neighborhood," Mackenzie said.

Danner glanced ahead. "The trash truck?"

"It's almost nine, pretty late for a garbage route. In rich neighborhoods, people complain if a truck wakes them up at four A.M. They bitch to their local reps, wave money around to get the city to shift the route later in the morning."

"Don't people in poor neighborhoods wake up when the trash truck comes through at four A.M.?"

"Sure," Mackenzie said. "But the city doesn't listen to their complaints. And their local reps have more important shit to worry about."

"Where'd you learn that?"

"From a Journy driver, actually."

Danner veered around the truck. "Did you read up on Moreau's background?"

Mackenzie nodded. "Cassiopeia Moreau, real name Catherine Moore. Met Trevor at a party six years ago, they started dating, she joined the company soon after. Journy's CMO for the last three years."

Danner leaned down, gazing through Mackenzie's window. "I think we're here."

The façade of the property was unobtrusive—Ipe wood and sanded concrete. The house itself was elevated and hidden by a terrace of clever landscaping. An opaque gate of metal and glass barricaded a driveway. Danner parallel parked in front of it and they got out.

Danner was dressed almost identically to the day before: black tie, black shoes, gray suit. The gold Patek Philippe glinted from under a cuff.

A black intercom panel sat on a wall near the driveway. Mackenzie pressed a small red button; after a moment, a woman's voice answered. "Good morning! Is this Mackenzie?"

Mackenzie leaned toward the intercom. "Hello! Yes, it's Mackenzie Clyde, from Hammersmith Venture."

"Great! Follow the path up the driveway. I'll meet you at the top of the elevator."

The gate slid into the adjoining wall with a dull buzz. Mackenzie and Danner stepped inside, and the gate whirred to a close behind them.

CHAPTER 12

Twenty-four days after Trevor Canon's death

The driveway curved around the base of the house and led them to a covered entryway next to the garage.

"I'm surprised there's not more security," Mackenzie said.

"Canon also bought out his neighbors," Danner said. "On either side, *and* across the street."

"He bought himself a moat," Mackenzie said.

A pair of elevator doors rested in the covered entryway. Mackenzie and Danner looked but found no call button on the wall. They stood for a moment, confused, until the elevator quietly slid open, beckoning them inside.

"Automatic sensors," Danner said.

Mackenzie nodded. "Anything less would be uncivilized." Danner gave a small smile.

The elevator dumped them into a short hallway. Ahead lay a broad, bright, open-plan area, the vibe identical to Journy's headquarters: refinished wood, smooth white surfaces, glass walls, mid-century furniture.

"Welcome!"

Cassiopeia Moreau greeted them from the kitchen, where she stood behind a granite island the size of Mackenzie's bedroom. Cassiopeia held a Vitamix filled with thick green goop, which she poured into a pint glass.

"Just finishing my breakfast," she said. "It's been *such* a crazy morning."

Mackenzie had to raise her voice awkwardly to be heard across the expanse. "No problem."

Cassiopeia walked toward them, barefoot and smiling. "Can I get you guys anything?"

Mackenzie glanced at Danner, who shook his head. "We're fine," Mackenzie said.

Cassiopeia led them to a U-shaped grouping of sofas and lounge chairs that orbited a sleek fireplace. Above rested the worst piece of art that Mackenzie had ever seen: chartreuse streaks haphazardly excreted across a black canvas.

"Make yourselves at home," Cassiopeia said. She dropped into an Eames lounger and placed her glass of goop on a marble coffee table. Mackenzie and Danner took spots on an adjacent sofa.

Cassiopeia Moreau was white, round-faced, with large, square teeth and oversized green eyes. She was petite and wore a blue, flowing Stevie Nicks romper that Mackenzie couldn't make sense of. Cassiopeia's defining feature was her hair: bright red and chopped into a short, unflattering, asymmetrical shape.

Cassiopeia smiled at Mackenzie, bangs bouncing. "I've been *so* excited to chat with you."

"Likewise," Mackenzie said.

"I know some of the folks at HV," Cassiopeia said. "But I don't think we've met before, right?"

Cassiopeia's voice was pitched with perfect corporate confidence. Her eye contact was unforgiving. She spoke like she was giving a TED Talk.

"I wasn't involved in the Journy Fund," Mackenzie said. "But I work closely with Roger. This is a space that he's really enthusiastic about."

Cassiopeia pursed her lips. "It's a huge opportunity, inherently scalable. We're empowering people to invest in themselves, really. Which is *always* a growth area."

Mackenzie understood none of what Cassiopeia said. "Totally."

Cassiopeia moved her eye contact, finally, to Danner. "And what do you do at HV?"

Danner sat in his customary ramrod position, upright on the edge of the sofa. "I'm not with Hammersmith Venture," he said. "Special Agent Jameson Danner, FBI."

Cassiopeia's smile vanished. "You're with the FBI?"

Danner nodded. "I'm investigating the murder of Trevor Canon. I'm here because I'd like to ask you a few questions."

Cassiopeia's features suspended in place. Her eyes flashed back to Mackenzie. "What is this? Some kind of trick?"

"HV is assisting the FBI in their investigation," Mackenzie said. "As you know, we had a lot invested in Trevor. Roger was very close with him."

"You told my assistant you wanted to meet about my incubator," said Cassiopeia.

"I do," Mackenzie said. "But I thought we could do two birds with one stone. Save you the time of setting up a separate meeting with Agent Danner."

Cassiopeia crossed her arms. She bit her lower lip. "This feels like a bait and switch."

"I apologize if that's how it feels." Mackenzie stripped any trace of sympathy from her voice. "I assumed you'd welcome the opportunity to help Agent Danner with his investigation."

"I do." Cassiopeia's TED tone slipped. Her voice broke slightly. "I want to help. I'm just surprised. I had a presentation ready."

"I'd still like to hear it." Mackenzie kept her expression neutral. "Roger has a hundred million earmarked for the coaching space. He wants to lock in a portfolio by end of year."

A glimmer appeared at the corner of Cassiopeia's eye. "That's great to hear."

"But Roger's also keen to find Trevor's killer, as I'm sure you are."

"I am, of course . . ."

Danner jumped in. "My questions can wait until after you and Mackenzie discuss your other endeavor."

Tactful, Mackenzie thought. Much different from Danner's approach the day before.

Cassiopeia gave Danner a wary look. "Just a few questions?"

Danner nodded. "I'll wait here. You and Mackenzie can meet first."

Mackenzie saw caution weighing against avarice in Cassiopeia's green eyes. Mackenzie imagined Cassiopeia's lawyers had told her not to speak to law enforcement.

But Mackenzie also thought it probable that Cassiopeia had been screwed by Trevor's dead money clause. She and Trevor had never married. The trappings of Cassiopeia's life were awash in money, but on paper, Mackenzie surmised, very little belonged to her. An investment from Hammersmith in her new coaching venture would be immense.

One thing that didn't factor into Cassiopeia's calculation, Mackenzie sensed, was of course the very thing that should have driven it: a desire to find her boyfriend's murderer.

"Incubator first," Cassiopeia said. "Then Agent Danner and I can talk." She locked eyes with Mackenzie, the TED Talk energy returned. "I'm eager to show you what I've put together."

"I'm eager to see it," Mackenzie lied.

For the next fifty-two minutes Mackenzie engaged in another professional skill that she'd spent years developing: the art of autopiloting through a conversation.

Cassiopeia led Mackenzie into a large workspace that she referred to as the "foundry." Mackenzie listened attentively. She asked questions. She smiled and shook her head at the right junctures. All the while, her mind was focused entirely on other things.

What Danner was going to ask.

The Tesla glowering on her street.

The dark crimson of Canon's blood on his office floor.

Occasionally a snippet of Cassiopeia's sales pitch would find its way through Mackenzie's cerebral defenses, exploding in her mind like a grenade of technobabble nonsense.

"It's all about intentionality, right? Feeding your inner creator."

"I leverage the leader that lays dormant within clients, embodying the wholeness of lived experience to manifest a corporate identity in ways they've never crystallized."

"I have to unwind the conditioning that my clients have internalized, often without even being mindful of how it's stunted their growth opportunities."

One wall of the foundry was covered in Post-it notes, a single word or phrase scrawled on each. "This is the ideation oasis," Cassiopeia said.

Mackenzie scanned the wall, taking in phrases like *mindful irrationality, liberate your essence, rebellious intention.*

"Very impressive," Mackenzie heard her autopilot saying. "It's rare to see such an advanced expression of values so early in a company."

"Exactly," said Cassiopeia.

After fifty-two minutes Cassiopeia led Mackenzie back to the living room. In a hall Mackenzie spotted the first sign of Trevor Canon she'd seen: a framed photo of Trevor and Cassiopeia in neon snow gear on a white glacier, surrounded by penguins.

"Antarctica," Cassiopeia said. "Trevor took me for my thirtieth birthday."

"I've always wanted to go," Mackenzie said. It was the first thing she'd said in an hour that she actually meant.

"Go soon," Cassiopeia said. She moved ahead, Stevie Nicks romper billowing behind her. "It's been discovered now. Won't be the same."

They returned to the living room. Danner waited on the sofa, staring at his phone.

"At the end of my meetings," Cassiopeia said, "I like to do an exercise. Come join us, Agent Danner."

Danner hesitated. "What is it?"

Cassiopeia smiled. "Step over here." Cassiopeia extended an open hand to her side. "Take my hand."

Danner moved around the sofa and grasped Cassiopeia's hand. With her other hand Cassiopeia grabbed one of Mackenzie's. Then she gestured at Mackenzie and Danner to clasp their free hands together.

Mackenzie did as directed. Danner's hand was considerably better manicured than her own.

The three of them stood in a tight triangle. The air smelled like celery. Cassiopeia's glass of goop still rested on a nearby table.

"I call this a Moment of Gratitude," Cassiopeia said. "We close our eyes, and for a few seconds we stand together."

Cassiopeia closed her eyes. Mackenzie hesitated before doing the same.

"How grateful are we," Cassiopeia continued, "to have this morning together?" Her voice slowed into the rhythm of a yoga teacher. "We had the opportunity to connect, to learn, to simply *be* . . ."

Mackenzie stole a glance at Danner. Both his eyes were wide open; he stared at Cassiopeia like she'd grown a second head.

Cassiopeia babbled for a while longer before opening her eyes and releasing her grip. She took a deep, dramatic breath. "Okay, Agent Danner. Now we can talk."

They resumed their earlier places in the living room. Cassiopeia reclined on the Eames, bare feet curled under her, gaze open and calm.

"How can I help?" Cassiopeia smiled. In no way did she resemble a person whose boyfriend had just been murdered.

Danner pulled out his phone and began his note-taking. "How did you and Canon originally meet?"

Cassiopeia's smile turned knowing. "At a party. From the start, our connection was undeniable." She looked away. "That was six years ago."

"What drew you to Canon?" Danner asked.

"Everything," Cassiopeia said. "Trevor wasn't like anybody else. He was one of one." She took a breath, bringing her eyes back to Danner. "Trevor's mind was always working. Our conversations were incredible. We could just sit and talk for hours, about any topic. Trevor was so much more than just Journy. He was a true polymath."

Mackenzie suppressed her eightieth eye roll of the day. "I've been told," Danner said, "that most of Canon's time was dedicated to the company."

Cassiopeia shrugged. "That's life as a founder."

"Did it ever bother you?" Danner asked.

"I'm not a teenager, Agent Danner. Journy is the most exciting company on the planet. I'm on the executive team. I know the demands of the job."

Danner stopped typing and placed his phone on the sofa cushion. "When did the two of you move in together?"

"About four years ago."

"After you'd joined the company."

Cassiopeia nodded. "I joined Journy six years ago."

"Soon after you started dating."

Cassiopeia's eye twitched. "Yes."

"Did anyone at Journy resent you for that?"

"Why would they?"

"Because you were dating the CEO," Danner said. "And within a few years, you became an executive."

"I *earned* my position," Cassiopeia said. She'd expected the question; her indignation had been loaded and ready. "I worked my way up. On my own." Her cheeks flushed. "I've been completely qualified for every job I've had."

Danner's features were stoic as ever. "I don't mean to impugn your qualifications. I'm trying to gauge how other people at the company may have perceived you."

"I don't care how I was perceived." Cassiopeia's lie was so transparent that Mackenzie almost felt bad for her.

"I'm just getting the lay of the land here, Miss Moreau. Your perspective on Canon's behavior could be invaluable."

"What do you mean?"

"You were with Canon every day, right?"

"Pretty much. Sometimes he worked late, or early . . . but even then, I'd see him at the office."

Danner's voice was flat. "Were you surprised that Canon put the dead money clause in his will?"

Cassiopeia hesitated; Mackenzie caught a tightening in her shoulders. She was sure Danner had caught it as well.

"Not really," Cassiopeia said. She squirmed on the lounge chair, shifting positions.

"Did you know that Trevor had changed his will before he died?"

"No." Cassiopeia's voice softened a touch. "Trevor and I never talked about money. It wasn't important to us."

Mackenzie stifled a cough as Danner continued. "What was your reaction when you heard?"

Cassiopeia dropped her eyes to the floor. Her cadence changed, the words breaking her veil of self-confidence. "If you want the honest answer, Agent Danner, it made me incredibly sad."

"Why?"

"Because clearly Trevor was scared about something." She lifted her head, eyes wide. "Why else would he do that?"

"Had you noticed any change in Canon's behavior in the weeks before he died?"

Cassiopeia sighed heavily. "Yes," she said. "Trevor hadn't been himself. For months."

Mackenzie glanced at Danner; it was the same thing Eleanor and Hector had said.

"How had he changed?" Danner asked. He picked up his phone, resumed typing.

"He became much more secretive. Protective. Irritable. He'd disappear without telling me, gone for entire nights. He'd say he'd been at the office, even though it was clearly a lie."

"Pardon me for asking," Danner said, "but did you ever wonder about—"

"Infidelity?" Cassiopeia shook her head. "Trevor wasn't wired that way. I'm positive."

"Then what triggered the change in his behavior?"

"I don't know," Cassiopeia said. "I've asked myself that a million times. Months ago, and also now . . ." She trailed off and turned her head. Tears formed at the corners of her eyes. "Now that he's gone."

"Had there been any big changes? Maybe with friends, or the company?"

Cassiopeia threw up a hand, voice breaking. "I knew he was acting weird, but I never thought . . . Oh *god*."

To Mackenzie's surprise, Cassiopeia began to cry. She heaved backward in the lounge chair, body crumpling into the leather as she sobbed. Danner froze awkwardly on the sofa.

Mackenzie grabbed her purse off the floor. Finding a small pack of tissues, she reached across the coffee table and handed it to Cassiopeia.

"Thank you," Cassiopeia said. She gave a weak smile. "God, how embarrassing."

"It's totally natural," Mackenzie said.

"I just . . ." Cassiopeia wiped at an eye. "I just can't believe he's gone, sometimes. I know it's been weeks now, but . . ."

"We understand," Mackenzie said.

Danner chimed in. "We can finish another time, if you prefer."

Cassiopeia shook her head. "I'd rather just get it over with."

Danner nodded. "What was Trevor's relationship like with the rest of his executive team? Did he ever talk about them?"

"Rarely," Cassiopeia said. She smirked, still wiping her eyes with the tissue. "The other executives and I were peers. Trevor said it wouldn't be fair to them."

"But you formed your own opinions, safe to say."

"Sure. In any job, you like some people more than others."

"What about Stanley Yoo?"

Mackenzie's attention sharpened at the mention of Yoo's name.

"Stan and Trevor were best friends," Cassiopeia said. "He used to come by the house all the time. Stan's always been a free spirit."

"How so?" said Danner.

Cassiopeia smiled, eyes dry. "One time Stan decided he was going to rollerblade across Japan. He announced it to the whole company. For a full year he wore Rollerblades in the office. He'd rollerblade between meetings, down the halls. You could hear him coming a mile away. Then, after a year, he went and did it."

Mackenzie snorted. "He rollerbladed across *Japan*?"

"Yep." Cassiopeia chuckled. "When Stan does something, he does it all the way. Trevor always knew how to make the most of it. He'd put Stan on special projects, let him go deep on things. When Stan came over he and Trevor would stay up all night, nerding out, talking about crazy ideas."

"When's the last time you saw him?" Danner asked.

Cassiopeia's eyes flitted between Danner and Mackenzie. "Why? Is he okay?"

"Nobody's seen him for a while," Danner said.

Cassiopeia's brow lifted with surprise. "He's missing?"

"Appears so. Nobody's been able to get ahold of him."

"That's strange," Cassiopeia said. "I haven't heard from him since Trevor passed. But he travels all the time. Maybe he's just off the grid."

"That's possible," Danner said, still typing. "What about the rest of the executive team? What were your impressions?"

Cassiopeia relaxed in her chair. "Eleanor's the rock. She was like Trevor's older sister. She's been great to me since he died. Great to everyone, really."

"She and Trevor were close."

"Very. Eleanor ran more of Journy than Trevor did. She took care of all the day-to-day. Let Trevor focus on the bigger picture. He always said she was invaluable."

"What about Hugo Chamberlain?"

Cassiopeia shrugged. "Hugo looks out for Hugo," she said. "Very competent. Very selfish." Cassiopeia raised her eyebrows, lips pursing. "Have you talked to Brady yet?"

"Brady Fitzgerald? No, not yet."

"You need to," Cassiopeia said.

"Why?"

"He and Trevor were fighting," Cassiopeia said. "Just a few days before Trevor died, he told me Brady was pissed at him."

"Fighting about what?" Danner asked.

"Brady's a child," Cassiopeia said. "He's insanely jealous of Trevor. He thinks that since he co-founded Journy, he should have just as much status. He resents being put on a shelf."

"As chief innovation officer," Danner said.

Cassiopeia rolled her eyes. "Right. Every few months, Brady gets drunk and yells at Trevor. They get into it."

"That doesn't sound uncommon," Mackenzie said. "Walk into any coffee shop around here and you'll find co-founders with axes to grind."

"Sure," Cassiopeia said. "But Brady is also in *love* with Trevor. He's jealous of *me*. He wants to go back to their twenties, just him and Trevor, bro-ing out in their apartment and writing dumb ideas on a whiteboard."

Mackenzie had a vision of the Post-its in Cassiopeia's "ideation oasis," but she let it pass.

"So if Brady and Trevor fought often," Danner said, "what made this time different?"

"Trevor said it was a bad one," Cassiopeia said. "He told me that Brady confronted him in his office."

"When?" Danner said.

"Not long before Trevor died. Under a week."

"What did Trevor say about it?"

"Brady was drunk and blew up at Trevor in his office. That's all Trevor told me. But it was the first time in a while that I can remember it spilling into an in-person thing."

"Trevor didn't say how it resolved?"

Cassiopeia shook her head.

Mackenzie leaned forward. "Do you think that could've been what made Trevor paranoid? Maybe Brady threatened him, scared Trevor into changing his will?" She didn't mention the elevator protocol to Canon's office. Danner hadn't said anything about it in front of Cassiopeia.

"I can't possibly imagine how Brady would really scare Trevor," Cassiopeia said. "Like I said, Brady's a child."

Danner interjected. "Yes, but if the confrontation happened a week before Trevor's death, the timing would line up."

And Brady's a member of the executive team, Mackenzie thought.

Danner typed on his phone. "What about Roger Hammersmith?" he asked.

Cassiopeia's eyes moved to Mackenzie. "You mean—her boss?"

Danner nodded. "What was Trevor's relationship like with him?"

Cassiopeia gestured at Mackenzie. "She'd probably know better than me. Trevor always liked Roger. Considered him a mentor, I guess. Beyond that, nothing unusual."

"Okay," Danner said. He finished typing, then looked up. "I just have one last question."

"Good," Cassiopeia said. "I'm exhausted."

Danner's face remained impassive. "Can you tell us your where-abouts on the night that Trevor died?"

Cassiopeia didn't hesitate. "Sure. I was at Serafina."

"Serafina?"

"It's a wellness retreat," Mackenzie said to Danner.

Serafina had started in the sixties as a hippie commune but had now evolved into a popular "wellness resort," one where tech elites like Cassiopeia shelled out thousands for the privilege of sitting bare-assed on boulders while drinking mushroom tea.

Cassiopeia nodded. "I go every few months. You can call them and check, if you'd like."

"We will," Danner said.

Cassiopeia pulled her phone out of her pocket. "I also posted while I was there. On my StoryBoard feed."

Danner and Mackenzie leaned forward as Cassiopeia hit play. The video was a panoramic shot of the Serafina grounds just after sunset, a collection of low wooden buildings perched on a cliff above the Pacific.

"That's still up on your page?" Danner asked.

Cassiopeia nodded. "Yep, feel free to check the time stamp."

Danner tucked his phone into his jacket. He rose and Mackenzie followed him.

"If you think of anything else, in particular any explanation for Canon's paranoia, please contact us."

"Of course," Cassiopeia said. She looked to Mackenzie. "And we'll be in touch after you speak with Roger?"

"Definitely," Mackenzie lied.

CHAPTER 13

Twenty-four days after Trevor Canon's death

"So," Mackenzie said as she folded back into the sedan, "what did you make of all that?"

Danner took the driver's seat and shrugged. "Lot to process. Canon's paranoia, this new stuff with Brady Fitzgerald, her reaction to the dead money . . ."

"You're forgetting the Moment of Gratitude."

Danner smirked as he started the engine. "Moreau's either the fakest person I've ever met, or she actually believes all the nonsense she spews."

Mackenzie smiled as Danner pulled off the curb. "The answer is both."

"Either way, she's hiding something."

"You think so?"

Danner nodded. "She had her alibi packaged up and ready to go. Even told us to check the time stamp."

"Maybe she knew you'd ask."

"Or maybe she created an alibi specifically to cover her tracks."

Mackenzie looked at him across the car. "You think Cassiopeia's a suspect?"

The customary shrug. "Not sure yet."

Mackenzie shook her head. "She may be ridiculously self-absorbed, but I can't see her killing Trevor."

Danner was flat-faced. "Impressions can be misleading."

"But what reason would she have?"

"A hundred million reasons, just like the others." The sedan waited at a four-way stop. "When I asked about the dead money, she flinched."

"I saw it, too."

"That house, the art, the surrounding properties—Canon paid for all that. It's not hers."

"But if she was motivated by money," Mackenzie said, "her better move would've been *marrying* Canon, not killing him. Then she owns half of everything. At much lower risk."

"Maybe." Danner tilted his head, considering the point. "Regardless, you don't live *and* work with someone and not know more about what's going on with them. She's definitely keeping something from us." Danner paused, then glanced over at Mackenzie. "I was impressed, by the way. With how you handled her in there."

A compliment? Mackenzie felt her suspicion rise.

"Thanks." She settled into the cheap cloth of the passenger seat. "I told you yesterday, there's a hierarchy in this industry. Unspoken, but always there. Roger Hammersmith is near the top, because of his track record and his money. I leverage his name every chance I get."

Danner kept his eyes on the road. "You came at her with complete confidence."

"That's the only option," Mackenzie said. "Cassiopeia's spent the last six years living in a billionaire's cocoon. Everyone in the cocoon is one-hundred-percent convinced of their own importance at all times. All their ideas are good ideas. All their decisions are the correct decisions. They operate on their own level."

"Your boss's level."

"Right. You want to get anywhere with people like that, you have to carry their same confidence."

Danner guided the sedan through SoMa. "I've been meaning to ask: How did you end up working directly for Hammersmith?"

Mackenzie glanced over at Danner. "What do you mean?"

"No offense, but you haven't been at his firm for that long. And you've risen pretty high."

"I could say the same about you and the FBI."

Danner gave a slight nod. "Fair."

"And I haven't risen that high," Mackenzie said. She gazed back out the windshield. "I'm an investigator. There's nothing that special about my job."

"You report directly to Hammersmith. You're close enough to leverage his name. That's something."

"I guess." Mackenzie shrugged as she decided which version of the story to tell. "A few years back there was a founder we'd invested in. Roger wanted to get out of it, but the lawyers couldn't find grounds for terminating the contract. I did some digging, found some stuff about the founder that got us out of the deal. After that, Roger made me an investigator."

"What kind of stuff did you find?"

Mackenzie chuckled. "You know I can't talk about it."

Danner smiled, eyes still on the road. "What's he like to work for?"

Mackenzie noted Danner's interest in Hammersmith. She filed it away for later.

"Roger's a living legend in VC," Mackenzie said. "Started off with a bang in the nineties, lost it all during the crash in the early 2000s, then built himself back up. Founders respect him because they know Roger's an entrepreneur himself. He's been to the bottom, lost everything, and then climbed back up through sheer self-belief. They see themselves in his story."

"So just like Cassiopeia, Hammersmith thinks all his ideas are good ideas."

Mackenzie smirked. "Roger's self-assurance makes Cassiopeia look insecure."

"How so?"

Mackenzie kept her gaze out the windshield as the sedan sank into a traffic jam. "When I joined HV, one of the old-timers at the firm told me a story. She went to Stanford with Roger; they had an English Lit class together. They were studying the work of this famous, reclusive writer, a woman named Daria Santorella."

"Never heard of her."

"Doesn't matter," Mackenzie said. "Anyway, the professor gave Roger a D for his analysis of a Santorella story. Told Roger that he'd totally misinterpreted it. Roger argued that his interpretation was actually the correct one—his professor was wrong."

"Okay."

"The professor told Roger to fuck off, so Roger took it up the ladder, all the way up to the president of Stanford. The president, like everybody else, told Roger to take the D and move on. But Roger didn't stop. He tracked down the author, Santorella herself."

"You're kidding."

"All of twenty years old, he flew to Italy and found a train to the remote village where Santorella was holing up. He badgered her until she admitted that Roger's interpretation of the story was the correct one—not his professor's."

"All this over a D?"

Mackenzie shook her head. "Can you imagine? Famous writer, enjoying some peace and quiet in nowhere Italy. Gets a knock at the door. Opens it up and finds some smug little asshole in a Stanford polo."

Danner laughed—a dry, half-hearted chuckle, as though he'd been reluctant to part with it. But it was better than another shrug.

"To get Roger off her back, Santorella calls up Stanford and tells the English department that Roger's interpretation was the correct one. Everyone had to admit they were wrong and Roger was right. Professor, president, all of them. Roger's D was turned into an A."

"And that was it?"

"That was it."

Danner shook his head. "All that over a grade."

"It wasn't about the grade," Mackenzie said. "When Roger decides he's right about something, he doesn't let anything get in his way."

"That's how he built himself back up, after the crash. Self-belief."

"Exactly. And it's why founders like Trevor Canon gravitate to him."

The sedan inched through the thick of gridlock.

"Let's reset," Mackenzie said. "Go over what we know, what we don't." She gestured at the surrounding traffic. "Might as well use the time."

Danner nodded. "Okay."

"We know that someone on the executive team killed Trevor."

"I sent Moreau's alibi to the office. We'll check it out."

"What about Eleanor's?"

"Eden's clear," Danner said. "She was at the gala all night. We've got time-stamped photos of her until well past midnight. And she sent over Journy receipts for her ride home. One A M."

Mackenzie nodded. "I left around midnight. She was still there."

"Do you recall what time you spoke to her?"

"In the bathroom line?"

"Yeah."

Mackenzie's voice was dry. "Not really. But I recall that I went straight to the bar afterward."

Danner smirked. "Was it awkward running into her?"

Mackenzie stared forward. "It's always weird when you see someone you dated. Even if it wasn't serious." Mackenzie paused. "I do remember one thing: The bar told me it was last call. I left after that drink."

"When was last call?"

"I don't remember. But you can probably call the venue and ask."

"Good idea." Danner fell quiet as he eased the car forward. "We still need to talk to Brady Fitzgerald and Hugo Chamberlain. And we need to verify Moreau's alibi."

Hammersmith's voice echoed in Mackenzie's head. She still didn't buy Danner's new openness. But she was happy to leverage it.

"We also need to find Stanley Yoo," she said.

"We're searching. Yoo took out a few thousand in cash right after Canon died. Since then he's been completely off the grid. Digital and financial."

"Crypto," Mackenzie said.

"Probably. Regardless, if he's running, he's doing a good job of it. So far."

"Do you think he is? Running, I mean."

Danner tilted his head. "It's hard to excuse the timing. But Yoo had to know it'd look bad. And by all accounts, he's a smart guy. If he killed Canon, he should know better than to think he can run from it. We'll find him."

"You think so?"

"We always do."

Mackenzie paused as a Journy Scoot zipped past her window, splitting lanes of traffic.

Danner continued. "We know Canon was afraid of something, paranoid. Frightened enough to change his will and restrict access to his office."

"And he was disappearing for long stretches."

"But we don't know where he was going."

"Or what caused his paranoia."

"No," Danner agreed. "Though we have this new story about Fitzgerald confronting him."

Danner's phone rang. The caller ID popped up on the infotainment system: ELEANOR EDEN.

Danner pressed a button and answered. "You're on speaker, Miss Eden. I've got Miss Clyde here in the car with me."

"Oh." Eleanor paused awkwardly. "Hello, Mackenzie."

"Hi," Mackenzie said, equally awkward. She caught Danner trying to suppress a smile.

"Were you able to meet with Cassiopeia this morning?" Even over the speakers, ragged fatigue was evident in Eleanor's voice.

"We just left her house," Danner said.

"Did you get what you need?"

"Got enough for now."

"Good." Eleanor shifted gears. "If you still want to talk to the other execs, I've got something for you. Brady's assistant admitted to Gaia that Brady's been spending most of his time at a bar."

Danner and Mackenzie glanced at each other. "A bar?" Danner asked.

"Yes. Apparently Brady's been 'working from home' there quite frequently."

"What bar?" Mackenzie asked.

"A place called Balboa Cafe," Eleanor said. Mackenzie groaned. "Do you know it?"

"I know it," Mackenzie said.

"Does Brady's assistant think he'll be there this afternoon?" Danner asked.

"It's very possible," Eleanor said.

"We'll check it out," Danner said.

"There's more," Eleanor said. "Tomorrow morning I'm doing a Q&A at the Futurist Summit in Palo Alto. Hugo is also going to be there."

"Chamberlain?" Danner asked.

"Yes. He's appearing on a panel. Could be a good opportunity to speak with him."

"Interesting." Danner pressed his lips together. "You're sure he's going to show up?"

"Undoubtedly," Eleanor said. "If there's one thing that Hugo likes more than listening to himself speak, it's *other* people listening to him speak." Mackenzie snickered as Eleanor continued. "A lot of big names will be there. Actually, Mackenzie, your boss is one of them."

"Hammersmith?" Danner asked.

"He's on a panel, too," Eleanor said.

"Who *isn't* on a panel?" Mackenzie asked, and Eleanor laughed.

"We'll be there," Danner said.

"Great. Gaia will send you the details."

Eleanor hung up. Danner glanced across the sedan cabin. "You know how to get to that bar she mentioned?"

"Unfortunately, I do."

"Good. Let's go find Brady Fitzgerald."

CHAPTER 14

Mackenzie sat in the back row of the lecture hall and watched the students file in. It was easy to identify her fellow 3Ls versus the first- or second-years. Body language gave it away.

It was March. Like all third-years, Mackenzie had sewn up her post-law-school plans. She'd spent the last two years currying favor with professors, putting in endless hours during a summer internship, scrapping for the handful of As on Georgetown's curve. She'd attended every study group, gone to every office hour, burned every drop of the midnight oil in the law library.

Mackenzie didn't have any passion for the law, but she'd relished the competition of law school. Many of her classmates hailed from wealthy coastal enclaves, or had connections to the Hill or the Street. Mackenzie didn't have her classmates' pedigrees, but she knew she was just as smart as they were. And to prove it, she outworked all of them. For her efforts she'd landed one of the best jobs of anyone in her class: associate at Parks Andrews, among the biggest law firms in the world.

But now it was March. The competition was over for Mackenzie and her fellow 3Ls. Like Mackenzie, they drifted to the back of the lecture hall, grabbing seats wherever comfortable.

The first- and second-years were still in the midst of their odysseys. They chattered nervously, elbowing for front-row seats where they could better catch the notice of the professor. Or, in today's case, her guest.

The lecture hall was packed. Late-coming students were forced to lean awkwardly on the aisle stairs. In her time at Georgetown, Mackenzie had never seen a crowd like it.

The source of the student enthusiasm was sitting in a swivel chair near the front of the lecture hall, speaking quietly with a professor. An aide helped them set up microphones. At six p.m. on the dot, the professor stood.

"Welcome, everyone." She gave a big smile. "I'm Adriana Cortez, a professor of law and politics here at Georgetown. I can tell from the crowd that our guest this evening doesn't need any introduction."

Light laughter as Professor Cortez gestured behind her. "But she deserves one all the same. You know her as the former COO at Spyder, one of the world's largest tech companies. Her new book, *A Seat at the Table*, has spent the last eighteen months on bestseller lists. She's also a proud graduate of Georgetown Law, class of nineteen—"

Eleanor Eden yelped from her chair onstage. "Don't! They'll know how ancient I am."

The crowd laughed with Professor Cortez. "Then we'll leave it a mystery. Please join me in welcoming Eleanor Eden!"

The hall filled with rapturous applause. From her perch in the back Mackenzie kept her arms crossed, hands tucked under her elbows.

Eden stepped to the podium. She appeared as unremarkable in person as she did in photographs. Plain features, brown hair. Blue eyes that matched her blouse.

Eden began by reading an excerpt from her book.

"'For my final interview at Spyder, I met with Tobias himself. I was intimidated. Spyder was still a startup, but Tobias already had a reputation for being a brilliant visionary. His technical acumen and foresight were legendary.

"'Meanwhile, I'd spent the last few years working for the secretary of commerce, a job as unglamorous as it sounds. I felt woefully unprepared to meet with someone of Tobias's stature.

"'But the interview was not what I expected. Tobias and I went for a long stroll around the Spyder campus while he asked me a series of unusual questions. Things like, "How lucky are you?" and, "If your goal was to set foot on Mars in the next decade, how would you try to achieve it, starting now?"

"'Toward the end of our walk, Tobias asked me a different question. He said, "If you were to take this position, you'd work with an executive staff that is entirely men. Do you feel that as a woman, you'd be at a disadvantage?"'"

Eden glanced up as the lecture hall filled with angry murmurs. She smiled and continued reading.

"'There were many ways I could respond to Tobias's question. One option that leapt to mind was telling him to go screw himself.'"

Eden paused again, looking up at the audience. "I suspect that's the option many of you would have chosen." More laughter.

"'Or I could have answered Tobias honestly, and told him it was obvious I would be at a disadvantage. Told him I would face obstacles that no man would. Explained the very real systemic challenges that women face in the corporate environment. Shared the studies showing that successful women are perceived as unlikable in the workplace, while successful men are perceived in the reverse.

"'But I didn't do any of those things. Instead, I looked Tobias in the eye and I lied. I told him no, I wouldn't be at a disadvantage—not at all.'"

Mackenzie felt a low rumble of anger in her gut. Eden continued at the podium.

"'Why did I lie? Why didn't I take the opportunity to explain to Tobias the systemic issues at play? Why didn't I flip the question, and ask Tobias why only men were in the leadership positions at Spyder?

"'The answer is simple: I wanted the job. Answering no was my best path to getting it. I decided that if I wanted to actually *do* something about systemic inequality, then I should start with myself. If I wanted Spyder to have more women in leadership positions, then I should become the first. Forget the systemic problems. If I wanted to actually achieve my goals (goals I shared with millions of women in the corporate world), then getting the job and kicking ass was my best path. I wouldn't tell Tobias about the systemic disadvantages I faced. I would simply show him that I was strong enough to overcome them.

"'Looking back, this was a critical juncture in my journey. When faced with an overwhelming challenge, it can be tempting to simply throw up our hands and scream. Rage against the inequality machine.

"'But what I discovered at Spyder was this. If we want to actually confront workplace inequity, then it's better to lower our arms, roll up our sleeves, and get to work. Because that's how change actually happens: incrementally, bit by bit, over time. It's not pretty. It's not fast. And it's not fair. But it works.

"'Too often, a woman in my position would have been honest with Tobias. She would have underestimated her own ability, as an individual, to overcome the systemic disadvantages she'd face. Studies have shown that a man would never do that. Men rarely underestimate their own abilities in the workplace. Women underestimate them all the time. In my conversation with Tobias, I was simply answering as a man would. Screw the disadvantages. I'm tough enough to overcome anything Spyder could throw my way.'"

An edgy, nervous twitch crept from Mackenzie's shoulders down through her arms, reaching the tips of her fingers.

"'Here's the truth,'" Eden continued. "'To effectuate change in modern corporate structures, we must first assert our position within them. If we want to change the composition of the table, then first we must take a seat at it.'"

Eden closed her book as the lecture hall exploded into another wave of applause. Mackenzie felt a pounding in her ears as she watched her classmates. All of them, it seemed, were enraptured by Eden's insights, faces glowing with admiration.

Eden retook her seat for a moderated Q&A. Professor Cortez read questions gathered from students over the prior week.

"First question," Professor Cortez said, reading from her laptop.

"'Eleanor, I imagine you've had to work with a number of difficult men. It's one thing to earn a seat at the table. But what if the table is full of men who don't treat you as an equal?'"

Eden nodded from her seat, microphone in hand. "I've worked with plenty of men over my career. Many decent. Some not. Here's how I approach it: I work hard enough that they don't matter. I simply outproduce them. And I rise above their nonsense."

Mackenzie bounced her foot nervously, trying to channel her bubbling frustration.

"'Eleanor, as a woman starting at a law firm in the fall, what one piece of advice would you have for someone like me?'"

"Keep your head down and produce," Eden said. "In every workplace there's a ton of gossip, rumors, politics. Ignore it and focus on what you're actually getting done. Produce good work. The results will come."

Mackenzie crossed her arms, leg bouncing furiously beneath the desk. She could sense her temper reaching its threshold; she forced herself to breathe.

"'Eleanor, how does your advice apply to mothers? How do you achieve work-life balance when it comes to raising children *and* pursuing a meaningful career?'"

Eden uncrossed and recrossed her legs, shifting in her seat. "Zoe and I have two kids, so I can speak directly to this. As women, we often force the either-or upon ourselves. I saw women at Spyder who built tremendous careers and then preemptively stopped asserting themselves because they were just *trying* to have a child—even if they weren't pregnant yet! It becomes a self-fulfilling prophecy. The bottom line is that a woman can be successful in her career *and* successful as a mother. Balance is achievable. We just have to be intentional about creating it."

The pounding in Mackenzie's ears grew into a dull roar. It overwhelmed the sound of Eden's voice. Mackenzie tuned it out, forcing her blood to cool.

The Q&A came to an end. The students of Georgetown Law erupted into a final round of jubilant applause, and the room began to break. Professor Cortez stood with Eden near the podium.

"I know many of you brought copies of *A Seat at the Table* with you," Professor Cortez said. "Eleanor has graciously agreed to sign them, if you'll form a line."

Mackenzie hung back as other students clambered forward, eager and shiny in their ardor, hardbacks of *A Seat at the Table* clutched in their hands. Mackenzie lingered at the end of the line, letting everyone go before her.

At the podium Eden cheerfully signed each book presented to her, basking in the chorus line of ass-kissing. It was all big smiles and forced laughter.

Progress was slow. After fifteen minutes Professor Cortez left. The line dwindled to ten students, then five. Mackenzie kept her place at the back, ensuring she'd go last.

Finally only one student remained between Mackenzie and Eden. A short girl with oversized teeth and straightened hair bounded up to the podium. Mackenzie judged her to be a 1L, based on her buoyancy.

"Oh my god, Miss Eden, I'm such a huge fan of yours, thank you so much for coming today."

Big smile from Eden. "Please, call me Eleanor. And thank you for being here." Eden took the book and opened the front cover. "What's your name?"

"Amara."

Eden signed the inside. "Amara, it was my pleasure. Always enjoy coming back here to visit."

"Your book changed my life. It's just been so *empowering* to listen to you speak."

"It's empowering for me to meet young women like you," Eden replied.

Mackenzie almost retched.

Amara made a merciful exit. Now, at last, Mackenzie found herself alone with Eden.

Eden beamed at Mackenzie from the podium. "Last but not least."

Mackenzie didn't smile back. She stepped to the podium, flats echoing in the empty lecture hall. Eden was of middling height.

Mackenzie towered over her, but Eden gave no sign of intimidation. She leaned casually against the wooden podium, features serene. She noticed that Mackenzie was empty-handed.

"Nothing for me to sign?" Eden asked.

"Nope."

Eden smiled warmly. "Just wanted to chat?"

Mackenzie nodded. The two of them were separated by a meter of fake mahogany.

"Everything you said tonight," Mackenzie said, "was total bull-shit."

Eden's eyebrows shot upward with surprise. She straightened at the podium, but her smile remained. "Oh?"

"Your book was bullshit, too. You're peddling crap."

Eden stepped back from the podium and folded her arms together. She tilted her head upward to better consider Mackenzie's face. "Which parts, exactly, do you disagree with?"

"All of them." Mackenzie kept her voice level. This isn't an emotional argument, she told herself. It's a factual one. "You've taken a complicated issue like gender equality and dumbed it down to a solution as moronic as pulling ourselves up by our collective bootstraps. You've convinced people to ignore everything that's wrong with our system, just because you got lucky."

Mackenzie watched as Eden's eyebrows fell, the smile fading from her lips. "Your decision to take the Spyder job is a magnificent rationalization. Somehow you've spun it as benefiting the cause when it was actually driven entirely by personal ambition. You *should've* told Tobias to go fuck himself, but you didn't. Not because it was better for working women, but because it was better for *you*."

Eden's face grew serious as she regarded Mackenzie. "Go on."

"Then you blame mothers for not being *assertive* enough." Mackenzie leaned forward. "My mom worked every day of her life to give me an opportunity. Since I was eleven I've been taking care of myself, because she was always on the road. It was the only way she could provide for my future, create a path for me to eventually attend law school at a place like this." Mackenzie gestured to the empty Georgetown lecture hall surrounding them.

"She couldn't *assert* her way to getting more time at home. She had to make a choice. Because women *are* forced to choose. Choose whether to be honest with an ass like Tobias or swallow it in pursuit of the job. Choose whether to take their maternity leave or fight for a promotion. Choose whether to work harder than their peers, sacrificing other parts of their life, to get the same money and the same recognition.

"Men never have to make those choices," Mackenzie said. "They cruise right through the system because they're the ones that built it. We shouldn't be fighting for a seat at *their* table. We should be flipping the goddamn thing over."

Eden stared hard at Mackenzie from across the podium, unblinking. Mackenzie had difficulty reading her expression. There was something at the corners of her eyes, a sparkle of fire that Mackenzie couldn't peg. Was it anger? Or something else?

"What's your name?" Eden asked.

"Mackenzie Clyde."

"Mackenzie Clyde," Eden repeated. "You're a 3L?"

Mackenzie nodded.

"What's your class rank?"

Mackenzie hesitated. She hadn't been sure how Eden would react. But certainly not like this.

Eden repeated the question. "Class rank?"

"At the top," Mackenzie said.

"*Where* at the top?"

"First."

Eden gave a slight nod, as though it was the answer she'd expected. "I assume you have a firm lined up. After graduation."

"Parks Andrews."

Eden paused, appraising Mackenzie for another long moment. Finally she moved toward the door and motioned Mackenzie to follow.

"Come with me," Eden said. "We need to talk."

CHAPTER 15

Twenty-four days after Trevor Canon's death

Balboa Cafe was busy.

Real estate agents ate power salads. Sixty-something suburban-ites sipped mimosas, down from Marin for the day in their Cay-ennes. Bros inhaled burgers while arguing about crypto. It smelled old. The air was ripe. Wooden floorboards creaked under Macken-zie's feet, sticky with decades of bad decisions.

"I hate this place," she said.

"Why?" Danner asked.

"This neighborhood is where original thought goes to die." Mac-kenzie used her height, scanning the room for Brady.

"There," Danner said. He pointed to the far corner. A guy sat alone at the bar, laptop open. "That's him."

Mackenzie led them through the sea of Ann Taylor and Bonobos. As they reached the back, Brady Fitzgerald came into clearer focus.

Brady had easy brown eyes, a prominent nose, and a strong chin carrying a few days of stubble. A Red Sox hat was perched over short brown hair. He wore expensive, un-scuffed leather boots, the type favored by men who consider themselves outdoorsy because they take an annual trip to the Yellowstone Club. Throw a stick in this neighborhood, Mackenzie thought, and it'd hit a dozen other white guys just like him.

Brady sat on a barstool next to the wall, focused on his laptop. A nearby rocks glass contained a finger of diluted brown liquid.

Mackenzie sidled onto an open stool to Brady's left. Danner took the next one over. Mackenzie glanced at Brady's screen—he was watching a Chainsmokers concert on mute.

Brady looked up and gave Mackenzie an unembarrassed once-over. "Hi there," he said.

"Hi," Mackenzie replied.

"You're very tall."

"Taller than you," Mackenzie said. She gestured at Brady's T-shirt; block letters read ANTIFRAGILE across the chest. "Big fan of Taleb?"

Brady grinned. "Of course."

"*Black Swan?*"

Brady swiveled on his barstool, opening his body toward Mackenzie. His grin widened.

"*Black Swan* is for gen pop," Brady said. "I go all the way back. *Fooled by Randomness.*"

"Ah."

Danner watched from his stool; Brady paid him no attention. He leaned an elbow against the bar. "How about you?"

"I started *Black Swan* but couldn't get through it."

"Why?"

Mackenzie shrugged. "Taleb's an insufferable prick."

Brady's face froze with surprise, then burst into an explosion of laughter. He extended a hand. "I'm Brady."

Mackenzie shook. "Mackenzie Clyde, from HV." She leaned back, gesturing to Danner. "And this is Federal Agent Danner."

Danner leaned forward. "Special Agent Jameson Danner, FBI," he said. "We'd like to ask you some questions about the murder of Trevor Canon."

Brady froze again, his eyes snapping between Danner and Mac-

kenzie. The shit-eating grin remained plastered on his face. "You guys
are fucking with me, right?"

Danner shook his head. "We're not."

Brady looked at Mackenzie. "This for real?"

Mackenzie nodded. "Real as rain."

The smile fell from Brady's face, the mirth in his eyes morphing
into shrewdness. Don't underestimate him, Mackenzie told herself.
He's not as dumb as he looks.

Brady flung his laptop closed. "Let's talk." He grabbed the rocks
glass, downed the last swirl, and thudded it back on the bar. "But first
I need a drink."

Brady flagged the bartender and pointed at the empty glass. "Another one, Donny."

The bartender gave a curt nod. Brady settled against the wall as
Mackenzie and Danner rearranged their stools into a cramped triangle.

Brady crossed his arms casually across his chest. "What do you
want to know?"

"To start," Danner said, "where were you on the night of Canon's
death?"

Brady smirked. "You want an alibi."

"Yes."

"You can talk to Donny." Brady pointed in the direction of the
bartender, who was perched on a ladder, reaching for a bottle of
whiskey. "I was here that night."

"The whole night?" Danner asked.

"Went to the Giants game," Brady said. "Got here around nine-
thirty. Stayed till close."

"Till two A.M.?" Mackenzie asked.

Brady nodded. "Donny can tell you."

Danner had his phone out, dutifully taking notes. "Did anyone
else see you?"

"I assume so." Brady pointed to the corner above them. A discreet
camera was embedded in the wall. "But you don't have to take my
word for it. Footage is probably in the cloud somewhere."

Donny arrived with a large pour of whiskey. Brady grabbed it and
took a long sip.

"What was your reaction when you heard Canon had died?" Danner asked.

"What do you think? I was crushed. How would you feel if your best friend was murdered in his own fucking office?"

Brady took another sip, then set the glass back on the bar. He sneered at Danner. "And since then, you government types haven't done shit to find his killer."

"I'm not SFPD," Danner said. "The FBI just took over the case."

Brady waved a hand. "SFPD, FBI, it's all the same. Bureaucrats sitting around with their dicks in their hands."

Danner flinched on his stool, and Mackenzie jumped in.

"What was your title at Journy?" she asked Brady.

Brady didn't hesitate. "Co-founder."

"Co-founder?"

"Yes," Brady said. "I co-founded the fucking thing. It was me and Trevor. The cars, bikes, golf carts. The app. All of that was *our* idea."

Mackenzie chose her words carefully. "We were told that your current title is a little different."

"Chief innovation officer." Brady spat the words. "Crock of shit."

"So CIO wasn't your idea."

"Hell no." Brady's expression darkened. "I should be running Product. Did you know that Trevor wanted Journy to only be bikes and scooters? He wanted to just drop 'em on street corners and let people rent 'em by the mile. It was *me* who said we also had to have cars, with actual drivers, that people could summon with the click of a button. Taxis were begging to be disrupted—you wanna talk about a shitty product."

Brady took another sip; only a few minutes had passed but the glass was nearly empty.

"Cars didn't fit with Trevor's grand vision." Brady chuckled. "He'd always say 'The car is the telegraph of our generation. It's begging for obsolescence.' And I'd say 'Who gives a shit? Sometimes you don't wanna pedal your ass to work.' We fought about it, but I won." Brady leaned back against the wall. "The rest is history."

"So why aren't you running Product?" Mackenzie asked. Danner had fallen quiet.

"Because Trevor hired a bunch of corporate assholes. I told Trevor we should be moving fast, breaking shit. Not wasting our time with fucking RASCI charts.

"But Trevor was under pressure. He said CIO was the best way to keep me on the executive level while 'freeing up my day-to-day.' He tried to spin it as good for me. But I knew what he was doing."

"What was that?"

"Putting me out to pasture," Brady said. "In the big old field with nothing to do but chew the cud."

He finished the whiskey and dropped it on the bar. He rapped a knuckle on the wood to alert Donny, then pointed at the glass.

"That must have been difficult," Mackenzie said.

"It is what it is."

"So you're on the executive team. But as a co-founder, I imagine your stock arrangement is different than the other executives'."

Brady gave Mackenzie a rueful smile. "Nice try. No, I didn't know about Trevor's little stunt with his will. The dead money provision, or whatever the fuck. As for my stock: It's no different than the rest of the executive team."

Mackenzie frowned. "But as a co-founder, wouldn't you have original shares from when you guys started the company?"

Brady shrugged. "I sold most of them to Trevor."

"When?"

"Six or seven years ago," Brady said. "I wanted to liquidate. Diversify."

Mackenzie kept her features still as her mind roiled. Brady had sold the shares back when Journy was much smaller; they would've been worth nothing compared to now. Brady's shortsightedness had likely cost him hundreds of millions. Billions, even.

Danner interjected. "You're 'put out to pasture,' as you call it. You already sold the majority of your stake. So why don't you quit and do something else?"

Brady regarded Danner like he was an idiot. "Because it's my fucking company, too."

Donny arrived with a fresh whiskey and Brady lurched for it, eagerly downing another gulp.

"Agent Danner is asking," Mackenzie said, "because it sounds like you carry some resentment toward the company."

Brady frowned. His eyes still carried the same shrewdness, though perhaps with a growing sheen.

"I don't resent the company," Brady said. "I resent the assholes Trevor hired. They've sucked the heart right out of Journy, turned it into any other soulless corporate tech bullshit, like Spyder or Story-Board."

"What about Trevor?" Mackenzie asked. "Do you resent him, too?"

Brady took a deep breath. "I've never resented Trevor," he said. "We lived together for years. Started Journy together. Dreamed together. He was my brother." He raised his palms. "We fought sometimes, but that's how brothers are. When you've been through a lot of shit together, it adds up."

Mackenzie kept her tone light. "What did you fight about?"

"Journy, my role, its direction. The people Trevor surrounded himself with. As smart as he was, Trevor had terrible judgment in people." Brady straightened on his stool. "But I never resented Trevor for Journy's success. My name's attached to it, too. Journy's success is my success."

Delusion, Mackenzie thought, is a helluva drug.

"We heard the two of you had been fighting more intensely," Mackenzie said. "That you confronted Trevor in his office."

Brady rolled his eyes, shaking his head. "I know who told you that. 'Cassiopeia Moreau.'" His voice was sopped with derision. "Or, as she's *actually* named, Katie Moore. You know she made up that name, right?"

Danner nodded. "We do."

"Did you guys go see her in the Temple That Trevor Built?"

"This morning."

Brady scoffed. "She's got real balls squatting in that place. Didn't spend a dime of her own money on it." Brady's eyes glistened. "But that's how their whole thing went. When Trevor made her CMO it was so embarrassing. Everyone in the company knew she didn't deserve it." Brady glanced back at Mackenzie. "Did she tell you about her 'coaching incubator'?"

Mackenzie nodded, and Brady snickered. "At exec meetings she used to make everyone get together and do a Moment of Gratitude.

She'd stand there with her eyes closed and the rest of us would just shake our heads. Even Trevor would roll his eyes."

Brady shrugged. "I tried to tell him about her for years, but he wouldn't listen. She even tried to get him to invest in her new thing. Thankfully he still had some sense left."

"Her new coaching venture?" Danner chimed in. "Moreau tried to get Canon to invest in it?"

"Oh yeah," Brady said, smiling at the memory. "She pushed him on it, but Trevor knew better. When he passed, Cass was furious."

Danner took notes as Mackenzie continued.

"So is she lying?" Mackenzie asked. "You never confronted Trevor?"

Brady set his drink down on the bar, then folded his arms together. "It happened," he said. "But it wasn't some huge deal."

"Go on."

Brady looked up to the ceiling. "Look, Trevor and I were still buds, even after the CIO thing. We'd smoke pot, go to Warriors games, jet down to L.A. for a night, have dinner at the Battery."

Brady reached up and removed his Red Sox cap, scratching at his hair. Mackenzie noted it was thinning. "Few months ago, though, Trevor started ghosting me. Wouldn't reply to texts, kinda disappeared. Stopped hanging out." Brady replaced his cap and snapped his fingers. "Just like that."

"Was that unusual for Trevor?" Mackenzie said.

"Yeah. 'Cassiopeia' can talk whatever shit she wants to, but Trevor and I were still close. It wasn't like him to go MIA."

Mackenzie snuck a glance at Danner. "We've heard similar things from your colleagues," Danner said. "A few months before his death, Trevor became increasingly paranoid."

"Huh." Brady blinked at him. "I wouldn't call it that." Brady paused, then reached for his drink again. "He was just vague as fuck. I could tell he was keeping something from me."

"Did you have any idea what it was?" Mackenzie asked.

"Not exactly," Brady said. He tilted his head slightly. "But I had a good guess."

"What?"

"I think Trevor was working on something," Brady said. "Something big, that he didn't want anyone to know about. I saw Trevor go into this mode back in the early Journy days. If he was into a new idea, he'd block everything else out. Head down, full bore, locked in. It was like the new idea was the only thing in his entire life that mattered." Brady shook his head. "This time I wasn't inside whatever he was working on. But his behavior was the same."

Danner's fingers flew over his phone. "But you don't know what this new project might be?" Mackenzie asked.

"I asked him a few times why he was being so weird. He just pushed me off."

Danner looked up from his phone. "Do you think anyone else at Journy had an idea that Canon was working on something?"

"I'm the only one who would've figured out that he was working on something new. I knew him the best."

"Do you think it was something related to Journy?" Mackenzie asked. "Maybe an IPO?"

Brady chuckled. "Definitely not. Trevor never gave a shit about the finances. He let Eleanor handle the money." Brady rubbed his neck. "I know Trevor was up to something, though. And a few weeks before he died, I got proof."

CHAPTER 16

Twenty-four days after Trevor Canon's death

Brady brought the glass to his lips, finishing off his second whiskey of the conversation. Mackenzie observed a slow glaze accumulating in his eyes, like dew gathering on a windshield.

"I went down to Serafina," Brady said, "to clear my head."

"Serafina?" Mackenzie said. "That's where Cassiopeia was the night Trevor was killed."

Brady tilted his head. "Really?"

"She posted a StoryBoard from there the night Trevor died."

"That's her alibi?" Brady asked. Mackenzie nodded. "Huh. Well, this was a few weeks before all that. I went down to Serafina, and one morning I went for a hike in Big Sur. There's a spot I know that's deep in the forest, remote as hell. Trevor and I used to go there back in the day, take mushrooms, go for a walk. We'd never see anybody.

"The hike is an out and back. I'm on my way back to the start, and in the distance, I see two other people on the path. They're way ahead of me, walking toward me, talking to each other. And I recognized both. One was Trevor."

"Trevor?" Danner asked. "You ran into him."

Brady nodded. "Trevor was the only other person who was aware of this trail, far as I knew. Coincidence that we'd be there at the same time, though."

"Who was the other person?" Danner asked.

"Indira Soti," Brady said.

Mackenzie's shoulders tightened. "Soti?"

"It was Soti. One hundred percent. When he and Trevor saw me they turned and booked it out of there. I tried to catch up to them, but I was too tired."

"Sorry," Danner interjected, "but refresh my memory on Indira Soti?"

"Soti's the biggest name in venture capital right now," Brady said. "Every hot shit startup wants to work with him. Does deals with all the celebrities, sits courtside at Warriors games, etcetera."

"He's my boss's biggest rival," Mackenzie said.

"Exactly," Brady said. "Roger Hammersmith and Trevor were super tight. So it was weird to see Trevor talking to Soti."

"What do you think they were talking about?" Danner asked.

"Don't know," Brady said. "But it had to be connected to whatever Trevor was working on. He was meeting Soti in the middle of nowhere. Clearly he didn't want anyone to know."

"Did you ask Canon about it?"

Brady leaned back against the wall. "That's what Cassiopeia told you about." His lip curled. "After the Soti thing, I had to talk to Trevor. So I went to see him in his office."

"During the workday?" Danner asked.

"Evening," Brady said. "It was just getting dark."

"And when was this? You said a week or so before Trevor died?"

"Less. This was more like three, four days before."

"What happened next?"

"Trevor barely acknowledged me. I told him I knew he saw me in Big Sur. I asked him why he was meeting with Soti." Brady shook his head. "Trevor acted like he had no idea what I was talking about. Denied the whole thing."

"He lied," Mackenzie said.

Brady nodded. "I was pissed. Trevor and I had been through a lot together. He was always honest with me. Even on the CIO shit, he told it to me straight."

"We've been told that he was blunt to a fault," Mackenzie said.

"Right." Brady slouched on the stool, torso melting into the wall behind him. "When he lied to my face, it got ugly. I told him he was full of shit. I knew he was working on something secret, and that he was meeting with Soti for a reason."

"How did Trevor react?"

"He told me to get the fuck out of his office." Brady grinned. "It devolved from there. I ripped him a new one. Trevor just stood there and took it, like it didn't faze him." Brady stared at the floor. "After I was done, he gave me this . . . *look*. Like he was the parent, and I was the child. He said he had another meeting. And that was it."

"Did your argument with Canon ever turn physical?" Danner asked.

Brady shook his head, raising a finger. "No. I yelled, sure. Raised my voice. But that was it."

"How did you leave things?"

"Like I just told you." Brady shrugged. "I left. That was the last time I saw him."

Danner plowed ahead. "Canon said he had another meeting. Did he say who it was with?"

"No," Brady said, "but I ran into him on my way out. He was coming off Trevor's elevator as I left."

"Who?" Mackenzie said.

"Roger Hammersmith," Brady said. "He came by Trevor's office all the time. Like I said before, they were tight."

Brady moved suddenly, sliding off the stool. "I gotta take a piss," he declared. He disappeared toward the back of the bar.

Mackenzie glanced at Danner. "What do you think?"

Danner finished typing on his phone. "He's clearly resentful. Of Journy and Canon both."

Mackenzie nodded. "But their big confrontation was only a few days before Trevor died. He'd already changed his will. So Brady's threats couldn't have been the motivating factor."

"Yes," Danner agreed, "but this is all Fitzgerald's version of events. And he's clearly not the most reliable narrator."

"Fair." Mackenzie paused. "Do you buy what he's saying? That Trevor was working on something new, something big?"

"It would explain why Canon had been so secretive before his death." Danner pressed his lips together. "But it's hard to believe anything that comes out of Fitzgerald's mouth."

Sitting on a barstool had taken its toll. Mackenzie hopped off and stretched, lifting her arms and rotating her neck. She pushed her right hand backward, trying to loosen up her wrist, as her eyes scanned across the room.

The crowd had thinned but the place was still busy. Not for the first time, Mackenzie wondered if anybody in San Francisco ever *worked* during the day. As she gazed to the far end of Balboa Cafe, she caught eyes with a guy seated at the opposite end of the bar, near the entrance.

The guy was tall, white, long-faced, with a blond buzz cut. He wore a black button-up with the sleeves rolled, revealing a colorful tattoo on his left forearm. Mackenzie wouldn't have noticed him, but she caught the distinct impression that he'd been staring at her.

Mackenzie couldn't be sure. But she felt a trace of heat in the back of her neck. And when their eyes met, the guy immediately looked away, staring too intently at the menu above the bar. Mackenzie's instinct told her that until that moment, he had been looking her direction—and for quite some time.

A chill filled her stomach as she thought of the black Tesla looming outside her window, the dark silhouette watching her from within.

Danner broke Mackenzie's reverie.

"Did Hammersmith tell you that he went to visit Canon? The night Fitzgerald says he saw him?"

Mackenzie shook her head. "He wouldn't have. He was at Journy HQ frequently, saw Trevor all the time."

"Sure. The timing is interesting, though. Especially if Fitzgerald is right, that he saw Canon with Indira Soti. You say Soti is Hammersmith's biggest rival?"

Mackenzie's voice was matter-of-fact. "Roger and Soti hate each other."

"Why?"

"Competition," Mackenzie said. "And more. Roger is old school.

He's been in the game for a long time. Soti is the new money on the scene. He's got a podcast, wears Yeezys, hangs out with YouTubers. Roger thinks Soti is all style and no substance. Soti thinks Roger's a dinosaur, overdue for a meteor."

Brady returned, moving back to his barstool.

"I gotta wrap this up," Brady said. "I'm meeting somebody here."

"Just a couple more questions," Danner said.

Brady nodded. "Donny!" He rapped his knuckles on the bar again, yelling at the bartender. "I'm gathering dust over here!"

Mackenzie wondered how much Donny would pay for a chance to punch Brady in the face.

"Earlier you said that Canon hired some corporate types," Danner said. "Were you talking about the other members of the executive team?"

Brady made a face. "There were a couple I liked. Couple I didn't."

"Who didn't you like?"

"Hugo Chamberlain," Brady said. "He's a stiff. Only cares about his résumé. Never gave a shit about Trevor or Journy."

"Did he have any particular grievance with Trevor?"

"He didn't have reason to. Hugo barely worked. Every week he was speaking on a panel, attending a conference. He delegated everything. Eleanor basically ran the Product team."

"Eleanor Eden?"

Brady nodded. "At first I didn't like her, either. She's like a soccer mom. Has little birthday parties for all her staff. It's cheesy as fuck." Brady shrugged. "But she was good at her job. Insulated Trevor, let him focus on the big picture, while she kept the trains running. How it should be."

"And what about Stanley Yoo?" Danner said. "Are you aware that he's been missing?"

Brady frowned. "Stan's missing?"

"Nobody's heard from him since Canon died," Danner said. "He told Eleanor he went to Hawaii, but he was supposed to return a few days ago."

Brady's brow lifted. "Ah, okay. I mean, that's just kinda Stan. He's always done his own thing."

"How so?" Mackenzie asked.

Donny appeared, expression dour. This time he held an entire bottle of whiskey. He slammed it on the bar and walked away.

Brady, impervious to Donny's irritation, opened the bottle and poured himself another. "Stan's smart as hell. But he's a grinder. Great at executing something if you tell him what to do. But he doesn't think big."

Doesn't think big, Mackenzie thought. In tech, it was perhaps the worst thing you could say about someone.

Brady lifted his hat, scratching at his hair. "Trevor gave him way too much rope. Stan was gone every fucking summer. Retreats in Tulum, villas in Bali. Two weeks at Burning Man, every damn year. It set a bad example."

"Every year?" Danner asked.

"Every year," Brady said. "Didn't matter what was going on at the company. Never missed it. Like clockwork." Brady shrugged. "He's probably doing ayahuasca in Kauai as we speak."

Near the windows, the crypto bros had escalated into a rowdy game of quarters. A brassy fake tan at the bar ordered a skinny cosmo, whatever the hell that was. Mackenzie was reaching the limits of her time in the Balboa Cafe.

Danner apparently felt the same. He stuffed his phone in his pocket and stood. "That's all the questions we have, Mr. Fitzgerald. We'll be in touch."

"Oh." Brady blinked. "That's it?"

Mackenzie sensed that Brady had enjoyed the captive audience. She wondered how often he had that experience.

"Contact us," Danner said, "if you think of anything else."

Brady raised his glass in a half-salute. "Will do, Agent Danner."

Mackenzie slid off her stool and Brady grinned at her. "You're welcome to stay."

Mackenzie nodded toward the open bottle of whiskey. "You've got all the company you can handle."

Brady laughed. Then his eyes popped open and flipped to Danner. "Oh hey, one more thing."

Danner stopped at his stool. "What?"

"You said Cassiopeia was at Serafina the night Trevor died," Brady said. "She posted a StoryBoard from there. That's her alibi, right?"

Danner narrowed his eyes. "Why do you ask?"

"Because it's bullshit," Brady said. His voice was rich with satisfaction, as though uncovering a long-buried secret. "At Serafina they take your phone. It's a digital detox retreat; no tech's allowed."

"Maybe she snuck her phone in," Mackenzie said.

Brady shook his head. "No way. They're real tight-asses about it. I'm telling you: The StoryBoard's bullshit."

"I'll take that into consideration," Danner said. He motioned to leave. "We'll be in touch."

As they exited the bar, pushing through the throngs of highlights and man-buns, Mackenzie looked for the guy with the sleeve tattoo. She wanted the guy to ignore her as she passed. That way she could quiet her overactive subconscious, thaw the chill that had lined her stomach. She could tell herself she'd been imagining their eye contact, that there'd been nothing odd about him.

But Mackenzie couldn't do any of that.

The guy with the sleeve tattoo had disappeared.

CHAPTER 17

Twenty-five days after Trevor Canon's death

Mackenzie rose from bed and moved straight to the bay window, slowly opening the curtains. She saw nothing but stark sunlight and gestating traffic. The night had passed quietly; no sign of the Tesla. Still, she'd slept poorly.

She was glad she hadn't told Danner about the Tesla, or about the sleeve-tattoo guy at Balboa Cafe. Mackenzie wouldn't go to Danner on intuition alone. And she certainly wasn't going to say anything to Hammersmith. Last night she'd texted him with updates about Cassiopeia's and Brady's alibis.

Roger Hammersmith: What about Yoo?
Mackenzie Clyde: nothing yet
Roger Hammersmith: Find him.
Mackenzie Clyde: on it

Hammersmith hadn't replied.
Mackenzie exited her apartment to the sight of Danner's silver

sedan rumbling on the curb. She bent into the passenger seat and Danner moved them into gear.

"We checked the alibis," Danner said.

He wore a black suit, but no tie. Improvement, Mackenzie thought.

"Cassiopeia and Brady?"

Danner nodded. "Fitzgerald's checks out. We got videos from the Balboa Cafe for the evening Trevor was murdered. Fitzgerald was there the whole night." Danner smirked. "Same exact seat at the bar."

"What about Cassiopeia?"

"More complicated," Danner said. He guided the sedan along the same path as the day before, heading toward the Embarcadero. "Serafina's manager won't confirm if Moreau was there on the night that Canon was killed. Gave us the privacy runaround. I'll have to get a subpoena."

"Will that be a problem?"

"No. But it'll take a bit." Danner paused. "The manager did confirm that guests are required to relinquish all their tech, including phones."

"Maybe Brady wasn't full of shit."

"Still not sure about that," Danner said. "He admitted that he confronted Canon in his office."

"But you just said his alibi holds up."

"That doesn't mean I'm ready to believe everything he said. He's a barely functioning alcoholic, he's full of resentment, and he had extra motive to kill Canon, considering his shares."

"So you caught that, too," Mackenzie said. "I can't believe he sold all his co-founder shares to Canon that early on. Probably cost him nine figures, at least."

"Maybe he wanted to get some of them back." Danner shrugged. "But you're right: His alibi is solid. Moreau's might not be."

"We need to talk to Moreau again," Mackenzie said, "and Hugo Chamberlain." She thought of their morning destination. "Do you know when Hugo's scheduled to speak today?"

Danner glanced at the clock on the dashboard. "Eden's panel is at nine, then Chamberlain's is right after. Back-to-back, same room."

"What's the plan?"

Danner shrugged. "We go to Chamberlain's panel, find him on-stage after. We can talk with Eden while we're at it, update her on Cassiopeia and Brady."

Hammersmith's last text floated into Mackenzie's mind. "What about Stanley Yoo?" she asked. "Any updates there?"

"Nothing," Danner said. "And nothing on Canon's laptop."

"Great." Mackenzie sighed.

Traffic was thick as ever. Minutes passed in silence as they plowed toward the freeway on-ramp.

"How did you and Eden originally meet?" Danner asked.

Mackenzie glanced across the cabin. "Do you really care?"

Danner gestured at the traffic. "We've got time."

Mackenzie paused in recollection. "I was in law school at George-town. Eleanor was an alumnus, came to campus for a book reading."

"*A Seat at the Table*," Danner said. "You've read it?"

Mackenzie nodded. "I found it very inspiring, obviously. So I chatted with Eleanor after the talk, one thing led to another, and . . ."

"How long did you date?"

"Very briefly."

Danner fell into an awkward silence as they finally reached the 280 freeway. Mackenzie sensed that, like Hammersmith, Danner had more questions but was unsure of an appropriate way to ask them. Instead, he changed the subject.

"How did you end up at Georgetown?"

"Scholarship," Mackenzie said. "I applied to each of the top fif-teen law schools and chose the one that gave me the most money."

Danner accelerated south. "Sounds like a very clinical approach."

Mackenzie shrugged. "Not all of us are legacies at Yale."

Danner dipped his head. "Fair enough." He paused. "What about undergrad?"

"NYU."

"Why NYU?"

Mackenzie turned and gazed out the passenger window, watch-ing the dusty pastels of Daly City flash by. "I grew up in Reno. I wanted to go to school somewhere that was as directly opposite as possible. Somewhere I could be anonymous. Blend in."

"I take your point on Yale, but NYU isn't cheap, either."

Mackenzie shook her head. "My mom helped me out. Saved up to send me wherever I could get in."

"Are you and your mom close?"

"We were," Mackenzie said, keeping her gaze fixed out the window. "She passed away."

Danner's voice fell. "Oh. I'm sorry."

"It's okay."

"Was it recent?"

"Few years back."

"I'm sorry to hear it," Danner said.

"Thanks."

Danner fell silent again. The sedan curved south into the gaping suburban maw of the Peninsula, the landscape transforming into a consumerist monotone of big-box stores, auto dealerships, and fast-casual restaurants.

"I wish I wasn't, by the way," Danner said.

Mackenzie glanced over at him. "Wasn't what?"

"A legacy," he said. "Obviously, yes, it got me into Yale. But I wish it hadn't."

Mackenzie studied Danner from across the cabin. "Did you join the FBI because your dad didn't want you to?"

Danner smiled thinly. "I'm that easy to peg, huh?"

Mackenzie shrugged. "I'm good at my job."

"Me and my dad . . . it's complicated. But I guess everybody says that about their father."

Danner glanced over at Mackenzie, inviting her to agree. "I wouldn't know," she said. "Never knew mine."

"Oh." Danner returned his gaze to the road. "Sorry. Again."

"Don't be. My mom was always open about it. Was a fling during a business trip to London. She told him, but never wanted him to be a part of it. I haven't really thought about it since I was a teenager."

"Did you ever try to track him down?"

"Once, online. Years ago. But when I saw his photos, I didn't feel any sense of connection. The opposite, really." Mackenzie watched the capitalist sprawl scroll by her window. "It taught me something important. There's no such thing as closure."

Danner raised his eyebrows. "Closure?"

"It's a bullshit concept," Mackenzie said. "Invented by psychologists to indulge people who can't move on. Everybody's got shit in their past."

"Isn't that the point, though? To confront the past, so you can move on from it?"

"You can't confront the past. It already happened. 'Seeking closure' is just an excuse to wallow in it." Mackenzie settled back into her seat. "You want to move on from the past, you just do it. Move on. My mom always said, 'You get one life. So get the hell on with it.'"

The Futurist Summit was held at a vanilla hotel in downtown Palo Alto. Everything was tidy, sterile, and expensive. The type of place, Mackenzie thought, you forget about the instant you leave it.

Danner left the sedan with the valet and they entered the lobby. The conference was a wasteland of chinos and lanyards, the air thick with the stench of professional networking. Mackenzie was enveloped by awkward smiles and desperate laughs. A Sheryl Crow song blared in the background.

Danner found the welcome table and grabbed the visitor passes that Eleanor had left for them. Mackenzie slipped the lanyard over her head as the chorus kicked in—*all I wanna do, is have some fun*—and felt a piece of her soul die.

"Chamberlain's scheduled for the main stage," Danner said, glancing at the Patek Philippe. "Eden's there now. We'll catch the end of her Q&A and find her after."

They moved down a wide hallway and came to a set of double doors. A large easel held a programming sign: A SEAT ON THE ROCKET SHIP: ELEANOR EDEN AND REBECCA KESSLER ON TRIUMPH AND TRAGEDY AT JOURNY.

The hotel ballroom had been outfitted with rows of chairs and a stage for the conference. Behind the stage a giant backdrop read FUTURIST in neon pink.

Eleanor sat onstage in a lounge chair, microphone attached to

one ear. She was flanked by an opposite chair that seated her interviewer: Rebecca Kessler, founder of the *Blender* news outlet. Kessler
possessed a sharp tongue and a gift for cultivating sources that made
her the tech industry's preeminent journalist. Mackenzie had always
found her slightly terrifying.

The auditorium was packed, every seat filled. Even the back was
lined with standers. Mackenzie and Danner found an open spot and
leaned against the wall.

"I appreciate your candor today," Kessler said, her voice echoing
through the ballroom. "I know it's not easy to talk about, but I'd like
to discuss Trevor's legacy, and how it impacts the future of Journy."

Eleanor relaxed in the lounge chair, hands in her lap. "I'm happy
to discuss it."

Kessler's hair was cut short. She wore thick-rimmed designer
glasses and gold hoop earrings that caught the stage lights. "Then let's
start with this: What do you think Trevor Canon's legacy will be?"

"That's self-evident," Eleanor said. "Trevor was a brilliant mind,
one of the great innovators of our time. His work at Journy was revolutionary. Trevor changed the world."

Kessler blinked at her across the stage. "You don't think it's more
complicated than that?"

"Not really," Eleanor said, smiling. "But it sounds like you do."
The audience laughed, slightly uncomfortably.

Kessler smirked. "Journy has been massively successful, sure. But
the company's level of success has been matched by its level of criticism. You have a laundry list of issues."

"Any successful company garners its share of critics."

"But Trevor went out of his way to invite criticism," Kessler said.
"Some said he relished the fighting."

Eleanor remained perfectly still, expression sanguine. "It's hard
for me to respond when we're not talking specifics."

"Okay. Look at the company's legal and policy issues."

"You and I have spoken many times about our regulatory situation."

"Yes, but city officials all over the world still *hate* Journy. They hate
how Canon barged into their cities with all aggression, zero negotia-
tion." Kessler consulted a tablet resting on her lap. "Trevor was once
quoted as saying this about the head of New York's Metropolitan

Transportation Authority: 'Sometimes I wish he'd throw himself in front of one of his subway trains, but they're so old and slow that the impact wouldn't kill him.'"

A brief silence hung in the ballroom. Eleanor remained unperturbed. "We have a dedicated policy team that's committed to building relationships with local governments."

"Okay," Kessler said, "then what about the safety issues? There have been tons of accidents with Journy vehicles. Some fatal."

"I've previously spoken about those incidents as well. The safety of our passengers is our highest priority."

Kessler lifted her tablet. "I'm not trying to hammer you, but the list of issues is just so *long*. This business with the driverless cars, which Trevor was touting for *years*. Trevor sold investors on the premise that autonomous cars were going to become Journy's profit center. Now we're years into it, and . . . where are they? All Journy's done on self-driving vehicles is burn cash—"

Eleanor interjected. "Look, Rebecca, success invites criticism. It also demands self-reflection. We've acknowledged our mistakes and taken steps to rectify them."

The audience was silent. Most Q&As at conferences like the Futurist were puff pieces. Kessler and Eleanor appeared to be engaging in a rare moment of honest back-and-forth.

"But that's my point," Kessler said. "When the company has made mistakes, or let's be honest, when *Trevor* made mistakes—*you're* the person who fixes them. It wasn't him."

"What do you mean?"

"Do a Spyder search. Any time Journy has faced controversy, *you've* been the face of the company's response. Not Trevor."

Eleanor was the picture of serenity. "I'm not quite sure what you're saying."

"I'm saying," Kessler said, tone sharpening, "that Trevor was the young, charismatic founder of Journy. He did the rah-rah stuff, raised the money, launched the products. But any time he made a mess, he sent you to clean it up. Older, wiser, more experienced, and, of course, a woman. To soften the company's public image and clean up its mistakes, Trevor leveraged your reputation as a prominent woman executive."

"Is there a question in there?" Eleanor said.

Kessler leaned forward in her seat. "Doesn't that bother you? That's the question. Doesn't it bother you that Trevor got the glory while you cleaned up after all his mistakes? Doesn't it bother you that some people refer to you as Trevor's 'Hatchet Woman'?"

Eleanor smirked. "You mean, doesn't it bother me that *Blender*—which is *your* company, I might add—called me Trevor's 'Hatchet Woman.'"

"Sure. But you know it's not just us."

Eleanor didn't hesitate. "To be honest, Rebecca, no, it doesn't bother me. I've been in the public eye for a long time. I can't control how the media perceives me, and frankly, I don't have the bandwidth to worry about it. If you're successful, you're going to have critics. End of story. I just focus on producing the best work I can."

"That's fair." Kessler adjusted her glasses. "But that sounds like the old Teddy Roosevelt line that founders use to excuse their behavior: 'It is not the critic who counts. The credit belongs to the man—or, in this case, woman—who is actually in the arena.'"

"I'm not excusing anything," Eleanor said. "As I said before, at Journy we've taken steps to rectify our mistakes. As for me personally, I can't worry about what *Blender* calls me. I focus my energy on being the best colleague, leader, and mother I can be. And I get my validation from those audiences."

Kessler laughed lightly. "That's very mature," she said, glancing out at the crowd. "I wish I could say I had the same approach." The audience laughed with her as Kessler continued. "Taking it back to Trevor. Considering your role, did you ever feel like you had a responsibility to steer Trevor in a better direction?"

Eleanor smiled. "I gave Trevor my counsel every day."

"Some say that you could have done more to prevent Trevor's mistakes. Trevor was very open about viewing you as a mentor."

"Trevor didn't need much mentorship," Eleanor said. "He had tremendous instincts. He built the fastest-growing startup in history."

"Sure, but do you think you should have taken more responsibility for steering Trevor away from some of his negative behavior?"

Eleanor paused. "If you're asking whether I shoulder responsibility for Journy's track record as a company, then the answer is definitively yes. I'm proud of our success, of the lives we've changed. Trevor made mistakes, but so does everyone."

Eleanor's tone softened, voice cracking slightly. "But working alongside Trevor was a privilege. He made me better. Stronger. The results of our partnership speak for themselves. And I'm just so unspeakably sad that it had to end like it did."

An awkward silence fell over the ballroom. Kessler sensed it.

"Let's end there," she said. "I want to thank you again, Eleanor, for speaking today about Trevor and Journy, especially given the difficult circumstances."

Eleanor gave a sad smile. "It was my pleasure."

Kessler looked out at the audience. "Okay, Futurists, let's hear it for Eleanor Eden." Thunderous applause filled the ballroom.

Danner and Mackenzie filtered through the crowd as it dissipated, weaving to the stage. Eleanor spotted them and excused herself from a crowd of well-wishers.

"Follow me," Eleanor said.

She led them behind the stage, ducking into an alcove formed between the metal latticework of the backdrop. Upbeat ambient music played from the stage speakers.

"One sec," Eleanor said. Opening a water bottle, she took a few long sips and smiled. "Sorry. All that yakking." She sighed, collecting herself. "Good morning."

"Good morning," Danner said.

"Tough interview," Mackenzie said.

Eleanor raised her eyebrows. "What, with Rebecca?"

"Yeah," Mackenzie said. "All the questions about Trevor, and the company's mistakes."

Eleanor waved a hand, unfazed. "Goes with the territory."

Danner looked at his watch. "Chamberlain's panel should be starting soon. Will you be joining us?"

Eleanor made a face. "About that. Hugo's panel was canceled, actually. The moderator is sick."

Danner's brow fell. "When did that happen?"

"Just a few hours ago," Eleanor said. "But good news: Hugo's still here, and he told me he's willing to meet."

"Today?"

Eleanor nodded, pulling out her phone and swiping it open. "This afternoon. The conference gave him a suite here."

"That'll work."

"I believe Hugo plans to bring his lawyer."

"That's fine," Danner said. "Any word from Yoo? Or anything on Canon's laptop?"

"I was hoping maybe you'd have news."

Danner gave a small shake. "None yet."

Gaia, Eleanor's assistant, appeared from around the stage corner. "You have that thing with Citibank," she said.

"Thank you, Gaia." Eleanor finished the water bottle. "Gotta run. Gaia will send you the details on Hugo."

Eleanor rushed away. Mackenzie and Danner drifted back to the heart of the ballroom. It was largely empty, but a few clusters of people lingered, huddled together on the patterned carpet.

Abruptly Danner's head swiveled, eyes fixing on a back corner.

"What is it?" Mackenzie asked.

"Your boss," Danner said. He took off on a beeline. Mackenzie followed.

Roger Hammersmith stood deep in conversation with two other men his age. Like Roger, they were dressed in unshapely button-ups and billowing slacks.

Danner stopped short of Hammersmith and his counterparts, hovering in their peripheral vision. Mackenzie kept a few steps behind. She couldn't make out the details of the conversation, but it appeared to be a jocular one. One of Hammersmith's cohorts said, "Fuck off, I can still piss strong enough to cut a diamond," and Roger unleashed a trademark *HA!* that echoed across the ballroom.

Mackenzie also noticed Hammersmith wasn't wearing a lanyard. He was the only person she'd seen at the conference without one. It was exactly the type of petty, idiosyncratic privilege most coveted by the mega-rich. Any dolt could pull up in a Maybach. Going badge-less at the Futurist Summit was a mark of true influence.

Hammersmith ignored Danner, though Mackenzie was certain he noticed the FBI man hovering. After six more minutes of bullshitting, Roger and his companions parted ways.

Danner moved in. "Good afternoon, Mr. Hammersmith," he said.

Roger ignored him, glancing past Danner to Mackenzie. "Hello, Mackenzie. What brings you to Palo Alto?"

"Just going where the investigation takes me," Mackenzie said.

"Good." Now Hammersmith turned to regard Danner, studying the federal agent. "You're Danner, then."

"Yes, sir," Danner said. "Special Agent Jameson Danner, FBI."

"It's rude to hover," Hammersmith said.

"I apologize, but I'd like to ask you a few questions." Danner's voice was flat and officious as ever; Mackenzie knew Roger would take poorly to it.

Hammersmith strode away, moving toward the ballroom exit. "You want to ask, go ahead. But don't expect any answers without my lawyer."

Danner hustled to stay at Hammersmith's shoulder, following the wider man as he moved into the hallway. Mackenzie stayed a step behind.

"When was the last time you saw Trevor Canon?" Danner asked.

Hammersmith said nothing. He headed toward the lobby.

Danner repeated the question. "When was the last time you saw Canon? Was it in his office?"

Hammersmith ignored him. A familiar-looking woman gave Hammersmith a warm hello. Roger returned it and kept moving.

"We've heard," Danner said, "that you went to see Canon in his office before he died. What did you talk about?"

Hammersmith stopped at an elevator bank. He pressed the call button.

"Did you talk about Indira Soti?"

The elevator doors opened. Hammersmith stepped inside, Danner and Mackenzie following. Hammersmith pushed the button for the top floor. The elevator rose upward.

"Did you know that Canon was meeting with Soti?"

Hammersmith didn't answer, and the elevator ride passed in silence. They exited at the penthouse level, and Mackenzie wondered where Hammersmith was leading them.

"Soti is your biggest rival," Danner continued. "If Canon met with him, that had to piss you off."

Hammersmith moved through a hallway, then opened a glass door marked HELIPAD. He scaled a short flight of stairs and approached another door, this one made of thick metal. Danner and Mackenzie followed.

"Or maybe you came to see him about the dead money," Danner said. A trace of frustration crept into his voice. "Maybe Trevor told you he was changing his will."

Hammersmith opened the metal door and suddenly they were bathed in sunlight. They stood on the roof of the hotel. Nearby, a large platform rested a few meters above the surface. Parked on the platform was a gleaming helicopter, every inch of it painted white—tail, rotors, skids, and all.

The *Hammer Angel,* Mackenzie thought. Of course Hammersmith wouldn't *drive* to the conference.

They were met by a broad, pugnacious-faced man with a crooked jawline. "Good morning, sir," the man said to Hammersmith. He gave Mackenzie and Danner a suspicious glance.

"Did he tell you?" Danner asked, leaning toward Hammersmith. He was like a dog with a bone, Mackenzie thought. "Did Canon tell you about the will?"

The security guy pointed at Danner. "Sir, is this man bothering you?"

Hammersmith smiled. "No, Alex. But thank you." He looked to the platform, where his helicopter lay waiting. "We ready to fly?"

Alex kept one eye on Hammersmith as he glowered at Danner. "The *Angel*'s ready when you are, sir."

"Then let's go."

Alex turned and signaled the pilot as Hammersmith moved toward the helipad. Danner began to follow, but Alex stepped into his path.

"Nope," the security man said.

Danner didn't push forward, but instead leaned around Alex to get a last glimpse at Hammersmith as he walked toward the *Hammer Angel.*

"I'm trying to further the investigation," Danner called. "Why aren't you being more cooperative?"

Hammersmith stopped. He turned and stepped back toward Danner, expression stern, his jovial features set with irritation.

"Let's get something clear," Hammersmith said, raising a thick finger. "I'm not one of your daddy's fuck-around fraternity brothers. I'll answer your questions when you can answer one of mine. *Where the fuck is Stanley Yoo?*"

"Uh, well—" Danner began to stammer.

"Trevor gets murdered; Yoo flees the coop. Now he's missing, and you don't have a clue where he is." Hammersmith lowered his hand. "You want to further the investigation? Then stop wasting your time and go do your goddamn job. Or else I'll call your daddy and replace you with someone who can."

Hammersmith spun toward the *Hammer Angel* and walked away.

CHAPTER 18

Nine years before Trevor Canon's death

Eleanor and Mackenzie sat across from each other at a small wooden table.

The table was in a wine bar: cozy, dimly lit, sunken below street level. Between her height and enormous winter coat, Mackenzie had felt uncomfortably bulky when they entered. Perhaps sensing this, Eleanor picked a table near the front, where a broad window made the bar less claustrophobic.

Eleanor had ordered two Sancerres while Mackenzie had bobbed her leg nervously. Ten minutes had passed since Mackenzie had unleashed her tirade in the Georgetown lecture hall; Mackenzie had spent them battling a wave of anxiety. She hadn't meant to go as far as she did after Eleanor's Q&A. It had all just . . . poured out.

Your temper, Mackenzie told herself. Again. Now look where it's gotten you. Embarrassing yourself in front of Eleanor Eden—author, role model, massively successful business executive. What the fuck did you just do?

Eleanor looked around the bar. "I came here all the time in law school," she said. "I'm glad it's still here."

"Listen," Mackenzie said, leaning across the table, "I want to apologize. I didn't mean to—"

"Stop." Eleanor raised a hand.

"Really, though, I feel a bit embarrass—"

"Don't apologize." Eleanor's voice was kind but firm. "It was the most honest thing anybody's said to me in years. I'm not going to let you backtrack out of it."

Mackenzie fell against her seat back.

Eleanor fixed her eyes on Mackenzie. "Your mother," she said. "You said she worked every day of your life, was on the road constantly. What did she do?"

"She was an accountant," Mackenzie said. "Worked for Braniff."

"Tell me about her."

Mackenzie settled in her chair. "Her family was from rural Nevada, where the only future was working the fields or the casinos. She started dealing cards at sixteen. Took the bus an hour each direction. Was the first in our family to graduate high school—"

"Sixteen?" Eleanor looked bemused.

Mackenzie nodded. "She lied about her age. By the time they found out, she was eighteen, and the regulars loved her." Mackenzie's leg bounced furiously under the table. "Dealing cards put her through college. Started at the local community college, finished at UNR."

"UNR?"

"University of Nevada, Reno."

The server arrived, placing two elegant wineglasses on the table. Mackenzie waited for Eleanor to take a sip and then did the same.

"Go on," Eleanor said.

"She liked dealing cards because she had a thing for numbers. She worked the casino at night, got her accounting certificate during the day. Braniff opened an office in Vegas for the big gaming companies; my mom scored a job in the mail room. Stayed there for twenty-five years."

"Worked her way up from the mail room?"

"Bookkeeper, junior accountant, all the way up. Staff accountant was as high as she could get." Mackenzie shrugged. "She didn't have the pedigree. Working your way up from the mail room sounds nice, but it's not the kind of thing you tell a Fortune 500 CEO about the accountant who's deep in their books."

Eleanor took another sip of her wine, expression inscrutable. "You sound like you were very close with your mom."

"We were."

"Can I ask why you speak about her in the past tense?"

"I don't see her much anymore," Mackenzie said.

Eleanor paused. "Did she pass away?"

"No."

Mackenzie didn't elaborate, and Eleanor took the hint. "Braniff has a reputation for working people hard."

Mackenzie nodded. "My mom's main clients were in New York and London. She wasn't home much. She wasn't a typical mom, in that way. But all we had was each other. Everything she worked for was for me. She saved enough to send me to NYU."

"And then Georgetown Law," Eleanor said.

"That part I did on my own."

Eleanor raised her eyebrows. "Scholarship?"

"Full ride." Mackenzie felt like she was being interviewed. It was strange, but there were worse things than catching the interest of Eleanor Eden.

"Your mom was in Nevada with Braniff. Is that where you grew up?"

Mackenzie nodded. "Reno."

"Why'd she stay in Reno? Why not move somewhere bigger, where a client was based?"

Mackenzie shrugged. "Reno was home. She was fond of it."

"And what did you think of Reno?"

"I couldn't wait to leave, and I haven't been back."

Mackenzie had a growing sense that the conversation carried implications far greater than a chat over a glass of wine. She tried to calm her legs. Eleanor sat across from her like a Buddha, fully comfortable. Mackenzie felt like a squirming teenager.

"Do I get to ask a question, at some point?"

Eleanor smiled. "Go ahead."

"With all due respect, I can't be the first person to tell you that *A Seat at the Table* is bullshit."

Eleanor's smile broadened. "You'd be surprised."

Mackenzie reached for her glass, nearly finished with her Sancerre. She told herself to slow down. "I guess most people do love your book, if my classmates are a barometer."

"Most," Eleanor agreed, nodding. "But not you."

"No, not me." Mackenzie laughed awkwardly.

"Obviously I value your perspective," Eleanor said, opening her hands, "or we wouldn't be here now."

"But I guess that's my question," Mackenzie said. "*Why* do you value it?"

Eleanor's eyes grew heavy. "Because *A Seat at the Table* is not a genuine expression of my worldview. I agree with you. It's crap."

Mackenzie felt a prickle of surprise. "What?"

"There's very little in that book that I actually believe to be true."

"Why did you write it, then?"

"Because people like fairy tales." Eleanor grabbed her wineglass, draining it. "The narrative isn't anything new. Everyone's eager to feel like they're in control of their own destiny, if they simply work hard enough. People have been peddling that nonsense since the dawn of capitalism. I just put it in a modern context."

"But all the writing, the interviews, the book tours . . . This whole time, you haven't actually believed any of it?"

Their server appeared and Eleanor reordered two of the same.

"I'll explain more later," Eleanor said. "For now, all you need to understand is that the book was a means to an end."

"But what end?"

Eleanor gave a knowing smile. "We'll get to that, too." Her eyes were a dull slate blue, and they sank into the growing darkness of the bar. "Let me ask you something else."

"Go ahead," Mackenzie said.

"Do you have many friends?"

"Do I have many friends?" Mackenzie hesitated. "That's a weird question."

"I know. Just answer honestly."

"Well," Mackenzie said, "no. Not really."

"What about when you were in school? Your level of academic achievement—usually that requires some kind of sacrifice."

Mackenzie nodded. "I didn't really socialize. Even back in high school. I studied, I played basketball, and I worked. That was it."

"Why?"

"I knew what I wanted," Mackenzie said. "Hanging out at parties wasn't going to get me where I wanted to go."

"Out of Reno."

"Right."

The server deposited two fresh glasses of wine on their table as Eleanor continued. "Why law school?"

"It was the shortest path," Mackenzie said. She forced herself to hold Eleanor's eye contact.

"Shortest path to where?"

"A graduate degree. Access. Connections."

"And money," Eleanor said.

"And that." Mackenzie paused. Eleanor had already lauded her honesty. Why was she sugarcoating it? "To be blunt, money was the primary motivation. Law school was the quickest path to the most money possible."

"Ah." Eleanor leaned back in her seat. "There are those who say money isn't everything."

Mackenzie scoffed. "The only people who say 'money isn't everything' are the people who have too much and didn't earn it themselves."

"Fair," Eleanor said. "And what do *you* say?"

"About money?"

"Yes."

"Maybe money isn't everything," Mackenzie said. "But it's a good fucking start."

Eleanor laughed. "Am I right to assume you have no particular passion for the law?"

Mackenzie started in on her second Sancerre. "Law school is a means to an end."

"Well played." Eleanor tilted her head. "But to echo your own question: What's the end?"

"I asked you first," Mackenzie said.

"Indulge me," Eleanor said. She leaned forward, folding her hands together. "All the work, the drive, the schools, the big firm. Why?" She stared at Mackenzie, eyes intent. "What is it, exactly, that you want?"

Mackenzie heard her mother's words echo in her mind. *You work yourself into the right places, get connected to the right people. Eventually, you'll be met with an opportunity. . . . A chance at something truly big.*

"I want to control my own destiny," Mackenzie said. "I don't want a seat at the table. I want to build my own."

Eleanor smiled. "I thought you wanted to flip it over."

"I have a bit of a temper," Mackenzie said, returning the smile.

"So . . . how?" Eleanor asked. "If you want to build your own table, it takes more than just money."

"I don't know yet," Mackenzie said. "But I know I can't just 'keep my head down and produce.'"

"No," Eleanor agreed. "You made your point there. But what's the alternative?"

Again, Mackenzie's instincts told her to play her cards close to the vest. At the same time, Eleanor had taken a keen interest in Mackenzie *because* of her honesty. This could be the type of opportunity her mother had been talking about.

"When I was growing up, my mother gave me some advice," Mackenzie said. "She told me that I should work my way up the ladder, get connected to the right people. Find adjacency to the spheres of power in our world. And then, wait."

"Wait?"

Mackenzie nodded. "One day, she said, I'll be met with an opportunity. Something that will give me the chance to build my own table, instead of sitting at someone else's."

Eleanor's eyes sparkled. "And what are you going to do, when you see this opportunity?"

"Grab it," Mackenzie said. "Whatever it takes."

Eleanor fell silent, staring at Mackenzie in the quiet of the wine bar. Mackenzie heard the loud falsetto laughter of a woman near the back, the clink of glasses being rearranged, the *thwop* of a cork popping from something sparkling. She willed her eyes to maintain contact, her hands to remain still, her leg to stop bouncing under the table.

"Parks Andrews is a mistake," Eleanor said finally.

"A mistake?" Mackenzie said. "It's one of the best firms in the world. There's an accelerated partner track, and my starting salary—"

"None of that matters." Eleanor cut her off. "You don't want to go there."

"I should choose a different firm?"

"No," Eleanor said. "All the Big Law firms are the same. You don't want any of them."

"But . . ." Mackenzie tried—unsuccessfully, she suspected—to keep confusion from overtaking her features. "Why not?"

"Because," Eleanor said, matter-of-fact, "they all belong to the old world. And the old world is dead."

Eleanor took a long sip from her wineglass. "Big Law was sustained by the empires of the old world," she said. "Now those empires are gone. The oil barons, the newspaper tycoons, the bankers, the manufacturers, the industrialists, the ranchers, the Rothschilds, the Rockefellers, all the big Manhattan families that used to grab the world around the neck and just *squeeze* . . ." Eleanor blinked at Mackenzie. "All of them are dead. Or they're dying, and just don't know it yet."

Eleanor leaned back in her chair, recrossing her legs. "Tech's killing them all. Each piece of the old world is being swallowed up whole by a few lines of code and a cartoony app. The tech industry is an expanding, carnivorous beast devouring everything in its path."

Mackenzie laughed lightly. "That doesn't sound very pleasant."

"It's not." Eleanor's expression was serious. "But that's not the point. It's where everything is going. Money, power, influence. It's all gravitating west. And faster than anyone realizes."

"And you're saying that's where I should go."

"If you're looking for something big, that's where it'll be."

Mackenzie felt a prickle of doubt. She hunched her shoulders. "I get what you're saying. I mean, I use Spyder all the time. But still . . ."

"You're skeptical," Eleanor said.

Mackenzie shrugged. "Yeah, a little."

Eleanor sipped her wine. "Understandable."

"Parks Andrews is a known quantity. I spent years working to get this kind of a position, with a firm like them."

"I get it."

"People said all this same stuff about tech back in the nineties. And it turned out to be a bullshit bubble."

Eleanor smiled. "The nineties were a long time ago."

"You know what I mean, though," Mackenzie said. "You're acting like this is all just obvious. Inevitable. And you seem incredibly confident."

"I am."

"Why?" Mackenzie asked. "How can you be so sure?"

"Because I've seen it." Eleanor paused. "I grew up in Indiana. I'm not some naïve California hippie. But I've been in it myself. And it's undeniable."

Eleanor leaned across the table, a new intensity overtaking her features. "The world is still underestimating the impact of the internet. We can't fathom how dramatically it's reshaping everything. I'm talking about a paradigm shift on the level of the wheel, or electricity." She paused. "Let me tell you something I'm not supposed to. Do you know what the biggest company in the country is right now?"

"I'm not sure. Exxon?"

"Close. Walmart, then Exxon. Do you know where Spyder is?"

Mackenzie shook her head. "Thirty-ninth," Eleanor said. "But based on Spyder's internal numbers, in three years Spyder will be bigger than Walmart."

"Three years?"

Eleanor nodded. "Within six, Spyder will be bigger than Walmart and Exxon *combined.*"

"Jesus." Mackenzie was stunned. "You're sure about that?"

"Like you said." Eleanor's gaze was steady. "Inevitable."

"How is that possible, though?" Mackenzie asked. "Is Tobias just that big a genius?"

Eleanor smirked, leaning back in her seat. "Tobias had one good idea, years ago. And he wasn't even the first to have it. He was just the first person barbarous and narcissistic enough to manifest that idea into reality."

Eleanor sniffed. "Tobias has the emotional intelligence of a doorstop. But he had the right idea, at the right time, in the right *place.* From there, his own ruthlessness and the limitless potential of the internet took it the rest of the way. The technology is that powerful."

"Even if you're right," Mackenzie said, "what do I *do* about it? What are you telling me, exactly?"

"I'm telling you that you're headed for the salt mines when there's a gold rush happening just over your shoulder." Eleanor's eyes were locked onto Mackenzie's, unrelenting. "You say you're looking for opportunity. In tech, the opportunities are flowing as broad and fast as the Amazon. You don't have to be a genius to capitalize on them. You don't even need a great idea. You just have to jump into the river, be in the right place at the right time. The right place is San Francisco. And the right time is *now*."

"So you're saying I should turn down Parks Andrews, move to San Francisco, and . . . What? Try to land a job at Spyder?"

"Doesn't have to be Spyder," Eleanor said. "With your résumé, you should be able to go wherever you want. You might try venture capital. From there you can see thousands of companies, get broader exposure."

Mackenzie hesitated again. She scratched the back of her neck. "Bailing on Parks Andrews is a pretty big risk."

Eleanor stared at her from across the table, unsmiling. "So was telling Eleanor Eden that her book was total bullshit."

Mackenzie laughed. "Can I say I'll think about it?"

"Sure." Eleanor nodded, but Mackenzie caught a tinge of disappointment in her tone.

Mackenzie sensed they were nearing the end of their conversation. It was time to finally ask the question that had spent the last hour rattling around the back of her mind.

"Why are you doing this?" Mackenzie shifted in her seat. "Why me? What do you want from me, exactly?"

Eleanor drained her second glass and flagged the server for the check.

"Do you have any idea," Eleanor said, "how many conversations I've had with people about *A Seat at the Table*? How many Q&As, how many interviews, how many readings?"

"I'm guessing a lot."

"Well over a thousand," Eleanor said. "And in those conversations, how many people have seen through it? Realized it's bullshit?"

"I'm guessing not a lot."

Eleanor smiled. "Nope."

"So, what—you wrote *A Seat at the Table* as a test? To see if anyone would see through it?"

"No. I wish I was that clever. But after the book was published, I realized that it served as an interesting filter."

The server reappeared with the check. Mackenzie made a half-hearted motion toward her bag, but Eleanor waved her off. She handed over a credit card.

"Few people," Eleanor said, "are realistic enough to see our world for what it is, rather than constructing it into something they want it to be. Your eyes are clear, Mackenzie. You see through the fairy tale." Eleanor smiled. "And you've got guts. Those are rare qualities. I need them."

"Need them for . . . what? Are you trying to hire me?"

Eleanor shook her head. "I'm not asking you to work for me. I'm asking you to be my ally. My friend. You can consider me a mentor, if you want. Someone who sees the world the same way. Because here's the truth, Mackenzie. You and I have the same goal. I don't want a seat at the table. I want to build my own. I want to do something *big*."

"Haven't you already? Spyder, the book . . ."

Eleanor's gaze was steady. "Those were just the first steps. And I've learned that if you want to do something big, it's hard to do it alone. You need people you can trust."

The server returned and Eleanor signed the bill. Then she removed a white business card from her wallet, placed it on the table, and slid it across to Mackenzie. "This is my personal contact info. Few people have it. Please treat it with discretion."

Mackenzie took the card, holding it delicately. "I will."

Eleanor rose from her chair. "You have real potential, Mackenzie. It'd be a shame to waste it on a law firm." Eleanor hoisted her purse over a shoulder and gave Mackenzie a final smile. "Come west. And when you do, get in touch."

Eleanor Eden glided out of the bar and disappeared into the growing chill of the D.C. night.

CHAPTER 19

Twenty-five days after Trevor Canon's death

Hugo Chamberlain's hotel suite at the Futurist Summit was filled with an abundance of light and a dearth of personality. In the distance to the west, Mackenzie spied the white, mission-style pillar of the Hoover Tower rising above the center of Stanford campus. Fitting, she thought, that Silicon Valley missed the irony in erecting a literal ivory tower in the middle of its most storied university.

Hugo was short, wiry, Black, wearing glasses, and much younger than Mackenzie had expected. He wore a tailored suit, bright blue.

Danner and Mackenzie were met at the suite's door by Hugo's lawyer. He was white, silver-haired, puffy-faced, and wearing a suit even more expensive than Hugo's. For once Danner wasn't overdressed.

"Gaylen North," the lawyer said. "Mr. Chamberlain's attorney." North guided them to the suite's dining table; bottles of Fiji waited at each of the four seats, their square edges placed at exact parallel to the table corners.

Hugo rose to shake their hands and introduce himself, giving Danner and Mackenzie each a stiff nod. He carefully pressed his suit as he retook his seat.

Before Danner could begin, North spoke. "At the outset, we'd like to share some information. In the interest of assisting your investigation, Agent Danner."

Danner seemed unexcited. "Go ahead."

Chamberlain remained silent, watching Danner carefully. "We assume," North said, "the FBI is interested in Mr. Chamberlain's whereabouts on August first, the night Trevor Canon was killed."

"You'd assume correctly," Danner said.

North nodded. "We're ready to supply that information, provided that you can keep it confidential." Mackenzie felt a spark of intrigue. "The details of Mr. Chamberlain's whereabouts that evening are extremely sensitive."

"I understand," Danner replied smoothly. "I assure you that Mr. Chamberlain's whereabouts won't be shared outside the investigation."

There was a pause. Hugo gave North a nod, and the lawyer continued.

"On the evening of August first, Mr. Chamberlain was engaged in a business meeting. There were multiple witnesses present, including myself. It was held in a private room at Toronaga"—North name-dropped a three-Michelin-star omakase restaurant—"and lasted from eight P.M. until midnight."

"Who was the meeting with?" Danner asked.

"Executive leadership from Spyder," North said. "Including Divakar Patel, CEO, and Tobias Nilson, founder and chairman."

"What was the meeting regarding?"

"Employment," North said. "Mr. Chamberlain signed a contract to begin working at Spyder."

Danner and Mackenzie both straightened in their chairs. "You're leaving Journy?" Danner asked Hugo.

North answered for him. "Yes. The meeting at Toronaga was to finalize Mr. Chamberlain's impending role."

"And what is that impending role?" Danner asked.

"Head of the autonomous vehicles division," North said.

Jesus, Mackenzie thought. No wonder Hugo's squirrelly about his alibi. He's packing up everything he knows from Journy and taking it to compete against them—at the biggest company in the world.

She blurted out the question. "Spyder is going into driverless cars?"

Hugo glanced over at North, who continued smoothly. "We'll get to that, Miss Clyde. First we want to establish that Mr. Chamberlain had nothing to do with Trevor Canon's tragic death."

North reached into his coat, withdrawing a small piece of paper. He passed it across the table to Danner.

"The Web address and password," North said, "for a secure server. On it you'll find written affidavits and video footage confirming Mr. Chamberlain's presence at Toronaga. Each file will be available for a single download. And Spyder will track the downloading device to ensure it traces to the Bureau.

"After accessing this link," North continued, "you will have exactly fifteen minutes to download the files before the server disappears. Please make sure your technical colleagues are aware."

Danner pulled out his phone and took a photo of the Web address. He left his phone on the table in front of him.

"I understand Spyder is a big deal," Danner said, "but these security measures seem extraordinary."

North glanced toward Mackenzie. "I believe Miss Clyde can help explain why." He smiled, his teeth wide and polished. "That's her role, is it not? To shed light on the inner workings of the technology industry?"

Danner tilted his head. "You're well informed."

"It's my job to be," North replied. He nodded at Mackenzie. "Go ahead."

Mackenzie obliged. "Conventional wisdom," she said to Danner, "is that autonomous vehicles will be the next big innovation to emerge from Silicon Valley. The next iPhone, the next social media. Think about how much of our world is structured around the car: entire landscapes, entire cities, countries, *everything*. Now imagine how driverless, autonomous cars could completely reshape that structure. No more human drivers. No more accidents. No more parking lots. It's a new frontier for transportation."

"I've read about it," Danner said. "But where does Journy come in?"

Mackenzie stole a quick glance at Hugo; he was studying her carefully from across the table. "For years, Journy has been burning cash. Rebecca Kessler even mentioned it onstage today."

"Isn't Journy worth seventy billion dollars?"

"Yes, but that doesn't mean it's making a profit yet. Like many startups, it's operating off its venture capital investment, not its own revenue generation. When someone like Roger invests money into Journy, he's betting the product will grow fast enough that in the future Journy *will* be profitable—immensely so. The same trajectory that many startups have followed, Spyder among them."

"Okay."

"Journy brings in a ton of money, but it also spends a ton of money." Mackenzie caught Hugo nodding across the table. "The margins are thin. Especially in Journy's biggest business, which is cars: people hailing a ride on their phone. Do you know what Journy's biggest expense is?"

"The drivers," Danner said. "They get seventy-five percent of each ride."

"Yes," Mackenzie said. "But imagine if you cut drivers out of the product entirely. A customer calls a Journy Car, but it's autonomous. No human driver. The car gets the passenger to their destination with no accidents, no wrong turns. And most important—"

"No seventy-five percent," Danner finished.

"Exactly. Journy would print money. That's why Kessler said what she did earlier. Journy's investors, like Hammersmith Venture, know the company is burning cash. But Trevor sold them that autonomous vehicles would eventually turn on the money faucet."

"Brady Fitzgerald said Canon 'didn't believe in cars,'" Danner said. "That it didn't fit with his vision."

"Yes," Mackenzie agreed.

"Canon had a phrase he used . . ." Danner swiped through his notes.

Hugo Chamberlain broke his silence. "The car is the telegraph of our generation."

Hugo flashed a thin smile across the table. "Trevor was fond of his pet phrases. In this case, he wasn't wrong. A human being driving a giant hunk of metal is the most inefficient form of transportation imaginable." He gave a slight nod to Mackenzie. "Please continue."

Mackenzie turned back to Danner. "Everyone knows driverless cars are a massive opportunity, so there's a race to see who can develop them first. Canon bet a lot of Journy's future on his ability to win that race. But there are other companies competing against Journy."

"Like Spyder," Danner said.

Mackenzie nodded. "Poaching Hugo to head up their new autonomous vehicles division is a very aggressive first move. Spyder jumping into the race like this . . . It's going to make a lot of waves."

Gaylen North stepped in. "Mr. Chamberlain is considered one of the smartest product minds in the industry. When Journy hired him, it was a big deal."

"And losing him will be an equally big deal," Mackenzie said.

"Just so," North said. "We expect that everyone connected to Journy will take the news badly. Investors, particularly."

"It'll be a gut punch for Journy," Mackenzie said. "Especially coming on the heels of Trevor's murder."

"Now you can understand our need for discretion," North said.

"Okay," Danner said. He grabbed his phone. "We'll check out the alibi—discreetly. But I still have other questions."

"Ask away," said North. He leaned back in his chair, folding his hands together. His portion of the rodeo was over. "Mr. Chamberlain is happy to assist however he can."

Danner adjusted in his seat, looking at Hugo across the table. "When did Spyder first begin recruiting you?"

"Six months ago," Hugo replied.

His posture was perfect, Mackenzie noted. Shoulders square, back straight, hands folded neatly. When Hugo spoke, only his mouth moved. The rest of his body remained rigid as a statue. A man always in control, Mackenzie thought.

"How did it happen?"

"Divakar Patel reached out to me," Chamberlain said, "via encrypted messaging."

"We've heard that lately Canon was acting more paranoid than usual. Secretive. Disappearing for long stretches. Did you notice that?"

Hugo paused. "Can't say that I did. But I'm not the best person to ask. Trevor and I didn't work closely together over the past year."

"Why not?" Danner asked.

"Differences of opinion," Hugo said, blinking behind his glasses.

"Do you think there's any chance that Canon knew you were talking to Spyder?"

"You're wondering if that was the impetus for his paranoia," Hugo said. "Not possible. Divakar and Tobias were extremely cautious. As was I. And if Trevor *had* found out I was talking to Spyder, his reaction wouldn't have been paranoia."

"What would it've been?"

"Rage," Hugo said.

There was a brief silence before Danner continued. "You and Canon had differences of opinion. Can you elaborate?"

"Trevor and I shared a vision: Autonomous vehicles were the future of the company. It's why the AV program was part of my remit. But"—Hugo's voice flattened slightly—"Trevor and I had different ideas about how to execute on that vision."

"How so?"

"Trevor had the opposite problem of many others: He couldn't see the trees for the forest. He was so obsessed with thinking *big*, with constantly 'pushing the envelope,' that he was incapable of executing on something day-to-day. He thought he could simply *will* projects into existence.

"There was a pattern," Hugo said. "Every few months Trevor would storm in with a new idea. He'd shift all the company's resources to it. A month would go by, he'd get a progress report. Then he'd explode."

"Explode?"

"He'd declare that the team wasn't thinking big enough, our people weren't smart enough, we weren't moving fast enough. Often, his 'feedback' was more like verbal abuse. Eleanor had to speak to him about it." Hugo sighed. "A few days later he'd scrap the entire project and move on to the next shiny object."

"Is that how Trevor operated with your autonomous vehicles initiative?"

"Essentially," Hugo said, his voice still calm. "It's important to understand how big a challenge it is to develop something like a driverless car. You can't simply talk your way to success. To use layman's terms, you have to build a robotic car from the ground up. It requires an immense amount of technology, radar, sensors. Then, even more difficult, you have to train that robotic car to drive like a human. There's no playbook, nothing to build off from the past. It's immensely time-consuming. A project like that will always be a marathon."

"And Canon didn't like that."

"Trevor never had the patience. He was only interested in shortcuts to the finish line. With his leadership style, the AV initiative was doomed from the start."

"If Canon was this difficult to work for," Danner asked, "why'd you take the job at Journy to begin with?"

"Isn't that obvious?" Hugo gave another thin smile. "At the time, Journy was a rocket ship. Trevor gave me stock options that nobody would've turned down." Hugo gave a slight shrug. "Besides, I've worked with difficult people before. I'd heard rumors about Trevor, but I assumed he couldn't be worse than the others. I was wrong."

Something about Hugo's answer nagged at the back of Mackenzie's mind.

"It sounds," Danner said, "like you didn't think much of Canon as a leader."

Hugo considered the question. "As a salesman, Trevor was unparalleled. As a leader, he was destructive. As a human being, he was one of the biggest assholes I've ever met."

Mackenzie stifled a laugh.

"Pretty strong words," Danner said.

Hugo blinked at Danner. "You asked, Agent Danner. I answered."

"Is that why you decided to leave?" Danner asked.

"It wasn't just Trevor's personality. It was the consequences of that personality on the company."

"How so?"

"Journy is failing," Hugo said matter-of-factly. "The company is going in the tank."

Hugo's words hung in the dry, sterile air of the suite. Mackenzie and Danner both shifted in their seats, the surprise evident on Danner's features.

"Failing?" Danner repeated.

"Growth has stagnated," Hugo said, "and the user base is actually shrinking. Has been for over a year."

Mackenzie cut in. "But Journy is huge. Most successful startup in history. Seventy billion valuation."

"Not for long," Hugo replied.

"But what about the Journy Fund?" Danner asked. "The five billion from Hammersmith Venture?"

"Trevor's spent all of it," Hugo said. "The five billion's gone."

Mackenzie nearly gasped. "No," she said.

"It's true," Hugo said. He twisted the cap off his Fiji water and took a long slug.

"But . . . how?" Mackenzie was incredulous. "I know startups can be irresponsible with cash, but how do you burn *five billion*?"

For the first time, Hugo gave a genuine smile. "Humans have yet to discover a sum of money large enough that they couldn't find a manner of wasting it. Trevor found all sorts of ways to waste the Journy Fund. He bought smaller companies on a lark, because he knew one of the founders. He made lavish promises to recruits, like me. He poured money into new projects and initiatives, then canceled them months later. He spent, and he spent, and he spent. And now it's gone."

"But this can't be right," Danner said. "About the money or the growth."

"The internal numbers don't lie, Agent Danner. I'm simply reporting what they say."

"If they're so dire," Danner said, "how has nobody else told us about them? We've spoken to everyone else on the executive team. You're the first to say anything about these numbers."

"I suspect they haven't seen them." Hugo's voice carried a measured strain of contempt. "Cassiopeia couldn't read a spreadsheet if her life depended on it. She only speaks in nonsense: *vibes, culture, mantras.*

"Brady," Hugo continued, "is a drunk. Stanley is too detached to care. He considers himself to be above things as prosaic as a profit-and-loss sheet. And Eleanor . . ." Hugo tilted his head, thinking. "Eleanor probably knows the numbers. But I bet she's so desperate for them to be wrong that she's not fully processing them. Like a mom who can't bear to watch her kids fighting."

Now Mackenzie realized what bothered her about Hugo's earlier answer: *"At the time, Journy was a rocket ship." At the time. Was.* Hugo was speaking in past tense. Now the rocket ship was about to fall back to Earth.

"What about Roger Hammersmith?" Danner asked. "He can't be happy that Canon burned through all his money."

"I don't know if he's aware," Hugo said. "He and Trevor had a unique relationship. Very close." He shrugged. "I wouldn't have given Trevor five billion dollars, but the levers of power move in mysterious ways."

Danner glanced over at Mackenzie. "Has he said anything to you about it?"

"Roger?" Mackenzie shook her head. "Hell no. This is the first I'm hearing about it."

Danner returned his gaze to Hugo. "And what about the dead money?"

"The dead money?" Hugo replied. Chamberlain and his lawyer frowned in unison.

"The provision Canon put in his will, a week before he died."

"I don't know what you're referring to," Hugo said.

"Canon amended his will," Danner said. "Inserted what's known as a dead money clause. It stated that if Canon was killed, all of his assets—including his controlling shares of Journy—would be frozen until someone was tried for his murder."

Hugo let out a dry laugh. "You're kidding."

"None of Canon's shares can be transferred," Mackenzie said. "Nobody controls the company. Journy is in limbo."

"All of Trevor's shares in Journy are just . . . sitting there, frozen?"

"Over twenty billion dollars' worth," Mackenzie said. "Hence the term 'dead money.'"

"That's why you're talking to the executives," Hugo said. "Without this dead money provision, each of us would've gotten a good chunk of Trevor's shares after he died." Hugo calculated in his head. "My guess is . . . a hundred mill, each?"

Danner paused for a moment before answering. "About that, yes."

"And you think *that* was the motive for killing him." Hugo looked up to the ceiling, enjoying himself as he reasoned through it. "So you're trying to figure out who knew about the dead money provision, and who didn't . . . Because if someone *didn't* know, then they would've killed Trevor to get themselves a nice chunk of change—"

Gaylen North cut in. "What Mr. Chamberlain *means* to say is that we have already ascertained his alibi on the evening in question. So his knowledge, or lack thereof, of Mr. Canon's will is moot."

Hugo's shoulders shook as he began a low, earthy chuckle. His face crinkled as the chuckle grew in intensity, boiling into a full-bore laugh.

"What's so funny?" Mackenzie asked.

"I just put something together," Hugo said, his eyes brightening. "You're focused on the dead money because of the stock. Trevor's shares—that's where all the money is. You have to solve his murder so that it can get unlocked and transferred to the right pockets." He looked at Mackenzie. "That's how you became part of this investigation. Hammersmith shoehorned you in."

Mackenzie paused. "More or less."

Hugo's face broke into a broad smile. "You don't see the irony?"

"No," Danner said.

Hugo looked between them. "I just told you: The company's circling the drain. Journy's as good as done. So Trevor's shares aren't going to be worth twenty billion. They're going to be worth *nothing*. All this swirl about his stock, and the dead money . . . it's all for nothing. Don't you see?"

Hugo leaned back against his chair, expression gleeful. "There *is* no dead money. There's no money at all."

CHAPTER 20

Twenty-five days after Trevor Canon's death

A sullen darkness permeated the sedan as Danner drove them north. Mackenzie and Danner sat in frustrated silence, each stewing over the interview with Hugo Chamberlain.

Mackenzie waited until they'd reached San Mateo before she spoke. "Do we think Hugo's right? About Journy going in the tank?"

Danner stayed quiet, so Mackenzie answered her own question. "What did Cassiopeia say about him? 'Hugo looks out for Hugo.' That seems about right. But, he has no reason to lie. He knows we could easily check on it ourselves. We need to ask Eleanor about it ASAP."

"I agree," Danner said.

"If Journy's headed for nowhere, I can't believe the other execs had no idea. Eleanor, Cassiopeia, Brady . . . They couldn't be completely oblivious."

"No."

"And now we have a motive problem. Our theory has been pretty straightforward: Exec kills Trevor, they get a big chunk of Trevor's stock, worth hundreds of millions. But if Hugo's right, and that stock is going to be worthless . . . and the exec *knows* it's going to be worthless, then . . . what's their motive?"

"We don't know." Danner scratched his chin. "Is Chamberlain right about the value? If the company's going downhill, will Canon's shares really be worthless?"

"He's not far off," Mackenzie said. "Trevor's shares in Journy are only worth what you can sell them for. And once word gets out about their numbers and the five billion they burned, they're toast. No bank is going to underwrite their IPO. No investor is going to pay for the shares. Everything unravels quickly." She glanced back over at Danner. "Look at companies like WeWork, or all the crypto bullshitters. One day they're worth billions. The next, they don't even exist."

"You think that could happen to Journy?"

"I don't know," Mackenzie said. "But in tech, companies rise fast and fall even faster."

They reached the exosphere of San Francisco, the landscape littered with the detritus of the tech industry: billboards advertising cloud storage services, anodyne office parks housing lesser-tier peddlers of B2B software.

"Brady said that he saw Trevor meeting with Indira Soti," Mackenzie said. "Maybe Trevor was trying to raise more money for Journy."

Danner's voice was skeptical. "I doubt either Soti or Hammersmith would be okay sharing a portfolio company with the other, based on what you've told me."

"You're right."

"And Soti is particular about his investments. No matter how much he loved Trevor, no way he'd throw money into a ship that was already sinking. He's never done it before."

"No." Mackenzie glanced across the cabin. "I'm impressed."

"Why?"

"You're picking up the VC dynamics pretty quickly."

Danner shrugged. "I did some reading last night." He paused. "We know Canon was disappearing in the months before he died. Paranoid. Fitzgerald said he thought Canon was working on something. Maybe he was working on stopping the bleeding at Journy. Turning the ship around."

"Maybe." Mackenzie nodded. "But why be so secretive about it? Why the paranoia?"

"He didn't want the rest of the company to know."

"I guess. But Brady told us he suspected Trevor was working on something *new*."

"True. But all of this is contingent on Fitzgerald's version of events. I'm not sure that's reliable."

Mackenzie thought about their interview with Brady the night before. "You know, we don't really have a motive problem. Even if they knew Trevor's shares weren't going to be worth much, a lot of people on the executive team had reason to hate Trevor."

"That's true."

"Cassiopeia wanted Trevor to invest in her new business. Plus with his disappearances we can't rule out some kind of affair."

"Agree."

"Brady clearly had some strong feelings for Trevor—obsessive, almost. Plus he sold all his shares to Trevor way too early, and resents being pushed aside."

"Agree."

"Hugo told us straight up that he thought Trevor was an asshole, hated him as a leader."

"Agree." Danner nodded. "They all hate each other. Cassiopeia Moreau hates Brady Fitzgerald; Fitzgerald hates Moreau. Moreau doesn't think much of Hugo Chamberlain. Fitzgerald doesn't think much of anyone. Neither does Chamberlain."

The traffic smoothed out and Danner accelerated past the airport. "But forget motive," Danner said. "We have a bigger problem."

"Alibi."

"Chamberlain, Moreau, Eden, and Fitzgerald can all account for their presence elsewhere when Trevor was killed. Though we still need to verify Moreau's story."

"Have you heard back on the subpoena for Serafina?"

Danner shook his head. "Should be soon. One of our agents did check with the venue for that *Fortune* gala, though. Last call was at eleven-thirty. Combined with the photographs, Eden's clear."

"So if Serafina confirms Cassiopeia's story, then all four execs have solid alibis. Leaving only one."

Danner's voice was heavy. "Stanley Yoo."

"We need to find him."

"I know."

"Have you searched his apartment?"

Danner shook his head. "Lawyers won't let us. Yoo told people he was leaving town, so he's not technically 'missing' enough that the lawyers say we can bust down his door."

Mackenzie studied the dry, sparse hills of South San Francisco as they sped by. She had a sudden thought. "We're still sure that it *had* to be an executive?"

Danner nodded. "We went deep on it. Went back over the security protocols, rechecked everything. Our original logic is still sound."

"Then we're missing something," Mackenzie said.

"We're missing Yoo."

"More than just Yoo. Something's not adding up."

"When things aren't adding up," Danner said, "it's usually because somebody's lying." He turned his head, fighting to shift lanes as they entered the boundaries of San Francisco proper. "Moreau is still a wild card."

"Brady told us her alibi wouldn't hold up," Mackenzie said. "And we should ask her about the company being in trouble. If anyone would've known that, it would've been Trevor's partner."

"Agree."

"And this new autonomous vehicles element," Mackenzie said. "It feels like there's something more to that."

"Agree," Danner replied, and the sedan once more fell quiet. Danner guided them into the city. Mackenzie flexed the fingers on her right hand, stretching her wrist as her mind wandered.

"Did you break that?" Danner asked.

Mackenzie glanced over at him. "What?"

"Your right hand," Danner said, nodding toward her. "You flex it a lot. Twist it, stretch it. Like you broke it once."

"Not my hand." Mackenzie replaced her hands in her lap. "My wrist."

"How'd you break it?"

"Basketball," Mackenzie said. She returned her gaze to the window.

"Figured you might've played," Danner said. "But didn't want to assume."

Danner hesitated, as though waiting to be congratulated for his tact. Mackenzie remained silent.

Her phone vibrated in her pocket. She pulled it out and looked at the screen: ROGER HAMMERSMITH.

Danner glanced over. "Go ahead."

"Sure you don't mind?"

"I don't care."

Mackenzie scrambled to grab her AirPods out of her purse, jammed them into her ears, and answered.

"Where are we?" Hammersmith said.

"We just spoke to Hugo Chamberlain."

"Anything of note?"

Mackenzie thought of Danner's promise of discretion with Hugo and his lawyer.

"He's got an alibi," she said. "As solid as they come."

"Hugo never struck me as a likely suspect," Hammersmith said. "Why?"

"Too risk averse. Too driven by self-interest. Hugo calculates the probability and always does what's best for him. That's also why he could never make it as a founder."

"He came across as very controlled," Mackenzie agreed.

"That's one way of putting it," Hammersmith said. "Then everyone's got an alibi, it seems. Eleanor, Cassiopeia, Brady, Hugo. Everyone except Stanley Yoo."

"Cassiopeia is still iffy," Mackenzie said. "Danner and I are following up."

"Ah, yes. Danner. How did you describe him? Has the entire tree up his ass?" Hammersmith scoffed. "After his little ambush at the conference today, I understand what you meant."

Mackenzie cast one eye toward Danner at the wheel and changed subjects. "We're making progress," she said.

"What about Yoo? I assume there's no progress there?"

"Not yet," Mackenzie said.

"That's unacceptable. We need to find him."

"I know."

"Stanley's not D. B. Cooper. Danner's got the entire FBI at his disposal and he can't find an eccentric software engineer?"

"Yoo's been good at hiding."

"How hard is Danner looking? Has he been in Yoo's apartment yet?"

"No," Mackenzie said, glancing again across the car. "Waiting on the lawyers to clear probable cause for going in."

Roger scoffed again. "Blaming the lawyers. Always the mark of someone who's not trying hard enough." Hammersmith's tone intensified. "You need to push him, Mackenzie."

"I am," she said neutrally. "Every chance I get."

"Push harder," Hammersmith said. "Yoo is the key. That's growing more obvious by the day."

"The instant we hear anything, I'll let you know."

There was a long pause over the phone. When Hammersmith spoke, his voice had grown venomous.

"I'm under extreme pressure here," Hammersmith said. "From multiple directions. Do you understand?"

"I do," Mackenzie replied.

"I'm getting squeezed on both sides. I've got Soti to deal with, and on the other hand . . ." Roger paused. "I won't spell it out for you."

"You don't need to," Mackenzie said. "I understand."

"Then get it done. Is there anything else?"

"One other thing," Mackenzie said. "Hugo Chamberlain says Journy is failing, going in the tank. Says the numbers are bad and getting worse." Mackenzie paused. "Is he right?"

"Hugo is always complaining about something," Hammersmith said. "Every time Trevor had a new idea, Hugo was there to tell him why it couldn't be done. He never understood how to 'start with yes.'"

Mackenzie heard a voice in the background that sounded like Hammersmith's assistant. "I've got another call. But I wouldn't give too much credence to anything Hugo said. He's never had the balls for the startup world."

Hammersmith hung up.

"Sounds like he's in a pleasant mood," Danner said.

"Same as ever," Mackenzie replied.

A few minutes later Danner pulled up to Mackenzie's building. Mackenzie turned to him as she opened the door. "I want to be there when you talk to Cassiopeia again."

Danner nodded. "I'll call you."

Mackenzie exited the sedan and walked to her building's front door. Casually, she looked around for the black Tesla, but saw nothing. And she felt nothing: no prickle of intuition, no sixth sense.

Mackenzie climbed to her apartment, unlocked the deadbolt, twisted the door open, and stepped inside. She kicked off her flats and walked down her long hallway. Her apartment was warm, baked by the afternoon sun from her south-facing windows; she decided to crack one to let in a breeze. She moved into the living room.

Something was wrong.

Mackenzie always left the curtains in a specific position: slightly drawn to either side, so the middle window was partially exposed.

Now, however, the curtains were pulled wide. The entirety of her bay window was exposed to the sun, which explained the unusual heat in her apartment.

Mackenzie froze, heart pounding as the realization hit her.

Someone had been in her apartment.

She stayed perfectly still, body paralyzed with terror. The fingers on her right hand tingled.

Someone had been in her apartment *today*. Maybe hours ago. Maybe less. Maybe they were still there. She thought of the bulky shadow in the Tesla and held her breath, listening for any sound of movement.

Then she noticed something else.

Taped to the center bay window, directly in the middle, was a single sheet of paper.

There was something typed on the paper, small font. Mackenzie moved quickly to the window to read it.

A message was typed in block letters. It consisted of only three words:

WE ARE WATCHING

CHAPTER 21

Twenty-five days after Trevor Canon's death

"You should've told me earlier," Danner said.

"I know," Mackenzie said.

"You *really* should've told me earlier."

"I *know.*"

Mackenzie and Danner moved through the lobby of the Royal Harbor hotel in downtown San Francisco, Mackenzie's large suitcase rolling alongside.

After reading the note, Mackenzie had immediately called Danner. Twelve minutes later, Danner and two other federal agents had piled into her apartment. Thirty minutes after that, Danner had checked Mackenzie in to a hotel. Now Danner excoriated Mackenzie as they headed for the elevator bank.

"When you saw the Tesla you should've called me right away," Danner said. "You have to trust your instincts."

"I thought it sounded ridiculous," Mackenzie said.

"I told you at the outset, this investigation is as serious as it gets.

We can't screw around. When you see anything off, you need to tell me. Immediately."

"I get it," Mackenzie said.

Danner's expression grew dark, voice laced with frustration. "'We are watching.' Why that message?"

"I don't know."

"You have no idea who it's from?"

"No clue."

"No idea who might want to intimidate you?"

"I was hoping you would."

"You can't hold out on me." Danner gave a stiff shake of his head. "First the Tesla, now this . . . You asked me to keep you in the loop. That goes both ways."

"*Okay,*" Mackenzie said. She stopped walking, luggage gliding to a halt. Danner stopped with her.

"I get that I fucked up, okay? I get it." Mackenzie rubbed her fingers through her dark hair, eyes falling to the lobby floor. "I'm sorry I didn't tell you about the Tesla. But I didn't want to waste your time." Mackenzie scoffed, bringing her eyes up. "I mean, my last investigation was about a founder's solarium. You know this isn't my area of expertise."

Danner's features softened. "I'm sorry for being harsh. I'm just frustrated. It wasn't your fault."

"I'm doing the best I can here."

"I know." Danner took a deep breath. "We'll see if forensics get anything from your place." He reached into a pocket, withdrawing a key card. He handed it to Mackenzie. "For now, you're staying here. Hotel security knows you're with us."

"Okay."

"Go get unpacked, meet me back down here in the lobby. We can talk about what's next."

Mackenzie rolled her bag up to the eighth floor. Her room was modern and had a decent view of the Ferry Building. Most important, Mackenzie noted as she exited, there was a deadbolt *and* security bar on the door. She shuddered as the reality of her situation resurfaced in her mind.

My apartment was broken into.

They broke through the deadbolt. But they locked it again on the way out.

They found a way past it. Or worse, they had a key.

WE ARE WATCHING

Mackenzie tried to shake the thought away as her elevator descended to the lobby. You knew this would be dangerous, she told herself. You can't blink now. Not when you've come this far.

Danner was waiting near the elevators, a renewed energy in his face. His jacket was buttoned, car keys in hand.

"What's happened?" Mackenzie said.

"Ibarra and Eden just called me," he said. "Canon's laptop got powered on. Just twelve minutes ago. They tracked its location."

"Where is it?"

"Stanley Yoo's loft."

Stanley Yoo's building was on the east side of the Mission neighborhood, a wide grid of post-industrial warehouses that had been Brooklynized into tasting-menu restaurants, obscenely priced lofts, and goopy wellness studios.

Danner double-parked the sedan at the building entrance, then opened his jacket and removed his pistol, features taut. Mackenzie realized it was the first time she'd seen Danner actually holding his gun.

Danner did some kind of preparatory motion to check the pistol, his movements hard and efficient, then re-holstered it. He exited the car, Mackenzie following. Danner was brimming with anticipation, every step carrying a new force of purpose.

"You can come in with us," he said to Mackenzie as they moved to the front door, "but hang back when we go into Yoo's apartment. You're not trained for this."

Mackenzie thought of Danner's gun. "Fine by me."

Two of Danner's colleagues met them out front: a stocky forty-something with graying hair, and a slimmer Latino guy with a shaved head.

A heavyset, bearded man emerged from the foyer. "Which one of you is Agent Danner?"

Danner looked at the man. "You're the building manager?" The bearded man nodded. "Let's go."

The manager led them into a small, modern lobby with concrete floors. An elevator rested next to a door marked STAIRS.

"How many exits?" Danner asked the manager.

"Just two. This one, and one at the end of that hall." The manager pointed down a long hallway that ran straight back off the lobby.

"Back stairs come out down there, by the other door?" Danner asked.

"Yep," the manager said. "But like I told you on the phone—Stanley isn't here."

Danner ignored him, turning to his two fellow agents. He pointed at the gray-haired man. "Cosetta, stay here, watch the exits." He looked at the younger agent. "Fernandez, with me." Fernandez nodded and Danner turned back to the manager. "Let's go."

"I'm telling you," the manager said, "Stanley isn't here. Nobody's seen him for ages."

"Stairs," Danner said. The manager sighed and opened the door to the stairway. "Which floor?" Danner asked.

"Fourth," the manager said. "Unit 404."

Danner led them up the stairway, Fernandez behind, Mackenzie and the manager bringing up the rear. Danner and Fernandez scaled the steps quickly, half-running.

They reached the fourth-floor landing. Mackenzie and the manager followed Danner and Fernandez through a metal door and into a carpeted hallway. Warm LED lighting shone from the ceiling. Along either wall, Mackenzie spied the wooden doors to the loft units.

Danner looked at Mackenzie, voice quiet. "Wait here until I call for you. If anyone comes in your direction, don't do anything. Just get out of the way."

"Can do," Mackenzie said.

Danner looked to the manager. "Stay behind us."

The manager protested once more. "There's no need for all this. Stanley *isn't here*. I can just let you into his place."

Danner ignored him and set off. Mackenzie stayed put, leaning against the frame of the stairway door. Danner and Fernandez crept down the hallway and then came to a stop, assembling on either side of a door. Each agent drew their gun. The manager waited a few steps behind, on the opposite side of the corridor.

Danner gave three firm knocks on the door, the sound echoing in the quiet of the hallway.

There was no response.

Danner knocked again, raising his voice. "FBI. We have a warrant to enter the premises." He waited in the quiet.

No response.

Danner nodded sideways at the manager, who stepped forward and stuck a key into the door, turning it. He stepped back as Danner turned the handle, pushing the door open.

Danner and Fernandez each straightened their arms, guns pointed ahead, postures alert, expressions tense. Danner disappeared from the hallway into Yoo's loft. Fernandez followed behind.

Mackenzie waited at the far end of the hall. She found herself holding her breath, waiting for a sound of confrontation. A gunshot; a man yelling; the sound of glass breaking.

But there was nothing. Only silence.

Another minute passed; still nothing. The building manager shook his head and leaned on the wall by Yoo's doorway, staring at his phone. Mackenzie heard the distinctive pings of Candy Crush.

Danner's head popped back into the hall. He looked toward Mackenzie. "You're good."

Mackenzie walked down the hallway as Danner glanced at the building manager. "Yoo's not here," Danner said.

"I told you," the manager replied. "He hasn't been here for months, far as I know."

"Months?" Danner asked. "You're sure it's been that long?"

"Months," the manager repeated. "Haven't seen him since the spring. I would know—dealing with his mail is a real pain in the ass."

"Okay," Danner said. "Wait here." He motioned Mackenzie to come inside. "Take a look."

Mackenzie followed Danner down a short entry hall and into the kitchen, which was modern and outfitted with high-end European appliances. More warm LED lighting shone from above. A handful of photographs were taped to the fridge. On the kitchen counters Mackenzie spotted a German espresso machine and a block of pricey Japanese knives. None of it looked like it'd ever been used.

In the main living area, the ceiling disappeared above Mackenzie, rising to twenty feet. The floors were polished concrete. Massive windows were covered by a thin shade. A scruffy sectional sat atop a white shag rug, facing a wall-mounted flat screen.

Everything was organized, tidy, but coated with a thin layer of dust. In the corner, a banana plant had dried to a husk, the floor littered with brown leaves. The space was bathed in gentle darkness, night filtering through the window shade.

Danner wiped his forefinger across a kitchen counter and shook his head. He looked at Mackenzie. "Check out the upstairs and meet me back here."

A spiral staircase led to the loft's open second floor. Mackenzie moved upward, noting more dust on the handrail. Fernandez passed her, headed the other direction.

Mackenzie felt uneasy as she moved through Yoo's living quarters. She was prowling through a stranger's home in the fading darkness, unsure whether that stranger was even still alive. The feeling was compounded by how dead the space felt: There were no glimpses that someone had recently occupied the space, not even a ghost of Yoo's presence. No scattered pillows, no indentations in the mattress, no missing socks that fell out of the laundry basket. The space felt hollow.

Yoo's bedroom was neat and dusty, as was the monochrome bathroom. The shower was bone dry. A thick ring of rust surrounded the water in the toilet.

Mackenzie walked into Yoo's spacious closet. Colorful retro Nikes lined the floor. Mackenzie chuckled, thinking of Japan as she spied a pair of Rollerblades in the front corner. There were jeans, suits, button-ups, a few pairs of chinos.

And then she finally spotted something of interest: Stanley Yoo's costume collection. It was, by far, the most populated segment of the closet. Mackenzie riffled through a dozen elaborate outfits, each carefully placed on a cedar hanger. Mackenzie saw an elf, a sea captain, a Pokémon character, and a giant purple outfit that, after several seconds of examination, she identified as an eggplant emoji.

All the costumes looked handmade. The fabrics felt substantial in Mackenzie's fingers, plush and double-stitched. None of the twenty-dollar Amazon throwaways that most people wore for Halloween.

Near the end of the costume row Mackenzie stopped, eyes caught by one of Yoo's outfits. It was a zip-up unicorn onesie, the fabric fuzzy and neon yellow. Attached to the onesie's hood was a plastic purple unicorn horn. Other neon accents were stitched across the body and limbs.

Mackenzie stared at a purple symbol stenciled onto the breast of the costume. It was a centaur holding a bow and arrow, aim facing up and to the right. The symbol triggered something familiar in the back of Mackenzie's mind, but she couldn't place it.

"Mackenzie." Danner's voice called to her from the stairs.

"Be right there," Mackenzie said. She descended to the kitchen, where Danner and Fernandez waited. Cosetta had come from his post downstairs to meet them.

"Fernandez and I did a first sweep," Danner said, glancing at Mackenzie. "No sign of the laptop."

"No sign of anything," Mackenzie said. "Feels like nobody's been in here for months."

Danner addressed his colleagues. "Full bore," he said. "Every drawer, every cabinet. Start upstairs." Fernandez and Cosetta nodded and moved away. Danner looked back at Mackenzie. "Don't think we'll find much, but you never know."

Struck by a thought, Mackenzie moved to the fridge and opened it.

The kitchen was pummeled by the stench of rotting food. Mackenzie squinted against the smell, forcing herself to examine the contents. A carton of milk sat on the main shelf; she spun it with a finger and looked at the expiration date.

"This milk is over three months old," Mackenzie said.

"Close that," Danner said, voice strained. He typed urgently on his phone.

Closing the fridge, Mackenzie studied the photos pasted to the door. Between the Christmas cards and wedding invitations her eyes fell on a familiar scene: Stanley Yoo and Trevor Canon arm in arm, the background an explosion of electric lighting. Same photograph from Trevor's office, she thought.

First time around Mackenzie hadn't noticed their outfits—but now she saw that Yoo was wearing the unicorn onesie from his closet, his neck ringed by a collar of fuzzy yellow fabric.

Mackenzie drifted back to the living room, scanning the space. Something else was off about Yoo's apartment, but she was having trouble placing it.

"He's not here," Danner said. He stood in Yoo's kitchen, speaking into his phone. His face was lined with frustration. "No sign of the laptop, either." A pause. "Mm-hmm. How tight is the geo-location? . . . Okay."

Danner ended the call and looked at Mackenzie. "Our office connected into Journy's geo-location system that activated on Canon's laptop. They confirm the laptop was here."

"But not anymore," Mackenzie said.

"Seems not."

"When exactly was it activated?"

Danner looked at his phone. "Thirty-six minutes ago."

"And how long did the signal transmit?"

"About thirty seconds."

"So what do you think?"

"Several possibilities," Danner said. "One, Yoo left the laptop here, came back for it. Realized his mistake when he turned it on, got the hell out."

"Manager didn't see him," Mackenzie said. "He says Yoo hasn't been here for months."

"Manager doesn't live on-site," Danner replied.

"Okay. But Yoo's an engineer. Wouldn't he know that Canon's laptop would trigger geo-location if he turned it on?"

"Possibly."

"And why would Yoo leave the laptop here to begin with? And come back for it now, when he knows people want to find him?"

"I don't know," Danner said.

"Doesn't add up," Mackenzie said. She looked around at the stillness of the loft. "Does this feel like a place anyone's been in recently?"

"No," Danner said. "Every indication is that Yoo hasn't been here for a long time."

"He said he was going to Hawaii just a few weeks ago. But this feels like it's been empty longer than that."

"Yes," Danner agreed. "Between the manager and the milk in the fridge, I'd say it's been months."

"So all summer long, Yoo was working at Journy, doing his normal job, but . . . he wasn't living here. So where was he living?"

"Good question," Danner said. "Brady Fitzgerald said that Yoo often worked remotely. Maybe he was doing that."

"Eleanor would've mentioned it," Mackenzie said. "Plus, we also know someone else who wasn't home a lot over the last few months."

"Trevor Canon."

"Maybe he and Yoo were together somewhere."

"It makes sense," Danner said.

Something clicked in Mackenzie's mind. "Another thing," she said. "Yoo was a brilliant technical mind, according to everyone. So"—Mackenzie gestured to the space around them—"where's all his gear?"

"Gear?"

"Guys like Yoo have tons of tech. Computers, servers, headphones, monitors, all sorts of shit. There's none of that here."

"There's the TV," Danner said, nodding toward the living room.

"Even your grandmother has a flat screen," Mackenzie said. "Doesn't count."

"Maybe he kept all his gear at the office."

Mackenzie shook her head. "He'd have his own stuff here. Especially if he often worked remote. So where is it?"

Danner looked around. "Simplest explanation is that Yoo took it all with him, whenever he left."

Mackenzie nodded. "He knew he was going to be gone for a while, and it wasn't a vacation. He needed all his gear, because he was working on something."

"With Canon," Danner said. "Fitzgerald said he was certain that

Canon was working on something new. Maybe he and Yoo were working on it together."

"The pieces fit," Mackenzie said.

"There's a second possibility for the laptop," Danner said. "The geo-location gets down to about eighty feet. Maybe the laptop was turned on within eighty feet of here, but wasn't actually *in* the loft."

"You think someone came to Yoo's building with the laptop, turned it on, and then left?"

"It's possible."

Mackenzie moved to a corner of the expansive window, pulling back the shade. Four stories below she saw the silver sedan double-parked at the building entrance. "You're right. They wouldn't even have to get out of their car."

"Whoever had the laptop could've driven up, turned it on, waited thirty seconds to be sure the geo-location kicked in, turned it off, and then driven away."

"But why do that?"

"Because they wanted us to come here," Danner said. "They wanted us to think Yoo had Canon's laptop."

"Just to be clear about this theory: Whoever has the laptop, and would go to the trouble of doing this . . . they're the same person who killed Trevor. Correct?"

Danner blinked at her. "Almost certainly."

"So we don't think it was Yoo, then."

Danner moved back into the kitchen, heading for the hallway. "It's just a theory. The first possibility could still be true." Danner clenched his jaw, tiny fissures of frustration emerging through his self-assuredness. "Maybe Yoo came back here, maybe he didn't. Either way, he isn't here now. So where the hell is he?"

Danner and Mackenzie exited Yoo's loft. "I'll have Fernandez and Cosetta see if there are any cameras outside the building, anything with a view of the surrounding streets." He shrugged. "Maybe we'll get lucky and pick up a car that idled for a while."

"You don't sound optimistic," Mackenzie said.

"I'm not," Danner said. "I'm going to drop you back at the hotel. If we find anything, I'll call you. But it could take most of the night."

Mackenzie was prepared to argue, but she didn't have the energy.

Exhaustion had overcome her. The Futurist Summit felt like it had been ten weeks ago, rather than ten hours.

She and Danner spent the ride back to the hotel in a familiar silence. Twelve minutes later they reached the front of the Royal Harbor, Danner pulling the sedan to the curb.

Mackenzie turned toward Danner as she prepared to exit. "What are you thinking?"

"I'm thinking that this investigation is starting to piss me off," Danner said. "I know it was an executive. I know how they killed Canon. But I can't find Yoo. Don't know where Canon was disappearing to. Everyone's got an alibi. Dead money might be a dead end. Someone broke into your apartment, threatened you. And now we're wasting time turning over Yoo's loft."

"We're swimming through shit," Mackenzie agreed. "But someone once said to me: 'If you're swimming through shit, keep swimming.' Eventually something will break for us."

"Yeah," Danner said, his voice flat. "Guess you're right."

Danner let his head fall against the headrest, the hotel's light reflecting off his smooth, clean-shaven cheeks. He looked to Mackenzie like a young boy, rather than an FBI agent investigating a homicide. Not Special Agent Jameson Danner, but Osiris Danner, Jr., son of Ozzie Danner, with the weight of his name and his father and the entire D.C. power apparatus heavy on his shoulders.

"I'll see you tomorrow," Mackenzie said.

"I'll meet you in the lobby, eight A.M."

When Mackenzie entered her room she texted Hammersmith an update on Yoo's apartment. Hammersmith didn't immediately reply, so Mackenzie threw her phone on the bed.

She took a long shower and guiltlessly ate a forty-three-dollar risotto from room service. After dinner she latched the deadbolt, flipped the security bar, turned off the lights, and closed the curtains.

The bed was divine. The room was pitch dark. Her stomach was full. She was exhausted, satiated, comfortable.

But as Mackenzie closed her eyes, a series of images began rotating through her mind, cutting through the comfortable darkness, unyielding and stark.

The black Tesla, a silent shark in the night.

The man with the sleeve tattoo, watching her from across the bar.

And then, blazing across the horizon of her mind's eye, bright and fiery and laced with menace, three inescapable words.

WE ARE WATCHING

She slept like shit.

CHAPTER 22

Six years before Trevor Canon's death

The entirety of the visitation room at Dublin Federal Correctional Facility was beige, from the low, tiled ceilings, to the cheerless linoleum of the floor, to the faces of the guards as they watched from the corners. The room was awash in harsh fluorescent light that reminded Mackenzie of a bad dental office. The walls were bare. The air was cold, the room barely heated by a single ceiling vent.

The tables were rubber and particleboard, tops covered by faux wood veneer that peeled at the edges. The chairs were hard-backed and plastic, almost intentionally uncomfortable, as though engineered to dissuade occupants from lingering.

Two vending machines neighbored a water fountain in the front corner. Mackenzie's typical cache sat on the table before her: two plastic bottles of Diet Coke, a bag of Doritos, a box of Swedish Fish, and a paper cup of water. She'd arrived early enough to nab a corner spot near the doors. Her leg bounced beneath the faux wood.

FCI Dublin was a low-security federal prison. It housed only white-collar criminals, all of them women. Shawshank it wasn't. Still, Mackenzie hated the feeling she got each month when she stepped inside its walls. It was like entering another dimension.

At exactly ten o'clock a set of double doors swung open. A short line of FCI Dublin inmates entered the visitation room, each in a drab uniform of the same beige as the rest of the prison.

Janine Clyde was fourth in line.

Mackenzie's mother had aged significantly in the last month. Janine's dark hair was stringy and frayed. Her skin was ashen, face riddled with lines. Her features had always been pinched—like Mackenzie's—but now they'd fallen inward, mouth growing tighter, brow contracting. Her eyes, at least, were still crackling with intelligence. Janine spotted Mackenzie and walked slowly to the table, stooping as she weaved between plastic chairs. When Mackenzie greeted her with a hug, she felt her mother's rib cage press against her chest.

Mackenzie had the dismal sensation that her mother's body was shrinking into itself, collapsing like a dying star.

And she knew exactly what it meant. She swelled with apprehension, trying to think how to broach the topic she knew her mother would refuse to discuss.

Janine sat and twisted the cap off a Diet Coke. "Thanks, honey."

Mackenzie nodded, smile tight. "No problem."

Janine took a long gulp then tore open the Swedish Fish, popping two of the small, strange red candies into her mouth. Her eyes closed with satisfaction as she chewed, body melting against the hard back of the chair.

Mackenzie chuckled. "Never understood what you see in those things."

"It's the way they make 'em." Janine opened her eyes as she swallowed. "The sugar hits your bloodstream in a different way—"

Janine straightened suddenly, raising an elbow to her mouth. She coughed violently, the noise echoing across the visitation room.

Mackenzie leaned forward, putting a hand on her mother's shoulder. "You sound terrible."

Janine brushed Mackenzie's hand away and resettled, grabbing another handful of Swedish Fish. "How's work?"

Mackenzie paused. "It's fine."

"Fine?"

"Yeah."

Janine eyed her daughter. "Doesn't sound fine."

Mackenzie shrugged, looking away. "We've talked about it before."

"So? I've got nowhere else to be. Talk about it again."

"I'm busy. I've got plenty of work. The other lawyers at HV are . . . They're okay."

"They're lawyers," her mom said.

Mackenzie gave a small laugh. "Right. I'm still doing the same stuff. Form agreements, contracts, dealing with all the idiots at the companies we've invested in."

"I read something about a company," her mother said. "It was in the news. Had a terrible name. Claremont, Clearly . . ."

"Clarifyde," Mackenzie said.

"Yeah. I read about them in *The Wall Street Journal*. It said Hammersmith Venture invested in them."

Mackenzie nodded. "It was a big round. They got a nice valuation."

"If it made the *Journal* it must be a pretty big deal."

"I don't get to work on the investments themselves," Mackenzie said. "I don't get any of the fun parts. I just write the legal language for the investment agreements. It's incredibly boring."

"Still, those are big numbers. I saw the investment was hundreds of millions."

"Yeah, three hundred million."

Mackenzie's mother tilted her head, taking another sip of the Diet Coke. "That's a lot of money."

Mackenzie shrugged. "It's typical for tech these days."

"Hmmm." Her mother looked at her. "What about the big boss, Hammersmith? You ever see him?"

Mackenzie shook her head. "Not really. He doesn't engage with the lawyers much. And I'm the most junior, so . . . No, I don't see him."

"You should go talk to him," Janine said.

"Talk to him?"

"Go to his office. Introduce yourself."

Mackenzie chuckled, shaking her head. "That's not how it works, Mom."

Her mother waved a hand. "I've read all about the tech industry, Kenz. They love to pat themselves on the back about their open offices, flat structures."

"HV has an open plan, sure," Mackenzie said. "But Roger Hammersmith isn't part of it. He's got an office. A big one, with a view of the whole fucking bay, from what I hear."

"You haven't seen it yourself?"

Mackenzie shook her head. "Can't just waltz in there."

"Why not? Is there security stopping you?"

"It's just not how it works." Mackenzie paused. "Tech's whole 'flat structure' thing is a mirage. Places like HV are just as hierarchical as any other industry."

Janine was struck by another violent cough, body convulsing against the edge of the table. Several of the other tables glanced over, eyes drawn by the noise.

"Jesus," Mackenzie said, placing a hand on her mother's shoulder. "Mom, come on. Drink something."

Janine reached for the Diet Coke and took a slug. She swiped Mackenzie's hand off her shoulder. "I'm fine. Stop." She took another drink, straightening in her chair.

Mackenzie stared at her mother. "Mom. We need to talk about this."

"In a bit. First things first."

"Seriously. The work stuff isn't important."

"You're wrong," Janine said, voice sharp. "It's the *most* important." She cleared her throat. "Now go on."

"Are you sure?"

"Yes." Despite her mother's condition, Mackenzie detected the old ferocity in Janine's eyes. "Tech. Hierarchy. Continue."

Mackenzie sighed. "Okay. Well, it's not just 'open offices.' Tech loves to pat itself on the back about *everything*. The VCs talk about entrepreneurship like it's the last bastion of meritocracy. 'In Silicon Valley, the best ideas win,' they say." Mackenzie scoffed. "But it's all bullshit. At HV, most of our investments can be traced back to Hammersmith's old boys' network from Stanford. Like that company you mentioned a minute ago, Clarifyde."

"What about them?"

"The founder is the son of Hammersmith's golfing buddy. And do you know where he got the money to start Clarifyde?"

Mackenzie's mother gave a wan smile. "A loan from daddy."

"A loan," Mackenzie affirmed, "but for the *third time*. His first two companies went belly-up. But now everyone suddenly says he's a genius."

"Money begets money," her mother said.

"Exactly." Mackenzie let the disgust run free in her voice. "It's all just money. The whole fucking thing. The entire tech industry is a giant, soulless, self-propelling machine that runs on its own bullshit."

Janine finished her Diet Coke and set the empty bottle on the table, features drawn. "You sound disillusioned," Janine said.

"I have been for a while," said Mackenzie.

"So what are you thinking of doing?"

"I'm thinking of quitting."

Mackenzie expected her mother to wince, but Janine's expression was unchanged. "Quitting and doing what?"

"Going back to a firm," Mackenzie said. "D.C., or New York. Maybe government. Just . . . something else. Anything else."

Her mother unscrewed the second Diet Coke, taking a swig. She stole a glance at the clock above the door, then grabbed the Doritos and ripped them open. "You still friends with that Eden woman?" she asked.

"Eleanor?"

"The smart one."

"Yeah. I am."

Three years had passed since Mackenzie's conversation with Eleanor at the wine bar. Mackenzie hadn't followed her advice immediately. She finished Georgetown, took the bar exam, prepared herself for the move to New York and her new job at Parks Andrews.

Mackenzie remembered the exact moment she decided to come west. She'd received an orientation packet from Parks Andrews in the mail, a three-ring binder thick enough to stop a bullet. The cover was dark burgundy leather, the front embossed with PARKS ANDREWS in ornate gold type.

The orientation binder had seven pages about the workplace attire at the firm's Midtown offices.

It had fourteen pages about billable hours—how to differentiate between the time Mackenzie would spend thinking about Lockheed Martin while sitting on the toilet versus the time she'd spend thinking about Philip Morris while downing a club sandwich.

It had one line about the workplace culture at Parks Andrews: "striving to create a communal sense of achievement through a tireless ambition to deliver the best possible outcomes for our clients."

As Mackenzie turned the pages, a single phrase had thundered across her mind: None of this matters. And then she'd recalled something Eleanor had said: *You're headed for the salt mines when there's a gold rush happening just over your shoulder.*

Mackenzie called Eleanor that very afternoon. Two weeks later she moved to San Francisco. A day after that, she started at Hammersmith Venture.

Mackenzie's mother popped a Dorito into her mouth. The visitation room was quiet, every table striving for privacy in a place that proffered none. "So what does Eleanor think about your plan to quit?"

Mackenzie hesitated. "I haven't told her yet."

"Why not?" Janine blinked at Mackenzie, obviously aware of the answer.

"Haven't gotten around to it."

"Or you know what she'd say. Which is the same thing I'll say."

"And what's that?"

"That quitting now would be the dumbest fucking thing you could do."

"You don't know that."

"Of course I do," her mother said. "You've only just begun. You're building a foundation. Quitting on it would be a huge mistake."

Janine delivered the lines simply, as though reading from an encyclopedia. The ocean is wet. The sky is blue. Quitting would be a huge mistake.

Mackenzie's shoulders tensed. "You haven't been listening to me."

"I've been listening to you for months," Janine said. She popped another Dorito, teeth snapping the corn with a noisy crunch. "Tech's not a meritocracy. People in the industry say one thing and do another. Founders get loans from their rich daddies. Your boss golfs."

"It's more than that."

"Not really." Her mother blinked at her. "Meritocracies don't exist, Kenz. Don't waste your time looking for one. You won't find it."

"It's *more* than just that," Mackenzie insisted. "You don't understand how self-important the industry is, how these people *talk*. Everyone in tech acts like they're working on the most important—"

"Like they're working on the most important thing in the whole wide world," Janine finished. "That's not new, either. Every industry is that way. I ran the books for tons of 'em. Big pharma, insurance brokers, even the oil companies. They've all developed a taste for their own bullshit. Tech's no different."

"Oil companies don't drape their mission statements from a banner in the lobby."

Janine shrugged. "That's cosmetic. Maybe the tech industry is fueled by a steady stream of its own bullshit, but hey—that's capitalism, honey. It's nothing but money, all the way down."

"Fine," Mackenzie said, raising a hand. "But let's say you're right. If tech isn't any different than the rest of the corporate world, then why shouldn't I leave?"

Janine crunched the last Dorito. "Isn't that obvious?"

"Not really."

"The money, Kenz." Finished with the Doritos, Janine went back to the Swedish Fish. "Numbers like three hundred million to a brand-new company. Junior employees, kids only a couple years out of college, making seven figures off stock options. *That's* different. Maybe tech is a machine running on its own bullshit, but it's a *growing* machine. It's getting bigger, and faster. And you're part of it now. You just need to be patient. Abandoning it now would be just plain stu—"

Janine's body spasmed into another coughing fit, the sound booming across the visitation room. She doubled over at the table, box of candy falling to the linoleum.

Mackenzie grabbed the water cup off the table, pushing it into her mother's hand.

"Drink this," Mackenzie said.

"I'm fine," her mother choked.

"Goddammit, Mom, drink it."

Her mother acquiesced, taking the cup. She sipped at the water, cup shaking in her hand. She remained folded over in her chair.

Mackenzie pushed the snacks to one end of the table. "You've gotta stop eating this shit."

Janine gave no reply. One thin hand lay on her chest, the other still gripping the paper cup. "Take it easy," she said. "I'm drinking it."

Mackenzie leaned forward. "Tell me right now: What's going on? Something's changed."

"Nothing," Janine said. "Nothing's changed." She emitted another cough, though weaker and quieter than before.

Mackenzie gritted her jaw. "Every month I come here but we never talk about what's *actually happening with you.* The medical liaisons won't tell me; they say it has to come from you. So tell me right now: What the fuck is going on?"

"Fine," Janine said. She moved her eyes away, staring at the cheap metal legs of the table. Her voice softened. "They say it's back. And it's gotten worse."

"Worse?"

Her mother nodded. "They did some tests."

Mackenzie's voice broke, anger receding. "Tests? What kind of tests?"

Janine's mouth curled. "They say they found it in the lymph nodes. And on from there."

"What?" A wave of dread fell over Mackenzie, body stiffening in the chair. "Why didn't you tell me?"

"I just found out." Janine's eyes were still on the table. "They told me yesterday."

"Mom . . ." Mackenzie felt tears welling in the corners of her eyes. She propped her elbows on the table, dropping her forehead to her hands.

It'd been five years since the initial diagnosis. A decade of breathing casino smoke had led to a predictable denouement: Janine Clyde had lung cancer.

The first years after the diagnosis had been a blur. There'd been tests. There'd been treatments. Rounds of chemo. Signs of recovery. Signs of relapse. More tests. More treatment. Hospital beds, IVs, cheap gowns and expensive pills. Stone-faced doctors hurrying between patients. Kinder nurses rushing through their tasks. Waiting. Endless, endless waiting.

Then, a few years after the initial diagnosis, the second hammer had fallen. Mackenzie had been in law school at the time. She wasn't naïve to the realities of the case against her mom. But Mackenzie had hoped the judge would show leniency, given her mother's cancer.

Instead, the entire court process had been transactional. There were no arguments. No deliberation of the unique circumstances. There wasn't even a defense. On advice of counsel, Janine Clyde pled guilty. The judge rubber-stamped the exact median sentence for her mother's category of crimes: seven years. It was justice the modern way, mass-produced in the factory and shoveled out the ass end, one size fits all.

Since moving into federal prison her mother's cancer had grown more opaque. Mackenzie could only track Janine's condition via rare, noncommittal updates from FCI Dublin's medical staff, and her own observational skills during her monthly visits. For a while, Janine's health seemed to stabilize. She'd resembled a passing version of herself.

It was only in the last few visits that her condition had deteriorated. And now, Mackenzie knew why.

"What stage?" Mackenzie asked. "I know they told you. They had to."

Janine's expression was resigned, mouth set in a thin frown, eyes dragging with fatigue. "Stage Three minimum," she said. "More likely moving into Four."

"Fuck."

"They say I have a few months left."

Mackenzie buried her face in her hands again, letting the tears flow. She pushed her chair back, dropped her head to the cheap laminate of the table, and cried. Mackenzie sensed her mother adjusting her position and felt a hand rest on her shoulder.

"I'm sorry, Kenz," her mother said.

A stern voice spoke behind them. "No more contact, Clyde," a guard said. "I've let it slide enough."

Mackenzie felt her mother's hand move away. She took a moment to gather herself, wiping her face with the sleeve of her hooded sweatshirt. She forced a deep breath.

"Okay," Mackenzie said. Her mind whirred back into action. "So what do we do?"

"Do?"

"What do the doctors say? Another round of chemo?"

Janine shook her head softly. "I'm not doing that again."

"I know how brutal it is, Mom, but if it's the best—"

"No," her mom said. "Not again. Not in here."

"We have to do something. The doctors must have recommended some kind of treatment."

"Kenz, there's nothing to be done."

"Don't say that," Mackenzie said. "I'm sure there's something we can do."

Her mother stared at her, features tight. "I've only got so much time left. I'm not spending it in the infirmary."

"Maybe they'll let you out."

"I'm not even halfway through my sentence."

"I can petition them."

"So I can go from one hospital bed to another?" Her mother shook her head again. "No."

"Mom." Mackenzie felt her eyes watering again. "You can't just *die* in here. Not in here. It's not . . ." Mackenzie's voice broke. "You don't deserve this. You don't deserve to *be* in here. It's just . . . It's not fucking *fair*."

"Fair?"

The word triggered something in Janine. Her back straightened, eyes sparking.

"Kenz, don't you remember what I taught you? Fair *doesn't exist*."

Janine leaned forward, her voice quiet and resolute. "Our world isn't built on fairness. It's not built on right and wrong, hard work, smarts. It's built on one thing and one thing only: *ruthlessness*. Our system rewards those who sacrifice. Those who are ruthless enough to give things up in pursuit of their goal. Give up their friends, give up their time, give up their ideas about the way they thought their life was supposed to go."

Janine's eyes bored into Mackenzie's. "I'm in here because I sacrificed. I knew exactly what I was doing. And I'd do it again."

Mackenzie sniffed, shaking her head. She gestured to the beige nothingness of their surroundings. "How can you say that? You're in *prison*, Mom." Mackenzie laughed with disbelief. "Sometimes I feel like you don't even *get* that."

Janine's expression was placid. "That's because I always knew prison was a risk."

Mackenzie frowned. "Then why did you do it? If you're doing something that could send you to prison, then isn't it maybe not worth doing?"

"I just told you. You have to be ruthless. You have to sacrifice." Janine's expression shifted. "Let me ask you a question: How do you think I paid for NYU?"

"You saved up. We made the deal when I was thirteen."

Her mother smirked. "NYU was over forty grand a year. You think I saved up two hundred thousand while you were in high school?"

"I . . ." Mackenzie froze. The answer crystallized in her mind. "Wait." She gaped at her mother. "*That's* how you paid for my college?"

Janine Clyde had been convicted on multiple felony counts of what her lawyer called the surf-and-turf of white-collar crime: fraud and embezzlement.

It started when Braniff, Janine's accounting firm, stumbled on irregularities in Janine's work for Obsidian Investments. Janine had worked closely with Obsidian for over fifteen years. Both Janine's employer and client were surprised: Though only a "staff accountant," Janine was known for her attention to detail.

When Braniff and Obsidian dug into the irregularities, they discovered something even more surprising. Across a period of seven years, Janine Clyde had systematically stolen over three hundred thousand dollars of Obsidian's money. And until that moment, one of the world's most reputable investment firms—and their equally reputable accounting partner—hadn't the faintest idea.

"That's exactly how I paid for it," Janine said. "Obsidian called themselves a 'financial services firm,' but they were nothing but thieves. They were too busy stealing other people's money to pay attention to their own. So yes, Kenz, I stole from them. I used the money to do what I said I'd do. I paid your way into college, somewhere good enough to give you a leg up, without the yoke of debt weighing you down for the rest of your life. And you know what? I don't regret it. Never have."

Mackenzie closed her eyes, falling back against the hard plastic of her chair. The familiar guard strolled past their table. "Five more minutes, Clyde." Janine nodded in acknowledgment.

Mackenzie pinched the bridge of her nose, head down, overwhelmed by her mother's admission. "Why are you telling me this now?"

Her mother gave a sad smile. "Because you need to wake up. Don't you remember what I told you all those years ago, back home, when we were drinking by the Christmas tree?"

"Wait for opportunity," Mackenzie said. "And then seize it."

"That's right."

Mackenzie shook her head, scoffing. "So that's how you're excusing what you did? Your idea of seizing opportunity is stealing other people's money?"

Her mother's voice hardened. "It doesn't need to be excused," she said. "I worked myself as close to power and wealth as I could. It was going to be the best opportunity I got. I knew there was a chance I'd be caught. But I also knew what that money was for."

Janine gave a genuine smile, eyes brightening. "I got you as far ahead as I could. And look at you now. You're plugged into the fastest-growing industry in history. Literally *surrounded* by money. In San Francisco, people younger than you and dumber than you are falling ass-backward into wealth. You want to control your own destiny, live your own life? Then you're in the right fucking place."

Mackenzie's mother leaned back against her chair, smile fading. "The opportunity will come, Kenz. Be patient. I waited for years. Decades. And I didn't have nearly the start that you do. So don't quit now. You're just getting started. Work your way into the right spots. Be ruthless. Be prepared to sacrifice. And when the opportunity comes, you'll be ready."

CHAPTER 23

Twenty-six days after Trevor Canon's death

Mackenzie woke early and checked her text messages. Hammer-smith still hadn't replied to her from the evening before. He texted like a Boomer—sporadically, with unnecessary punctuation—but it wasn't like him to not reply.

She met Danner downstairs at eight sharp. Danner looked haggard as he emerged from the elevator. The faintest trace of stubble appeared above his upper lip.

"Ready to go?" Danner said. His tone was gruff.

Mackenzie nodded. Five minutes later they sat in their customary positions in the sedan as Danner pulled into SoMa traffic. The weather fit Danner's mood. The air was brisk and wet, the sky low and thicketed with dense clouds. Summer in San Francisco.

"Late night?" Mackenzie asked.

Danner grunted. "Spent hours looking through security footage from Yoo's building, trying to find a car that idled nearby. But we got nothing. There's only one camera and it has a bad angle. Someone in a car could've easily been out of scope, and still triggered the geo-location."

Mackenzie watched the familiar sludge of morning traffic. A middle-aged guy on a Journy Scoot buzzed past her window, nearly clipping the mirror. "Where are we headed?"

"Moreau's house."

Mackenzie flipped her eyes back to Danner. "The subpoena came through?"

Danner nodded. "That was the rest of my night. We spoke to the manager of Serafina."

Mackenzie raised her eyebrows. "What'd she say?"

"Moreau stayed there for three nights, including the night when Canon was murdered."

"So Cassiopeia was telling the truth."

"Not entirely." Danner pushed the sedan through an orange light. "On the evening of August first, Moreau left Serafina for a while. Took off. She was gone several hours and didn't return until late."

"What? But that's . . ."

"The exact window of time when Canon was killed."

Mackenzie stared at Danner. "Where did she go?"

"That's what you and I are going to find out."

"How does Serafina's manager know Cassiopeia left?"

"The no tech policy," Danner said. "When you enter Serafina, they hold your tech for you at reception. Moreau came to get her phone before she took off. Gave it back when she returned."

"What time did she get back?"

"The night porter thinks it was around one A.M."

"Trevor was killed a little before eleven-thirty," Mackenzie said. "Serafina's a couple hours from here."

"It's tight," Danner agreed. "Moreau would have had to kill Canon, then immediately hightail it back to Serafina. But regardless, we're paying her another visit." He paused. "Have you heard any-thing from your boss?"

"Not since our drive back from the Futurist Summit yesterday."

"Okay," Danner said. "I heard from forensics on your apartment, by the way. They didn't find anything useful. Whoever broke into your place knew what they were doing."

"Forensics didn't find *anything*?"

"Nothing," Danner said. "No fingerprints, no fibers."

"How'd they get into my place?"

"They picked the lock."

"But I deadbolted my door. I'm sure of it."

Danner glanced over at her, expression patronizing. "Whoever did this is a professional. A deadbolt's as much deterrent as a BEWARE OF DOG sign."

Mackenzie let Danner have his moment of mansplaining. "But isn't that odd? My apartment and Canon's office . . . both bone dry on the forensics? Not even a single hair?"

Danner shrugged. "Maybe."

"That's not unusual?"

Danner kept his eyes on the road, expression inscrutable. "Happens more often than you'd think."

He fell silent as they pulled up to the familiar Ipe wood façade of Moreau's property. Danner parked exactly where he had two days prior. He stepped quickly out of the sedan, Mackenzie following, and loped over to the intercom panel, jabbing the red button.

There was no reply. It was gusty and Mackenzie huddled in her jacket, bracing against the chill. Danner jabbed the button again.

Another fifteen seconds passed, then twenty. "Are you worried about her running?" Mackenzie asked.

"Moreau?" Danner made a face. "No."

Finally, a crackle from the intercom. Cassiopeia's voice echoed into the damp morning. "Hello?"

"Special Agent Danner, FBI."

"Uh, yes, Agent Danner." Moreau's voice was hesitant, wary. "We don't have an appointment, do we?"

"No," Danner said. His tone was direct. "I need you to answer a few follow-up questions."

Another long pause. "Now's not a good time. You can follow up with my assistant—"

Danner cut her off. "You weren't at Serafina when Canon was killed. You can let us in and answer questions here, or I can take you into custody and we do this from federal holding. Your call."

Another long beat passed. Danner stood tensely near the inter-com, Mackenzie at his shoulder.

"Come in," Cassiopeia said, and the driveway gate whirred to life.

Cassiopeia was waiting for them in the kitchen. She stood behind the massive granite island, hands braced against the edge. There was none of the sunny welcome of their prior visit. Cassiopeia rocked on her feet, eyes downcast. Giant windows amplified the mournful clouds outside.

Danner and Mackenzie took standing positions across the island from Cassiopeia. Journy's chief marketing officer was wearing little makeup, her short red hair messy and un-styled. She wore pajama pants and a Journy green T-shirt that read BITCHES WHO CODE.

Cassiopeia met Danner's eyes. "I can explain," she said.

"Lying to a federal agent is a felony," Danner replied. "Up to five years in prison."

"I didn't *lie*," Cassiopeia said.

"You said you were at Serafina when your boyfriend was mur-dered. Turns out you weren't. That's pretty cut and dried."

"I *was* at Serafina." Cassiopeia raised her hands off the island, palms out. "Just, yes, okay, not the *whole* time."

"You also told us that you and Canon never talked about money. But that wasn't true, either. You asked Canon to invest in your coach-ing startup. And you were pissed when he said no."

Cassiopeia's mouth fell open. "How do you know that?"

"It's true, isn't it? When Canon told you he wouldn't invest, you took that personally. It'd be impossible not to."

"No," Cassiopeia said. Her eyes closed. "Not in the way you think. Just, hang on—"

Mackenzie's attention was diverted by a set of expensive Japanese knives that rested on the counter behind Cassiopeia. They were the same brand as the ones in Yoo's loft.

"That's two lies so far," Danner said. "What else did you lie about?"

"I can *explain*."

"Then let's hear it."

Cassiopeia took a deep breath and closed her eyes. She placed one hand on her sternum while returning the other to the island. "I told you that Trevor had been disappearing. Lying. Secretive. After a while, I started to get suspicious."

Danner watched Cassiopeia carefully. "Of what?" Danner said. "You told us Canon had never been unfaithful."

"I didn't know that at the time," Cassiopeia said. "After all those months, all those nights where I'd wake up at three A.M. and Trevor still wouldn't be home . . . I started to wonder." Cassiopeia's eyes softened. "I'm only human, Agent Danner."

Danner exhibited no sympathy. "So you got suspicious. What then?"

"One night I decided that enough was enough. I followed Trevor."

"The night he was killed? That's why you left Serafina?"

"No," Cassiopeia said. "This was a few weeks before he died. I got a Zipcar and waited outside the office. Near the back alley, Prince. Trevor always had his Journy Cars pick him up there."

"We know Prince."

"I waited there for hours. Around midnight, I saw Trevor come out of the alley. But he wasn't in a Journy Car. He was in a Buggy."

Mackenzie interjected. "He was in one of the golf carts?"

Cassiopeia nodded. "That was the first moment I knew something was off. Trevor *never* drove himself. He always took Journy Cars. But there he was, puttering along in a Buggy."

"Why would Canon take a Buggy instead of a car?" Danner asked.

"Didn't want a driver dropping him off at his destination," Mackenzie said. "He didn't want anyone to know where he was going."

"I followed him," Cassiopeia continued. "He went east, then south, all the way down to the piers in Bayview."

"What's down there?" Danner asked, glancing toward Mackenzie.

"By the piers?" Mackenzie paused. "Old shipyards, I think. But I've never been."

"That's why I started to get nervous," Cassiopeia said. "I'd never been down that way before. Neither had Trevor. At least, not with me. And it was dead quiet. Nobody was around, and it was late. I had no idea where Trevor was going. I started getting the creeps."

Cassiopeia's eyes glazed, as though reliving the memory. For the first time since meeting her, Mackenzie had the feeling that every-thing Cassiopeia said was true.

"Trevor knew where he was going. He didn't stop—just drove straight on ahead. Finally we passed a big recycling facility, and Trevor turned down a little alleyway. It ran between a bunch of old warehouses that were all dark. They looked totally abandoned. Then Trevor parked the Buggy and hopped out."

Cassiopeia shook her head. "I was too creeped out to follow him down the alley. Plus I was scared about what he was doing. Scoring drugs? Going to some kind of weird party? I had no idea. So I just kept driving. I went past real slow and tried to see where Trevor went."

"What did you see?" Danner asked.

"Trevor walked up to one of the big warehouses. It had one of those wide roll-up garage doors, like you'd see at a mechanic's, and then a smaller, regular-sized door right next to it. Everything was dark. But when Trevor walked up to the smaller door, it opened from the inside. And light poured out."

"The door opened to meet him?" Danner asked. "Someone was waiting for him there."

"Yes."

"Who was it?"

"I don't know," Cassiopeia said. "They were backlit, so I could only really see a silhouette. But it looked like a man."

"It was Stanley Yoo," Mackenzie said.

There was a brief silence as both Danner and Cassiopeia turned to face Mackenzie. "The other day," Mackenzie said to Cassiopeia, "you said that Stanley used to come over here all the time."

"That's right," Cassiopeia said.

"*Used to*," Mackenzie said. "As in, Stanley didn't come around the house *anymore*."

Cassiopeia tilted her head. "That's true. Stanley used to come over like once a week. But he hasn't been here for a long time."

"When would you say is the last time Yoo was here?"

Cassiopeia thought. "April, around Easter. He came over for the Big Wheel Race."

"Spring," Mackenzie said. "Four months ago. And would you also say that's around the same time that Trevor started acting weird?"

Cassiopeia's eyes widened. "Yes, actually. It was right around then."

Mackenzie looked at Danner. "And we know that Yoo hasn't been in his loft since at least May. It lines up."

"Stan hasn't been home since May?" Cassiopeia asked. "Where did he go?"

"I think he was living in that warehouse," Mackenzie said.

"Hold on," Danner said. His voice was firm, and he stared at Cassiopeia across the island. "All you've told us is that you followed Canon one night. But that doesn't explain where you were on the night he was actually killed."

Cassiopeia nodded. "After I saw Trevor go in the warehouse, I was freaked out. I went straight home. I didn't see Trevor until the next morning. I asked him where he'd spent the night. He lied and said his office. I didn't push him on it."

"Then what?"

"Weeks went by," Cassiopeia said. "I tried to forget about it. Clearly Trevor didn't want me to know what he'd been up to. I tried to rationalize it away. But it festered in me. I could barely talk to Trevor. It's why I decided to get away to Serafina, clear my head."

Cassiopeia took another deep breath. "But even Serafina didn't help. All my favorite things—transcendental foraging, the circle of self-inquiry—I couldn't *do* any of them. I just kept thinking about that goddamn warehouse. Finally, I couldn't take it anymore. I left Serafina and drove back to San Francisco."

"So you were in the city," Danner asked, tone sharp, "on the night Canon was killed?"

"Yes, but not *here* here. I went to Bayview. To the warehouse."

"You went to go look for Canon?"

"I wasn't sure if he was going to be there. But I had to go look for myself."

"How did you find it? By memory?"

"It took me a while," Cassiopeia said, nodding. "It was dark. I got lost a few times and almost gave up. Luckily I found the recycling plant. From there I knew where to go."

"What time did you find it?"

Cassiopeia thought for a moment. "I think around ten."

"Then what?"

"I parked at the end of the alley, on the main road. Then I walked up to the warehouse door."

"Did you see anyone?"

"No," Cassiopeia said. "The whole area was dead, just like the first time. I went up to the door—the regular one, not the big rolling one—and knocked. But there was no answer. I tried again, waited a few minutes, but there was nothing. I put my ear to the door, but didn't hear anything."

"Did you see any lights?"

"None."

"Did you try to look inside?"

"There aren't any windows."

"What about the sides or back?"

"One side was blocked by a chain-link fence. The other side had a path, but I was getting too freaked out." Cassiopeia stepped back from the island, shoulders curling into a shell. "The whole place was creepy and I was alone. I realized it had been a dumb idea. So I got in my car and got the hell out of there."

"Just got back in your car, went straight back to Serafina?"

"Yes."

"You didn't go anywhere else?"

"No."

"Serafina says you didn't get back till around one A.M."

"It's a long drive." Cassiopeia was now leaning back against her kitchen counter, arms crossed, shoulders raised. Full defensive position.

Mackenzie jumped in. "If we can find some record of you stopping, that would help us corroborate the timing of your story."

Cassiopeia shook her head, but then stopped. Her brow lifted slightly. "Wait. Actually, yes. I got gas."

Danner withdrew his phone from his jacket. "Where?"

"A Shell," Cassiopeia said, face lighting up. "Just past the airport, off 101. I chose it because it was super bright, lights everywhere."

Danner typed a quick note. "We'll check it out." He looked back at Cassiopeia, voice flat. "Now for the million-dollar question, Miss Moreau. Why didn't you tell us all this when we were here two days ago?"

"I don't know," Cassiopeia said. She shifted on her feet. "I should have. It was a mistake."

"A big mistake," Danner said.

"I know," Cassiopeia said. "I guess I just panicked, okay? I knew it would look bad if I told you I was poking around some abandoned warehouse, by myself, on the night Trevor died.

"And I didn't *lie*. You asked me where I was the night Trevor was killed, and I said I was at Serafina. That was technically true."

Danner's voice was polar. "'Technically true' doesn't cut it. Your boyfriend was murdered. We're the ones trying to find his killer."

"It was a mistake."

"Forget the felony charge," Danner said, staring daggers across the island. "If you really cared about finding who killed your boyfriend, then you should've told us about the warehouse."

Cassiopeia threw her hands in the air. "Fine. I was *embarrassed,* okay?" Her eyes bugged with frustration. "I was fucking *embarrassed.*"

Cassiopeia rubbed her face. "Trevor and I were together for years. Lived together, worked together. And yet I had no clue what he'd been up to—for *months*. I knew *nothing*. I mean, doesn't that sound ridiculous?

"Do you have any idea how hard it is to date someone like Trevor? *Nobody* respects your relationship. They whisper it's all about money. They whisper I'm only CMO at Journy because I'm fucking the founder. When Trevor started disappearing, and started lying to me, all of those whispers bounced around in my head."

Cassiopeia's voice softened, her eyes falling again to the floor. "Then he was murdered, in his own office. And I knew *nothing*. Had no idea what he might have gotten himself involved in, had no idea where he'd been disappearing to. Even if that's what got him killed."

She looked up at Danner. "I should have told you the whole story from the jump. I was just embarrassed. And scared. I'm sorry. Really."

Danner appeared entirely unmoved. "Okay." He turned away

from the island, placing his phone back in his pocket. "Get your things together."

"What?" Cassiopeia said. "Why?"

"You're coming with us."

"You're *arresting me?*"

"No," Danner said, shaking his head. "At least, not yet. But you're going to take us to that warehouse. Right now."

CHAPTER 24

Twenty-six days after Trevor Canon's death

They waited while Cassiopeia went to change. Alone for a moment, Mackenzie looked at Danner.

"It was Stanley Yoo in that warehouse," she said. "The night Cassiopeia followed Trevor there. It had to be."

"I think you're right," Danner said.

"Yoo moves out of his loft in spring, stops coming over here. Trevor starts acting weird, disappearing, becomes paranoid. They were working together on something new. And they were doing it at the warehouse."

"It lines up."

Mackenzie recalled something else. "Cassiopeia said that Trevor put Yoo on special projects. Let him go deep on things."

"That's right." Danner paused. "In either of Moreau's little performances, today or the other day, did you ever get the impression that she's honestly torn up about her boyfriend getting murdered?"

"No. I do think she's telling the truth, though. Today, at least."

"So do I," Danner said. "But I also think she'll say anything necessary to save her own skin."

Cassiopeia reappeared in the entryway. She'd applied makeup and was wearing ludicrous designer clogs.

"Let's go," Danner said.

They took Danner's sedan. Cassiopeia rode shotgun with Mackenzie relegated to the back seat. Cassiopeia led them southeast into the diagonal jumble of the Bayview piers, a labyrinth of empty lots, hulking warehouses, and long, unending spans of chain-link fencing.

After fifteen minutes they arrived at the alley. It was made of loose, dusty gravel, and lined on either side by rows of warehouses that stretched back ten deep. The warehouse fronts were tall; the alley ran straight between them like a canal through a canyon.

Mackenzie looked around. Zero pedestrians, no sidewalks, no trees. No other cars. Across the road from their parking spot there was nothing but a vast span of concrete, colorless and infinite as the morning sky above.

If Trevor Canon wanted to keep something secret, he'd chosen well. They were only a few miles from the burritos and bongos of Dolores Park, but Mackenzie guessed that ninety-nine percent of San Francisco's tech industry had never set foot in this part of town.

"What is this place?" Mackenzie asked.

Danner took measure of their surroundings. "Industrial warehouse rental."

"You've seen these before?"

Danner nodded. "Industrial rental spaces used to be very popular with criminals. People would rent 'em by the month and produce drugs, store weapons, traffic all sorts of illicit materials. But since 9/11 any facility like this is carefully monitored. FBI and local police make sure the property owners keep records on who's renting what, and when."

Danner pulled out his phone. "There'll be a paper trail. We can find out who's renting the warehouse."

Danner stepped away, phone to his ear, while Mackenzie looked around. Even in morning, the facility had a menacing presence. The warehouses were towering dark metal, and utterly opaque, with no windows. Narrow paths ran between them, snaking off the central alley. Everything was stark and gray: the gravel, the sets of concrete stairs at the warehouse entrances, the rolling metal doors that dominated their façades.

Mackenzie saw no garbage, no footprints, no tire tracks. The facility felt utterly devoid of life.

Danner finished his call and strode back to the others. "Let's go."

They moved down the alley, gravel crunching beneath their feet. As they passed the first warehouse on their left, Mackenzie spotted one of the paths Cassiopeia had mentioned. It ran between two buildings, narrow and barred off by chain-link fencing. Then they came to the second warehouse, its garage door wide and tall enough to accommodate a truck.

A concrete slab extended into the gravel, twelve inches high. Danner, Mackenzie, and Cassiopeia stepped onto the slab and walked to the warehouse's front door.

The door was made of the same metal as the rest of the warehouse. A small stencil labeled it as 2F. There was no bell.

Danner knocked. They heard the sound echo inside the warehouse. There was no response.

They waited a few seconds, then Danner knocked again.

Nothing.

Danner pulled on the door's metal handle, but it stayed in place. When Danner tried to push the door open, it didn't move.

"Deadbolt," he said.

"Can we pick it?" Mackenzie asked, half-joking.

Danner ignored her. "Let's go around back. Places like this have to have fire exits. It's code."

They moved to the far side of the warehouse and followed a scrubby, dirty path that led them straight back, knifing between 2F and its neighbor. At the end they reached a small open area. It was unimproved ground, more scrub checkered with weeds. Across, Mackenzie saw the backs of the next row of warehouses, their faces as austere as the fronts: all metal, no windows, no lights. As Danner predicted, each warehouse had a fire door set into its back corner. Where the front doors were metal, the back doors were plain wood, painted the same charcoal as the rest of the buildings.

But 2F's fire door had been destroyed.

The framing around the door was busted. The door itself hung askew, lowest hinge torn from the frame. The entire lock mechanism was battered, as though clobbered with a sledgehammer.

Danner stopped and held out a hand; Mackenzie and Cassiopeia halted behind him. Danner quietly reached into his jacket and withdrew his gun. He did the same jerky motion with the gun that Mackenzie had seen in the car.

Danner's voice was low. "Wait here."

Danner crept to the fire door, gun before him. He reached the threshold and stopped, listening, then used the muzzle of his pistol to nudge open the wood. The door swung inward, revealing nothing but gloomy darkness.

Danner disappeared inside.

Mackenzie and Cassiopeia waited in the dusty scrub behind 2F. Mackenzie felt a combination of tension and inutility as the seconds passed in silence. Her wrist began to ache; she forced the pain out of her mind. Cassiopeia pulled out her phone, scrolling through photos on her StoryBoard.

A light turned on inside the warehouse. Danner re-emerged from the fire door.

"It's clear. You'll wanna see this."

Mackenzie stepped through the battered fire exit and into the warehouse.

The interior was as large and industrial as the exterior had indicated. The ceilings were high; the slate morning sky filtered in through reinforced skylights. The floors were finished concrete, the walls metal and bare. There was a small bathroom on the distant wall, jammed between the entrance and the garage door.

Mackenzie stepped deeper into the warehouse, Danner in front and Cassiopeia trailing. It was clear that her prediction had been right. Whoever occupied the warehouse had been working on a project—and it was highly technical.

Danner had his phone out, taking photos. "It's a workshop," he said. "Or whatever the tech equivalent is."

The warehouse was sparsely furnished. Near the east wall stood a chain of five standing desks arranged in a half circle. Each desk held a huge monitor on its surface, screen dark. Under each desk sat a boxy computer tower, humming quietly.

Two rolling desk chairs rested at the center of the half-circle of desks. A coffee table and a couch were placed haphazardly in the middle of the room. An old, beat-up mini-fridge squatted next to them, plugged into a floor outlet.

On the west wall Mackenzie saw a router, networking devices, and racks of servers organized into a tall, buzzing cube. She wasn't an expert, but it looked like a hell of a lot of computing power.

Wires and cables ran all over the place: up the walls, along the floor, into the corners, out of the server racks, into the monitors. The cords snaked across every surface of the warehouse, spreading like invasive vines in a jungle.

Mackenzie walked past the standing desks to a series of four whiteboards. They were arranged end-to-end in a neat row. Three of them had been hastily erased; the boards were smeared with traces of black pen, but nothing decipherable.

The fourth whiteboard, at the farthest end, stood slightly detached from the other three. A single word was scrawled in big, thin letters across its surface:

M1ND

"That's Trevor's handwriting," Cassiopeia said, staring at the board. There was an evident sadness in her eyes. She was being confronted with Trevor's secrets, the pieces of his life that he had chosen to hide from her. And the pieces were substantial.

Mackenzie kept her voice gentle. "Do you see anything else that confirms it was Trevor and Stanley here?"

Cassiopeia pointed to the middle of the floor, where the mini-fridge rested near the couch.

"That," she said.

"The fridge?"

Cassiopeia nodded as they walked toward it. "It was Stanley's. He had it at HQ for years; engineers used to fill it with Red Bull for all-nighters." She pointed at the front. "Those were his stickers."

The fridge door looked like a teenager's notebook, riddled with a colorful mishmash of overlapping logos, flags, symbols, and phrases, few of which Mackenzie understood. But then her eye caught on a familiar image: a neon yellow centaur on a purple background. The centaur held a bow and arrow, facing up and to the right. An image of Stanley Yoo's yellow unicorn costume floated through her mind.

"Come check this out." Danner's voice carried from the opposite corner. He stood just inside the rolling garage door, where a massive tarp covered a large, low object. As Cassiopeia and Mackenzie approached, Danner grabbed the tarp and yanked it free.

It was a car. A white Prius, draped head to toe in equipment. A dozen cameras were affixed to the roof in an exoskeleton of mounts. The sides and back of the Prius were a jumble of circular discs, each made of a metallic, mesh-like material.

"What the hell is it?" Danner asked.

"It's a self-driving car," Mackenzie said. "Or at least, a prototype. Look at all these cameras. Those aren't run-of-the-mill lenses. They're lidar, or some equivalent. And all of these discs are sensors."

"How do you know?" Danner asked. He'd stopped on one side of the hood.

"I told you autonomous vehicles are the next big thing," Mackenzie said. "I've researched them at HV." She ran a hand over the roof. "Maybe Trevor and Stanley decided that Hugo Chamberlain wasn't up to cracking autonomous vehicles. Maybe they decided to do it on their own."

Cassiopeia kept her distance from the car, like it was a dangerous animal. "You know what's weird?" She gestured to the broader warehouse around them. "I don't see a Journy logo. Haven't seen a single one anywhere in here."

"Yoo and Canon weren't doing it for Journy," Danner said. "They were doing it for themselves."

Cassiopeia raised her eyebrows. "What? Outside the company?"

Danner glanced at Mackenzie, sharing an unspoken thought. *Yes, because Journy was a sinking ship. Yoo and Canon were building their own lifeboat.*

But Danner simply said, "Based on their secrecy, that would be my guess."

Mackenzie nodded. "The pieces fit."

Cassiopeia's face darkened. Wordless, she wandered away, back toward the center of the warehouse.

"Don't touch anything," Danner called after her. "Could be evidence." Cassiopeia didn't reply.

Mackenzie stared at the car. She kept her statement vague, since Cassiopeia was still in earshot.

"This is it, right?"

Danner nodded. "I think so."

Her implication was unsaid, but clear. This, an autonomous vehicle prototype, was what Canon was hiding. This is what he was paranoid about keeping secret, what had demanded all his attention.

And, the logical conclusion that followed: This is what got him killed.

Mackenzie glanced at the tarp that Danner had tossed aside. "If this was the prototype, why cover it up with a tarp? Wouldn't they be messing with it constantly?"

Danner shrugged. "Maybe they were worried about someone sneaking on the roof. Taking pictures."

"Hmm." Mackenzie resumed pacing around the perimeter of the car. "Look at all the lenses. They're dusty."

"It's not as bad as Yoo's loft," Danner said, "but there's a little dust on everything in here. Feels like nobody's been here for a while, either."

"Except whoever destroyed the fire door."

"Let's check the bathroom," Danner said.

The bathroom was as spartan as the rest of the warehouse. A pedestal sink, a shelf with paper towels, and the type of blocky, low-to-the-ground toilet that reminded Mackenzie of junior high.

Danner moved to the sink. "Look."

Mackenzie stepped next to him. Across the white porcelain rim of the sink she saw a splatter of dark burgundy dots. They were pooled together like red raindrops. The color was unmistakable.

"Blood," Mackenzie said.

Danner bent down so that his eyes were only inches from the stains. "Several weeks old, at least. Probably more."

"How can you tell?"

"You can tell a lot from bloodstains." He pointed a finger. "They're dime-sized. Even circles, no splatter around the edges. That means they were stray drops, not gushing from a bigger wound. And they fell from just above the sink. Probably a nose, a lip, something on the face." Danner paused. "It's turned brown, but it's not flaking. It's not ancient, but it's been here awhile."

Danner stood abruptly, pulling out his phone. He took a few photos and then began typing. "We'll get forensics in here, see if we can match DNA."

"You can find out whose blood it is?"

Danner nodded as he typed. "But I'm pretty sure we already know."

"Trevor, or Stanley."

They stepped out of the small bathroom and Danner stared across the warehouse. "Let's check out the technical equipment."

They moved to the server hub. Six racks stood in a two-by-three hive, lights blinking, humming in a dull roar. Danner circled around them as Mackenzie studied the cables coming to and from. The server rack appeared to be the nexus of all the wiring that enveloped the warehouse.

Danner squatted at one of the racks, peering at devices on the lower shelves. He withdrew his phone again, taking pictures.

"You know what any of this stuff is?" Mackenzie asked.

"They built a closed network," Danner said to Mackenzie's surprise. "Fairly standard when you're working on something and don't want anybody outside to know what it is." Danner gestured to all the cables, then pointed at two that snaked away toward the Prius in the distance. "Everything in here is connected. Even the car."

"How do you know all that?" Mackenzie said.

Danner was about to answer when his phone rang. He stepped away to take the call.

"Say that again? Sagittarius? How the hell you spell that? Okay . . . Good. Keep digging."

Danner hung up, then looked at Mackenzie. "The warehouse is rented to a group called Circus Sagittarius. Mean anything to you?"

"Circus?" Mackenzie asked. "Are they sure about that?"

"Yep," Danner said. "Apparently they're a nonprofit organization, registered as some kind of artists' collective. But they don't have any online presence. Fernandez says they can't find anything on 'em."

"Never heard of it."

Danner nodded. "We'll keep looking." He stared up and past Mackenzie suddenly, eyes moving toward the busted fire exit. "Look at that."

Mackenzie turned and followed his gaze. A camera was placed high into the corner of the warehouse, facing down toward them. It was camouflaged by its surroundings—cables, HVAC ducting, overhead lighting. But it had a clear view of the warehouse floor.

"Might not be operational," Mackenzie said. "Remember, Trevor bricked all the cameras at Journy HQ."

"True," Danner said. "But let's see if it's alone."

They moved to the opposite corner of the warehouse, where another camera was tucked into the corner, hidden just as carefully as the first.

"That's two," Danner said.

A thorough sweep of the warehouse revealed no more. "Two cameras," Danner said. "Opposite corners. Enough to cover the space, but pretty bare bones."

"Isn't that odd?" Mackenzie asked. "Canon went apoplectic about the cameras in Journy headquarters . . . But put them up here, in his secret warehouse?"

"Maybe Canon didn't put them up."

"Then who?"

"Maybe Yoo insisted. Or someone else did."

"Who else?"

"I don't know."

Danner fell quiet. Mackenzie sensed he was doing the same thing she was: collecting the disparate elements of the warehouse and compiling them into a picture. Investigation is synthesis, Mackenzie thought.

"There's a lot here," Mackenzie said. "What do you make of all of it?"

Cassiopeia had taken refuge on the sofa, lying horizontal as she scrolled on her phone. She appeared wholly uninterested, but Danner kept his voice low.

"Canon and Yoo were working on autonomous cars, off the books, in secret. Taking great pains to hide it, which means they were getting somewhere. Someone else found out about it, busted in, and there was a confrontation. Either Yoo or Canon got bloody and they cleaned up in the bathroom."

"Why would somebody bust in here?"

"All sorts of reasons," Danner said. "They wanted whatever Canon and Yoo were working on. Or if Hugo Chamberlain was right, Canon was focusing on this while Journy was going down the tubes. Someone found out and was pissed."

"Or," Mackenzie said, "Yoo and Canon had a falling-out, and got into a fight here. Would explain the blood."

"But not the door," Danner said. "Someone busted the crap out of it. Neither Canon or Yoo would've had to do that."

"True." Mackenzie remembered something. "You said maybe someone else put the cameras in here. Brady Fitzgerald saw Trevor meeting with Indira Soti, in Big Sur. Maybe the 'someone else' is Soti."

"Why would Soti be involved?"

Mackenzie gestured to the warehouse. "Maybe he's bankrolling this whole thing."

"But they wouldn't need Soti. Canon's a billionaire."

"Only on paper," Mackenzie said. "And that paper is Journy stock. If Journy's circling the drain, then Canon isn't rich at all. Far from it. And all this shit is expensive."

"True," Danner said. "It's a good theory."

Mackenzie pointed at the camera above the fire door. "If this is a local network, insulated from the outside, then where would the footage go?"

Danner nodded toward the bank of standing desks, computers humming underneath. "Probably one of those."

He and Mackenzie marched to the standing desks. Cassiopeia remained supine on the sofa, lost in her phone.

Mackenzie examined the desks. When they'd entered the warehouse, all five had appeared identical. But now Mackenzie noticed small differences. The desk in the center had a webcam attached to its monitor. And the desk on the right . . .

Danner saw it at the same time. "On the right. There's no computer."

Mackenzie nodded. They could see a clear outline of dust where the computer used to sit. A disconnected power cord lay on the floor behind.

"After someone busted in here," she said, "Canon and Yoo must've realized the space wasn't secure. So they took everything on these computers and dumped it all onto one. Then they left with it."

"Put everything important on one computer and then took off."

"Explains why the fire door wasn't fixed. Why everything is dusty." Mackenzie pointed at the other four computers, their power lights still glowing green. "Why the other computers are still on. Why the servers are still active. They packed up and left in a hurry."

Mackenzie stared at the center monitor, eyeing the webcam atop its frame. She stepped to the keyboard on its desk and pressed the space bar. The monitor resurrected from its hibernation.

"What are you doing?" Danner asked.

"This one has the webcam. They must have used it to talk to someone remote, via videoconference."

"You want to see who they were talking to. See if your theory's right."

"If they had an investor, they'd need to show updates."

Danner stepped to her shoulder. The monitor lit up with the desktop background, a span of dark gray with four small letters tucked into the top right corner: M1ND. The letters were neon green DOS font, like they'd been imported from *The Matrix*.

A pop-up in the center of the screen demanded a password. Mackenzie's fingers floated above the keyboard.

"Any ideas?" Danner asked.

"I always try this one first." She typed *password* in all lowercase letters, hit return.

The monitor beeped in rejection. The pop-up blared at them:

INCORRECT PASSWORD: ATTEMPT 1 OF 3

"What does a guy like Canon use for a password?" Danner said. "No clu—"

"It's seventeen." Cassiopeia's voice echoed in the warehouse. "Trevor's password for everything is seventeen."

Mackenzie twisted toward her. "Seventeen?"

Cassiopeia remained horizontal on the sofa, eyes adhered to her phone. "The number—spelled out."

"Why?" Mackenzie said.

"I don't know," Cassiopeia said.

Mackenzie turned back to the monitor and typed the keys, careful with her fingers. Danner watched over her shoulder. Mackenzie hit return.

The pop-up disappeared.

"We're in," she said.

She opened the Finder and began exploring the hard drive. "Everything's empty," she said. "It's been wiped. Not many applications left. Except for this one."

Mackenzie clicked on an icon for something called Encrypto-Call, a red-and-black logo with a video camera symbol. The app opened to reveal a simple, unsophisticated interface. There was a black window with few options: Direct Call, Conference, and Settings.

"Videoconferencing?" Danner asked.

Mackenzie nodded. "They wouldn't use an app like SpyderChat if they were working on something sensitive."

"Why didn't they delete it?"

Mackenzie shrugged. "Maybe you're right, they were in a hurry."

"Check the call history."

Mackenzie clicked on Direct Call. There was a column labeled History, but it was empty. "Not that easy," she said.

Mackenzie poked around the app, checking the top menus until she found something called Address Book. Like the call history, it was an empty column—nothing there. Then she went to Encrypto-Call's general preferences and saw a section for Address Book. There were just a few menu options, but one stuck out: a small button that read RESTORE CONTACTS.

She clicked on it and a pop-up appeared. RESTORE CONTACTS FROM LAST SAVE?

"Good thinking," Danner said.

"Worth a shot," Mackenzie replied. She clicked YES.

A second later, the Address Book refreshed. The column was no longer empty. A single name beamed out from the monitor in stark, black letters:

INDIRA SOTI

CHAPTER 25

Twenty-six days after Trevor Canon's death

"We're getting closer," Mackenzie said.

"Yes," Danner agreed. "But we've still got problems."

They idled on a Potrero Hill curb. Danner had his phone out, typing furiously. Cassiopeia had remained silent, expression glum, until they dropped her off.

"Look at everything we just learned," said Mackenzie. "We know Trevor was paranoid because he was working on the autonomous vehicles project with Stanley Yoo. We know he and Stanley were both disappearing to the warehouse in Bayview. We know Indira Soti was likely bankrolling them. We know someone found out about it and confronted them—violently."

"Yes, but we still have our original problem." Danner yawned, his eyes still red. "Five execs. Four good alibis."

"You found the gas station?"

Danner nodded. "Moreau's Mini Cooper was at a Shell station near SFO at eleven-twenty the night Canon was killed. She's on security tapes, clear as a bell."

"That rules her out."

"Yes."

"And we're positive about the time of death?"

"Rock solid."

Mackenzie paused. "Still no trace of Stanley Yoo?"

Danner shook his head. "Nothing." A grudging admiration crept into his voice. "Disappearing is much harder than people think. They underestimate the logistical difficulties, their inevitable digital trail. But Yoo's done it."

"Everybody says he's brilliant."

"Appears so," Danner said. "Gone for days, tons of resources dedicated to finding him, and we've got nothing."

Mackenzie fell silent. She thought about the warehouse, the blood in the sink, the autonomous Prius covered with more sensors than a heart transplant. Something wasn't adding up, but she couldn't articulate what.

"Have you heard anything from your boss?" Danner asked.

With a twinge of surprise, Mackenzie realized she hadn't. She'd texted Hammersmith a long update on the return from Bayview, but, like her update from the previous night, it had gone unanswered. "No," she said.

"Is that unusual?"

"Yeah. He's always busy, though." As Mackenzie said it, she knew it wasn't true. Hammersmith had castigated Mackenzie and Danner about finding Stanley Yoo. And now, even after the discovery of the warehouse, he was radio silent.

"Now we know why Canon changed his will," Danner said. "If the change came right after an attack at the warehouse, that would mean the attack happened . . . eight or nine days before he died. That would mean they fled the warehouse a month ago."

"It fits," Mackenzie said. "Fits with the dried blood, with the dust. We have a timeline. We're getting closer."

"In that respect, yes." Danner prepared to shift the car out of park. "We need to talk to Indira Soti."

"Where are we going?" Mackenzie asked.

"His office."

"Indira Soti doesn't have an office."

Danner stopped, one hand still on the gear shift. "What?"

"Soti doesn't have an office," Mackenzie repeated. "His firm is small. Just him and a handful of associates."

"Where does he work?"

Mackenzie shrugged. "Nowhere. Everywhere. Expensive restaurants. The offices of his portfolio companies."

"Where does he meet with founders?"

"He goes to them. Or he has them to his house."

"So let's go to his house. The office can track down his address."

"Won't work," Mackenzie said. "I've heard Soti has a dozen different houses around the country. No idea which one he's at."

Danner sighed. He opened his phone and hit a button. A ringtone echoed through the sedan's cabin.

"Who are you calling?"

"Eden," Danner said. "We need reinforcements."

Eleanor Eden answered on the second ring. "Agent Danner. And, I'm assuming, Mackenzie as well?"

"Both of us," Danner confirmed. "I need a minute."

"Of course."

Danner gave Eleanor an overview of the warehouse. He left out the violent details—including the busted door and the blood in the bathroom—but included everything else.

"Trevor and Stanley were working on AVs together?" Eleanor's surprise was clear. "And they were being backed by Indira Soti?"

"That's our working hypothesis," Danner said.

"But that's . . ." Eleanor fell quiet. "Why would they do that?"

Danner glanced at Mackenzie. "We're not sure yet. But we're pretty confident."

"Trevor was always big on driverless cars," Eleanor said. "He was obsessed with it, almost. But we'd invested a ton in it at Journy. We were making progress."

"I can't speak to Canon's motivations," Danner said. "But I know that we need to talk to Indira Soti. Do you know where to find him?"

"I'm afraid I don't," Eleanor said. "I've heard he takes meetings at one of his homes, but I don't know where they are. I'm sure the FBI could find them."

"Yes," Danner said, "but we don't have time to check them one by one. We need to speak to him as soon as possible."

"I'm sorry," Eleanor said. "I'd help if I could."

Danner's shoulders drooped in his seat. "You don't know anywhere we can find him?"

"I know he goes to the Battery. But other than that—" Eleanor stopped. "Actually, wait. I have an idea."

The sound of Eleanor typing echoed in the sedan. "Indira's a minority owner of the Warriors," she said.

Mackenzie straightened in her seat. "That's right."

Danner frowned. "As in the basketball team?"

"Yes," Eleanor answered. "They have an exhibition game tonight. Here in town."

"He'll be there," Mackenzie said. "That's it."

"Why?" Danner said.

Mackenzie looked at him. "Courtside at a Warriors game is like a Met Gala for tech people," she said. "VCs, founders, executives, they all jockey for the best seats."

"Why do they care?" Danner said.

"Why do they care about anything?" Mackenzie said. "Status. Courtside tickets are insanely expensive. You're on TV during the games. The Warriors are trendy. See and be seen."

"Tonight's the first game of the year," Eleanor said. "I'm sure he'll be there."

"Worth trying," Danner said.

"How do we get in?" Mackenzie asked. "To get to Soti we'll need to be on the court."

"Journy keeps a pair of courtside seats," Eleanor said. "I'll get the tickets to you this afternoon."

"That works," Danner said. He paused. "Another thing: The warehouse was rented to a group called Circus Sagittarius. Does that mean anything to you?"

"Sagittarius?" Eleanor asked. "Like the astrological sign?"

"Yes."

"Can't say that it does," Eleanor said. "But I'll think on it."

"Please do," Danner said. "One last question. We've been told that

Journy is actually doing much worse than public perception. That it's in financial peril."

An earthy chuckle came from the speakers. "I can guess who told you that," Eleanor said. "Hugo."

"How did you know?"

"Hugo's a fatalist. He was always pessimistic about everything. Since his first day on the job, he's had one foot out the door."

Now it's two feet, Mackenzie thought.

"Hugo thought that his autonomous vehicles work was the only important thing happening at Journy. When Trevor scrapped some of it, Hugo was incensed."

"So is Chamberlain wrong?" Danner said. "About the company's finances?"

Eleanor sighed, her voice dripping with its familiar bone-deep exhaustion.

"It's complicated," Eleanor said. "Has growth slowed? Yes. Have we been as judicious with capital as I'd have liked? No. But there are still millions of people using Journy every day. We still have excellent revenue numbers. And we have options."

A hint of defiance rose in Eleanor's voice. "Journy was never headed light speed toward world domination. That was Trevor's rhetoric, and I always tried to hew him closer to reality. That's always been my job, Agent Danner. Ignore the hype and navigate us forward. Help us mature. Take care of the thousands of people that work for us. That's still my job, now that Trevor's gone. And with your help I intend to finish it, despite the doomsday predictions of Hugo Chamberlain."

CHAPTER 26

Twenty-six days after Trevor Canon's death

The Warriors arena was a gleaming hunk of glass and steel. It was airy, modern, and choked with a prosperous sterility that evoked the feeling of an under-visited museum.

Mackenzie and Danner sat in courtside seats, metal folding chairs gussied up with foam covered in blue leather. Unflattering arena lights blared from overhead. Upbeat pop music blasted from the speakers. A jumbotron the size of a mega yacht ran a highlight reel. The whole place was a flash-bang of noise and color. Danner typed urgently on his phone, head down.

The Warriors players warmed up nearby, relaxed and jovial. A current of nostalgia swept into Mackenzie, her memory taking her back to the small Nevada gyms of high school.

"No sign of Soti yet," Danner said.

Mackenzie watched as a stream of the tech industry's wealthiest filed in through the VIP entrance. Rich white people of every size and shape seeped across the edges of the court. Mackenzie saw pimply-faced crypto bros, well-heeled senior VCs, dressed-down angel investors. She saw product designers in short suits, influencers in puddle pants and wide-brimmed hats. It was a parade of expensive labels and exposed ankles. Outside of Danner and the players on the court, Mackenzie couldn't find a single man who appeared to be wearing socks.

Mackenzie spotted the Warriors' majority owner across the way, a hedge fund barracuda who'd been one of the original partners at Obsidian Investments. A thought of her mother drifted into Mackenzie's mind, but she pushed it away.

"You're sure Soti's coming?" Danner said.

"He'll be here," Mackenzie said.

Indira Soti arrived just before tip-off. Mackenzie pointed him out to Danner as he strode out of the VIP tunnel. Soti wore an oversized Off-White hoodie, black joggers, and bright red vintage Nikes. He was tall, Indian American, and flanked by two men Mackenzie didn't recognize, each dressed in a black T-shirt and jeans.

"Who's he with?" she asked.

"Security," Danner said.

Soti and his companions made a halting journey toward the court, stopping every few feet for a handshake or fist bump. Soti's face was lit with a perma-smile, posture comfortable and open. He was a man returned to his domain, reveling in the eyes that followed his slow procession toward center court. His skin was clear, eyes dark and shiny, hair carefully styled. His laugh revealed a set of celebrity teeth, whiter than the ice caps. Soti wasn't an attractive man, but he was popular, stylish, and obscenely rich. It was easy to see why Hammersmith hated him.

And then, like that, Soti was gone.

Soti didn't take a courtside seat. As the game started he simply left the court, retreating back through the VIP entrance.

"Where's he going?" Danner asked.

"Maybe he forgot something," said Mackenzie. "I'm sure he'll be back."

The game began. Mackenzie and Danner watched for Soti to re-emerge, but there was no sign. The minutes ticked by.

"We should go look for him," Danner said.

"Just wait a minute," said Mackenzie. "At least till the first time-out."

One of Soti's security men emerged from the VIP tunnel. The game broke for free throws, and the man shimmied along the sideline. He came to a stop before Mackenzie and Danner, kneeling on the court.

"Agent Danner, Miss Clyde," the man said. "Good evening."

Mackenzie realized that Indira Soti's security had identified them long before Soti had ever considered taking his seat.

"Indira would like to invite you up to his suite on the club level. He says there's something the three of you need to discuss."

Danner didn't hesitate. "Let's go."

The man smiled and stood. "Follow me."

They moved back through the VIP tunnel, up an elevator, and down a carpeted hallway. Mackenzie spied the man's counterpart standing on one side of the hallway, quiet in his matching outfit. An attendant greeted them at a door on the opposite side.

"Agent Danner, Miss Clyde," the attendant said. "Good evening. Would you care for any refreshments?"

"We're good," Danner said.

The attendant pressed his hands together in a slight bow. "Very well. Please be welcome. Indira is waiting for you inside."

The door opened automatically. The security detail waited in the hallway as Mackenzie and Danner entered, door closing behind them.

Indira Soti's club suite was of a piece with the rest of the Chase Center. Gray marble, light wood, dull furniture, banal art. Every other wall held a flat screen tuned to the game. A sleek kitchen lay opposite a long beige sectional. A marble-topped island rested between them, counter height.

Indira Soti waited on the far end of the sectional. He looked up as they entered, expression unreadable, legs crossed, arms spread wide across the back of the leather.

"Make yourselves comfortable," Soti said. "Did Gerald offer you something to drink?"

"We're good," Danner repeated. He remained standing, leaning against the island, while Mackenzie took a seat on the near end of the sofa, facing Soti.

Mackenzie was momentarily struck by the oddity of sharing a private audience with Indira Soti. She imagined it was the last thing Hammersmith had in mind when he assigned her to liaise on the investigation. Thinking of Hammersmith made her quickly check her texts—still nothing from him.

Soti looked between Danner and Mackenzie. "Agent Danner, Miss Clyde. I assume we're all familiar with each other, so let's skip introductions. Instead, why don't you just tell me what you know."

"Hold on," Danner said, irritated. "First, how did you know we were here?"

Soti flashed a catlike smile. "I'm one of the owners of the arena, Agent Danner. I was notified the moment you entered."

Mackenzie interjected. "But how did they know to look for *us*? How did you even know who we were?"

"The warehouse cameras," Soti said. "The system notified me there'd been motion. Imagine my surprise when I saw Agent Danner prowling across the floor, gun drawn."

"So you *are* connected to the warehouse," Mackenzie said.

"Of course I am," Soti replied. "But we'll get to that." He looked back toward Danner. "First: Tell me what you know."

"That's not how this works," Danner said.

Soti's expression was even more rigid than Danner's. "I'm not interested in a pissing contest, Agent Danner. I know who you are. I know what you're investigating. Tell me what you know, and then I'll answer your questions."

"All our questions?"

"You found the warehouse. Clearly I've decided that it's worth my time to have a conversation. So let's not waste it."

Mackenzie watched Danner calculate, deciding how much to divulge. Tell him everything, she thought.

Danner did. "We know that Trevor Canon has been working on a secret project with Stanley Yoo at the warehouse. It was extremely high stakes, and Canon became deeply paranoid once it began. He spent virtually no time at home or Journy headquarters because he was devoted to the warehouse project. Stanley Yoo moved out of his loft and was living full-time at the warehouse. We know that you were bankrolling it—"

Soti interjected. "How did you discover that?"

"Brady Fitzgerald saw you and Canon in Big Sur, just a few weeks before Canon was killed."

"That doesn't prove anything."

"We also found your name," Mackenzie said. "On one of the computers in the warehouse."

Soti looked at her. "They wiped those."

"I restored the last save of the address book in the videoconferencing system," Mackenzie replied. "Yours was the only name in it."

Soti pursed his lips, nodding to Danner. "Continue."

"Roughly ten days before Canon was killed, someone busted into the warehouse and violently confronted him and Yoo. We know that it got bloody. Afterward, Canon and Yoo packed up everything important and fled. A day or two later, Canon changed his will and restricted access to his office. A week after that, he was killed."

"And Stanley Yoo?"

"Yoo told Journy staff he was going on vacation. Hasn't been seen since."

"You don't know where he is?"

Danner hesitated. "No."

Soti settled into the beige leather of the sectional, dark eyes traversing between Danner and Mackenzie.

"So you've found the warehouse. But do you understand what's in it?"

Danner frowned. "You saw us walk through it."

"Yes." Soti nodded impatiently. "But do you understand what the warehouse was *for*?"

"M1ND is the name of the project," Mackenzie answered, pronouncing it *mind*. "It's what Trevor and Stanley were working on."

Soti's eyes challenged Mackenzie. His voice was smooth, professorial—it reminded her of Georgetown. "But what is it, *exactly*, that you think M1ND is?"

"Autonomous vehicles," Danner said.

"No," Mackenzie said. Danner glanced over at her, expression quizzical.

Mackenzie paused. Soti's questions were a test. But Mackenzie knew the answers.

"That's what it looked like," Mackenzie said to Soti. "There was the Prius. And at Journy, driverless cars had been one of Trevor's obsessions. But I don't think that's what M1ND actually is."

Soti's eyes glimmered with intrigue. "Why not?"

"One, M1ND is a terrible name for driverless cars. Trevor cares about names. He plastered Journy's branding everywhere. He even loved the slogan: 'It's not the destination—it's the Journy.' He'd never give AVs a name as bad as M1ND."

Soti remained still. "And two?"

"The Prius is still there," Mackenzie said. "It's not secure. Trevor and Stanley wiped the computers, took all their data. But they left the Prius. If the tech on it was really their focus, there's no way they would've left it behind. And there's no way *you* would've let them."

Soti stared up at the ceiling for several seconds, saying nothing.

"Everything we discuss from here on out cannot leave this room," Soti said finally, eyes still facing upward.

"I can't promise that," Danner said. "If there's information directly related to who murdered Canon, I have to share it with my colleagues."

"Obviously." Soti waved a hand, dropping his gaze to Danner. "But I'm going to disclose some extremely sensitive information about a technological innovation. I have to trust that the details of it stay in this room."

"All I care about," Danner said, "is finding Canon's killer. Any technical details will stay with us."

Soti nodded, then looked past Danner. He pointed at a TV above the bar. "I assume that you're both familiar with Steph."

Danner and Mackenzie glanced at the TV. Stephen Curry, the Warriors' superstar point guard, was dribbling up the court.

"The job of a venture capitalist," Soti said, "is deceptively simple: Identify the outlier. Our systems, whether they be business or basketball, are designed to produce predictability. They're built on rules and norms that govern behavior. Everyone plays by the rules, everyone knows what to expect."

Soti continued, still watching the screen. "Occasionally, someone comes along who can operate outside that system. They can subvert the rules, the weight of expectations, and do things in a manner that nobody would've imagined. They are the outliers."

On the screen Curry now stood near center court, several feet behind the three-point line.

"Steph is an outlier. He has a rare ability: He can shoot from long distance with such proficiency that it challenged the fundamental expectations of how basketball should be played. For years, conventional wisdom was clear: The closer to the hoop a player was, the better. But Steph changed that equation."

As if on cue, Curry stepped back from his defender and launched a shot. The hoop didn't even appear on the screen when the ball left his hand. It arced high through the air, soaring above the court, and then splashed through the net with a perfect *swish*.

"Steph altered the underlying math that drives the systems of basketball. He's such an outlier that he literally changed the way the game is played."

Soti dropped his eyes from the screen. "Trevor Canon was like Steph—an outlier. He was a brilliant entrepreneur. Relentless, creative, audacious. His ability to think freely and openly was unparalleled. He had a true growth mindset—he saw the world not for what it was, but what it could be."

Mackenzie hid a smirk. It was much simpler, she thought, to see the world for "what it could be" if you never had to actually experience the world as it was. It's a lot easier to be a visionary when you're at the top of a skyscraper than when you're battling for elbow room on the street.

"I recognized Trevor's outlier brilliance in the earliest days of Journy. When I missed out on the opportunity to invest, I was deeply disappointed." One of Soti's Nikes bobbed above his knee, the red nylon unnervingly clean. "So when Trevor came to me with a new project, you can imagine my excitement."

"What was the project?" Mackenzie asked.

"You're correct that Trevor was working with Stan Yoo. They'd scrapped the autonomous vehicles initiative within Journy. Trevor decided to take the project external. Just him and Stan. And they were using a new approach.

"For many years, work on autonomous vehicles has followed a similar path. Most people start with the car's hardware. Lidar, sensors, navigation, more."

"Like a robot," Mackenzie said, thinking of Hugo Chamberlain's description.

"Robots on wheels," Soti said. "That's how the layman thinks of autonomous vehicles. But the hardware is the easy part. Plenty of people have built cars that can drive themselves on predetermined routes." He paused. "The real challenge is training the car to operate in the *human* environment. To adapt to its surroundings. The soft skills of driving. Gauging whether the pedestrian lingering at the corner actually intends to enter the crosswalk. Anticipating when another driver is going to change lanes—before they use their blinker. To read, react. Drive as a human would.

"This is the path that AV has always taken. To grossly oversimplify: First, you create the car. Then, you teach the car to drive like a human."

Danner listened from the island. "What does that have to do with Canon?"

Indira Soti smiled, teeth incandescent in the mood lighting of the suite. "Trevor's genius," Soti said, "was flipping the calculation on its head. Forget the vehicle. Rather than build a car and teach it how to drive like a human, Trevor endeavored to do the opposite. He would build a human, and then teach it how to drive a car."

A thick curtain of silence fell over the suite, Mackenzie and Danner digesting the implications of Soti's illustration.

"Trevor was working on artificial intelligence," Mackenzie said. Soti nodded.

"That's what M1ND is," Mackenzie said. "Trevor wasn't working on autonomous vehicles. He was working on AI."

"Not just working on it," Soti said. "He'd done it. He and Stanley Yoo built an artificial intelligence. That's why Trevor was killed."

CHAPTER 27

Twenty-six days after Trevor Canon's death

For a few moments, nobody spoke.

"Canon was creating an 'artificial intelligence,'" Danner said finally. "So what?"

Soti blinked at him. "I'm not sure I understand."

"AI isn't anything new." Danner held up his phone. "I ask my house to play jazz, Alexa makes me a playlist. I ask my phone how to make spaghetti carbonara, Siri gives me a shopping list. On Spyder I can have a full conversation with a chatbot. AI's everywhere. So what if Canon was building another one?"

"The fact that you would even make those comparisons, Agent Danner, indicates your limited understanding of the topic." Soti sniffed, his tone indignant. "I'm not talking about parlor tricks. I'm talking about *real* intelligence. Innovation on the scale of the wheel, or fire. It will change the essence of what it means to be human."

Danner frowned; Mackenzie sensed his frustration growing. "Stop condescending and answer my question. If you're saying that

Canon was killed for his AI, then you need to explain what it is that Canon and Yoo actually *built*."

Soti sighed, recrossing his legs. "Yes, Agent Danner, M1ND can help you make *pasta*." Soti spat the word. "Yes, it can converse—far beyond the Wikipedia regurgitations that Spyder is offering. But chatbots and digital assistants are the most simplistic expression of artificial intelligence. Trevor and Stanley have built the first AI with the capability to move *beyond* that, into far more powerful applications."

"Like what?"

"Name an industry, Agent Danner. Let's take medicine." Soti folded his hands on a knee. "Current AIs are the equivalent of talking to a doctor at a cocktail party."

Mackenzie sensed this wasn't the first time Soti had discussed the practical applications of M1ND. There was something unnerving about it, like watching a child exploring a dangerous new toy.

Soti continued. "They can spout reams of complex medical knowledge: the strange history of a rare disease, the ethical debates over a new pharmaceutical. They are information repositories that cobble data into coherent, humanlike expressions. But that is where they stop. They cannot take their information and *apply* it directly to the world around us. There's a significant difference between a doctor chatting idly at a cocktail party and that same doctor diagnosing a cancer patient in their office."

Mackenzie interjected. "And you're saying that's what M1ND can do? It can diagnose a patient?"

"Yes," Soti said simply.

"How?" Danner asked.

"M1ND replicates the doctor's actions, but better. It studies a patient's individual biology, their imaging, their data, the context of their lifestyle, their reported symptoms, and—in the span of a microsecond—analyzes *all* of it against millions of other patients that have come before. Then it makes a diagnosis. Faster, and more accurately, than any human doctor is capable of."

"It can do this *now*?" Mackenzie asked.

Soti nodded. "It has the capability now; it simply needs the data.

This isn't a theoretical application. And it applies equally to other industries. M1ND will buy and sell securities, argue legal cases, write code. And once it learns from those experiences, it will do even more. Eventually, M1ND could be trained to do almost anything a human does. It could develop cutting-edge science, make new breakthroughs. It could create art, play music, write novels. It could negotiate peace settlements."

"Or fight wars," Mackenzie said.

"Or fight wars," Soti agreed, nodding. He stared at Danner, dark eyes blazing, voice growing heavy. "Agent Danner, this would be a technological breakthrough that has no comparison. A discovery worth killing for."

Danner's eyes darted to Mackenzie. "You agree with all this?"

"I do," Mackenzie said.

"It's not bullshit?"

"No," she said. "If it's true . . ." Mackenzie shrugged. "It could be the biggest thing to ever come out of Silicon Valley."

Danner folded his arms. "Eden said there are no original ideas in the tech industry. If this is such a big deal, how come Canon and Yoo were the only ones working on it?"

"They weren't," Soti said.

"Tons of people are working on it," Mackenzie added. "Like you said, AI isn't necessarily new. But taking it to the next step, like he's describing"—Mackenzie gestured at Soti—"that's a huge challenge. Nobody's been able to make much progress yet."

Danner's eyes moved back to Soti. "You're saying Canon and Yoo cracked it?"

Soti hesitated. "They're not all the way there," he said. "But Stanley Yoo's been working on M1ND for years, secretly, outside his work on Journy. He and Trevor have come much, much further than anyone else. M1ND has a foundation of intelligence that's simply never been seen before."

"Fine," Danner said. "Let's say M1ND is a huge innovation, the biggest technology ever. Where is it?"

Soti blinked at him. "What do you mean?"

"I mean physically. Where is it right now?"

"I don't know," Soti said.

Danner was incredulous. "You don't *know?*"

"No," Soti said. "For security purposes, Stanley distributed their work across a range of servers and locations. There's a key to unlocking it, compiling it all together. And that key was on a computer in the warehouse."

"The computer that Yoo and Canon took with them," Mackenzie said.

"Yes."

"So where'd they take it?" Danner asked.

"I don't know," Soti said.

"They didn't tell you?"

"Stan took it, but I don't know where."

Danner didn't hide his skepticism. "And you were okay with that?"

"I didn't have much choice. Everything happened very fast, Agent Danner."

"You're bankrolling a piece of technology that is literally going to 'change humanity,' and you don't know where it is? I find that hard to believe."

"I don't care if you believe me." Soti sniffed. "We scrambled to get them out of the warehouse as fast as possible. A week later Trevor was killed, and everything went to hell. Then Stan disappeared."

"So you don't know where Yoo is, either," Mackenzie said.

Soti shook his head. "Not for lack of trying." He gestured toward the exit, where his security waited in the hall. "I employ a dozen security people, all of whom served in the highest levels of intelligence and defense. As good as they come. They've been searching for Stan for days."

"Yoo is wanted for questioning by the FBI," Danner said. "*We're* looking for him."

Soti shrugged. "So?"

"So," Danner said, tone growing hostile, "I don't want a bunch of amateur mercenaries getting in my way. What if one of your guys spooked Yoo and sent him deeper into hiding?"

"They wouldn't make such an obvious mistake."

Danner scoffed. "Maybe they're not as good as you think they are. They haven't found Yoo."

"Neither have you," Soti said sharply. "All the resources of the FBI to bear, and it's been half a week with nothing to show for it. Tell me again, Agent Danner: Who are the amateurs?"

Danner locked his jaw, saying nothing.

"Don't underestimate Stanley Yoo," Soti continued. "I've been in this industry since I was a teenager. Stan's the most brilliant technical mind I've seen. When he and Trevor joined forces, they were unstoppable."

"Earlier you said Trevor came to you with the idea for M1ND," Mackenzie said. "But you also said Yoo had been working on it for years."

"That's right," Soti said, shifting his gaze to Mackenzie.

"Why wouldn't Yoo have come to you before then? On his own?"

"Stan is happiest when he's alone behind a keyboard. He has no understanding of how to channel his brilliance into commerce. Trevor does—did, rather."

Mackenzie continued. "Do you think there's any chance that Trevor and Stanley had a falling-out?"

"Impossible. They were like brothers."

"Brothers fight," Mackenzie said, thinking of Brady Fitzgerald. "Sometimes worse."

Soti shook his head. "Didn't happen."

"So Trevor came to you with M1ND," Mackenzie said. "But why?"

"Why what?"

"Trevor had a close relationship with Hammersmith," Mackenzie continued. "If Trevor wanted someone to bankroll his work on M1ND, why would he go to you instead?"

Soti raised his eyebrows, eyes twinkling with amusement. He glanced toward Danner, head tilting. "Isn't that obvious?"

"Isn't what obvious?" Mackenzie said.

Before Soti could continue, Danner changed the subject. "So why did Canon and Yoo leave the warehouse?"

"You already put that together," Soti said. "There was a break-in. It got violent. The warehouse was no longer secure. Obviously, Trevor and Stan had to leave."

"When did they tell you about the break-in?"

"They didn't have to tell me," Soti said. "I watched it happen just after the fact, on the security feed."

Mackenzie leaned forward. "It was your idea to put those cameras in the warehouse. The same ones that saw us this morning."

Soti nodded. "Trevor wasn't happy, but I insisted. Obviously I'm glad I did."

"If you put the cameras in," Danner said, "where did you send the footage?"

"The cloud," Soti said. "It was the only data that left that warehouse."

"Can you access it from your phone?"

"Of course."

"Show us the break-in," Danner said.

Soti opened his mouth then closed it. "Okay."

Soti stood and moved to the island, swiping his iPhone and placing it on the marble surface. Danner and Mackenzie huddled over it, staring at the screen. It was a still image of the inside of the warehouse. Perfect clarity, full color. The angle was from above the now-busted fire door.

Soti hit play and the footage rolled. A small time stamp showed the hour as 21:09.

Trevor Canon stood at one of the standing desks. He stared intently at a monitor. He was typing, but otherwise still. Next to the standing desks sat the row of whiteboards, covered with scrawled writing. Mackenzie spied M1ND in big letters on the rightmost. Stanley Yoo reclined on the sofa, some twenty feet away.

Mackenzie felt strange seeing the two of them, like she was glimpsing echoes of the past. The murdered entrepreneur and his missing partner. Ghosts captured in the machine.

For several seconds nothing happened. Trevor typed furiously, his wiry frame dressed in a black T-shirt and black pants. Stanley scrolled his phone, long hair splayed out to either side of his face. The time stamp ticked forward.

Then Stanley reared up on the sofa, head snapping toward the camera. He was focused on the fire door, just below their vantage point. Now Mackenzie heard a tinny *thump* echo from the iPhone speaker. Then Stanley yelled something, turning toward Trevor.

"The sound quality is embarrassing," Soti said. "The cameras have terrible mics."

Trevor swiveled toward the fire door, just as Stanley had. Stanley stood from the sofa, phone still in hand. Both men were clearly alarmed at what they heard or saw.

Another tinny *thump*, then a crash of motion from the bottom of the picture. Mackenzie realized it was the fire door swinging open, the wood barely hanging from its hinges. A man strode through the wreckage and entered the frame.

Mackenzie felt a rush of heat in her chest as the man came into view. For a moment her vision flashed red, as though a filter had been snapped over her eyes. Her limbs stiffened.

The man was huge. He looked as tall as Mackenzie, and was built like a linebacker, with broad shoulders, long arms, and a thick, squatty neck. A black Dri-Fit tee accentuated his physique. The camera angle didn't reveal the man's face, but his hair was short, buzzed into a military cut.

Mackenzie caught Danner glancing at her sideways. She realized she was holding her breath and forced herself to exhale.

"Who is that?" Mackenzie asked.

"Just wait," Soti replied.

The man stopped on the inner threshold of the warehouse, head twisting as he took in the scene. Trevor and Stanley stayed rooted to their spots, thirty feet away. The man began stalking toward Trevor with long, purposeful strides.

Stanley shouted something indistinct, pointing with anger while still holding his phone. The intruder bore a straight line for Trevor, but Stanley stepped into his path, blocking his way.

The man didn't stop. With a flash of motion, he pumped one of his enormous arms and punched Stanley square in the face.

The punch was a quick jab, with no windup. Still, Yoo looked as though he'd been struck by a grenade. His head snapped backward, body crumpling to the ground. His phone flew from his hand and skidded across the concrete floor.

The man didn't look down as he stepped over Stanley's body. He kept moving toward Trevor, who remained frozen by the standing desks.

Danner turned to Mackenzie, voice quiet. "The blood in the bath-room." Mackenzie nodded in agreement.

Stanley Yoo writhed on the warehouse floor, holding his face. The enormous man stalked toward Trevor and held out a meaty hand, one finger raised. He wagged the finger at Trevor, saying something. Trevor responded.

The man stopped just short of the standing desks. His body was faced away from the camera, at an angle. Trevor shrunk backward, shaking his head. The two of them stood only feet apart. The conversation was inaudible, but the body language was clear enough: Trevor and the man were arguing.

Now the man swept his hands outward, gesturing to the rest of the warehouse. Then he strode back to the form of Stanley Yoo.

Yoo had pulled himself up onto all fours. The man approached him and, without hesitation, swung a giant foot into Yoo's abdomen. Mackenzie winced as she watched the force of the collision. Yoo's body lifted into the air and then collapsed back to the polished con-crete.

Then the man reached for his waistband and withdrew a gun.

Trevor sprang away from the standing desks, hustling around the man and stepping between him and Yoo. Trevor raised both hands in front of his chest, shaking them in a clear gesture of capitulation. The man re-holstered his gun. They argued some more. Trevor was acqui-escing, in some way. Behind them, Stanley Yoo had rolled himself up from the ground. One hand on his face, the other on his stomach, he began limping toward the bathroom at the back of the warehouse.

The linebacker's body language calmed; he stood listening to Trevor. Then he shoved his finger into Trevor's chest, forcefully, and stalked back toward the busted fire door. Now the man's face finally came into focus. Soti paused the video, tapping at the screen, and the picture zoomed in. They had a clear view of the intruder.

He had graying hair, deep-set eyes, and features that would char-itably be described as rugged. His mouth was wide and curled into a resting frown. His nose was askew, his expression bellicose. Macken-zie guessed he was in his late forties.

His features were all hard edges, as though decades of confrontation had settled them into a mask of permanent aggression. He looked like an aging boxer, or a prison guard. Not the type of person you saw talking to tech founders in San Francisco.

"Who is he?" Mackenzie asked again.

Soti looked at Danner, as though expecting him to speak. But Danner kept his focus on the screen, saying nothing. Finally Soti looked back to Mackenzie. "His name is Vitaly Kovalev."

"How do you know?" Mackenzie asked.

"One of my portfolio companies builds facial recognition software. Homeland Security uses it. I ran the face through their systems."

Soti hesitated again, glancing at Danner. But now Danner was glued to his phone, typing rapidly.

"Kovalev is a Russian national," Soti continued. "Former KGB. Now he runs security for a consortium of Russian oligarchs."

"Oligarchs?" Mackenzie asked.

"Billionaires," Soti said. "Incredibly wealthy Russians who've made their money through dark methods. Exploiting natural assets, crooked deals with the government. Usually they mix in other activities, too. Arms trading. Financing terrorists. Drugs." Soti sniffed. "They're no different than thugs. Like a wealthier version of the mob."

"I know who the Russian oligarchs are," Mackenzie said. She pointed at the screen, the image of Kovalev's craggy jawline frozen in place. "What I meant is, why the hell did their head of security break into Trevor and Stanley's warehouse?"

Soti gazed back at her. An odd look came over his face. "I don't know."

"How do Russian oligarchs, or their security guys, possibly have anything to do with Trevor?" Mackenzie frowned. "How would someone like Kovalev be connected to all this?"

"That's a good question," Soti said. His voice was strange, almost patronizing. He turned and stared at Danner. "I've been wondering the same thing."

Danner ignored Soti, finishing something on his phone. He looked up briefly and pointed at the image of Kovalev. "I'll need a copy of that footage."

Soti paused, as though deliberating. "I'll send it over."

Danner's voice grew hostile. "Why didn't you share any of this with us earlier?"

Soti returned his gaze. "I'm sharing it now."

"You had Canon and Yoo working on a secret project in the warehouse. You knew this guy, Kovalev, broke into the warehouse and assaulted them. And you knew it happened just a week before Canon was murdered. You've known all of it for nearly a month."

"Yes," Soti said. "And?"

Danner's face fell, eyes darkening. "You didn't *tell* anyone. Even after Canon died, and Yoo disappeared, you didn't contact the FBI. Why?"

Soti's tone was pedantic. "Because it would've been a waste of time."

"A waste of time?" It was the most animated Mackenzie had seen Danner's face. "You've gotta be—"

"Let me finish," Soti said. He stood at one end of the island, leaning against the marble. "You act, Agent Danner, as though I'm not taking this seriously. The opposite is true. M1ND is revolutionary. It's worth billions. Trevor and Stanley had the keys to it. Now Trevor is dead, and Stanley is missing. I'm taking this *incredibly* seriously. I've put all my own resources to bear. My security team. The defense companies in my portfolio. My contacts—not just in defense agencies, but in the highest levels of government. People more important than even your father, Agent Danner."

Soti gave a wan smile. "If I want to find Stan, or find Trevor's killer, I know I'm going to have to do it myself. My resources are certainly going to go a hell of a lot further than anything scraped together by the FBI."

Soti leaned forward, his posture challenging. "From what I hear, Agent Danner, you've spent the past few days gallivanting around the Bay Area with Roger Hammersmith's lackey, asking questions about dead money and Journy stock." Soti's features dripped with condescension. "Like I said: a waste of time."

Soti grabbed his phone off the island, swiped, then dropped it where it was visible to all three of them. He'd panned back to the beginning of the warehouse footage. Trevor Canon stood at the monitor, Stanley Yoo reclined on the sofa.

"None of this has ever been about Journy. It's never been about Trevor's stock. It's never been about 'dead money.'"

Soti thrust a finger toward the screen. "*That's* what it's about. Trevor and Stanley's work. Their breakthroughs on artificial intelligence. Their creation of M1ND. That's why Trevor's dead."

CHAPTER 28

Six years before Trevor Canon's death

Fort Scott Field was tucked into the northwest corner of the Presidio, only a stone's throw from the Golden Gate Bridge. Today it hosted a packed agenda of youth soccer games. The fields were a kaleidoscope of noise and color and sound.

Mackenzie spotted Eleanor standing on a distant sideline. Most of the parents congregated together, near midfield, but Eleanor had chosen a private area nearer the corner.

The air was warm, an Indian summer pushing out the normal drapery of chilly fog. The sun was high and swollen, the afternoon glowing with a radiant shimmer that Mackenzie had always found unique to California. Eleanor wore jeans, sneakers, and a black T-shirt that read BUMBLEBEES MOM in yellow letters.

"Go Bumblebees," Eleanor said as Mackenzie arrived. Her hair was tied in a scraggly ponytail. She wore no makeup.

"Go Bumblebees," Mackenzie agreed.

Mackenzie stood at Eleanor's shoulder, facing the field. Two dozen six-year-old girls stormed across the grass in a wild pack of shrieks and kicks. Half the girls wore black and yellow stripes, the other half wore bright blue. Occasionally, a Bumblebee parent down the sideline would shout a word of encouragement ("Good kick, Olivia!") but Mackenzie didn't know how they made any sense of what they were watching.

Eleanor stared at the dusty horde, chuckling drily. "There's a ball in there somewhere."

Mackenzie laughed. "Where's Genevieve?"

Eleanor waved toward the pack. "In with the rest of them."

"Sorry I'm late," Mackenzie said.

Eleanor shrugged. "We've got plenty of time. How did you get here, by the way?"

"Rented a Zipcar."

Eleanor gave a small smile. "That'll change soon."

"Journy?" Eleanor nodded, still smiling. "You took the job," Mackenzie said.

"Yep."

"Trevor Canon finally persuaded you?"

"No," Eleanor said, still watching the field. "The numbers did."

"So it's going well?"

"Very well. Potentially very, *very* well. But we can come back to that." She turned her head, looking at Mackenzie. "What's going on with your mom?"

The shrieking pack had migrated to the opposite corner, moving in unison, like a rolling neon tumbleweed across the plains.

"She could go any day," Mackenzie said. She took a deep breath, willing away the familiar wave of rage and depression.

"She still won't let them give her any treatment?"

"Only stuff that eases the pain. Nothing that'll actually help."

"I'm sorry."

Mackenzie shrugged. "She's stubborn. Always has been."

Eleanor reached out, raising her arm to bridge the difference in height. She placed a hand on Mackenzie's shoulder. "It's not on you, Mackenzie. You know that, right?"

"I know." Mackenzie kept her focus on the field. If she looked at Eleanor square, Mackenzie knew she'd cry.

"You've done as much as you could. As much as anyone could. She's made up her mind."

"You're right."

"It's not about you," Eleanor said. "I know it feels that way because she's your mother. But as someone with daughters"—Eleanor nodded her head sideways, toward the field—"trust me when I say it's not. She knows she's going. She's decided how she does it."

"I know," Mackenzie repeated. She used the sleeve of her T-shirt to wipe her eyes. "Rationally, I know all that. But it doesn't make it any easier."

"No." Eleanor dropped her hand, eyes back on the field. "No, it doesn't."

They stood in silence, watching the maelstrom of peewee soccer.

"How is Hammersmith treating you?" Eleanor asked. "Still restless?"

"Three years," Mackenzie said, "and nothing to show for it."

Eleanor waited a few beats. "How's the firm itself doing?"

"The firm is doing great." Mackenzie sniffed. "*I'm* not getting any of the action, but we're doing very well."

"Lot of activity?"

"Over a hundred deals this year alone. We land every target. Every new founder is beating down our door."

"But you're not inside any of the deals."

Mackenzie shook her head. "No."

Eleanor paused. "I assume Roger was pleased about the *Blender* piece."

Blender had run a feature on Hammersmith Venture headlined "Silicon Valley's Once and Future King." The piece detailed Hammersmith's career, starting with his rise in the nineties, chronicling his fall into insolvency during the dot-com crash, and then finishing with his triumphant return to the pinnacle.

"I'm sure he loved it," Mackenzie said. "Everyone in the office was buzzing about it."

"People love a rags-to-riches story," Eleanor said. "Poorhouse to penthouse."

Mackenzie scoffed. "There was no poorhouse, in Roger's case."

Mackenzie flattened one hand above the other. "It was penthouse to one floor below the penthouse then back to the penthouse again."

Eleanor smiled. "True."

Down the sideline, the Bumblebee parents rose in volume as the pack neared the opposing goal.

"HV's done over a hundred deals this year?" Eleanor asked.

"That's right."

"Do you have any idea how Roger's financing them?"

Mackenzie frowned. "What do you mean?"

"Money's going out," Eleanor said. "Lots of it, for all those investments. But is it also coming in?"

"It has to be."

"From where? It's been a while since one of HV's portfolio companies had an IPO. Or any other cash out."

"I guess. But StoryBoard was just a couple years ago. And it was massive."

"True. But getting back into the penthouse takes a lot of capital, no matter what floor you start from. Could be worth looking into."

Mackenzie shrugged. "There's plenty of cash flow. The numbers on these deals are huge."

"I'm sure you're right." Eleanor shifted her stance. "However you slice it, sounds like Roger's the king of the Valley again."

Mackenzie nodded, voice wistful. "And I'm just a pawn, toiling away in the depths of his castle."

Eleanor smirked. "The trouble with being king," she said, "is that someone's always coming for your crown. Have you ever heard the name Indira Soti?"

"No."

"You will."

The pack of Bumblebees and Neon Blues had lodged itself on the precipice of the Blue goal. Suddenly, as though escaping a black hole, the ball ejected itself from the swarm and rolled into the net. Goal, Bumblebees.

The sideline exploded with cheers. Eleanor pumped a fist, shouting and clapping. "Great job, Genevieve!" she called.

Mackenzie joined the applause. "Was Gen the one who scored?"

Eleanor dropped her voice to normal level. "Nobody will ever know," she said. Mackenzie laughed.

The girls resumed their starting places. The referee blew her whistle, and the Neon Blues kicked off. Within ten seconds, the roving horde congregated anew.

"At HV," Eleanor said, "you feel unimportant. Stifled."

"Yes."

"Like you came out for the gold rush, but you're stuck on the riverbank."

"Exactly." Mackenzie nodded.

"Is it bad enough that you're thinking of making a change? Leaving the firm?"

"I think so."

"Leaving tech altogether?"

"I don't know. It just feels like everyone here is so . . ." Mackenzie sighed with exasperation. "So full of *shit*. There's no substance to anything. Like the emperor has no clothes—but the entire town is emperors."

Eleanor laughed. "What does your mom think?"

"She thinks I'm being impatient. Says I need to ride it out."

They fell into another comfortable silence. Eleanor was one of the few people Mackenzie had encountered who seemed to enjoy periods of quiet in a conversation.

"You know," Eleanor said, keeping her eyes on the field, "you've never told me what your mother is in for."

"Haven't I?" Mackenzie knew she hadn't.

"No. I've never pushed. But I'll admit to being curious."

"I'm sure you could Spyder it."

Eleanor nodded. "But I haven't."

"Why not?"

Eleanor looked over at her. "Because you're my friend. One of my only *real* friends, if I'm being honest. And I figured you'd tell me when you wanted to."

"Oh." Mackenzie returned Eleanor's gaze. "Thanks."

Eleanor moved her eyes back to the field. Mackenzie took a long breath. "I haven't told you because I never talk about it. With anyone. 'My mom's in federal prison.' It's embarrassing."

Eleanor's voice was dry. "That depends on what she did."

Mackenzie watched the game, letting the Indian summer soak into her skin. The heat was liquid, almost viscous. To the north, she spied the international orange of the Golden Gate peeking over the eucalyptus groves. Her vista was an unspooled palette of lush greens and impossibly bright blues. In that moment, Mackenzie felt very far away from Reno. She liked the feeling.

"She stole," Mackenzie said.

"She stole?" Eleanor was surprised. "But I thought she was an accountant—oh." Eleanor stopped. "I see it now."

"They dress it up: 'embezzlement and fraud.' But basically, she stole."

"Who'd she steal from?"

"She worked on the books for Obsidian Investments," Mackenzie said. "None of it was that complicated. My mom wasn't a criminal mastermind. She moved money out of accounts, then backfilled it with other money. Shaved a deposit here, rerouted a payment there. Small stuff. Methodical. Over a long period of time."

"How long?"

"Seven years."

Eleanor laughed. "Seven *years*? How'd they find out?"

"Drawback of financial crimes," Mackenzie said. "There's always a paper trail, even if nobody's willing to hunt for it. White-collar crime isn't any smarter than violent crime—it's just a hell of a lot more boring. There's no adrenaline, no crime scene, no weapons. Instead it's deposit certificates and transfer confirmations."

Eleanor gave her an appraising look. "I didn't realize you knew so much about this."

"I had a personal interest." Mackenzie paused. "My mom got unlucky. A big Obsidian client sued them, and discovery dug up old accounting documents. Lawsuit had nothing to do with her, but some old numbers didn't match up and Obsidian's lawyers started sniffing around. That was the beginning of the end."

"How much did she steal?"

Mackenzie hesitated. "A lot."

"Like what a lot?"

Mackenzie cleared her throat. "Three hundred and sixty-two thousand dollars," she said.

Eleanor's mouth dropped in surprise. She burst out laughing.

"Your mom stole three hundred and sixty-two thousand dollars from the stuffiest firm on the Street?"

Mackenzie nodded.

"I don't think that's embarrassing," Eleanor said. "Quite the opposite."

"I guess."

"I'm serious. It's impressive, actually."

Mackenzie's voice sharpened. "I don't think there's anything impressive about dying in prison."

Eleanor's smile faded. "Fair," she said, nodding. "But it's all relative."

Eleanor adjusted her hair, then folded one arm over the other. She watched her daughter fight among the scrum of happy six-year-olds.

"My mother was a drunk from Terre Haute, Indiana. Never left the state—not once, her entire life. Was rarely sober enough to take care of herself, let alone me. I left the millisecond I turned eighteen. I never went back."

Mackenzie waited a beat. "Did you stay in touch with her?"

"No." Eleanor's tone was flat, words clipped. "One of her junkie boyfriends decided to cook meth in her trailer. Blew the whole place up—my mother included." Eleanor exhaled. "I was twenty-four at the time."

"I'm sorry," Mackenzie said.

"The worst part is that I had no idea. I'd started a whole new life, rid myself of where I grew up. Washed Terre Haute off me like grime in a shower. I ignored anyone from home who tried to contact me. So I didn't find out my mother was dead until a full week after it happened. My aunt—the cop—had to track me down."

"That must've been horrible."

"It was." Eleanor kept her eyes on the game. "I've never told anyone that before."

"Thank you for telling me," Mackenzie said. "And I'm sorry for snapping."

"It's okay," Eleanor said. "All I'm trying to say is that with your mom . . ." Eleanor took a long breath. "There are worse ways to go. For both of you."

They watched the game, each alone with their thoughts.

"Does your mom regret what she did?" Eleanor asked.

Mackenzie shook her head. "The opposite, actually. Like you said."

"My type of woman." Eleanor paused. "I have to tell you, as far as Hammersmith Venture is concerned—"

"You agree with her," Mackenzie said.

Eleanor chuckled. "I'm that obvious?"

"No. But you're like her, in some ways. You think like her."

"I'll take that as a compliment."

"You should."

Eleanor smiled. "Thanks."

"Go ahead," Mackenzie said. "Tell me why I should stay."

"Three years ago, when you moved out west—why did you choose Hammersmith Venture?"

"Because it was the best."

"Has that changed?"

"No," Mackenzie admitted.

"If anything, Hammersmith Venture has only become *more* successful."

"True. But I'm not seeing any of that success."

"Not yet."

"It's been three years of standing on the riverbank, like you said."

"I hear you," Eleanor said. "But it's still the right river. Things are happening, starting to coalesce. Now that I'm at Journy, if you stay at HV, we can start to reinforce each other's interests."

Mackenzie looked at Eleanor. "What do you mean?"

"Journy's a rocket ship," Eleanor said. "The product's incredibly sticky. Growing like a weed. It's going to be huge. Huger than huge."

"The numbers are that good?"

"Better than I imagined," Eleanor said. "I was right about Spyder, wasn't I? When we first met?"

"Yes. It happened like you said it would. Faster, actually."

"Journy's numbers are even better. It's going to be a monster."

"You sure?" Mackenzie made a face. "I've heard a little about Trevor Canon. Hasn't been good."

Eleanor waved a dismissive hand. "I've dealt with plenty of Trevors before. And even if he's a dipshit, I can get Journy where it needs to go." She laughed. "I don't say that to be immodest. It's why Trevor hired me. I'm not just there to be the adult in the room. I'm going to run the company."

"What's Trevor going to be doing, then?"

Eleanor rolled her eyes. "All the nonsense that twenty-nine-year-old founders want to do. The Met Gala. TED Talks. Heli-skiing with Dick Branson. I don't really care. Journy's going to be massive. And it's just a matter of time until we raise another round of investment. A big round."

"Do you think you could steer it to Hammersmith?"

"I've already started." Eleanor glanced over at Mackenzie, expression serious. "If HV leads a huge investment into Journy, both of our positions get stronger. Much stronger. We start to coalesce."

"Reinforcing each other's interests."

Eleanor nodded. "Exactly."

"If HV gets stronger, that's great. But that doesn't necessarily strengthen *my* position."

"No," Eleanor agreed. "That, you'll have to do on your own." She paused. "It might be time to get a little aggressive."

"How so?"

"If you don't like your position, find a new one. Recast yourself."

"It's not that simple. I'm a lawyer. That's what I was hired to do."

"You think that stops other people?" Eleanor snickered. "Everyone in this business is faking it, Mackenzie. Every single one. The smart ones have created fully separate versions of themselves. Alternate personas."

Mackenzie returned her gaze. "What's yours?"

"This." Eleanor gestured to the field, where the Bumblebees struggled to organize for a corner kick. "Soccer mom. Minivan driver. PTA president." She made a fist and pumped her arm, like Rosie the

Riveter. "Bestselling author of a book about how women *can* have it all, if they just work hard enough."

"You're saying none of that's real?"

"Of course some of it's real. I love my family." Eleanor's expression grew wistful. "But I do hate that fucking minivan."

Mackenzie laughed, and Eleanor smiled, nodding toward the field. "But that's exactly my point. I've made the suburban ideal the center of my brand. You can call it family-oriented, but you can also call it nonthreatening. A people pleaser. Soft. Someone content to roll up their sleeves and drown themselves in the American dream."

"A means to an end," Mackenzie said. "Just like *A Seat at the Table.*"

"Exactly."

"That sounds exhausting. And a little . . ."

"What?"

"Misanthropic."

Eleanor shrugged. "That's the corporate world. Everything is about how you project yourself. Personally, I find it useful. My persona is like a diversion. It protects me while I work toward my real pursuits. Nobody in the industry knows about Terre Haute. Nobody knows the truth about my book. Nobody knows what I really think, what I'm really focused on. Nobody knows how high I'm really aiming." Eleanor glanced at Mackenzie. "Except you."

Eleanor turned her eyes back to the field. "You need your own persona," Eleanor said. "Figure out who you want to be, and make it into reality."

Mackenzie waited a moment. She turned back to the game and found the shrieking horde was no more. The pack had finally broken, dispersing across the field.

"Thank you," Mackenzie said finally.

"For what?"

"For trusting me with all this."

"You've earned it."

Mackenzie smiled at Eleanor. "And you're my friend, too," she said. "My *only* real friend, if I'm being honest."

Eleanor returned the smile. "Thanks."

"It's hard for me," Mackenzie said. "To see through all the bullshit and just . . . swallow it. I have a temper."

"I know," Eleanor said. "Remember how we met?"

Mackenzie laughed. "My instinct is always to just burn it down. Say 'fuck it,' and leave it all behind."

"I understand that impulse," Eleanor said. "When I look back at some of the things I've had to do, sometimes I feel disgusted. All the things I've said—and the things I *haven't* said to people like Tobias, or Trevor, who are just so goddamn drop-dead certain they're infused with the brilliance of the gods themselves. Sometimes I wish I'd just told everyone to fuck off and burned a trail to the sun." Eleanor paused. "But then I remember: It's all part of the game. And it's still a game that I intend to win."

Eleanor looked at Mackenzie, her eyes suddenly hard, features set. "That first time we met, you asked, 'Why me?' Why, out of all people, had I taken a sudden interest in you? Do you remember what I told you?"

"Because I could see through the bullshit."

Eleanor nodded. "But seeing through it is only the first step. After that comes the interesting part."

"What's that?"

"Learning to navigate it. Taking all the bullshit and turning it on its head so that you can use it to your own advantage. And that's exactly what you and I are going to do."

CHAPTER 29

Twenty-six days after Trevor Canon's death

Danner shoved open the glass doors of the Chase Center and Mackenzie followed him into the night.

It was dark. The evening marine layer rolled in with force, and Mackenzie shivered in her black blazer. They walked across an empty plaza toward the parking garage.

"What was that?" Danner asked.

"What was what?"

Danner glanced at her. "During the break-in footage. You saw something that made you tense up. What was it?"

"Hold on," Mackenzie said. "I could ask you the same thing. Soti kept giving you weird looks. What was *that*?"

Danner pulled out his phone, reading a message on his screen. "I'm serious, Mackenzie. If you saw something, I need to know."

"I'm serious, too. I'll tell you, but you have to reciprocate."

"Fine. Go."

Mackenzie sighed. "The guy who broke into the warehouse. I've seen him before."

Danner stopped mid-stride. He froze on the new concrete of the plaza. "What? When?"

"Several years ago," Mackenzie said, stopping with him. "I don't remember exactly."

Danner's eyes bored through the dark. "Where did you see him?"

"At the HV offices. I was working late. As I got on the elevator to leave, he was coming off. I thought it was weird, someone coming to the office that time of night."

"You're sure it was him? The same guy from the warehouse."

"You don't forget someone like that," Mackenzie said. "We don't see American Gladiators strolling into HV on a regular basis."

Danner typed something on his phone. Then it began to vibrate in his hand. He stepped away from Mackenzie and raised the phone to his ear.

"Yes," he said, keeping his voice low. He continued drifting away from Mackenzie, and she strained to catch snippets of his conversation. "I agree . . . Yes. Unprompted . . . If we can use it as a link . . . Understood."

Danner ended the call and re-pocketed his phone. He resumed walking toward the parking garage, gesturing Mackenzie to follow.

"Who was that?" Mackenzie asked.

"I'll tell you soon," Danner said. "But for right now, we need to move."

"What about the reciprocation? You said you'd tell me why Soti was giving you weird looks."

"I will," Danner said. Seeing Mackenzie about to object, he continued. "I'm not freezing you out, I swear. But we need to go. I'll explain everything as soon as we get there."

"Get *where*? Where are we going?"

"We'll swing by the hotel and get your stuff," Danner said. "And then it's time for you to meet my boss."

Mackenzie and Danner spent the short drive to the hotel in silence. Mackenzie rested her head against the window, watching the new construction of Mission Bay flash past.

Her thoughts turned to Vitaly Kovalev. The image of him stalking into the warehouse, coiled muscle, oozing with menace. The flash of violence when he'd punched Stanley Yoo. The words of Soti: ex-KGB, head of security for a group of billionaire thugs. The traces of Yoo's blood spattered across the edges of the warehouse sink.

Mackenzie felt a slow drip of nausea pooling in her gut, her rational mind unable to reason it away. She knew exactly what the nausea represented: fear.

Mackenzie had known the Canon investigation would be dangerous. She was fully aware that she was treading in violent waters. But the note on her bay window, creepy as it was, had been abstract. She'd felt the danger indirectly.

As with the black Tesla parked outside her apartment. As with the sleeve-tattoo guy at Balboa Cafe. There'd been no direct confrontation. Danger loomed on the perimeter of her life, where she could keep it out of focus.

Hell, she'd never even *seen* Trevor Canon's body. Danner had sent her the SFPD files, but she hadn't looked at the photos. She hadn't watched the blood as it trailed across Canon's office.

But now Vitaly Kovalev had entered the picture.

The threat of danger felt real the moment he'd entered the camera frame. His physicality, the way he moved, the way he surveyed the warehouse, the way he interacted with Trevor—all of it had triggered primal instincts hardwired into the ancient subsections of Mackenzie's brain. The conclusion was inescapable.

Kovalev was a predator.

Mackenzie's intuition told her that he was circling. Confrontation was coming. It was inevitable. It felt very near.

Danner waited in the sedan, idling on the curb as Mackenzie entered the Royal Harbor. The lobby was broad and open. There were low couches, coffee tables, San Francisco trinkets, and vintage books. Tile floors with nautical rugs.

It was nearly nine P.M., a weeknight, and the building felt empty. Two staffers stood at the reception desk, laughing at something on a computer screen. Boomers played cards on a coffee table. Counting Crows whined in the background.

Mackenzie reached the elevator bank and pressed the call button. She spun around, facing out toward the lobby. The staffers were now swiping their phones. The Boomers shuffled. All was quiet.

Mackenzie checked her text messages. Still nothing from Hammersmith.

She heard a friendly, high-pitched *ding* as an elevator arrived. She turned and stepped into it, hitting the eight button as the doors closed behind her. The elevator lurched and then glided upward. Mackenzie's mind hummed with questions. Why did Danner want to get her stuff before seeing his boss? She was glad she'd barely unpacked.

The Royal Harbor was an old building, and Mackenzie found the elevators maddeningly slow. Impatient, she moved to the center of the doors. She was ready to step off the instant they finally opened.

But she didn't move anywhere.

The doors parted to reveal a man waiting at the threshold. He stood facing her, close enough to touch.

The man was her height, white, with short blond hair and a long face. He wore a black T-shirt that revealed an ornate, colorful sleeve tattoo running down his forearm.

It was the man from Balboa Cafe. The one that had been staring at Mackenzie from across the bar.

Kovalev, Mackenzie thought. Of course he isn't working alone. He never has been.

For a heartbeat, the two of them stared at each other. The man went through the same rapid-fire emotions as Mackenzie. First, surprise. Then, recognition. It was plain in the man's eyes—he knew exactly who Mackenzie was.

Mackenzie reacted first. And for one of the rare instances in her life, her long frame came to her advantage.

Mackenzie twisted her torso, swinging her right hand. She balled a fist as her arm shot across the threshold of the elevator.

And she punched the tattooed man square in the nuts.

CHAPTER 30

Twenty-six days after Trevor Canon's death

The tattooed man staggered backward, eyes bugging with surprise. He fell to the hallway carpet.

Mackenzie wasn't sure if she'd actually hurt him. She wasn't going to stick around to find out. She jabbed the button for the first floor. The doors closed and the elevator began its ponderous descent back to the lobby.

Mackenzie stood centered between the doors, heart pounding against her rib cage. Her hand stung. Through the adrenaline she felt the first traces of a stiff, familiar pain as it gathered deep in her right wrist.

What the fuck just happened? she thought. She pulled out her phone and dialed.

"Danner."

"There was someone waiting for me!" Mackenzie yelled into the phone.

"What? Where?"

"On my fucking floor!"

"Hold on," Danner said. "Who was waiting for you?"

"I don't fucking know!" Mackenzie said. "A man. I think he's with Kovalev."

Danner's voice grew urgent. "Where are you right now?"

"I'm in the elevator, coming back down to the lobby."

Danner hung up.

After an eternity, Mackenzie's elevator reached the ground floor. The doors opened and Mackenzie stepped out carefully, head on a swivel.

There was no sign of the tattooed man. No sign of Kovalev. The lobby appeared as dull as it had a few minutes prior.

Danner burst through the hotel entrance. Seeing Mackenzie, he jogged across the lobby, weaving between the leather sofas and potted dracaenas. Mackenzie met him a few paces from the elevator bank.

Danner's brow was furrowed. "Who was it?"

"I don't know," Mackenzie said. "A guy. I got to my floor and he was there."

"Are you okay?"

"I'm fine."

Danner glanced downward. "What happened to your hand?"

Mackenzie hadn't realized that she was holding her right forearm across her torso, hand positioned at a stiff angle. "I hit him."

"You *hit* him?"

A high-pitched *ding* echoed behind them, and both Danner and Mackenzie turned to face the elevator bank. Doors opened and Mackenzie felt her heart stop.

It was Sleeve Tattoo. He'd put on a jacket that covered his arms, but it was him. He stepped off the elevator, dragging something behind him. He saw Mackenzie and Danner and his eyes brightened with anger. He moved straight toward them.

He followed me down, Mackenzie thought. Her muscles tensed as she prepared to turn and run, but she was stopped by Danner's voice.

"Eagerly," Danner said. He looked across the lobby at Sleeve Tattoo, recognition in his tone. "What are you doing here?"

"She fucking hit me," Eagerly said. He reached Danner and Mackenzie, his expression dour. "Right in the balls."

Danner turned to Mackenzie. "This was the guy you ran into?"

Mackenzie frowned back at Danner. "You *know* him?"

"I was told to pick up her stuff," Eagerly continued. Mackenzie now noticed that the item Eagerly pulled behind him was, in fact, her suitcase. "What are *you* doing here?"

Danner sighed wearily. "Mackenzie," he said, "meet Special Agent Eagerly. Though it sounds like you two are already acquainted."

Mackenzie stared at Danner. "Hold on a second. This guy is with *you*?"

"Yes," Danner said.

"She was right there when the elevator opened," Eagerly said. "She hit me before I could say anything."

Mackenzie turned to Eagerly. "You were following me. What was I supposed to think?"

Now both Eagerly and Danner looked at her. "What do you mean?" Eagerly said.

"I saw you," Mackenzie said. "At Balboa Cafe. I remember the tattoo."

Danner shook his head and shot a look at Eagerly. "I told you."

"Bad luck," Eagerly said.

"I told you to cover that thing up on duty."

"I'm supposed to blend in," Eagerly said. "Look normal." He stared back at Danner. "Normal people have tattoos, Danner."

Danner's voice was dry. "Not like yours."

"How would you know?"

"Stop." Mackenzie raised her hands. "One of you, right now, tell me what the *fuck* is going on."

Danner waited a beat, thinking. "Everybody in the car," he said. "I'll explain on the way."

Ninety seconds later Danner turned the sedan onto Howard Street, heading into the thick of SoMa. Eagerly sulked in the back seat while Mackenzie rode shotgun, hand throbbing in her lap. She attempted to twist her wrist, pushing through the accumulating stiffness, but her nerves punished her with a jolt of pain. She winced as Danner glanced over at her.

"How's your hand?"

"It's fine," Mackenzie said. "Now tell me what the hell just happened."

"Agent Eagerly is from the San Francisco office. He was assigned to tail you."

"Tail me?"

Danner nodded. "Keep an eye out. Make sure nobody put you in harm's way."

"Since when?"

"Since the beginning."

"So Eagerly's been tailing me since *before* someone broke into my apartment."

"Yes."

Eagerly stewed in the backseat, arms folded.

Mackenzie thought. "Why were you concerned I might be 'put in harm's way'?"

Danner shrugged, flat-faced. "I told you this would be a dangerous investigation. You're not trained for this kind of thing."

Mackenzie stared at Danner as he drove. He kept his eyes on the road. "You're acting like this is standard procedure."

"It's not uncommon. I wanted you to have some extra protection."

"Bullshit." Mackenzie felt her blood rising.

Danner said nothing. The sedan cruised down Howard Street.

"You didn't seem that surprised when someone broke into my apartment," Mackenzie said. "And you didn't seem very surprised by the warehouse footage. You still haven't explained why Soti was giving you those weird looks."

"I've tried to be as open as I can," Danner said.

Mackenzie twisted to glare at Eagerly. "And you were supposed to be watching my back, not scaring the shit out of me."

"I was doing my job," Eagerly said, shoulders hunched. "They told me to get your stuff."

Danner cruised through Civic Center Plaza, then slowed in front of a large, utilitarian office building. It was tall for San Francisco—twenty stories, at least—and took up an entire square block. Mackenzie looked up to see a dull, repetitive grid of concrete and windows, most of them dark.

"Where are we?" Mackenzie asked.

"Federal Building," Danner replied. "FBI's field office is on the thirteenth floor."

"Why'd we have to get my stuff from the hotel?"

"Because it's not secure enough," Danner said. He pulled into an underground parking garage and rolled toward a security checkpoint. "You're staying here for the time being. The investigation has evolved."

"Evolved how?"

"You're about to find out."

CHAPTER 31

Twenty-six days after Trevor Canon's death

The FBI field office was a monotone bullpen of cubicles. Swivel chairs, coffee stations, televisions, and computer monitors. The shitty black Cisco landlines that never worked. Conference rooms covered by sets of venetian blinds.

Most of the bullpen was empty, chair backs covered with black nylon jackets that read FBI in yellow letters. But for the jackets, the office could've been home to anyone. Sales firm, consulting shop. Or the Federal Bureau of Investigation.

Danner guided Mackenzie toward a bank of conference rooms that lined an exterior wall. Eagerly headed the opposite direction, silently parting ways. Danner stopped in front of a wooden door. Plain, no signage. A glass wall lay to one side, its contents obscured by closed blinds.

Danner knocked. A deep voice echoed from within. "Come in."

Danner opened the door to reveal a modest conference room. Drop ceilings, thin carpet. Glass exterior wall, like the one facing the bullpen. A rectangular wooden table in the center.

A man sat at the head of the table, facing the door. He was Black, clean-shaven, thick-framed, with high shoulders. He wore a navy blue suit with a burgundy tie, silk in full Windsor. A laptop and smartphone lay on the table before him.

The man didn't get up. "Have a seat," he said, gesturing to the chairs. With his voice, Mackenzie sensed it was less an invitation than a command.

Danner and Mackenzie took seats on opposite sides of the table. The man looked at Mackenzie. She felt a jitter as his eyes fell on her.

"Miss Clyde," he said. "My name is Dedrick Whitaker. I'm the assistant director of the FBI's Criminal Investigative Division."

Mackenzie nodded. She tried to ignore the dull pain in her right hand. "Hello."

Whitaker and Mackenzie appraised each other. She guessed Whitaker was in his mid-fifties. His eyes were probing, studying Mackenzie with the sharpness she expected from someone in his position. But Mackenzie also detected something else in Whitaker's expression: an undercurrent of deep, world-worn pragmatism. It was the face of a D.C. bureaucrat; Whitaker's features carried the decades he'd spent fighting battles and climbing ladders.

"For the past fifteen months," Whitaker said, "I've led a special task force created within the Department of Justice. Agent Danner has been working under my supervision."

Mackenzie glanced at Danner, then back at Whitaker. "I thought Danner was with CID."

Whitaker didn't acknowledge the question. "I understand you had a bit of a scare tonight."

Mackenzie holstered a sarcastic reply. "Yes," she said instead. "I did."

"Danner tells me you've been an asset to the investigation. I asked him to bring you in tonight so I could brief you. After that, I'm going to ask you some questions."

"Okay."

There was a knock at the door. "Come in," Whitaker said. Agent Eagerly entered with an ice pack. Wordlessly, he handed it to Mackenzie.

"Thank you," Mackenzie said. Eagerly didn't respond as he exited.

Mackenzie put her hand on the table and placed the ice pack over it, the chill numbing the pain.

Whitaker's body remained still as he continued. Like Danner his posture was perfectly upright, straight as a pine. Bureau thing, Mackenzie thought.

"The focus of our task force," Whitaker said, "has been a specific form of criminal activity: the use of venture capital, particularly in the technology industry, to launder money on behalf of foreign actors."

"Okay . . ." Mackenzie furrowed her brow.

"For many years," Whitaker continued, "the FBI has suspected that some venture capitalists are funding startups using dark money. They're investing on behalf of drug peddlers, arms dealers, and more. Organized criminals. Syndicates. Cartels, even. Our task force has been investigating these venture capitalists and their associated sources of funding."

Mackenzie stared back at Whitaker. "You're saying that there are VCs connected to drug cartels?"

Whitaker nodded. "And worse."

"You're kidding."

"No." Whitaker didn't smile.

Mackenzie smirked. "I'm sorry, but have you *met* any VCs? It sounds kind of ridiculous."

"I can assure you it's not," Whitaker replied. His mouth was flat as the Mojave.

"Okay. But how does that even work?"

Danner chimed in from across the table. "Imagine a drug cartel," he said. "They're sitting on a ton of cash. What do they want to do with that money?"

Money begets money. "Make more," Mackenzie said.

"Exactly," said Danner. "How do they do that?"

"Sell more drugs?"

"We're not talking *Miami Vice*," Danner said. "These are sophisticated organizations. A modern cartel operates like a business, with billions in revenue. They need to diversify their income. And legitimize as much of their cash as they can, if they want to use it freely."

"I follow."

"So they approach venture capitalists. Provide money the VCs use to invest in startups. When the startup makes it big, the VC cashes out. And they distribute their payout back to the cartel. Nobody's watching."

"Nobody *was*," Whitaker added. "Until us."

Mackenzie lifted her left hand, the right still covered in ice. "Investing in startups is super risky. Why wouldn't the cartel just dump their money into Spyder stock?"

Danner shook his head. "Money goes into the market, a lot more eyes fall on it. Questions get asked. The SEC gets involved." Danner periodically glanced at Whitaker, as though checking for validation.

"Much easier," Danner continued, "for criminals to pour that same money through VC mechanisms. Comparatively, they're the Wild West."

"VCs are still regulated," Mackenzie said.

"When's the last time you read about a VC getting fined by the SEC?"

Mackenzie paused. "Fair."

"Besides, these organized criminals consider themselves businessmen. They see the funny money in tech. They see celebrities getting in, politicians, everyone. And they want a piece, just like everybody else."

Mackenzie considered Danner from across the table. She recalled her surprise at Danner's knowledge of the network infrastructure in the warehouse.

"How long have you been focused on this?" Mackenzie asked.

Danner hesitated and Whitaker answered for him. "Agent Danner joined the task force when it was first created fifteen months ago," Whitaker said. "He's been working on the intersection of financial crimes and venture capital for much longer."

Mackenzie kept her eyes on Danner. "Are you even a homicide investigator?"

"I've worked on homicide investigations."

"When?"

Danner's eyes flitted between Whitaker and Mackenzie. "In my early days at the FBI."

"But not recently."

"No."

"I understand your question," Whitaker said. His voice was firm, filling the conference room. "Why was Agent Danner assigned as lead agent to the Canon investigation? And what does it have to do with our task force?"

Whitaker used a hand to smooth his tie, burgundy rippling under broad fingers. "The reality, Miss Clyde, is that we already know who killed Trevor Canon. We've known for quite some time."

"What?" Mackenzie straightened in her seat. "Who was it?"

"Your boss," Whitaker said. "Roger Hammersmith."

CHAPTER 32

Twenty-six days after Trevor Canon's death

The words hung in the air like a fart at a funeral.

"That's impossible," Mackenzie said.

"Hammersmith didn't pull the trigger," Whitaker said. "But he orchestrated Canon's murder."

Danner's eyes were focused on the table. He looked sheepish.

"Why on earth," Mackenzie said, "would Roger want to kill Trevor?"

Whitaker leaned back in his chair. "There are elements of what I'm about to tell you that I can't explain further. DOJ lawyers will allow me to share only a streamlined version of events."

"Fine."

"Tonight's meeting," Whitaker said, "never took place. If it comes down to it, I will not think twice about hanging you out to dry. Nothing personal. Goes with the job."

Mackenzie's wrist pulsated under the ice pack. "I understand."

Whitaker nodded. "Are you familiar with the Ten?"

"Ten?"

"*Ten,*" Whitaker repeated. He pronounced the word like *tyen,* with a *y* jammed after the *t.* "Not the number. It's Russian for 'shadow.'"

"Never heard of it."

"Most haven't. To simplify, the Ten are the elite class of Russian organized crime. Professional, highly organized, massively wealthy, with close ties to the Russian government."

Whitaker spoke as though reciting something he'd shared many times before, in a thousand meetings with the thousand tentacles of the U.S. government.

"Though they began in Russia, the Ten now have a sizable presence on every continent. They are the modern front of organized crime: a syndicate that operates like a multinational corporation."

Mackenzie glanced at Danner. "The oligarchs that Soti was talking about."

Danner made a face. "The Ten go far beyond what Soti thinks he knows."

"Think of the Ten like a modern conglomerate," Whitaker said. "Some of their income streams have legal pretenses: construction, real estate, energy. But the vast majority of their revenue comes from professionalized criminal activity on a global scale."

Whitaker leaned forward, eyes locking onto Mackenzie's.

"It's important you understand me, Miss Clyde. These aren't guys with leather jackets and crowbars. If you met someone in the Ten's leadership, you would struggle to differentiate them from an executive at Exxon, or Obsidian, or even Spyder. They wear suits, sail on yachts, fly private. They're all over Sun Valley and Davos. They are fully ingrained into the highest echelons of money and power."

Whitaker leaned back. "The distinction is how they *make* that money. The Ten are arms dealers. They finance terrorists. They engage in drug trafficking, but also human trafficking. They've stockpiled uranium from the Soviet era and sell it on the black market. They steal, they blackmail, they torture. They kill without hesitation. I cannot emphasize this enough: The Ten are as dangerous as it gets."

An image floated into Mackenzie's mind. "Vitaly Kovalev," she said. "Soti said he worked for the oligarchs."

Danner nodded. "We'll come to him."

Whitaker continued. "Over a decade ago, Ten leaders were introduced to Roger Hammersmith. The Ten liked Hammersmith. They liked the idea of investing in American tech startups under the nose of the U.S. government. And they liked the returns they read about in the press: massive IPOs that turned seven figures into ten.

"Hammersmith was at a low point after the dot-com bust. The Ten provided him a path back to relevance. They had endless capital, and they needed someone to invest it for them. Someone who knew tech and was willing to look past any legal or ethical considerations."

Mackenzie lifted the ice pack off her wrist, rotating her hand. She raised the underside of her wrist to face the ceiling, then replaced the ice. She kept her motions slow and deliberate, taking advantage of the pause to gather her thoughts.

"I've worked for Roger for years," Mackenzie said. "He can't possibly be connected to a . . . I don't know what to call it. A group like this."

"Are you sure about that?" Danner interjected. "You told me when Hammersmith makes a decision, he doesn't let anything get in his way."

"I did," admitted Mackenzie. "But human traffickers? *Terrorism?*"

"Hammersmith doesn't see any of the Ten's day-to-day operations," Whitaker said. "But he sees the money. And he knows where it comes from."

Mackenzie shook her head slightly. "I'm not trying to be disrespectful, but this is hard for me to believe. Do you have evidence? Proof?"

"Not that I'm authorized to share with you," Whitaker said. "But we've been investigating Roger Hammersmith and his firm for many years. We have bank statements, wire transfers, travel records, and much more. His relationship with the Ten is not conjecture, Miss Clyde. It's fact."

Danner spoke, his voice quiet. "You saw Kovalev yourself, Mackenzie. Coming into your firm at off-hours. You didn't know who he was, but it creates a link."

Mackenzie tilted her head. "That's true."

"This is real, Mackenzie. Assistant Director Whitaker wouldn't be here if it wasn't."

Danner was more engaged in the conversation than Mackenzie had ever seen him. "Okay," she said. "This syndicate, the Ten. How long do you say Roger has been working with them?"

"Since his 'comeback,'" Danner said, using air quotes. "The Ten have financed almost every major investment made by Hammersmith Venture over the past ten years. Including the Journy Fund."

Mackenzie shook her head. "But that's billions of dollars."

"Five point two billion dollars," Whitaker said. "Virtually all of it stemming from Hammersmith's relationship with a criminal syndicate."

"I still don't understand how that's possible," Mackenzie said. "Why would the Ten even *want* to do that? So much money tied in one investment."

"For the same reasons that Indira Soti was desperate to invest," Danner said. "Journy was can't-miss. Fastest-growing startup in history."

"Hammersmith had established a track record," Whitaker said. "He made the Ten a lot of money. When he presented the Journy opportunity, I'm certain the Ten's leadership didn't hesitate."

"And nobody knew the Journy Fund was financed by organized crime?"

"Nobody knew," Whitaker said.

Mackenzie shook her head. "But . . . *how*? The SEC, Treasury? Somebody had to know."

"The world of venture capitalists avoids governmental scrutiny," Whitaker said. "And their political donations help keep it that way."

"What about Trevor Canon? Did he know?"

"Now we enter the next chapter of our story." Whitaker looked at Danner. "Go ahead."

Danner moved to the front of his seat, bright-eyed, like a pupil who knows the correct answer.

"Hammersmith invested over five billion dollars in Journy," Danner said. "For a while, everything was great. The company kept growing. Magazine covers, fancy offices, IPO rumors, all of it. But then the numbers changed. Journy's trajectory began to shift. Quite suddenly, the company wasn't a sure thing anymore."

"Hugo Chamberlain was right," Mackenzie said.

Danner nodded. "Journy was burning cash. Growth stopped. The user base began shrinking. The projections got very bad, very fast."

"And you think the Ten saw it happening."

"Journy was their golden goose. They kept a close eye on their investment. And when things began to sour, the Ten were livid. They pressured Hammersmith. And he pressured Canon." Danner paused. "We aren't certain when Canon learned who was behind the Journy Fund. We aren't certain how much he knew about the Ten and Hammersmith's corruption. But we know that at the very least, Hammersmith and the Ten were pressuring Canon to turn things around."

"We also know what happened next," Whitaker said. "A catalyzing event."

"The warehouse," Mackenzie said.

Both men nodded as Danner continued. "Hammersmith and the Ten learned that Canon wasn't even *trying* to save Journy. He was too busy working on his new project."

"M1ND," Mackenzie said. She paused before asking her follow-up. "How did they find out?"

"We aren't sure," Danner said. "We don't know if Hammersmith was aware of what, exactly, Canon and Yoo were working on. But we suspect he learned that Canon approached Indira Soti about funding."

"Brady Fitzgerald saw Soti and Trevor together. Maybe somebody else did, too."

"Maybe," Danner agreed. "However it happened, the Ten went from angry to apoplectic. Not only was Trevor Canon abandoning Journy for a shiny new object, he was bypassing them to finance it. Enough was enough. The Ten decided to get personally involved."

"Kovalev," Mackenzie said.

Whitaker reached below his chair. He brought a thin folder up and slid it across the table. "This is one of the few items the lawyers have authorized me to share."

Inside the folder was a dossier. At the top it read VITALY KOVALEV above a headshot. Kovalev's visage stared out at Mackenzie, features curled into their customary glower.

"Kovalev is one of the Ten's security operatives," Danner said. "Born in Belarus, educated in England, trained by twenty years in Russia's Federal Security Service. He's spent the past decade working for the Ten."

Mackenzie paged through the dossier. "What does he do for them?"

"Whatever's required," Whitaker said.

The dossier was broken into sections: headlines, background, associates. Mackenzie saw a label for KNOWN ALIASES. One phrase was listed: *the Bull*.

"Why's he called 'the Bull'?" she asked.

"Because he's a Taurus," Whitaker answered. After a beat he continued. "That was a joke, Miss Clyde."

"Oh."

"We assume it's due to the obvious physical resemblance," Danner said.

Mackenzie stopped reading. She stared at Danner across the table. "This is why Soti kept looking at you in his suite. He knew you were aware of the Russian criminal connections to Journy, and he assumed you knew who Kovalev was."

Danner didn't flinch. "Yes."

"How did Soti find that out?"

"His defense contacts. He's aware of our task force."

Mackenzie sharpened her tone. "Seems like everything we've learned are things that you already knew."

Danner looked away.

Whitaker cut in, pointing at the dossier. "I'll have that back."

Mackenzie closed the folder and slid it back across the table.

Danner continued. "We know that Kovalev entered the U.S. five weeks ago. From the timing, we can infer the warehouse was his objective. Intimidate Yoo and Canon. Make it clear that their side project needed to be shelved or given to Hammersmith and the Ten."

Mackenzie thought for a moment. "How did Kovalev know where to go?"

"We assume," Danner said, "that Hammersmith found the warehouse and passed the information on."

"How'd Hammersmith find it?"

"We don't know yet," Danner said. "I thought maybe they got sloppy, rented the warehouse under a name familiar to Hammersmith. But that's been a dead end."

"Circus Sagittarius," Mackenzie said. Sagittarius, she thought. And Taurus. Astrological symbols. There was a loose thread there. But Mackenzie had enough threads in her mind; she didn't have time for another.

"We still haven't found anything on Circus Sagittarius," Danner said.

Mackenzie considered the timeline, dots connecting like string lights. "So your theory is that Kovalev goes to the warehouse about ten days before Canon's murder. Kovalev intimidates Canon, roughs up Yoo. Canon and Yoo clear out of the warehouse, leave it behind."

Danner nodded as Mackenzie continued. "Canon's paranoia, already high due to his work on M1ND, goes up another notch. He changes his will to create the dead money. Plus he locks down access to his office. Restricts it to only people he trusts, who really need the access: the executive team."

"That's right," Danner said.

"A week passes." Mackenzie's mind hummed. "Something happens. Maybe Hammersmith and the Ten find out more about M1ND. Maybe Canon tells them to fuck off. Either way, the Ten decide that Trevor Canon has to die. And, what—they send Kovalev to shoot him?"

"Yes," Danner said.

"How?"

"Just as we laid out over the past few days. Kovalev uses a badge, goes up to Canon's office, shoots him, and leaves."

"But Kovalev would've needed an executive badge. Where'd he get one?"

"You missed something," Danner said. "A few days before Canon's death, Brady Fitzgerald went to Canon's office."

"Trevor brushed him off," Mackenzie said. "Why does that matter?"

"Because who did Brady Fitzgerald see as he was exiting Canon's office?"

Mackenzie froze. "Roger," she remembered. "I didn't think much about it—we were grilling Brady about his own fight with Trevor."

Danner nodded. "Fitzgerald saw Hammersmith getting off the elevator. This was only days before Canon's death—the badge protocol had already changed. Hammersmith only could've gotten up there if he had access."

"It would make sense for Roger to have an executive badge," Mackenzie said. "Trevor would've given him one at some point. Five billion dollars gets you free access to the founder."

"Exactly. And Canon *told* Fitzgerald he had another meeting. Hammersmith's visit wasn't impromptu."

"You think Trevor had Roger to his office so he could tell him to fuck off?"

Danner leaned back in his chair. "Trevor Canon wasn't the type of guy to back down from confrontation. I bet Canon told Hammersmith he wasn't impressed by Kovalev's intimidation. Maybe told him there was nothing he could do about M1ND. Few days later, Canon was dead."

A heavy silence settled in the conference room. Mackenzie looked up and saw a clock—it was almost midnight. She felt exhaustion begin to overwhelm her adrenaline.

"There's still one problem," Mackenzie said.

"What's that?"

"Why would Hammersmith care about solving Canon's murder if he *knows* Kovalev did it? He had me attached to the investigation. He had the FBI brought in."

Whitaker cut in. "No, he didn't."

Mackenzie turned to him. "No?"

Whitaker half-smirked. "Hammersmith has powerful friends, but he doesn't dictate DOJ jurisdiction. He did, however, use his connections to get *you* attached to the investigation as liaison."

"Oh."

Whitaker's voice was dry. "As I said before: political donations."

"Hammersmith doesn't care about Journy," Danner said. "It's a sunk cost." He leaned forward. "Think about it from Hammersmith's perspective. He finds out Journy is tanking. Five billion, squandered. The Ten, furious. Then he learns about Canon's secret project: M1ND.

He learns about Indira Soti. And he pivots. 'Forget Journy,' he tells the Ten. 'This new thing is going to be even bigger.'"

Mackenzie quieted. She fell against the back of her chair and sighed. "The dead money doesn't matter."

"It never mattered." Danner's eyes were bright with satisfaction. "Hammersmith sells the Ten on a new plan: Take M1ND for themselves. Kovalev goes to the warehouse to intimidate Canon and Yoo. Delivers the message: Give us M1ND, or else. But it doesn't stick. Yoo flees the coop and disappears. Canon pretends to acquiesce in the warehouse, but a few days later he summons Hammersmith and tells him off."

"Trevor sealed his own fate," Mackenzie said.

Danner nodded. "Hammersmith and Kovalev move to plan B. Kill Canon, get him out of the way. Stanley Yoo was the brains of the operation anyway. They find Yoo, they can *make* him hand over M1ND. Force him to play ball."

"How?"

"You've seen Kovalev in action," Whitaker said. "How do you think?"

Mackenzie moved the ice pack off her wrist, the pain suitably numbed. She felt her mind spinning and took a breath, trying to stay focused. "This whole time, Roger's never actually cared about the investigation."

Danner gave a thin smile. "Whenever you've briefed Hammersmith, what did he always push you on? Finding Canon's killer?"

Mackenzie's mouth fell open, as though the realizations were piling up like a car wreck. "No," she said. "His main directive was finding Stanley Yoo."

"Hammersmith and the Ten need Yoo. That's all he cares about. Hammersmith put you on the investigation because he wanted you to look for Stanley. But more important, he wanted to know the *instant* that we, the FBI, found him."

"Why?"

"So he and the Ten could get there first."

Mackenzie leaned back, delicately placing her hands in her lap. "They took Trevor's laptop in case it had anything related to M1ND."

"We think so," Danner said. "Either Hammersmith or Kovalev

activated it outside Yoo's apartment. They wanted to draw us there, see if we'd pick up a trail. You'd let Hammersmith know if we had. And then they could follow us to wherever Stan's been hiding."

Kovalev's face floated in Mackenzie's mind. She phrased her next question carefully. "You said Agent Eagerly was giving me 'extra protection,'" Mackenzie said. "That protection is from Kovalev and his syndicate. Isn't it?"

Danner hesitated, and Whitaker filled the brief silence. "Yes."

"The Tesla I told you about. You think that was Kovalev."

"They've been following you," Danner said. "In case you, or the investigation, leads them to Stanley Yoo."

Mackenzie shook her head softly. "But why break into my apartment? Why leave that weird message on my window?"

Danner hesitated again. He glanced at Whitaker, who gave a slight nod. "Intimidation," Danner said. "They didn't ransack your apartment. They just wanted to scare you. They knew you saw the Tesla. They wanted to hammer the message home."

Mackenzie's exhaustion engulfed her, the stress of the day finally taking its toll. She dropped her left elbow to the table and put her head in her good hand, closing her eyes.

Danner and Whitaker exchanged glances. "There's more to it," Whitaker said, "but it's late. We'll pick it up in the morning."

"I'm sorry," Mackenzie said. "It's a lot to process. My firm is funded by criminal money. My boss killed Trevor. He's using me to find Stanley Yoo." Mackenzie raised her head, blinking rapidly. "It's been a long night."

"We understand." Whitaker's words were more sympathetic than his tone. "From now on you'll stay here, for security. The fifteenth floor has been converted into temporary apartments for visiting Bureau personnel."

"Agent Eagerly has put your stuff in a room upstairs," Danner said.

Mackenzie was too tired to protest. "Okay."

Danner led her to a pseudo-apartment on the fifteenth floor. "This will be a good safe house," Danner said. "The building's secure twenty-four seven."

"Thanks."

"I'll knock on your door at seven tomorrow."

The quarters were big and bland. Eagerly had left her suitcase on a luggage rack near the bed. Within minutes Mackenzie was horizontal, head on the pillow.

She stared up at the bare ceiling above her, mind racing.

She thought about Trevor Canon. Brilliant visionary. Relentless. Charismatic. But also wasteful. Destructive. An asshole. And now dead, a bullet between the blues.

Stanley Yoo. Brilliant. Detached. Genius. Not a big thinker. The final piece of the puzzle, the missing key.

Eleanor Eden. Indefatigable. The adult in the room, the soccer mom. But also Trevor Canon's hatchet woman. Cleaning up his mistakes.

Cassiopeia Moreau. Speaks only in vibes. Embarrassing. Deeply insecure—but perhaps for good reason.

Brady Fitzgerald. Tech bro. Child. Drunk. But right about almost everything he'd said.

Hugo Chamberlain. Fatalist. Selfish. Only looks out for himself.

Then she thought about Roger Hammersmith. The once and future king of Silicon Valley. Titan of the industry. And a corrupt murderer, according to Danner and Whitaker.

She thought about Vitaly Kovalev, the Bull. Taurus, she thought again. The loose thread was still there, waiting to be pulled.

What words do people use to describe me? Mackenzie wondered. How will I be defined after this is all over?

And then she recalled something from Whitaker's introduction.

I asked him to bring you in tonight so I could brief you. After that, I'm going to ask you some questions.

They still hadn't asked her anything. Which raised another thought as she tossed in bed, considering the spare white ceiling of the FBI apartment.

Was it a safe house? Or a prison?

CHAPTER 33

Five years before Trevor Canon's death

Eleanor cut the engine and the rented speedboat slowed to a halt, drifting in the center of the lake.

Eleanor turned to face Mackenzie. "What do you think?"

Mackenzie looked around. They were totally alone. The chintzy attractions of South Lake Tahoe were kilometers away. The sky was as clear and deep and cerulean blue as the lake below.

Now Mackenzie understood why it had been her mother's favorite place. Away from the mayhem of its edges, Lake Tahoe had a serene, meditative quality. Mountain peaks encircled the lake like ancient gods huddled around a campfire. It made Mackenzie feel pleasantly insignificant. The terrain around her was so old, so massive, that the substance of her problems seemed ephemeral by comparison.

"Here's great," Mackenzie replied.

Janine Clyde had known when she was going to die. Ever practical, she had made her own arrangements. Now, six weeks after her mother's death, Mackenzie sat on a boat with a ceramic golden urn resting between her feet. The urn was modest, but it didn't feel cheap. It had weight to it. Janine Clyde had made sure of that.

Mackenzie grunted as she hauled the urn to her lap. A soft breeze eased the boat west. It was a good time for it, Mackenzie thought. A clear day, a still lake, nobody around. Tranquility. How her mother would have wanted it.

Eleanor stood at the helm. Mackenzie stepped past her to the prow of the boat. She knelt on a seat, leaning forward, straining to hold the urn over the surface of the lake.

"Should we say anything?" Eleanor asked. "A few words?"

Mackenzie could think of a million words.

Stubborn. Selfless. Foul-mouthed. Bullheaded.

Thief. Criminal. Felon.

A scrapper. The first Clyde to ever do anything besides turn the soil or turn the cards.

The first Clyde to go to prison.

Unapologetic. Fiercely pragmatic. A realist, to the death.

Someone who cut her own path and let the chips fall where they may.

But Mackenzie didn't say any of it. Her mother would've hated even the faintest trace of a soliloquy.

Instead Mackenzie said, "For most of my life, she was the only person I had. And she always made that enough."

Mackenzie dropped the urn into the lake.

"Under no circumstances," Janine had told Mackenzie, "are you to *spread my ashes* on the lake. I know that water. They'll never sink. My ashes'll float around the surface until they merge with the cigarette butts and used condoms over by Harveys."

Janine had shaken her head. "I bought the heaviest urn I could find, within reason. Drop the whole damn thing in the lake. Let it swallow me up."

The urn landed with a splash and began to sink. Mackenzie watched as the gold coloring twinkled in the clear mountain water. It faded slowly, glimmering as it melded with the Tahoe blue and sank below.

Eleanor watched in silence. She retook her seat at the helm, lounging against the leather.

Mackenzie lay horizontally along the prow. For five minutes the two of them sat in quiet, each enjoying a rare moment of open thought. Five minutes stretched to ten.

"Thanks for doing this with me," Mackenzie said finally.

Eleanor glanced her way. "What are friends for?" She smiled behind oversized sunglasses. "Real friends, I mean."

Mackenzie sat up. "Coming all the way up here. Renting the boat. It means a lot."

"You'd do the same for me."

"I would." Mackenzie stood and moved to the stern. "Thanks for driving the boat, too."

Eleanor smiled. "Don't you remember my book? There's a whole chapter about sailing in the Greek Islands."

"Must have blocked it out," Mackenzie said, and they both laughed. "How's Journy?"

Eleanor sputtered her lips. "The same. Trevor thinks he's a genius. He makes mistakes. I clean them up."

"Not what you imagined."

"I'm running the company, ninety percent. But Trevor fucks up his ten percent enough to make everything miserable."

"So why stay?"

Eleanor smiled. "The growth is crazy. If I can keep us on this trajectory, in spite of Trevor, the payoff will be worth it."

Mackenzie stared out at the lake. "We should talk about the other thing."

Eleanor removed her sunglasses and looked at Mackenzie with dull blue eyes, squinting in the sun. "Whenever you're ready."

"I did what you suggested," Mackenzie said. "I followed the money."

"The money that comes into Hammersmith Venture?"

Mackenzie nodded. "I looked into how Roger's been financing investments."

Eleanor tilted her head. "And?"

"It's complicated."

Eleanor half-laughed. She gestured to their surroundings. "I don't think we'll find a better place to unpack it."

"It's not just complicated. There are legal ramifications."

"So what?" Eleanor said. "We're a little past that. Wouldn't you say?"

"True." Mackenzie sighed. "I started with the recent investments. Venture capital is like a chain. Invest in a company. Earn an eventual cash out. Take those earnings and reinvest in something new."

"Sure."

"Financing for the new investments was easy to track. When Roger added a new link to the chain, I could dig backward, see where the money came from. Broadly speaking, the numbers worked. It added up."

Eleanor watched her intently from the helm. "I sense a 'but' coming."

Mackenzie nodded. "But then I went further back. Four, five years. And I found some weird stuff." Mackenzie shifted in her seat. "Right before I joined the firm, HV invested in a company called Crew."

"I remember it," Eleanor said. "Napster meets Myspace."

"HV put in $250 million. Roger was very proud of it. The problem is I couldn't find where the hell that $250 million came from. There weren't enough prior links on the chain. All the earlier income had been attributed to other new investments. It didn't add up."

"Maybe Roger used other people's money," Eleanor said. "Institutional investors. Banks."

"That's what I thought," Mackenzie said. "But if you bring in capital from someone like Citibank, there are records. I combed through our internal database. As one of the firm's only in-house lawyers, I have access to almost everything. But there was no record of that $250 million. So I went to the next layer."

"What's that?"

"The books themselves. All the accounting and banking records. For the firm, but also for Roger himself."

Eleanor's brow raised. "Your experience with your mom is bearing fruit."

"It helps," Mackenzie agreed. "But most of this is just knowing where to look and having the patience to dig through it."

"How'd you get all the information?"

Mackenzie hesitated. "It wasn't entirely legal."

Eleanor simply nodded. "Go on."

"Once I had the books, I found the money," Mackenzie said. "Deposits. Some into HV accounts. Some into Roger's personal accounts. Ranges all across the board, no rhyme or reason to the timing. Some for millions. Some for tens of millions."

"Random," Eleanor said. "Organic activity."

"Or designed to look that way," Mackenzie said. "I tracked down the accounts that these deposits came from. Then I followed where those accounts led. It was like one of those investigative boards from the movies, with the photos and the strings tying between them. Except instead of suspects, I had banks and account numbers, with names attached. Almost all of the account holders were companies: shells, mainly, which then led back to their *own* cascade of accounts, with more shells, and more accounts. It was like starting at the center and building dozens of spiderwebs, all at the same time."

"This must have taken you ages," Eleanor said.

"Two and a half months," Mackenzie said. "The broader the web grew, the more I knew I was onto something. This went far beyond how my mom covered her tracks: Someone was going to *extreme* lengths to hide where the money came from before it ended up at HV. I could look at a deposit in HV and trace it all the way back through a dozen different banks and shells. Corporations within corporations. Subsidiaries. Offshoots. Someone had built a labyrinth to hide it.

"I kept digging until I hit the bottom. The shell game of companies eventually stopped. And I began to assemble a list of accounts. The original source points of the money that poured into Hammersmith Venture."

Eleanor was transfixed. "How many accounts?"

"About ninety," Mackenzie said. "Not a single one is American. Most of them are held by banks in Cyprus, Panama, and the Caribbean. I tracked down the legal paperwork. Articles of incorporation, for the corporate holdings. Names, for the accounts and trusts. I began to cross-reference all the names I found. And quickly, something became clear."

"What's that?"

"All the accounts trace back to Russia," Mackenzie said.

"Russia?"

"Not directly," Mackenzie said. "But eventually, yes."

Mackenzie opened her phone, navigated to her recent Spyder search results, then handed the phone to Eleanor.

"Gregor Oberon," Eleanor said. "Management consultant in Tel Aviv." Eleanor looked up from the phone, puzzled. "Am I supposed to know who that is?"

"No," Mackenzie said. "But Gregor's the contact for a Cyprus trust that has sent over $60 million to Hammersmith Venture, all funneled through the maze of shell companies."

"Where's a management consultant get $60 million?"

"Gregor's brother Dmitri," Mackenzie said, "is an executive at Gazprom, the energy giant. Biggest company in Russia. Before Gazprom, Dmitri spent eighteen years in Russia's Federal Security Service, where he worked in the same unit as Russia's current president."

Eleanor stared at her. "You're kidding."

"There's more," Mackenzie said. She grabbed her phone back from Eleanor, then typed in another name. "Eight years ago a company called Cheung Industries opened an account in Panama. Since then, it's funneled over $33 million to Hammersmith Venture. One of the names on the articles of incorporation for Cheung Industries was Oleg Yelchin." Mackenzie held up her phone. The screen displayed a mugshot. "Last year, Yelchin was arrested by Interpol for selling weapons to terrorists."

Eleanor's eyes widened. "Terrorism?"

Mackenzie pulled up a *Foreign Affairs* article on her phone, handed it back to Eleanor. "Yelchin has ties to organized crime in Russia. He *also* has ties to a number of high-ranking executives in Russian corporations."

"People like the brother," Eleanor said. "Dmitri."

"Yes," Mackenzie said. She gestured to her phone. "And there are more like Yelchin. That article in *Foreign Affairs*—I talked to the writer. She told me there's a new form of organized crime coming out of Russia. Like the mob, but far more professional. Organized. Corporate. Closely connected to high levels of the government. And very, very wealthy."

Eleanor read Mackenzie's phone, expression grave. Mackenzie continued. "I gave the journalist two other names that appeared frequently on the shell accounts. A few days later, she told me that both names have ties to this Russian criminal group. And both names are on Homeland Security watch lists."

"These are the guys pumping Hammersmith Venture full of money?"

"Yes," Mackenzie said. "Each thread takes a different path. But the center of the web is always the same: money into HV."

Eleanor handed the phone back to Mackenzie, eyes blinking across the boat. "Are you telling me what I think you're telling me?"

"You wondered about where Hammersmith's money was coming from. I think I found out."

"Roger Hammersmith built his venture firm on dark money."

"Not just dark—criminal. I don't understand the full scope of this Russian organized crime network, but the *Foreign Affairs* writer said they're bad."

"How bad?"

"Drugs. Weapons. Terrorism. Human trafficking. Bad as it gets."

Eleanor stared at her for a long moment. "It's impossible to believe, if you hadn't just laid everything out."

"It sounds preposterous," Mackenzie said. "Roger working with organized crime? But the more I dug, the more it lined up. When he started Hammersmith Venture it became successful so quickly. *Too* quickly."

"It was overnight." Eleanor nodded. "All of a sudden he was splashing cash around like he'd never left." Her eyes moved skyward. "Hammersmith's dirty money is all over the Valley. Journy. StoryBoard. Hell, he even got a little into Spyder before they went public. It's everywhere."

She brought her eyes down. "This is incredible, Mackenzie. Seriously." Eleanor laughed. "I don't know whether to say it's magnificent or terrifying."

"I think it's both."

Mackenzie felt a strange mixture of relief and dread. After months of work it felt good to validate her theory with Eleanor. As she'd explained it, Mackenzie had become even more confident that it was true.

But truth has consequences.

Eleanor scooted to the edge of her seat. "Then let me ask you the important question, the one I'm sure you've been waiting for. What are you going to do?"

"I don't know," Mackenzie said. "That's why I wanted to talk to you."

"Let's talk options."

"Okay." Mackenzie thought for a moment. "I could take it to the Feds. Tell law enforcement."

"Sure," Eleanor said. "That's an option."

"It'd probably be the right thing to do."

Eleanor grimaced. "The right thing isn't always the smart thing. So you tell the Feds. What happens next? And how does it impact you?"

"They shut down the firm," Mackenzie said.

"Certainly," Eleanor said. "HV closes. It's a big, ugly story. And anybody associated with HV gets the stink on them. Including you. Meanwhile, what happens to the organized crime group? Nothing. It's not illegal to invest your money, and you don't have any proof how they made it."

Eleanor kept going, mouth moving as fast as her mind. "And Hammersmith himself? Maybe he'll do some time. But with his connections, and his lawyers, he could walk. Or cut a deal with the Feds."

"Taking it to law enforcement seems simple," Mackenzie said. "But it's actually complicated."

"Right."

"There's another option," Mackenzie said.

"Use it," Eleanor said. Her features burst with enthusiasm. "You have to *use* it, Mackenzie. This is the opportunity you've been waiting for. First time we met, what did you say? 'I want to control my own destiny.'" Eleanor stared at her. "This is your chance."

Mackenzie nodded. "I know."

"Confront Hammersmith. Leverage what you've learned to get a better position at the firm."

"It's not that simple."

"Sure it is." Eleanor pointed with a finger. "This is the chance to start building your persona. Everything we've talked about."

Mackenzie looked away, hesitating. "It's risky. Giving it to the Feds feels safer."

"No risk, no reward," Eleanor said. "Sometimes life is that simple."

Mackenzie didn't reply, her eyes scanning the lake.

"I understand if you're scared," Eleanor said. "But this is your *chance*, Mackenzie. You've been stuck for years. This is the pivot you've been waiting for." Eleanor opened her arms, gesturing to the lake around them. "Look at why we're here today, and answer this honestly. If your mother was still alive, and she was in your position—what would she do?"

CHAPTER 34

Five years before Trevor Canon's death

Three days after Lake Tahoe, Mackenzie sat in a small anteroom outside Roger Hammersmith's office. Hammersmith's longtime assistant, Gretchen, sat behind a nearby desk, pecking efficiently at a keyboard.

A door popped open to Mackenzie's left. Roger Hammersmith's round head emerged through the opening. His brown Yogi Bear eyes searched the anteroom before they landed on Mackenzie. He gave a broad smile.

"Mackenzie?"

"That's me," she said.

"Come on in."

Mackenzie entered Hammersmith's office and stopped short, overwhelmed by the view. It was midday, one of the impossibly bright afternoons where the bay glistens and the Golden Gate glows and, for a few hours at least, San Francisco looks like paradise. Sailboats glided across the water, passing in front of Alcatraz. Spare clouds tumbled across the sky.

Photographs of Roger stared out at Mackenzie from every surface. Hammersmith and Bono on the back of a yacht. Hammersmith and Condoleezza on a white helicopter. Presidents. Movie stars. Musicians.

What am I doing here? Mackenzie thought. A guy with this kind of office? This kind of power? I don't belong here.

She steeled herself. Opportunity, she told herself. Destiny.

"Have a seat," Hammersmith said. He plopped onto a couch and gestured to the one opposite. Mackenzie took a seat. A coffee table, big as a dumpster, rested between them.

Hammersmith crossed his legs and gave Mackenzie a soft smile, eyes crinkling behind his glasses. "I believe this is the first time we've met."

"Yes, sir," Mackenzie said deferentially.

Hammersmith winced. "Call me Roger."

"Yes, Roger, I think you're right."

"You've been on Legal for a few years, is that correct?"

"That's right."

Hammersmith nodded. "You get an amazing amount done for such a small team. Small but mighty, I always say."

"Thank you."

Hammersmith's hair was gray and poorly styled. He was stuffed into baggy black slacks and a white polo that he shouldn't have attempted to tuck in. Nothing about him was threatening. He looked like a guy at the nineteenth hole, sharing bad jokes over a couple of beers.

For a moment, Mackenzie wondered if her research had been accurate. This is the man responsible for flooding startups with criminal money? The man working with the modern evolution of Russian organized crime? Her stomach rumbled again, churning with uncertainty.

Hammersmith's tone changed slightly. "I'm always happy to make time for folks at the firm, but apparently you told Gretchen you wanted to discuss something urgent?"

"It's a legal matter," Mackenzie said. "Highly sensitive. I thought it best to bring this directly to you."

Hammersmith's eyebrows raised slightly. "Well, now you've certainly caught my interest." He laughed, a loud *HA!* that bounced off the floor-to-ceiling windows. Despite Hammersmith's smile, something shifted in his features, eyes narrowing a fraction of an inch.

"Go ahead," Hammersmith said. "I'm all ears."

Mackenzie forced her muscles to relax. Now or never, she told herself. Say the words.

"I know where the money comes from."

Hammersmith didn't react. His entire form stayed frozen: half-smile on his lips, eyes studying her from behind glasses, one slacked leg crossed over the other. If he breathed, Mackenzie didn't see it.

Hammersmith spoke. "What are you talking about?"

"You've been taking cash from a criminal syndicate for years. It's how you got back on your feet after the crash. It's how you built the firm. It's how you've funded nearly every investment. It's how you've done everything."

Now Hammersmith's smile disappeared. His eyes hardened, as did his voice. "What is it that you think you know?"

"I know you've built a labyrinth of bank accounts to hide the flow of money. I know how it's structured. I know its origin points. And I know the people at the origin points—the people you've been taking money from. Human traffickers. Weapons dealers. Terrorism financiers. The worst of the worst."

Mackenzie reached into her pocket and withdrew a thumb drive. She placed it on the giant coffee table, sliding it across to Hammersmith.

"It's all there," Mackenzie said. "Accounts, transfers, shells, subsidiaries. All created to hide the truth. That this entire firm—the most influential in the Valley, the king of venture capital—is built on blood money."

Hammersmith reached forward and took the USB drive, holding it between a meaty thumb and forefinger. He held it up to his eyes, then looked back at Mackenzie.

"Why should I believe you?"

Mackenzie nodded. "I thought you might say that."

So she walked him through it. The Crew investment, the accounts in Panama and Cyprus, Dmitri Oberon, Gregor Oberon, Oleg Yelchin, the political ties, Homeland Security. The only thing she left out was *Foreign Affairs,* to protect the journalist.

Hammersmith didn't move. He spent all of Mackenzie's explanation in silence, still holding the thumb drive in hand. Only when Mackenzie had finished did he speak.

"That's a lot of information." His voice still carried a measure of authority, as though unwilling to acknowledge Mackenzie's leverage. "Including personal information. Very little of it is publicly available."

"No," Mackenzie agreed.

"Then how did you get it?"

Mackenzie forced herself to maintain a front of complete confidence. "I called banks, your accountant, the corporate registry offices. I told them I was a lawyer at Hammersmith Venture. We'd received a tip we were going to be audited—the SEC was going to dig into our books. So I needed to outflank them. Double-check our numbers, get prepared for the audit."

"And they believed you?"

"Why wouldn't they? They looked me up, saw me on the firm website. I gave them my work email. It all checked out."

"None of them notified me."

"I told them not to bother you. Roger Hammersmith, dealing with the SEC? That's what he pays lawyers for. Like me."

Hammersmith snorted. "That's smart."

"Thank you."

"But it's fraudulent. You obtained information illegally, through fraudulent means."

"Sure." Mackenzie shrugged. "But look at it from the perspective of the Feds. My fraud? That's a little ground beef. But what's on there?" She pointed at the thumb drive, still in Hammersmith's grip. "That's prime rib."

Hammersmith considered the thumb drive, studying it like a bear holding a hornet's nest. He stood abruptly, moving to his desk. He leaned against it, back to Mackenzie, still and pensive. Mackenzie stayed on the sofa, coiled with tension. She studied the way Hammersmith's polo shirt strained against his belt, defying every law of physics.

"I don't think you've considered the full implications of your move here," Hammersmith said finally. He turned to face Mackenzie, features heavy but free of animosity. He looked stricken more than anything.

Mackenzie kept her voice steady. "I've considered them."

"You're entering very dangerous waters."

"I'm aware."

Hammersmith stared at her, then snickered. "You've got real balls," he said. "I'll give you that. Half an hour ago I didn't even know your name." He folded his short arms together. "Far as I can see, there's only one reason you're here right now. You want to deal."

No point dancing around it, Mackenzie thought. "Yes."

"Then out with it. What do you want?"

"A promotion," Mackenzie said.

"HA!" Hammersmith laughed aloud. "What: Fire Linda and install you as GC? You think you can blackmail your way up the ladder?"

"I don't want to move up the ladder," Mackenzie said. "I want to skip it altogether."

Hammersmith narrowed his eyes. "What do you mean?"

Mackenzie leaned forward. "Look at what I've put together," she said. "Has anyone else ever come close to what I've discovered here?"

Hammersmith frowned. "No."

"That's because I'm relentless. Once I found the thread, I didn't stop pulling. It took months. Every day, every night, piecing this together. Whoever these Russians are, exactly—they didn't make it easy. I dug through a rat's nest of paperwork. Incredibly dense. Multilayered. But I kept digging. Because I have the instincts to know *where* to dig. And I have the tenacity to *keep* digging until I hit bottom."

Hammersmith stayed quiet.

"Now imagine," Mackenzie continued, "that I took those same qualities and weaponized them—on *your* behalf. Imagine if I found leverage like this on other people. Founders, before we decide to in-

vest. Problematic executives. Bankers. Outside investors." Mackenzie
paused for effect, leaving Soti's name implied. "I could even dig into
our competitors."

A flash of intrigue passed across Hammersmith's features. But it
faded quickly. "I can't condone what you're doing here. It's extortion."

"It's not extortion," Mackenzie said. "It's proof of concept. For my
new role."

"As what?"

"Your director of investigations."

Hammersmith moved back to his sofa, retaking a seat. "Just you?"

"Just me."

"A team of one."

"A team of one."

Hammersmith pursed his lips, thinking. Got him, Mackenzie
thought.

"Reporting only to me," Hammersmith said.

"That's how I'd want it."

"How can I trust you?"

"You don't have to," Mackenzie said. "You'll get complete trans-
parency. I'll show you everything I do. Monitor the hell out of me.
Pay someone to watch me, if you want. I don't care. I'll work my ass
off and I'll rebuild your trust."

Hammersmith stared at her across the coffee table, still quiet.

"You don't like how this went down," Mackenzie said. "I wouldn't
expect you to. But ask yourself: Is there any other way I could have
done it? I came to you in person—no paper trail, no digital trail,
besides the thumb drive. I didn't go to the Feds. And if I just *gave* you
everything I discovered, without asking anything in return—would
you trust that? In all your time in this industry, have you ever encountered anybody *that* altruistic?"

Hammersmith dropped his head backward and stared up at the
ceiling. "I have stipulations."

Mackenzie celebrated inwardly. "Go ahead."

"One, you report directly to me, and *only* to me. You don't tell a
single other person, anywhere, what you're working on. Ever. Inside
or outside the office."

"Of course."

"Two, when I give an assignment, you take it. I say, 'Dig here.' You get your shovel."

"No problem."

Hammersmith lowered his chin, returning his gaze to Mackenzie. The irritation on his face had been replaced by a new emotion. Mackenzie felt a chill when she realized what it was.

Fear.

"Three isn't a stipulation," Hammersmith said. "It's a warning. The people you traced the money back to are more dangerous than you can imagine. I will only say this once, so remember it: They *do not fuck around*. They keep a close watch on the firm. They're going to wonder why a lawyer has suddenly moved into investigative work. And I'll have to tell them the reason. So if you ever fuck up. If you ever share any part of what we've just discussed. If you ever let something slip . . ."

Hammersmith leaned forward, expression grave. "It won't be me you answer to. It'll be them."

CHAPTER 35

Twenty-seven days after Trevor Canon's death

Danner knocked on Mackenzie's door at precisely seven A.M.

"Get your bag," Danner said. His suit was gone, replaced by khakis, sneakers, and one of the nylon jackets that read FBI in yellow letters. "We're going on a field trip."

Ten minutes later Mackenzie was in the back of the silver sedan, knees bumping against the passenger seat, which was occupied by Dedrick Whitaker. Instead of a black FBI jacket, Whitaker was draped in a tan-colored overcoat, the type Mackenzie had never seen on a man under fifty. He typed on his phone, silent.

They headed west on Lombard, bearing for the Golden Gate.

"Where are we going?" Mackenzie asked.

"Belvedere Island," Danner said. "To your boss's house."

Roger Hammersmith lived in a bay-front mansion in Belvedere, an island enclave near Tiburon that was home to the Bay Area's old money paragons. The home had previously belonged to Tony Bennett; Hammersmith and his wife made enemies of their neighbors when they unceremoniously knocked it down and replaced it with their own design.

"Are we going to talk to Roger?"

"Hammersmith's not there," Danner said. He glanced at Whitaker, who remained focused on his phone. "Two nights ago, one of Hammersmith's neighbors called the local cops. She was on her boat and saw a man on Hammersmith's dock. She says the guy was throwing something into the water. Something large and heavy. She yelled at the guy from her boat. He flipped her off and walked back up the dock to Hammersmith's property."

"She called the cops because he flipped her off?"

Danner followed Lombard as it curved north and merged onto the bridge. "She was pissed he threw trash into the bay. Littering. That's why she yelled at him."

"You're kidding."

Danner shook his head. "Local cops put it in the system. Eventually they saw the flag on Hammersmith's name, ran it up the chain. We found out about it this morning."

"Did she say it was Hammersmith on the dock?"

"No," Danner said. "Someone taller, more muscular."

"Kovalev?"

"Maybe."

"So we're going to see what was dumped in the bay?"

Danner nodded. "USERT—the underwater evidence guys—are already in the water."

Mackenzie gazed back out the window. "Why is there a flag on Hammersmith's name?"

"Because," Dedrick Whitaker said, his deep voice filling the car, "Roger Hammersmith has gone to ground."

Whitaker finished with his phone and gazed out the front windshield.

"We had agents watching Hammersmith. Two nights ago he disappeared." Whitaker paused. He didn't turn in his seat, but his tenor made it clear he was addressing Mackenzie. "Which raises a question: When is the last time you spoke to him?"

"Day before yesterday," Mackenzie said. "On the way back from the Futurist Summit. Danner was in the car with me."

"And there's been no other communication?"

"No. I've been texting him updates but he hasn't replied."

"Did you text him last night? After you met with us?"

"Of course not," Mackenzie said.

"So until thirty-six hours ago, you were in constant communication with Hammersmith. Updating him on the investigation."

"That was the whole point of me being assigned as liaison."

"And then he suddenly stopped replying."

"Yes," Mackenzie said.

"Did he say anything unusual? Tell you to switch focus?"

"No. He wanted me to find Yoo. Like I said last night, that's been his directive."

Whitaker turned his head, watching out the passenger window as Danner drove across the Golden Gate. It was a bright, cloudless morning. The boundless sapphire of the Pacific sparkled in the west.

"Was last night," Whitaker said, his focus still on the window, "the first time you'd heard anything about the source of Hammersmith's money?"

"Yes," said Mackenzie.

"You'd never wondered about it?"

"Didn't have reason to," Mackenzie said. "When I joined HV, the firm was the biggest deal in the Valley."

"Did you ever observe any connections to Russia?"

"Not that I can remember." Mackenzie shrugged. "Roger went to Moscow, I guess."

"How often?"

"Now and then. But he went everywhere now and then."

"You never saw anything else suspicious, anything that made you wonder?"

"No."

"In the course of all your investigative work for the firm, Hammersmith never gave you an assignment that struck you as odd? Made you pause?"

"No," Mackenzie said again. "It wasn't my place to question him. But I had no reason to. I spent most of my time scrounging for dirt on competitors. The usual."

"The usual," Whitaker said.

Mackenzie shifted in her seat, voice rising. "Look, Agent Whitaker—"

Danner cut her off. "Assistant Director Whitaker."

"Assistant Director Whitaker," Mackenzie corrected. She felt awkward addressing the back of Whitaker through the headrest, so she leaned forward for a better angle. Whitaker turned his head to accommodate her. "Yesterday was the first I heard anything about blood money, or criminal ties, or any of this crazy shit—pardon my language. You have to understand the context. Roger is one of the kings of the industry. Getting a job with his firm was a dream. I accepted that he was who he said he was. *Everybody* did. Do I wish now that I had asked a few more questions? Been a little more curious about the guy I was working for? Of course. I was up all night thinking about it. But I wasn't alone. Roger had everyone fooled. Not just me."

Whitaker took his time. Eventually he moved his eyes back to the front.

Mackenzie didn't stop. "While we're asking questions," she said, "I have a few of my own."

Whitaker scoffed. "I can't promise we'll answer them."

"When did you know that Hammersmith was involved in Canon's death?"

Whitaker said nothing but gave Danner a slight nod. "We assumed he was from the start," Danner said.

"Because of your task force," Mackenzie said.

"Yes," said Danner.

"When Trevor was murdered, you knew Hammersmith had a part in it."

"We had a strong suspicion. Given what we knew about the Ten, and Journy, and Hammersmith's connections to both. That's how we got jurisdiction."

"When did you *know* that Kovalev killed Trevor?"

Danner hesitated. "Go ahead," Whitaker said.

"When we saw the crime scene," Danner said.

Mackenzie frowned, watching Danner's eyes in the rearview. "When we went to Trevor's office?"

"Before that," Danner said. "When we saw the SFPD reports. And the photos of Canon's body."

"How did you know it was Kovalev?"

"Because there was no evidence," Danner said. "No fibers. No blood, no fingerprints. Nothing. And, more important, because of how Canon was shot."

"You said the gun was generic. A Glock 19 is a dead end."

"Not the gun. The bullet hole." Danner took the exit for Belvedere. "It was dead center, right above Canon's eyes. Based on the angle and blood trail, we expect the shooter was about fifteen feet away."

"So?"

"So that's a perfect shot," Danner said. "Fifteen feet doesn't sound far, but that's expert marksmanship. Single shot, dead center, middle of the forehead. Immediate kill. No casings. That's professional."

"Kovalev."

"Yes," Danner said.

They moved into the sloping, bucolic suburbia of Tiburon. Mackenzie cracked her window, breathing in a gust of clean marine air.

"You knew about the Ten," Mackenzie said. "You knew Hammersmith orchestrated the murder. You knew Kovalev pulled the trigger."

"Yes," Danner said again.

"So what the hell have we been doing?"

Danner paused, clearing his throat. Mackenzie watched Whitaker shift his position in the passenger seat.

"What do you mean?" Danner asked.

"Last night, during your dramatic reveal," Mackenzie said to Danner. "You looked almost sheepish. I just realized why: You felt bad. You knew everything we went through the last few days, the interviews, arguments at Journy's offices, the speculation, the mad dash around the bay . . . All of it was a show. Totally unnecessary."

"That's not entirely true—" Danner started, but Mackenzie cut him off.

"You *knew* who killed Trevor. So why drag me through the whole song and dance of the investigation?"

"Because we're professionals," Whitaker cut in.

He clipped his words, tone impatient. "Yes, we suspected Hammersmith was connected. Yes, we suspected Kovalev pulled the trigger. But we don't deal in suspicions. Our task force and the DOJ lawyers—our goal isn't arresting Roger Hammersmith. We want a *conviction*. We want Hammersmith behind bars. For that, we need evidence. We need to assemble proof. We need to explain motive and means."

"We didn't know about the AI project," Danner said. "We didn't know Journy was going in the tank, that Canon was jumping to something new. We had the beginning of the story, and the end. But we needed the middle."

The sedan coasted across the narrow isthmus that led to Belvedere Island.

"Fine," Mackenzie said. Whitaker emitted a grunt of impatience from the passenger seat. "But then why didn't you tell me?"

Whitaker twisted his head, glancing backward. "Tell you what?"

"What you were actually investigating," Mackenzie said. "I had no idea what you were really looking for. Hell, Danner played dumb the entire time. Acted like he knew nothing about the tech industry or venture capital."

"And this upsets you?" Whitaker asked.

"Of course it does," Mackenzie says. "I've spent the last week putting a puzzle together while you guys had the missing pieces in your pockets."

Danner glanced at Mackenzie in the rearview, then looked away. Whitaker took a breath, head shaking slightly. "Do you know why we didn't tell you?"

"No."

"Because *we didn't trust you*," Whitaker said. He emphasized each word, pounding them into the sedan's cabin.

"You worked closely with Hammersmith. He pulled strings to attach you to the investigation." Whitaker fired off the sentences hard and fast, like sprays from a machine gun. "What did you expect? That the FBI would simply open its doors, welcome in an amateur with close ties to our chief suspect?"

Mackenzie felt her cheeks go red. She stayed quiet.

"You came to us after the break-in," Danner said. "And after the Soti meeting, you told me that you saw Kovalev at Hammersmith's offices. That's an important link for our case." He glanced at Mackenzie in the rearview. "I assume you'll sign an affidavit backing that up, if we ask you?"

"I'll testify in court, if you need it," Mackenzie said.

Whitaker nodded. "As I said last night, you've showed yourself to be an asset." Whitaker snapped his focus back to the windshield. "So now you've been briefed. But if you felt out of the loop, don't expect an apology. At every step we've done what was best for the investigation."

Mackenzie turned and stared out the back-seat window.

Danner navigated them in silence through the winding roads of Belvedere, the sedan rising into an elevated network of snaking cul-de-sacs and dead ends. Danner turned down a long, narrow private drive. He brought the sedan to a stop.

"We're here," he said.

The three of them got out and walked to the top of a long driveway, significantly wider than Mackenzie's apartment. It ended at a big stucco garage maybe fifty yards away, downhill. She couldn't see the water; the private drive was surrounded by trees, and Hammersmith's property was protected by a high wall covered with sharp golden ornamentation. A large security gate sat ajar.

The top of the driveway was cordoned off by yellow tape. Two men stood near the center. One of them was Fernandez, from Stanley Yoo's loft.

Fernandez greeted Danner and nodded to Whitaker. "Good morning, sir."

"Where are we?" Whitaker said.

"Divers found something," Fernandez said. "They're bringing it up now. We'll meet them on the dock."

"Good," Whitaker said. "What about the neighbor?"

"I called her this morning." Fernandez pulled up his phone, reading the screen. "Name's Laura Glenellen. Lives two houses south."

"She confirmed her report?"

Fernandez nodded. "Same as what she told Belvedere PD. She was bringing her boat in after dinner in Sausalito, maybe ten P.M. She saw a man on Hammersmith's dock."

"Could she identify the man?"

"Just a silhouette, sir. She said he looked bulky. Definitely wasn't Hammersmith, but couldn't tell otherwise."

"Go on."

"The man threw something heavy into the water. Glenellen yelled at him, and he flipped her off. Then he walked back up the dock and disappeared into Hammersmith's yard." Fernandez looked up. "Glenellen said she's had issues with Hammersmith ever since he moved in. Called him a douchebag."

Mackenzie smiled to herself as Whitaker continued.

"What'd the divers find?"

"Better to show you, sir."

Fernandez led them down the driveway, following a stepstone path to the water's edge. Now the trees began to open up and Mackenzie got a better view of where the path led: Hammersmith's personal marina, thrumming with activity.

A boathouse stood at the entrance. Behind it a long, central pier extended straight into the water. Two shorter docks jutted northward off the central pier, giving Hammersmith's marina the shape of an uppercase *F*. Between the two docks rested Hammersmith's boat, bobbing in the waves of Richardson Bay.

The place was crawling with federal agents. Everywhere Mackenzie looked she saw yellow lettering on black nylon: FBI.

As they reached the water Mackenzie turned and looked back toward Hammersmith's house. It was a heaving stucco monstrosity, curvaceous and birdshit white. The house the Ten built, Mackenzie thought. No wonder the neighbors hate him.

The surrounding estate was a tasting menu of mega-rich living: gaudy fountains, putting course, two pools, clay tennis court. Mackenzie spied another hardcourt that'd been converted into a helipad for the *Hammer Angel*. The helipad lay empty.

Two women met the group halfway down the pier. One was dressed in standard FBI attire, though Mackenzie noted instead of black her jacket was royal blue. The other woman was in a still-damp scuba suit, wet hair slicked back against her head. Mackenzie spied an oxygen tank, flippers, and scuba mask in a large plastic bin behind her.

"Assistant Director Whitaker," Fernandez said, "this is Agent

Isaac and Agent Vangelos, from USERT." Fernandez gestured to the woman in khakis and the woman in the scuba gear, respectively. "Agent Isaac is the team lead, and Agent Vangelos just finished a dive."

"Good morning, sir," the agents said in unison.

"Good morning," Whitaker said. "Thank you for getting this done so quickly."

Isaac, the one in khakis, spoke. "Of course, sir."

"I understand you've got something," Whitaker said. "Show me."

Isaac and Vangelos led them down the pier. They turned at the outermost dock and passed along the starboard side of Hammersmith's boat. Two jacketed agents buzzed across the boat's decking, flipping over cushions and opening holds.

The USERT agents led them to a large cubic toolbox sitting on the wooden dock. It was steel, painted dark gray, two feet to a side. Its chrome latches were rusted and dulled, but it looked in decent condition for something that'd just been hauled out of the water.

"We found it this morning," Isaac said. The six of them assembled in a small circle around the toolbox. Isaac pointed at the water beyond the dock. "About five feet out from the end of the pier, straight down."

"How deep is the water here?" Danner asked.

"Only twenty-two feet," Vangelos said. "But there's a ton of eelgrass. Had to comb through a thicket before we spotted the box."

"Good work," Whitaker said. "Has anyone opened it yet?"

"No, sir," Isaac said. "We were waiting for you."

Whitaker nodded. "Let's go."

Isaac stepped into the center of the circle. She knelt down and unclipped two thick, metal latches that secured the toolbox lid. With a grunt she flipped the lid open, revealing the contents that lay inside. Mackenzie's breath paused as she joined the others in leaning forward.

Inside the toolbox rested two items.

The first was a pistol: matte black, polymer plastic. It was dirty and worn. Mackenzie didn't know much about guns, but the expression on Danner's face made it clear the gun was a Glock 19.

The second item, resting under the barrel of the Glock, was a laptop. A fifteen-inch MacBook Pro, still luminescent silver after two days underwater. An oversized sticker, faded from time, was clearly visible on the laptop's surface.

It was an italicized uppercase *J*, in the unmistakable Journy green.

CHAPTER 36

Twenty-seven days after Trevor Canon's death

Whitaker spent the next twenty minutes on the phone. He paced along the pier, tan overcoat flapping behind him.

Mackenzie watched the remaining divers from the FBI's Underwater Search and Evidence Response Team. Then she moved back to Hammersmith's boat, now empty of federal agents.

Mackenzie wasn't sure if Hammersmith's boat qualified as a yacht or something smaller. It seemed long, with multiple decks and an array of technical equipment slapped on top. Every inch of the hull was a clean, smooth white—just like Hammersmith's helicopter.

The boat's name was painted in gold italics near the front: *Hammer Hydra*. Beneath, in smaller letters, someone had painted a list of global landmarks the *Hammer Hydra* had navigated.

EQUATOR: 2014
PANAMA CANAL: 2011
TROPIC OF CANCER: 2012
TROPIC OF CAPRICORN: 2014

Mackenzie stood for a moment and stared at the list. Tropic of Capricorn, she thought. The phrase snagged on a corner of her mind.

"Danner."

Whitaker's summoning of Danner broke Mackenzie's concentration. Danner hustled over to meet Whitaker on the central pier.

Mackenzie moved casually in their direction. Danner and Whitaker seemed not to notice as she drifted within earshot, but their voices were low enough that Mackenzie caught only snippets of their conversation as she resumed her train of thought.

"What'd they say?" Danner asked.

"It's not enough," Whitaker replied.

"Not enough?" Danner's voice strained. "Are they kidding?"

"We need more." Whitaker's deep voice was laced with frustration.

"What more do they want?"

"They're U.S. attorneys. They always want more."

Tropic of Capricorn, Mackenzie thought, staring at the *Hammer Hydra*'s golden letters. Whitaker had said something about Vitaly Kovalev's nickname: the Bull. *Because he's a Taurus.* At the time Whitaker said he'd been making a joke; now Mackenzie realized the comment had been condescending.

Taurus. Capricorn. Astrological signs.

"We just found the gun and Canon's laptop," Danner said to Whitaker.

"Circumstantial, they say."

"Circumstantial? The murder weapon and an item stolen from the scene?"

"You know the gun isn't a slam dunk."

"Fine," Danner said. "But we have a witness who saw both being dumped *by* Kovalev on *Hammersmith's* dock."

"The neighbor couldn't identify Kovalev. Couldn't make out a face."

"What about the badge protocol? And the warehouse video? All our background on motive, with the new technology that Hammersmith wants?"

"Not enough," Whitaker said. In her peripheral vision, Mackenzie saw Whitaker shake his head, hands on his waist. "We need a direct link between Hammersmith and the violence, between the conspiracy and the murder itself."

Taurus, Mackenzie thought. Capricorn. Astrological signs. Where else had she—

Sagittarius.

Circus Sagittarius, the name of the mysterious group renting the warehouse.

Mackenzie had always found astrology to be unfathomably stupid. Now, for the first time, she wished she had paid it more attention.

Taurus, she thought. The bull was the symbol. But what was the symbol for Capricorn? Or Sagittarius? She pulled out her phone, opened a search.

"We have Kovalev on camera," Danner was saying, "at the warehouse, confronting Canon and Yoo."

"No audio," Whitaker said. "Need to know what they were saying to tie it back to Hammersmith."

"We have Kovalev striking Yoo."

"Do you want to get Kovalev on assault?" Whitaker said.

"No," Danner admitted. "But we could bring Kovalev in and go from there."

"Okay," Whitaker said. "Where do you suggest we find him?" Danner didn't reply. "We need a direct link," Whitaker repeated, "between Hammersmith and the violence. That means bringing Kovalev into the open."

"How?"

Mackenzie typed *Sagittarius symbol* and hit search.

"Stanley Yoo," Whitaker said. "We know the Ten need him."

"That's right," Danner said.

Stanley Yoo, Mackenzie thought. Stanley Yoo. Stanley Yoo. Everybody in San Francisco wants to find Stanley fucking Y—

Mackenzie froze.

The search results loaded, an image appearing on Mackenzie's screen. She stared at it with surprise. The loose thread in her mind finally came free, unraveling all that lay behind it.

"Yoo will draw out the Ten," Whitaker said. "As a witness, he can corroborate what happened at the warehouse. He can tie everything with Canon back to Hammersmith and the money."

"They're the links," Danner said. "Kovalev and Yoo. If we want to get Hammersmith, we need both of them."

"Yes," Whitaker said.

"But we still have our problem," Danner said. "We don't know where the hell Stanley Yoo is."

Mackenzie's voice cut through the quiet of the marina. "I do," she said.

Danner and Whitaker fell silent, their faces snapping to Mackenzie.

Mackenzie walked toward them, raising her phone to share the image on her screen. It was the symbol for Sagittarius: a centaur holding a bow and arrow, the aim pointed up and to the right.

"You know where Yoo is?" Danner asked.

"Yes," Mackenzie said. "I know where he is. Right now, as we speak."

"Where?"

Mackenzie gave a small, almost embarrassed smile. "Burning Man."

Danner's eyes popped. "Burning Man?"

"I just put it together."

"How?"

"This symbol," Mackenzie said, gesturing to the centaur on her phone. "It's the symbol for Sagittarius."

"As in Circus Sagittarius."

Mackenzie nodded. "I've seen this symbol before. On a unicorn costume in Stanley Yoo's closet."

Whitaker looked like he might jump off the dock. "A unicorn costume?"

"Neon yellow," Mackenzie said. "Custom made. Quality fabric, not cheap. It's the exact type of thing someone wears to Burning Man."

Danner looked at Whitaker. "Burning Man is a festival," Danner said. "Held every year in the Nevada desert. People camp, build elaborate art installations, wear costumes, do a bunch of drugs, listen to weird music. There's no money, no electricity, no running water. Everything is brought in."

Whitaker's voice was sandpaper dry. "I'm familiar."

Danner looked back at Mackenzie. "You saw the costume in Yoo's closet?"

"I also saw a photo of Yoo *in* the costume, on his fridge. He was with Trevor. The background was neon, and they were both wearing eye makeup."

"I saw it," Danner said.

"Same photo was in Trevor's office," Mackenzie said. "On his bookshelf. At first I thought it was a music festival. Now I realize it was Burning Man."

"Brady Fitzgerald said that Yoo went to Burning Man every summer. Two weeks."

"Like clockwork," Mackenzie added. "Never missed it. And Cassiopeia said that when Stanley Yoo does something—"

"He does it all the way," Danner finished.

"Hold on," Whitaker said, raising a hand. "Stanley Yoo has been missing. Our best people haven't found him. And now you think he's going to show up at a festival in Nevada? Would he be that stupid?"

"He'd be exactly that stupid," Mackenzie replied. "Burning Man isn't just a festival. For people in tech it's like a religious experience. Everyone goes. Celebrities, founders, executives. Tobias from Spyder goes every year."

"You might be right," Danner said, thinking.

"For many people it's the most important event of the year. Yoo had tons of other costumes in his closet. I bet he's one of those people. And even now, even with everything going on, he won't miss it."

Danner had a new excitement in his voice. "But Circus Sagittarius—how does that fit in?"

"I think it's the name of Yoo's camp." Mackenzie assembled the pieces as she spoke. "Burning Man is in the middle of the desert. Like you said: No food, no services, no water or electricity, so you have to bring everything in. People organize into camps that take collective action to set up infrastructure. They have a theme, and they coordinate everything together. Set up their RVs, tents, porta-potties, share meals, make art."

"They set all that up in the middle of nowhere?" Whitaker asked.

"You'd be amazed," Mackenzie said. "Some of the camps have been around for decades. They have leadership groups, fundraising, dues, whole thing. And most of them have physical spaces where they keep all their desert crap during the rest of the year."

"The warehouse," Danner said. "You think Yoo already had it—even *before* the M1ND project."

"It was Burning Man storage," Mackenzie said, "for Yoo's camp, Circus Sagittarius."

"We need more than guesswork," Whitaker said.

"I'm not guessing," Mackenzie said. She stared at Whitaker and Danner, five feet of Hammersmith's dock separating them. "I won't pretend to know where Yoo's been hiding out for the past few weeks. But I know where he is *now*. Burning Man started two days ago. Stanley Yoo is there."

Whitaker looked at Danner. "You agree with her?"

Danner gave Whitaker a stiff nod. "It lines up, sir. And it's the first real lead we've had on Yoo."

Whitaker pressed his lips together. "If we go, it's a significant commitment. Resources, time, manpower."

"So commit them," Mackenzie said, frustration mounting. "Like Danner says, it's our best bet so far."

Whitaker's eyes were heavy. "I can't operate on hunches."

"It's not a hunch," Mackenzie insisted. "Look at all the supporting pieces of information. The warehouse registration, the symbol—"

Mackenzie stopped. A new memory broke through: an image almost identical to the centaur's bow and arrow. She had seen the symbol before, she realized. Even before the Canon investigation began.

"I can corroborate this theory," Mackenzie said. She almost wanted to laugh. "Hold on."

Mackenzie held out her phone and moved closer to Whitaker and Danner. She looked up a contact and dialed, putting the phone on speaker.

"Who are you calling?" Danner asked.

"Kevin Reiter," Mackenzie said. "He's the founder of Lexie, the fintech company."

"I've heard of it," Danner said. "How do you know him?"

"Long story."

A man's voice answered the phone. "Office of Kevin Reiter."

"Hi there," Mackenzie said into the phone. "This is Gretchen, from Roger Hammersmith's office. Can I connect him?"

"Oh," the man said. "Gretchen. Uh, let me see if Kevin's available."

"Roger said it's urgent," Mackenzie said.

"Of course," the man said. "One moment."

Mackenzie, Danner, and Whitaker huddled around her phone. A few seconds passed.

"Roger." Reiter's reedy voice echoed through the speaker. "How are you?"

Mackenzie held the phone up to her mouth. "Hello, Kevin."

A pause. "Who is this?"

"Mackenzie Clyde. From the Battery. The solarium."

Reiter's voice grew acidic. "You."

Danner, watching at Mackenzie's shoulder, raised his eyebrows.

Reiter continued. "I don't know what game you think you're playing—"

Mackenzie cut him off. "Roger asked me to call. Need to ask you something."

"I already signed your fucking settlement," Reiter said. "I'm going to fire my goddamn assis—"

"One question," Mackenzie said. "Answer it, and you'll never have to speak to me again."

A pause. "One question."

"The night of our meeting," Mackenzie said, "your T-shirt had a symbol on the chest pocket. An arrow pointed up and to the right."

"So?"

"What was that arrow a symbol for?"

"Why are you asking?"

"Just answer, Kevin. Then we're done."

Reiter hesitated. "Circus Sagittarius."

"And what is that?"

"It's a Burning Man thing."

"Like a camp?"

Reiter scoffed. "It's not a camp. We don't sleep in the fucking *dirt*. It's a helluva lot more than that. You wouldn't know."

"Why wouldn't I know?"

"Because," Reiter said derisively, "Circus Sag isn't a bunch of hippies riding unicycles around the Playa. This is next-level Burning Man. Invite only. We don't talk about it with outsiders."

"The camp is happening this year, I assume?"

"I'm headed there in a couple days. Look, you said one question. I'm hanging up."

"One more thing," Mackenzie said. She leaned toward her phone. "Stanley Yoo. Is he connected to Circus Sagittarius?"

"Stanley Yoo?"

"The CTO at Journy. Worked very closely with Trevor Canon."

"I know who he is."

"Is Yoo part of Circus Sagittarius?"

Reiter laughed, the sound grating Mackenzie's ears. "You really don't know anything, do you? Of course Stanley Yoo is part of Circus Sagittarius. He founded the fucking thing."

CHAPTER 37

Twenty-seven days after Trevor Canon's death

Mackenzie opened the door of her rented Hyundai and stepped into the dust. She studied her reflection in the driver's window.

She wore white sneakers, pink yoga pants, and a feathery pink top she'd found at a Haight vintage store. She'd applied pink mascara and pink lipstick. For the coup de grâce, atop her hair rested a fuzzy pink hat in the shape of a flamingo's head, the neck and beak protruding outward over her face.

Mackenzie assessed her costume in the sedan's window. All in all, she made a passable flamingo.

If the shoe fits, she thought.

Behind Mackenzie lay the interstellar vastness of the Nevada desert, a sweeping landscape of dust and sagebrush and rock that shimmered in the unforgiving heat. The sun was beginning its descent, light growing softer in the ebbing hours of the afternoon.

To Mackenzie's side lay the entrance to Burning Man: a row of shipping containers retrofitted as check-in stations. And straight ahead, one hundred yards across the hard-packed caramel sand, lay Black Rock City, the patch of desert that every August was transformed into the temporary home of seventy thousand Burning Man acolytes. From her parking spot Mackenzie saw a half-organized sprawl of tenting and tarps, generators and water tanks, parked trucks and Jeeps and more RVs than she'd ever seen in her life. The whole thing looked like an REI store shaken up and dumped into the desert.

Mackenzie pulled a black backpack out of the car and checked her phone. No wifi. One intermittent bar of cell network. Just as she'd expected.

Not that it mattered. It was too late to change the plan anyway.

After Hammersmith's marina, Whitaker had made phone calls and the big oily bureaucracy of the FBI had churned into motion. The Bureau didn't have time to mount the type of comprehensive operation it typically preferred. They'd have to move fast.

"We're setting a trap," Whitaker had decreed. "We have two objectives: Get Vitaly Kovalev, and get Stanley Yoo. We know Kovalev will go after Yoo. So we provide Kovalev with a trail. We find Yoo. Kovalev finds us. We take both."

Danner had looked at Mackenzie. "You'll tell Hammersmith you're going to Burning Man. Tell him that you've found Yoo. It's what you'd normally do, yes?"

"Yes," Mackenzie had answered. "He'd expect me to tell him the minute I found Stan."

"Okay," Danner said. "Forget us. Pretend you're going to get Yoo on your own. What would you do?"

"I'd rent a car. Corporate account."

Whitaker cut in. "Rent the car. Tell Hammersmith where you're taking it. He'll tell the Ten, and Kovalev will follow your trail."

"So you're using Yoo as bait," Mackenzie said. And me, she thought.

"It's the only way," Danner interjected. "If you're right that he's at Burning Man, then he's already putting himself in danger."

"But I'll be leading Kovalev straight to him."

"You will," Danner agreed. "But we're giving ourselves a head start. By the time Kovalev and his team get transport and logistics together, they should be at least two hours behind us."

"You're forgetting something," Mackenzie said. "Kovalev and Hammersmith know I'm working with you. They'll suspect that following me to Yoo is a trap."

"That's possible," Danner said. "But even if they do, Hammersmith and the Ten want Yoo badly enough that they'll make a play for him. Like us, this is their first chance since Yoo disappeared."

Mackenzie had paused. "Two hours ahead of Kovalev," she said. "I'll have two hours to find Circus Sagittarius, find Yoo, and get him to the rendezvous point."

"Yes," Danner said. "Get to the rendezvous, hit the signal, and wait for us."

"And Kovalev," Mackenzie said.

"Yes," Danner said again. "But you probably won't see him coming. Kovalev won't burst in like he did at the warehouse. He knows what he's doing." Danner paused, then added, "But so do we."

So Mackenzie had hit the road in a rented beige Hyundai. As she pulled out of the downtown Hertz, she'd sent a text to Hammersmith.

> I know where Stanley Yoo is: Burning Man. Danner and
> the Feds think I'm crazy, but I rented a car and I'm
> headed there now. I'll text as soon as I find him.

Now, four hours later, Mackenzie stared at her phone through the desert heat. Hammersmith had never replied.

She thought back to Danner's last bit of insistence in the FBI field office: *but so do we.* It left Mackenzie far from reassured. Her mind returned to a visual that she'd found difficult to shake during her drive to Nevada: a mouse moving through a maze, searching for a piece of cheese while shadowy eyes observed from above. Danner and Whitaker's plan sounded straightforward, but Mackenzie hadn't voiced many of the questions that rose in her mind. Even if she found Circus Sagittarius, how would she get in? And once she found Stanley Yoo, how would he react?

They were questions Mackenzie couldn't answer. She and Danner and Whitaker couldn't plan for everything. A good part of what transpired over the coming evening was going to depend entirely on Mackenzie's ability to improvise. It was an unsettling reality.

Before leaving San Francisco, Danner had pulled her aside for a final word. "Kovalev and Hammersmith need Stanley Yoo alive. But you . . ."

Danner had left the rest unsaid. *But you? Not so much.*

"I know," said Mackenzie.

"Be careful," Danner said. Mackenzie sensed it was the closest he would get to a pep talk.

Now Mackenzie was on her own. She locked the Hyundai and stuffed her phone into her waistband. She threw her keys into the backpack, checking to make sure the flare gun was in there with them. Not an actual gun—Danner had informed her that the FBI couldn't lend a firearm to an unlicensed civilian. Mackenzie had replied that a gun would've been wasted on her anyway. She had no idea how to use one.

Mackenzie hitched the backpack onto her shoulders and trudged through the dust to Black Rock City. A mouse in a maze, she thought. Mackenzie couldn't pretend she was surprised. She'd known from the beginning that a scenario like this could be the ultimate outcome. And she'd made her choices anyway.

You get one life. So get the hell on with it.

Black Rock City was much bigger than Mackenzie had expected. The full diameter was nearly three miles, and shaped like a thick, circular horseshoe. In the center was an open circle of desert referred to as the Playa, half a mile across. And at the epicenter of the Playa lay the Man, a towering wooden edifice that was ceremonially burned at the close of the event. Mackenzie walked toward Black Rock City's entrance gate at the bottom of the horseshoe.

Two hours, she thought. Two hours to sift through a city of seventy thousand people, find Stanley Yoo, and get to the rendezvous point. Two hours for Danner, Whitaker, and the FBI to set their trap.

THROOONNNG.

Mackenzie jumped as a deep bass note thundered across the desert. It was incredibly loud; the bass reverberated off the rocky, prehistoric landscape and gradually settled in the marrow of Mackenzie's bones.

What the fuck was that?

Mackenzie waited a moment. Then she regathered herself and moved into the dusty, chaotic extravagance of Black Rock City.

Burning Man looked like the largest, dustiest campground Mackenzie had ever seen. Or a military base on acid. She saw trucks and trailers everywhere. RVs rested together at odd angles, parked front to back in a line, or placed into circles, surrounding a camp like elephants around a water hole.

She saw every form of tent imaginable, from two-person nylon numbers to humungous, pole-supported marquees. Some had full furniture sets beneath them—even rugs.

Mackenzie saw hundreds of generators, massive solar arrays. She heard the steady beat of electronic music emanating from countless speakers, so omnipresent that it seemed to originate in the desert floor itself.

She moved north along a main thoroughfare, heading toward the center of Black Rock City. The avenue was busy with traffic. Most people were on bicycles, each customized with colorful accessories and strange attachments. She saw a bicycle done up like Fozzie Bear, brown fur covering its frame. She saw a handful of unicycles.

There was dust everywhere. Dust already covering Mackenzie's legs, dust crusting on the flamingo beak above her head. Dust under her fingernails. Dust caking her lips.

Boomp. Boomp. Boomp. Boomp. The beat of the electronic music was inescapable, distant and near and everywhere in between. It seeped into Mackenzie's blood, infesting her cells, flowing into her heart and setting it to the rhythm of the desert.

She reached an intersection and turned west. At the field office she'd studied an online map of Black Rock City. Circus Sagittarius was clearly marked, and Mackenzie had felt confident she'd be able to find it.

Now that she was on the ground, she wasn't so sure. She felt adrift in a storm of neon hedonism. The lowering angle of the sun cast ev-

erything in long shadows, compounding her sense of entering another dimension.

She saw bars everywhere. Set up on tables, behind wooden shacks,
pulled on bicycle trailers. People clustered around them holding little
metal cups. She saw a big tent with a skull and crossbones and a sign
reading ABANDON ALL EGO, YE WHO ENTER HERE. She saw a camp
called Attention Deficit Order. She saw a booth advertising a Mis-
fortune Teller and a tent offering FREE HJS: INQUIRE WITHIN. She
saw an old-fashioned phone booth, red and polished, the kind you'd
see next to Beefeaters on the streets of London. A sign on its window
promised a DIRECT LINE TO GOD.

She passed a man who stood next to a giant water tank. He held
a hose. "Water blast!" he asked.

"No thanks," Mackenzie said.

Mackenzie quickened her pace, feeling self-conscious in her flamingo costume. She'd hoped to blend in, but now she realized that
the costume was woefully subpar. Everyone wore colorful hats and
zany sunglasses. Many people wore little else, choosing to beat the
desert heat in leotards and spandex—always in silver, gold, or a sparkly neon. She saw a hundred top hats, two hundred tutus. She passed
a guy dressed up in full Master Chief regalia. *Dune* costumes were
everywhere: She saw a half dozen Fremen and a guy in a papier-
mâché sandworm. She saw more animals than Noah's Ark, croco-
diles and giraffes and otters and camels. She saw a million unicorns
in every possible shade of neon, and thought of Stanley Yoo.

How the hell was she going to find him? She was surrounded by
anarchy. On the flip side, she felt even more certain that her hypothesis was correct: Yoo was here. He would feel confident that he could
remain anonymous, go unnoticed. It was the only place on earth a
man in a fluorescent unicorn costume could hide in plain sight.

THROOONNNG.

The deafening bass fell once more across Black Rock City. Mackenzie flinched and checked her phone: Twenty minutes had passed.
She kept walking.

The light slackened, the sun continuing its descent. It was still
impossibly hot. The electronic music thumped in her blood. The dust

rendered her white sneakers into desert camouflage. She kept walking.

Boomp. Boomp. Boomp. Boomp.

She stopped at another intersection. According to the map in her head, she'd arrived near the general location of Circus Sagittarius. But she saw no sign of the camp.

What had Kevin Reiter said? *Invite only. We don't talk about it with outsiders.*

There won't be a sign, Mackenzie thought. She circled around and found it within a minute. In a place like Black Rock City, attempting to be inconspicuous was the surest way to stand out.

Circus Sagittarius lay behind an impassable wall of four luxury RVs. After days at Burning Man their sides remained as glassy and white as Hammersmith's boat, windows covered to ward off lookie-loos.

Between the RVs rested a five-foot gap that served as entrance to the camp. A sign stretched across the opening and held a single image: a centaur with a bow and arrow, facing up and to the right.

Mackenzie approached a bouncer leaning against the tail of an RV. He was bearded, dressed in bright gold stretch pants and a black T-shirt. The same arrow logo as Kevin Reiter's appeared on the chest pocket. He held an iPad in one hand.

"Name?" the bouncer said.

"Mackenzie Clyde."

The man scanned the iPad. "Not on the list."

"You're not letting me in?"

"Private party," the bouncer said. "Invite only."

Mackenzie cocked her head to one side. "Isn't Burning Man all about community and togetherness?"

The bouncer smiled. "Sure," he said. He nodded behind him, where Mackenzie could see a huge marquee tent. There was string lighting, high-top tables covered in linen, and, most impressively, no sign of sand. The entire camp was covered in raised wooden decking, like the ballroom stage at the Futurist Summit.

"But we've got a lot of high-net-worth individuals," the bouncer said. "They value their privacy. If you're not on the list, can't let you in."

Mackenzie thought about arguing, but felt the clock ticking. Kovalev was still coming. No time for junking around. She threw her fastball.

"Here's what we're gonna do," Mackenzie said. "You're gonna find whoever's in charge, and tell them that Mackenzie Clyde wants to come in. Tell them I work directly for Roger Hammersmith, and he's demanded that I enter. You're going to check out my credentials, look me up on LinkedIn, and then you're going to come back here and welcome me inside."

The bouncer hesitated. "Roger Hammersmith, huh?"

"The very one."

The bouncer disappeared into the camp. Mackenzie waited, watching traffic filter by.

THROOONNNG.

The bass pounded off the metal sides of the RVs and Mackenzie jumped again, heart skipping a beat.

The bouncer reappeared, expression sheepish. "Come on in," he said.

Mackenzie didn't reply. She stepped past him and into the exclusive confines of Circus Sagittarius.

CHAPTER 38

Twenty-seven days after Trevor Canon's death

Mackenzie immediately felt a drop in temperature. Air conditioners blasted a chill through the marquee tent, fighting against the desert heat.

Mackenzie saw communal tables, designer furniture, potted plants. A sprawling buffet where a chef prepared sushi atop mountains of crushed ice. A large bar, above which an oversized monitor showed a live feed of the Playa, the open epicenter of Black Rock City.

Everything was clean. The coating of dust that permeated the rest of Burning Man was gone.

Mackenzie spotted a series of white igloo-like yurts, pipes connecting them to water tanks and bulky HVAC systems. A stable of generators whirred in a corner. The space was strangely uncrowded; maybe a dozen Burners drifted through the camp. Opposite the buffet, a tall Scandinavian DJ spun mellow electronic music.

There was nothing circus-like or astrological about the atmosphere. There was nothing *Burning Man*. She could've been in the atrium at Journy headquarters.

The clock ticked in her head as she moved through the marquee tent, looking for Yoo's face—or at least someone in a unicorn costume. Mackenzie checked her phone again: ninety minutes left. She thought for a moment about Kovalev and his team. Rationally, Mackenzie agreed with Danner's assessment: She should have plenty of lead time. There were only so many paths into Black Rock City. But she couldn't ignore her undercurrent of anxiety. Her right hand pulsed with pain, wrist tight and stiff even in the heat.

She pushed it out of her mind and refocused on her objective. Find Yoo. Get him to the rendezvous. Get the hell out.

She moved to the bar, where two men stood in patterned spandex. "Have you guys seen Stan?" she asked.

The two men looked at her blankly. "Stan?" one asked.

"Stanley Yoo."

The men shook their heads. "Sorry. Don't know him."

Mackenzie asked two women at the communal table. She asked a man watching the giant television. She asked the DJ.

Nobody had seen Yoo. Nobody even knew who he was.

Mackenzie felt a creeping onset of panic as she circled the marquee. Maybe she'd been wrong about Burning Man. So what if Yoo had started Circus Sagittarius? Maybe he wasn't, in fact, stupid enough to attend when he was hiding from Kovalev. Maybe this idea had been a colossal waste of time.

"Mackenzie!"

A familiar figure moved toward her. Short and sinewy, the man weaved between lounge furniture, gait unsteady. He was dressed in a Boba Fett costume that'd been recolored in lime green and electric blue. It took Mackenzie a moment to recognize him.

"Hugo Chamberlain," she said.

Hugo smiled wide and then, to Mackenzie's astonishment, stepped up and greeted her with a warm hug. As they separated, his eyes sparkled. Hugo's features appeared incapable of doing anything but smiling broadly, grin frozen in a slight underbite.

Mackenzie had lived in San Francisco long enough to recognize the signs. Hugo Chamberlain had ingested enough Molly to light up a Christmas tree.

"I didn't expect to see you here," Mackenzie said.

"I come every year!" Hugo said. He gestured to his costume. "All work and no play makes Hugo a dull boy!" He laughed at his own joke, then tilted his head. "Besides, I could say the same to you. Did you join Circus Sag?"

"No," Mackenzie said, thinking. Danner never told Hugo that Stanley Yoo was missing. And there's no way Hugo would know anything about M1ND, or the Ten. Hugo should, in theory at least, be unaware of the bigger picture.

THROOONNNG.

Mackenzie flinched again at the power of the bass note, and Hugo laughed. He seemed unaffected.

"What the hell is that?" Mackenzie asked.

"It's the Thunder of Zeus!" Hugo said, as though it was clear as the rising of the sun. "It's the world's biggest drum. They built it in the Playa, special for this year's Burn—"

Mackenzie regretted asking. "Actually, I'm just here to look for Stanley Yoo. Have you seen him?"

"Stan?" Hugo stopped, then looked around the camp. "I know he's here somewhere . . ."

"He's here?" Mackenzie felt an immediate wash of relief.

Hugo looked back at her. "Of course he is. This is his fourteenth Burn in a row." His eyes flashed. "Wait, I just remembered. I think he was headed to the Playa."

"The Playa?" Mackenzie brightened. If Yoo wasn't in the camp, the Playa would be the next best thing. Danner and Whitaker had designated the large, open circle of desert as the rendezvous point. "When?"

"Maybe an hour ago." Hugo paused. "I don't think he wants company, though. He's going to the Temple."

"What's the Temple?" Mackenzie asked.

"The Temple is a sacred place," Hugo said. His voice grew solemn, incongruous with his gleeful features. "It's where people go to honor those who passed away before this year's Burn."

Mackenzie was surprised something like that existed in Black Rock City. "It's where people pay respects to the dead?"

Hugo nodded. "People bring photos, letters, trinkets . . . It's a big memorial."

"How will I know where to find it?"

"It's at the north end of the Playa." Hugo smiled again. "And trust me, you'll know it when you see it."

Seven minutes later, Mackenzie stood at the edge of the Playa. Her head was sweating in the flamingo hat. She removed it and held it by the neck, beak dangling toward the desert floor.

The Playa was a big circle of open desert. Like the rest of Black Rock City, the ground was hard-packed sand. The last vestiges of light were clinging to the sky; the horizon faded into a rosy orange.

The Playa wasn't crowded, but only because it was so sprawling. Mackenzie estimated a thousand people in her vision, maybe more. She'd forgotten to ask Hugo what Yoo's costume was. If Yoo isn't in the Temple, Mackenzie thought, he won't be easy to find out here.

Mackenzie stood near the western side of the Playa. Straight ahead, she saw the Man statue rising above the center of the open dust: a tall, wooden effigy of an androgynous humanoid figure, several stories high. The Man served as Mackenzie's rendezvous point with Danner and his team. According to Danner, the Man's location in the center of open desert would allow them to see Kovalev coming and spring the trap.

There was something disquieting about the Man's shape—it dwelt in the uncanny valley between human and inhuman—so Mackenzie moved her gaze north. She saw the distant outline of a large cedar structure, even taller than the Man. The Temple looked like a pavilion, with multiple layers of pointed, ornate roofs.

Mackenzie extracted her phone from her waistband. She attempted to call Danner but got only a beeping noise. Not enough signal. Instead, she sent him a text.

Have a location on Yoo. En route to him now. Will meet at rendezvous. Be ready.

The text struggled in the poor reception before going through. Then, following the steps of Whitaker and Danner's plan, Mackenzie laid the trail for Kovalev. She flipped to her thread with Hammersmith and saw her last message to him, still unanswered.

> I know where Stanley Yoo is: Burning Man. Danner and
> the Feds think I'm crazy, but I rented a car and I'm
> headed there now. I'll text as soon as I find him.

She composed a new message.

> I was right. Yoo's at Burning Man.

Mackenzie hit send. She prepared to repocket her phone, but it vibrated in her hand before she could. Danner, she thought.

But it wasn't Danner. It was Hammersmith. He'd replied with only one word.

> Where

Mackenzie hesitated. What did Whitaker say? Operate according to standard working procedure. She checked the time. According to Danner, she should have over an hour before Kovalev and the Ten arrived. Mackenzie typed out a reply.

> He's heading to the Man, at the center of Black Rock
> City. I'm going to intercept him there.

She hit send and tucked her phone away. Then she stuffed the flamingo hat into her backpack and stepped onto the Playa.

The Playa was home to the hundreds of extravagant art installations that made Burning Man famous. They were dotted across the desert like exhibits in a surreal museum; Mackenzie walked past several as she cut northeast.

She passed a giant open hand, blue globes of light dangling above. She passed a rocket ship, an Eiffel Tower, an Egyptian pyramid. She passed a lotus flower that slowly opened and closed, the word *KIND* lit up in gold within its petals.

Some of the art also passed her. These were the mutant vehicles of Burning Man: moving art installations on wheels. All of them were equipped with their own flashing lights, dance platforms, and sound systems, creating a rolling cascade of electronic music that rotated around the Playa.

Boomp. Boomp. Boomp. Boomp.

Mackenzie saw a fluorescent pirate ship. She saw a galloping herd of zebra, a Komodo dragon with a dancer's pole. Then a squadron of yellow golf carts cruised past, each repurposed to look like a lunar lander. Mackenzie laughed aloud when she realized they were retrofitted Journy Buggies—the uppercase *J* logo still evident under the yellow paint.

Then her vision was caught by something else. Across the Playa Mackenzie saw the front half of an entire jumbo jet. It was a Boeing 747, the top carved out and replaced with an open-air dance platform. It was packed with people. Gyrating bodies danced atop the platform, in the plane cabin, even on the wings. Neon lights flashed from the nose, music blaring. Mackenzie saw the words AIR PLAYA stenciled on the fuselage as it cruised across the desert, like an apparition from a fever dream.

And then Mackenzie came upon the Thunder of Zeus.

Hugo Chamberlain hadn't exaggerated. It was the biggest drum Mackenzie had ever seen.

The Thunder of Zeus was twenty-five feet across and half as many thick. It stood vertically on its edge, supported by metal scaffolding. Its resonant head faced toward Mackenzie, a thick blue lightning bolt painted across the face. Mackenzie saw a bearded, white-haired man standing beside the drum. He wore a Greek toga and a golden crown.

As Mackenzie walked past, the bearded man grabbed a long, metal mallet and stepped away. He began to spin, swinging the mallet around like an Olympian doing the hammer throw, rotating with increasing velocity. Then, with astonishing precision, he brought the huge metal head crashing into the face of the drum.

THROOONNNG.

The noise almost knocked Mackenzie to the ground. She knelt in the desert for a long moment, waiting for the reverberations to fade. Then she rose and moved north.

The Temple emerged before her like an oasis in the desert. It resembled a towering Chinese pagoda, with five layers of pointed roofs, each lined with lanterns that burned red in the dimming light. A wide entrance was carved into the front. Mackenzie walked through it and stepped inside.

The interior was broad and square. More Chinese lanterns were strung from each corner, casting the space in a soft crimson glow. The floor was hard desert.

Mackenzie walked along the inside of the front wall, staring. The entire interior surface was a memorial. Photographs, drawings, paintings, poems, letters—all of it was attached to the four Temple walls, a rambling collage of mourning and remembrance. In each corner lay hundreds of small candles, the flames licking in the gathering darkness. There was no sound beyond the distant thump of music from the Playa outside.

Mackenzie found the scene to be starkly peaceful; almost diametrically opposed to the disorder of Black Rock City.

The Temple wasn't crowded. And as Mackenzie's eyes scanned the room, they fell upon a figure sitting near the back wall. The figure was staring forward, cross-legged, unmoving. They were wearing a bright white astronaut's uniform, plastic space helmet fitted over their head.

As Mackenzie approached, she noticed the astronaut wasn't wearing any shoes. Instead, resting on the ground next to them was a pair of bright silver Rollerblades.

Cassiopeia Moreau's voice echoed in her mind. *One time Stan decided he was going to rollerblade across Japan.*

Investigation is synthesis, Mackenzie thought.

She approached the astronaut and sat next to him in the dust. The astronaut was staring through his helmet visor at a photograph on the wall: It was the image of Stanley Yoo and Trevor Canon arm in arm, the neon spectacle of Burning Man in the background. It told Mackenzie all she needed to know.

Stanley Yoo, Mackenzie thought. She kept her body still as she celebrated inwardly. Stanley Yoo, Stanley Yoo, Stanley Fucking Yoo. The entire world's been looking and *I've* finally found you. I've got you now.

As long as I don't scare you away.

The Temple was impressively quiet. The steady beat of electronic music was barely audible. All Mackenzie could hear was the solitude of the Temple and a distant, whirring noise from somewhere on the Playa. One of the mutant vehicles, Mackenzie thought, passing by on its loop.

THROOONNNG.

Even the Thunder of Zeus felt quieter, though the bass still echoed off the Temple walls. Mackenzie waited for the noise to ebb, then pointed toward the photo of Canon and Yoo.

"Do you miss him?" she asked.

The astronaut waited a beat; he didn't turn to face Mackenzie. His voice sounded hollow inside the space helmet. "Yes and no," he said. "And I don't know." He shrugged. "It's complicated. Did you know him?"

"Not well," Mackenzie said.

The astronaut reached up and removed his helmet, revealing the long, wavy hair and easy features of Stanley Yoo. Still staring at the photograph, Yoo held the helmet between his hands. "He could be selfish, when he wanted something. Merciless, when he thought he was right. Most people thought he was an asshole. But they only knew him in the recent years. After the money."

"Not you?"

Yoo shook his head. "I knew him before all that. His brain and my brain . . . We just had a way of connecting, you know? I can't explain it. Something just clicked. It's how we became friends."

Mackenzie tilted her head toward the photograph. "When was that taken?"

Yoo smiled. "Way back. Before Journy, before the funding, before all the billionaire bullshit. Once all that happened, Trevor couldn't have normal relationships anymore. Everything became transactional. His co-founder, his girlfriend, his executive team . . . the money infected everything."

"Like a virus," Mackenzie said.

Yoo nodded. "All the founder stuff, the attention . . . he changed. The whole Journy experience made him a worse person."

Mackenzie chose her words carefully. "Some say an experience like that doesn't change your character. It just reveals what was already there."

"Maybe that's right." Yoo finally looked over at Mackenzie. "I don't miss Trevor for who he was with everybody else. But I miss Trevor for who he was with *me*. Does that make me selfish?"

"I think it makes you human."

Yoo shook his head, eyes moving back to the wall. "We're funny creatures. We can be completely different animals depending on the context of who's around us. It makes you wonder if there's anything permanent to us at all."

"If we even exist," Mackenzie said, "outside of the way that others perceive us."

"Exactly."

Mackenzie joined him in staring at the wall. She waited a beat before she spoke.

"You've got a lot of people looking for you, Stanley."

Yoo paused. "I know."

"I'm one of them."

"I know," Yoo repeated.

"Where have you been?"

"On a boat." Yoo shrugged. "The Pacific is sixty million square miles. You can hide on the ocean for a lifetime if you know what you're doing." He glanced at Mackenzie. "How'd you know I'd be here?"

Mackenzie returned the shrug. "It's my job."

Yoo nodded. "I figured as much, when you sat down. But I also figured you must be one of the good guys. Otherwise, I'd have never seen you coming at all."

"That's true."

"I didn't kill Trevor," Stanley said.

"We know," Mackenzie said.

"Who's 'we'?" Yoo moved his eyes back to Mackenzie. "Who are you with? Police?"

"FBI," Mackenzie said. She met Yoo's gaze. "We know everything, Stan. We know Journy was failing. We know that you and Trevor were working on a secret project. We know about the warehouse, M1ND, Indira Soti. We know that Roger Hammersmith found out. We know that one of his thugs, Vitaly Kovalev, showed up and assaulted you. And we know that Kovalev killed Trevor. We know all of it. The complete picture."

Yoo dropped his head, letting it fall toward the dirt between his legs. He made an odd sound, somewhere between groan and sigh. "I'm so fucking tired."

"Then come with me." Mackenzie stood and offered her hand. "I'm not the only one who knows you're here. Kovalev is on his way. He's coming for you. Let's get you somewhere safe before that happens."

Yoo hesitated. For a moment Mackenzie wasn't sure what he'd do. He'd been hiding out for weeks, evading everyone. Will he run? she thought. Will he tell me to fuck off?

But Stanley Yoo just shrugged.

"Okay," he said.

CHAPTER 39

Five years before Trevor Canon's death

Mackenzie punched in the security code and pushed through the front door to her building. Grabbing a wad of envelopes from her mailbox, she filed through them mindlessly as she ascended the stairs to her apartment.

Much had changed in the six weeks since her confrontation with Hammersmith. Mackenzie had received her new title and a private office with a sliver view of Nob Hill. Hammersmith had filled her plate with an immediate pile of investigative work: vetting a crypto founder, digging for leverage on a hedge fund, following up on rumors about internal strife at a Soti company.

Neither Mackenzie nor Hammersmith had said another word about what transpired in his office. There'd been no further mentions of blood money or Russian consortiums.

Hammersmith gave assignments. Mackenzie took them.

Mackenzie's hours had also changed. Now she regularly found herself working late into the evening. It was nearly ten P.M. as Mackenzie climbed her stairs.

Mackenzie had lived in her building for three years. She'd rarely encountered her fellow tenants. There'd never been suspicious visitors, strange noises, pulled fire alarms. In the vicinity of her apartment Mackenzie had never sensed even a whiff of danger.

This, combined with the monotonous routine of daily life, had bred in Mackenzie a certain complacency when it came to security. The door to her unit had a knob lock, so she never bothered with the deadbolt. It felt unnecessary—one additional inconvenience that stood between her and her bed at the end of a long workday. Mackenzie had never given it a second thought.

That was about to change.

Mackenzie thrust the key into her doorknob and twisted, pushing the door open. She tossed her mail on a console table. Staring at her phone, mind occupied by work, Mackenzie glided down her long hallway and into the living room.

She stopped.

The curtains were drawn across her bay window. Mackenzie always left her curtains in a specific position. This wasn't it.

She stared at the window dumbly, a mix of surprise and horror seeping into her mind. Then a light switched on behind her.

It had come from her kitchen.

Mackenzie's heart seized. Her instincts screamed out with a painfully simple message, one that her brain was too stunned to fully comprehend.

Someone was in her apartment.

Mackenzie turned as a giant stepped into her hallway.

The man was taller than Mackenzie, with buzzed gray hair and linebacker shoulders. His features were condensed into a scowl, eyes dark, near black. The man's bulky frame seemed to fill the entire hallway, blocking the light. Mackenzie had never seen him before.

Time stopped. For a split second, Mackenzie and the man stared at each other.

"Lock your phone," the man said, "and put it on the floor." His voice was deep, guttural, like a truck engine.

Mackenzie did as she was told.

The man moved toward her, striding down the hallway. Mackenzie instinctively retreated, backpedaling into her living room. The man paused at the threshold as Mackenzie kept moving. She stopped when she'd put as much distance as possible between them.

The man flipped a switch and the living room filled with light. He gestured to Mackenzie's sofa. "You may sit down, if you like." His English was excellent, though it carried a heavy Russian accent.

"I'll stand."

The man's gaze was calm, hands resting comfortably at his sides. He was dressed entirely in black: pants, sneakers, and a sleek hooded jacket. "Do you know who I am?"

Mackenzie shook her head.

"My name is Kovalev," the man said. "Hammersmith and I work for the same people. Do you understand?"

The Russian consortium, Mackenzie thought. Instinctively she'd known it from the moment Kovalev had stepped out of her kitchen. Hammersmith's warning rushed back to her.

I will only say this once, so remember it: They do not fuck around.

"I understand," Mackenzie said.

Kovalev nodded. "Hammersmith said that you know who we work for. Is this true?"

"Yes," Mackenzie said.

The man stared at her across the living room. "What do you know?"

Mackenzie forced herself to breathe. Everything about Kovalev reeked of danger: his frame, his countenance, his casual confidence. Kovalev's body was still, his speech unhurried. He was a man accustomed to being in this position.

"I don't know much," Mackenzie said.

Kovalev's face contracted, eyes darkening. "No games," he said. He stepped deeper into the living room.

Mackenzie raised a hand. "Wait." Kovalev stopped.

A new, overriding directive took hold in Mackenzie's mind: Tell this man whatever he wants and get him out of your apartment.

"I know enough," she said. "Where the money comes from."

"What about where it comes from?"

"I know the shell accounts. Dummy corporations. Trusts."

Kovalev didn't react. "Do you have names?"

Mackenzie hesitated. "Some, yes."

"Who?"

"Yelchin," Mackenzie said. "Oleg Yelchin."

Mackenzie paused. Kovalev's dark eyes watched her, unblinking.

"And Oberon," Mackenzie said. "Gregor and his brother. Dmitri."

Kovalev's eyes fell downward, as though considering the information. Mackenzie let her feet slip to the left, circling around the edge of her living room. She eyed the French doors that led to her bedroom, triangulating her position. There was another doorway from her bedroom out to the hallway, behind Kovalev. If she could get there before him . . .

Kovalev raised his eyes and Mackenzie froze anew. "I could kill you now. Normally, this would be my preference. It is the simpler path. Cleaner."

Kovalev paused, and Mackenzie's heart pounded in her chest.

"But," Kovalev continued, "Hammersmith says you will be an asset to us."

"I will," Mackenzie said. She heard the panic in her voice.

Kovalev drifted a step deeper into the living room. Mackenzie instinctively matched him, circling around the opposite side, keeping as much distance as she could. She willed herself not to glance at her bedroom.

"You've made an arrangement with Hammersmith. He has made your responsibilities clear."

Mackenzie nodded eagerly. "He has, yes. Very clear."

Kovalev slowly circled as Mackenzie matched him, two planets orbiting the sofa in the middle of the room. Kovalev maintained his angle on the hallway, but the French doors drew slightly closer to Mackenzie.

"You understand," Kovalev said, "what is required of you. Not just performance, but silence."

"Yes," Mackenzie said.

"Obedience."

"Yes." Mackenzie felt her head nodding involuntarily. "I understand. Completely."

Kovalev stopped for a moment, eyes still fixed to Mackenzie's. "I believe you," he said. "I believe that you understand *now*. But in months, years . . ." Kovalev tilted his head. "This conversation could fade. It is the nature of memory. Knots become loose, edges become dull. I need to make sure you won't forget your responsibilities."

"I won't," Mackenzie said. "I'll give you anything you want."

"But that is the problem," Kovalev said. His voice dropped an octave and Mackenzie felt her muscles tense. "You have no family. Your mother is dead. You have nothing to give me. So I must find another way."

Kovalev reached into his jacket and withdrew an object. He held it up for Mackenzie to see.

The object was a mallet hammer. The head was bigger than Mackenzie's fist, its metal dull in the soft light of her living room. The black rubber of the handle peeked between Kovalev's thick fingers.

Mackenzie bolted.

She sprang laterally, putting the sofa between her and Kovalev. She pushed off her long legs and dashed for her bedroom.

But Kovalev was faster. Impossibly fast for a man of his size.

He vaulted over the sofa and leapt across the room. In an instant he'd cut off Mackenzie, steps before she reached the French doors.

She froze.

Kovalev's expression remained calm. Before Mackenzie's brain could even process the motion, he jabbed his free hand outward. It struck Mackenzie in the high part of her stomach, just below the rib cage.

Air exploded from her lungs. A sharp, disorienting pain burst through her torso.

Mackenzie gasped and tumbled to the floor of her living room. She lay on her right shoulder, left hand reaching for her stomach. Her right arm fell across the creaky floorboards, palm facing the ceiling.

She couldn't move. Her lungs felt like an open air lock. Oxygen rushed out; none came in.

Kovalev knelt near Mackenzie's head. He adjusted the position of the mallet hammer, holding it in the air above the base of Mackenzie's motionless right hand.

Mackenzie willed her body to move, but nothing happened. She struggled for breath.

Kovalev spoke with the same measured calm he'd carried since the moment he'd appeared in her hallway. Mackenzie closed her eyes, frozen by panic.

"Remember," Kovalev said. "We are watching."

And he brought the hammer down.

CHAPTER 40

Twenty-seven days after Trevor Canon's death

Yoo wore socks, his silver Rollerblades carried in one hand. Mackenzie hitched her backpack higher on her shoulders. Together they strode out of the Temple and into a helter-skelter explosion of color.

Sunset fell over Black Rock City. The sky was afire with undulating layers of tangerine orange, carousel pink, periwinkle blue. The distant mountains melded into a smooth horizon of inky black.

The desert floor shimmered before them. The Playa was alive with light and energy. Every art installation and mutant vehicle had activated their LED light displays. It transformed the desert into a moving ocean of neon, a million Vegas strips stretched across the earth.

Mackenzie stopped outside the Temple, transfixed.

Yoo stopped next to her. "First Burn?"

"Yeah."

Yoo smiled. "Pretty fucking beautiful, isn't it?"

"Yeah," Mackenzie said again. To her own surprise, she meant it.

They kept walking. Mackenzie pointed in the direction of the

Man, the tall, unsettling humanoid looming in the distance. "That's our rendezvous point with the FBI team," Mackenzie said. "Then we'll get you out of here."

"Okay," Yoo said.

They walked in silence across the open desert. The Man stood directly ahead, and Mackenzie studied its shape as it grew steadily nearer.

Then she noticed something was wrong.

There was a new object in the desert. It was straight ahead, just a stone's throw from the Man. Mackenzie had noticed it when they left the Temple, but from a distance she'd assumed it was another mutant vehicle.

Now, however, they were close enough to see that it wasn't an art installation. It wasn't a mutant vehicle. It wasn't anything, in fact, that belonged on the Playa.

It was a helicopter. And every part of it, from nose to tail, was painted in a smooth, glossy white.

The *Hammer Angel*, Mackenzie thought. Roger's helicopter. And then reality hit her. How could she have been so stupid?

Hammersmith and Kovalev hadn't wasted valuable time arranging logistics. They'd just taken Hammersmith's helicopter and flown straight to the desert. That whirring noise she'd heard inside the Temple had been the *Hammer Angel* coming in for landing.

Kovalev and his team should be at least two hours behind us.

Wrong.

And then Mackenzie recalled what she'd texted Hammersmith, just minutes before.

Her stomach dropped. Three figures stood next to the *Hammer Angel*, heads up, postures alert, scanning the surrounding Playa. One of the figures was tall, broad-shouldered, shaped like a muscly triangle. Mackenzie's right hand flooded with a dull, familiar pain.

Vitaly Kovalev was here.

And Mackenzie had led him straight to the rendezvous point.

Mackenzie stopped in her tracks. Yoo stopped with her. He followed her gaze.

"Fuck," Yoo said. "Fuck, fuck, fuck."

"Hold on," Mackenzie said.

Yoo's entire face transformed. The color drained from his features, eyes bursting wide, blinking rapidly. His shoulders began to tremble.

"He doesn't see us yet," Mackenzie said. Her mind flooded with panic, but she kept her voice calm. If Kovalev is at the Man, then where the fuck is Danner?

She continued. "He can't just land in the center of the Playa. People will question what they're doing."

Mackenzie said the words but didn't believe them. Most Burners seemed to be keeping their distance. They probably think it's an art piece, Mackenzie thought.

Yoo was silent, jaw clenched tight. He watched Kovalev prowl the desert a hundred yards away.

A wave of adrenaline coursed into Mackenzie's bloodstream, like the breaking of a dam. She wanted to get away from Kovalev as fast as possible. We need to get back to cover, she thought. But open desert surrounded them in every direction. They were half a mile from the camps of Black Rock City.

Kovalev's team split up. One man stayed near the helicopter while Kovalev and a third man began to sweep the area. Kovalev wore his customary all-black outfit, replete with earpiece and tactical vest.

"Fuck," Yoo said.

"Stay with me, Stan."

Kovalev and his partner turned north, facing in Yoo and Mackenzie's direction. Kovalev stared straight ahead.

Directly at Mackenzie and Yoo.

"Fuck this," Yoo said.

Yoo dropped his Rollerblades and helmet to the desert floor.

He ran.

Mackenzie cursed as Yoo sprinted across the desert. Between his astronaut costume and sudden burst of speed, Yoo was the opposite of inconspicuous. Kovalev and his associate took immediate notice. They gestured to each other and ran in Yoo's direction.

Mackenzie cursed again and pumped her legs into gear. Her muscles protested but she ignored them, letting adrenaline take over.

Yoo was already thirty yards ahead and running fast, heading for the camps at the edge of the Playa. Mackenzie lengthened her strides, her abdomen and chest groaning at the exertion.

For a guy in his socks, Yoo was cutting a decent clip. But Kovalev and his partner were faster. They tore across the desert, moving at an angle to intercept Yoo. Sixty yards became fifty. Fifty became forty.

Where the *fuck* is Danner? Mackenzie thought. There was no sign of him. No Whitaker. Nobody from the FBI.

The thought of the FBI triggered something in her mind. She slowed and twisted the backpack onto one shoulder, withdrawing the flare gun. Still jogging, Mackenzie pointed it up into the fading light and pulled the trigger.

A red fireball launched into the desert sunset, tracing high into the air, above the Man, above the Temple, above the low, sprawling, thrumming hum of Black Rock City.

Nothing happened.

Mackenzie waited, looking toward the Man. There was no sound, no movement. Spring the trap! she thought. Danner, Whitaker, fucking *somebody*.

THROOONNNG.

Mackenzie jumped, the adrenaline and surprise lifting her a full foot off the ground. She gathered herself and kicked her legs back into gear.

Kovalev and his partner pursued Yoo across the Playa. Mackenzie trailed at an angle, blood pumping with fear and adrenaline and panic and rage.

Mackenzie's hand throbbed as she watched Kovalev run. She had no desire to get anywhere close to him. But she'd led them here. She was responsible. And she needed Yoo.

Mackenzie kept running.

Yoo darted through the long, sequined tendrils of a levitating jellyfish. He weaved past a pyramid, jumped over a sparkling gold python. Kovalev followed inexorably, like a lion across the savannah plain.

Yoo yelled at some nearby Burners, waving in the direction of Kovalev as he sprinted past. The Burners were both men, each in bright silver spandex. One of the spandexed men yelled at Kovalev. He stepped into the Russian's path.

Kovalev barely slowed—he dropped a shoulder and plowed through the man's face, running through him like a steamroller over a slug. The spandexed man screamed in pain as he was driven into the dust.

Yoo glanced over his shoulder, eyes widening. Kovalev snarled and kept running.

Mackenzie dragged behind, exhaustion draining her limbs. She cursed Danner with each breath. Where. The. Fuck. Are. You?!!

Suddenly Yoo veered again, changing direction. Mackenzie saw where he was headed.

The plane.

Air Playa taxied slowly across the desert, platform still packed with dancers, strobe lights and music still blasting from every orifice. *Boomp boomp boomp boomp.* At dusk the entire plane was lit with an outline of neon purple, the AIR PLAYA on its side glowing in bright LED green.

Yoo sprinted for the back, where a metal staircase was affixed to the sawed-off fuselage. Yoo caught the staircase and hopped on. He scrambled upward, disappearing into the cabin.

Kovalev barked at his partner. He thrust a finger at the front of the plane, then followed Yoo up the stairs. His partner looped around the side, running hard to get in front of the rolling behemoth.

They're pinning him in, Mackenzie realized. Stanley Yoo had trapped himself.

Mackenzie's abdomen shrieked in pain. She reached the back of the plane just as Yoo emerged on the platform above.

The dance floor of *Air Playa* was a snake pit of humanity cruising thirty feet off the ground. Dancers were packed shoulder to shoulder, squeezed together like sausage in a casing. The beat of the music was unceasing, echoing off the jet's metal plating. Mackenzie's senses were overwhelmed with color and panic.

Boomp. Boomp. Boomp. Boomp.

Yoo pushed his way through the crowd. He moved toward the nose of the jet, but it was slow progress.

Mackenzie realized that Yoo didn't know he was trapped. She

spotted Kovalev's partner running to the front of the plane. She kicked her legs and followed in his direction.

She saw a flash of motion above; Kovalev emerged at the near edge of the dance floor. The Bull windmilled his way through revelers. A Burner in a purple rabbit costume blocked his way, bobbing cluelessly in a musical trance. Kovalev shoved forward, but the rabbit didn't budge. Kovalev growled and the purple rabbit turned to face him. They exchanged words.

In a single furious motion, Kovalev lifted the rabbit up and threw him off the plane.

Mackenzie watched in horror as the man flew face-first over the edge. With a sickening *thud* his body splattered on the jet wing, fifteen feet below.

A cry of shock rose from the plane's dance floor. Burners turned to face Kovalev, gesticulating in anger. Kovalev responded by withdrawing a gun from his tactical vest. He raised it in the air and fired off a shot. The distinctive *crack* of gunfire pierced the beat of the electronic bass.

Kovalev's move had the intended effect. The dancers receded like an ebbing tide. Kovalev charged forward.

Yoo emerged on the nose. He shuffled forward on hands and knees, balanced precariously atop the jumbo jet. He has nowhere to go, Mackenzie thought.

Kovalev followed Yoo onto the nose. He was only fifteen feet behind.

Yoo twisted onto his butt, crab-walking over the cockpit. Looking back, he saw Kovalev and paused. Then, with a sudden motion, he dropped his butt onto the windshield and slid down the front of the plane.

It was a daring move—the nose ended a good distance above the desert floor. Yoo slid forward, gathering speed, and then plunged through the air. For an instant he looked like an astronaut untethered from his shuttle, hurtling through space.

Yoo landed hard on the dusty ground, falling to one side. He yelped in pain. And though Mackenzie respected Yoo's tenacity, his maneuver had been useless.

Vitaly Kovalev's partner was waiting.

The man leapt to Yoo's form, yanking him off the desert floor. He shoved Yoo into a standing position and moved behind him, wrapping his arms around Yoo's chest.

Vitaly Kovalev followed Yoo's path. He slid belly-down against the fuselage, legs first. He fell to ground and landed in a deft roll, deadening the impact. Then he rose and paced to Stanley Yoo.

Mackenzie glanced at the *Hammer Angel*, which rested near the Man a short distance away. It felt like hours had passed since she left the Temple. Where the fucking *fuck* is Danner? Where is the FBI?

Yoo was dazed from the pursuit. He slunk in the arms of Kovalev's partner, head down. Kovalev approached and spat angry words in Yoo's face. Yoo didn't respond. Kovalev slapped Yoo hard on the cheek.

Yoo looked up, arms restrained by Kovalev's partner. Mackenzie watched from her position thirty yards away, feet glued by fear and exhaustion to the dusty ground. The Bull reared back and launched a furious uppercut into the center of Yoo's abdomen.

Yoo retched as his body folded in half. Mackenzie's hand pulsed as she watched; she could almost *feel* the air bursting out of Yoo's lungs. Kovalev's partner held Yoo's body upright as he crumpled in pain.

Kovalev grabbed his gun and leaned forward. He tapped the barrel against Yoo's forehead, spat more vitriol into his ear. Yoo groaned, then staggered into a standing position.

Kovalev gestured with his gun, then circled behind Yoo and pointed it at the back of his head. Slowly, the three of them moved in the direction of the helicopter.

For the tenth time, Mackenzie found her mind consumed with a singular thought: Where was the FBI?

The Man and the helicopter were only a short walk away. Kovalev and his partner marched Yoo toward it, their progress slow but steady as Yoo stumbled forward. Together, the three of them formed a small triangle—Yoo at the front, Kovalev and his partner behind, at each shoulder.

Kovalev tapped his earpiece and snarled instructions. The rotors of the *Hammer Angel* slowly churned into motion.

The Playa was so vast and cacophonous that few Burners had even noticed the chase. The crowd on the plane watched from their perch, a few Burners tending to the fallen purple rabbit on the wing. But the jet kept rolling, taxiing away as Kovalev's trio marched in the opposite direction.

They've got him, Mackenzie thought.

All the days of searching, the prep, the coordination with Danner and Whitaker, her careful approach in the Temple—none of it mattered. They'd set a trap and it'd never sprung.

All her planning, all her sacrifice—for nothing.

The thought filled her with rage.

Mackenzie looked around, scrambling for an idea. Yoo can't get on that helicopter, she thought. If Yoo goes with Kovalev, everything is over. None of this will have been worth anything.

No risk, no reward. Sometimes life is that simple.

And then she saw it.

One of the bright yellow golf carts she'd encountered earlier—the Journy Buggies retrofitted as lunar landers.

One Buggy had peeled off from its group, the driver's attention caught by the commotion near the plane. Now he was parked a stone's throw away, sitting in the driver's seat as he watched Yoo and Kovalev stagger toward the helicopter.

Mackenzie sprinted over.

The driver greeted Mackenzie with a smile. "That was incredible, wasn't it?"

"I need your cart," Mackenzie said, breathing hard. She moved to the open driver's side.

The man seemed not to hear. "I heard they might have performance art this year, but holy *shit*."

"I'm with the FBI," Mackenzie said. "Give me your cart. *Right now.*"

"Oh fuck," the guy said. "Okay."

He sidled out and Mackenzie hopped behind the wheel. She buckled the shoulder belt and shoved the Buggy key into drive. Punching the gas, she peeled a track across the desert, bearing for Yoo and Kovalev.

Mackenzie had been in many Journy Buggies. They drove like any other golf cart: top heavy, jerky steering, electric motor. They topped out at a speed of about twenty-five miles per hour. Not fast.

But plenty for what she had in mind.

The triangle of Yoo, Kovalev, and his partner was nearing the *Hammer Angel.* The shadow of the Man loomed above.

Mackenzie pressed the gas to the floor. She looped around in a wide, careening circle, the cart lurching against the physics of the turn. Once she was directly behind the trio Mackenzie straightened the wheels and surged ahead.

Pedal to the floor, the Buggy streaked across the dusty Playa ground, seventy yards out and closing fast.

Sixty yards away.

Fifty.

A few shreds of color hung in the sky. Dead ahead, Mackenzie saw the two black tactical outfits of Kovalev and his partner. Between them, she caught the flash of a white astronaut costume, caked in Playa dust.

Forty yards.

Thirty.

One advantage of the Buggy's electric motor was its relative quiet—it emitted only a slight high-pitched whir, even at top speed. Against the thumping background of the Playa's electronic music, it was nearly inaudible.

Twenty yards.

Twenty-five miles per hour didn't sound like much. But Mackenzie knew an impact at that speed was more forceful than people realized. How forceful? She wasn't sure.

One way to find out.

Fifteen yards.

Ten.

Mackenzie gritted her teeth as the Buggy sped straight for the backs of Kovalev and his partner. She tensed her hands on the steering wheel, bracing for impact.

Vitaly Kovalev froze.

Maybe he heard the pitchy whine of the Buggy's motor; maybe it was instinct bred from a lifetime of violence. He turned his neck to look back.

His eyes went wide. Mackenzie's Buggy was an instant away. With incredible reflexes, Kovalev leapt to one side.

Mackenzie jerked the wheel, slamming the brake as the Buggy peeled out, flying horizontally across the sand. In the next breath—

Impact.

Mackenzie's Buggy smashed into the back of Kovalev's partner. His body ejected forward like it'd been launched from a cannon, rolling over and through the dust once, then twice, then three times. Finally he came to a stop. His body was contorted into an unnatural shape. It didn't move.

Mackenzie never saw any of it. The seatbelt saved her from the worst of the impact, but her forehead slammed against the steering wheel.

Everything went dark.

When Mackenzie opened her eyes, she saw three things.

First, ahead in the desert—the shape of Kovalev's partner, inert.

Second, near Kovalev's partner—Stanley Yoo on the ground, groaning and holding his leg.

Third, directly to her left, out the Buggy's open driver's side—Vitaly Kovalev.

He stood just eight feet away, the length of a dining table. His shoulders looked as broad and massive as ever. His black tactical gear was covered in Playa dust.

Kovalev's right hand held his gun. It was pointed at the desert floor.

Mackenzie stared at him. Kovalev stared at her. Recognition flashed across his eyes.

The sky faded into the black of night. Kovalev's face was lit by neon LEDs from the Man, which towered above them both, just steps away.

Mackenzie couldn't move. Still strapped to the Buggy, her right hand throbbed with familiar pain. Her entire body was frozen, rigid with fear and the realization of what was going to happen next.

She saw neon lights.

She heard the beat of distant electronic music.

She saw dust and stars and the open desert sky.

She saw the disturbing humanoid figure of the Man, watching from above like a terrifying god.

Kovalev didn't say anything. With calm, measured efficiency, he simply raised the gun, used his left hand to steady it, and pointed it at Mackenzie's head.

He prepared to pull the trigger. And then—

THROOONNNG.

The Thunder of Zeus boomed across the Playa, deep and rich and ear-crushingly loud. A waterfall of sonic power washed over the desert floor.

Kovalev hesitated—just for an instant.

And then his left eye disappeared.

The eyeball, the lid, the lashes—all of them were gone, replaced by a bright red circle of blood.

Suddenly, another circle of red appeared—this time on Kovalev's forehead.

Vitaly Kovalev's arms fell forward. His pistol clattered to the ground below.

Like the felling of a great oak, the Bull's body tumbled to the desert floor. Mackenzie watched, emotionless, as blood poured out of Kovalev's face. It streamed onto the Playa dust and gathered in a small pool near what remained of his head.

And then, emerging from the shadows under the Man, Special Agent Jameson Danner stepped into the neon light, gun drawn, eyes still fixed on Kovalev's lifeless form.

Mackenzie looked at him, unable to speak. Danner looked back at her, expression grave.

Mackenzie passed out.

CHAPTER 41

Twenty-seven days after Trevor Canon's death

Mackenzie and Danner sat in camping chairs. Night had fallen on the Playa; the euphoric neon palette of Burning Man had been replaced by the red, white, and blue of law enforcement. The mutant vehicles and costumed partyers were gone. In their stead lay ambulances and federal agents. Mackenzie's vision was a sea of black FBI jackets.

The Feds had closed off the entirety of the Playa. Now the desert looked less like the epicenter of a festival and more like it did the other fifty weeks a year: a wide, dark, barren sprawl of hard dust.

The FBI had whisked Mackenzie into the back of an ambulance for a medical evaluation. Then they'd put her in the camping chair, draped a blanket over her shoulders, and given her a bottle of water.

Twenty-five minutes had passed. Danner spent them in conversation with a rotating cast of black nylon jackets. Whitaker arrived, phone stuck to his ear.

"You don't have a concussion," Danner said. "But the medics say if you get any headaches, you need to let us know right away."

"What about Stanley?" Mackenzie asked.

"He's going to be all right," Danner said. "But his right leg is fractured."

Mackenzie groaned. "That's my fault."

Danner shrugged. "His choices were a broken leg or a helicopter ride with Kovalev."

Mackenzie paused. "What about Kovalev?"

Danner's voice didn't change. "He's dead."

"And his partner?"

"Broken pelvis, internal bleeding," Danner said. "But you didn't kill anyone." He paused. "The two Burners that ran into Kovalev are doing the worst. The guy in the rabbit costume got airlifted to Reno."

Mackenzie stayed quiet.

"You did very well," said Danner. "Even the stunt with the golf cart. It was insane, but you probably saved Stanley Yoo's life."

Mackenzie stared into the blackness of the Nevada desert. The lights of Black Rock City twinkled in the night, just a half mile away. Suddenly they felt very distant.

"What a fucking mess," she said.

"It was never going to be pretty," Danner said. "Place like this, multiple objectives, short notice. Mess is unavoidable."

Mackenzie turned to look at him. "Where were you? I texted you when I found Yoo. I sent up the flare. But you guys didn't show up. Not until it was almost too late."

Danner leaned forward, dropping his elbows on his knees. "They played us," he said. "They brought a truck in the front gates, plowed right through the check-in structures. Hit the entrance just minutes before the helicopter landed here."

"A diversion," Mackenzie said.

"By the time I got back to the rendezvous point, Kovalev was already chasing Yoo across the desert."

Mackenzie kept her eyes on Danner. "So you saw the chase."

"Some of it, yeah."

"Then why didn't you shoot Kovalev earlier?"

"Couldn't risk it," Danner said. He gestured to the surrounding desert. "Hitting a moving target, at that distance, with a handgun . . .

it's not like the movies. If I missed, my shot would've carried into the rest of the festival. A bullet can travel over a mile. There's no telling where it would've ended up. I had to wait until I was in close enough range."

Mackenzie thought. "What about when Yoo and Kovalev were walking toward the helicopter? They were moving slow. Stanley was hurt."

"Bad angle." Danner grimaced. "I was under the Man statue. Yoo was between me and Kovalev. And then you came up behind them, doing your charge in the golf cart."

"You didn't want to risk the shot."

Danner nodded. "Not until I was certain I'd take him down."

Dedrick Whitaker stood among a tight circle of nylon jackets, phone still to his ear. Then he hung up and the group broke. Several of the agents exchanged smiles or backslaps.

Whitaker spotted Danner and Mackenzie. He paced across the dust toward them, still wearing the long tan overcoat.

"Good news?" Danner asked.

Whitaker nodded. "We got him."

"Got who?" Mackenzie asked.

"Hammersmith," Whitaker said. "He was at a private airfield in Big Sky. Boarding a jet belonging to Dmitri Oberon."

"Oberon?" Danner sounded surprised.

"Am I supposed to know who that is?" Mackenzie asked.

"Executive at the biggest energy company in Russia," Danner said. "Former Russian Security Service. For a long time we've pegged him as one of the leaders of the Ten."

"Our assumption," Whitaker said, "is they were flying Hammersmith to Moscow."

"They knew the net was closing in," Danner said.

Whitaker looked at Mackenzie, expression stern but not unkindly. "You did well," he said, echoing Danner. "Figuring out the Burning Man connection. Tracking Yoo. The golf cart, at the end. It was good work."

"Oh." Mackenzie was surprised by Whitaker's sudden positivity. "Okay?"

Whitaker didn't smile, but he came close. "That was a compliment, Miss Clyde."

Mackenzie managed a tired smile. "Thanks."

Whitaker gave a stiff nod and walked away.

"We've got a long night ahead," Danner said. He gestured to the commotion on the Playa. "We'll set up in Reno for the night. You're welcome to ride with us."

"Thanks," Mackenzie said. "But after the past week, all I want right now is to be alone." She rose from the camping chair, her entire body sore. "I can manage the drive."

Danner nodded. "Whenever you get back to San Francisco, come by the field office. We'll get final statements. Shouldn't take more than a few minutes."

"Will do," Mackenzie said. She felt depleted from the adrenaline crash, and her legs screamed at her for chasing Kovalev across the Playa. One foot in front of the other, she began a slow walk across the Playa.

"See you soon," she said to Danner.

"Get some sleep," he replied.

Mackenzie traversed the Playa and moved through Black Rock City. She passed RVs, yurts, bars, bicycles. She passed hundreds of fanciful costumes and blissed-out revelers.

The beige Hyundai sat serenely in the parking lot, like nothing had transpired in the hours since she'd left it. Mackenzie found the keys and climbed in. She peeled off the flamingo shirt, threw on a hoodie, and started the engine.

She drove out the main gate. Two shipping containers at the entry had been destroyed. A large semitruck rested in the center of the wreckage. She ignored it.

Mackenzie guided the Hyundai along dirt and gravel and exited the desert. She drove an hour on back roads until she reached the bright lights and strip malls of Interstate 80. She merged and headed west.

Mackenzie drove at exactly the speed limit. There was little traffic, and she had plenty of gas.

She didn't stop in Reno. She cruised past the familiar skyline of her childhood and kept driving.

Mackenzie crossed the California border. She followed I-80 as it curled through a series of faceless towns with names like Floriston and Boca, places that were little more than a gas station and an old ski chalet, places that Mackenzie knew she'd never once set foot in, not if she lived a million years.

She took the exit for Highway 89 and followed it south as it snaked past Tahoe's most famous ski resorts. Their buildings were dormant in the summer, the slopes covered with patchy grass, chair-lifts motionless. She kept driving.

Mackenzie slowed as she reached the sleepy outskirts of Tahoe City. She passed grocery stores, chain restaurants, overpriced boutiques. Within a minute she cleared the town and burned south, hugging the western edge of the lake. To her left Lake Tahoe spilled out in the night, dark and empty and everlasting. Mackenzie smiled at the sight. She kept driving.

Exactly three hours after she'd departed Black Rock City, Mackenzie arrived at a small settlement called Tahoe Pines. It was no bigger than Floriston or Boca. There were no boutiques or fast-food joints. Not even a gas station.

All there was in Tahoe Pines was vacation homes. They were scattered among the pines on the western shore of the lake, most owned by families who'd passed them down through generations. Not a fancy place, by any means, but one of the few remaining in the vicinity of Lake Tahoe where a person could be left alone.

Mackenzie turned left off the highway. She drove east, straight for the lake. She didn't look at a map or consult her phone. It had only been a few months. She remembered the way.

She turned south onto a dead-end street. To her left sat a row of lakefront vacation homes. They were on big pieces of land, but the houses themselves were modest. The kind of places that had canoe paddles above the door, snowshoes in the garage, and beat-up charcoal grills on the patio. Lakefront Americana.

It was after midnight. The street was pitch black, the only light coming from the moon reflecting off the surface of the lake.

Mackenzie cruised to the fourth house on her left. She turned in to the driveway and parked the Hyundai next to another vehicle. Then she cut the engine and got out.

The house looked just as she remembered—no smaller or bigger than its neighbors. Detached garage on the left, two-story structure on the right, big pines creating a dense canopy above.

Mackenzie ignored the front door and cut past the garage into the backyard. It was a big open lawn, a hundred feet across, separated from the water by a rocky beachfront. Mackenzie walked across the grass, heading for a wooden dock that extended out into the lake. The mountain air was crisp in the last nights of summer.

Mackenzie reached the dock and stepped onto its faded wooden planks. She focused on the silhouetted figure that waited at the end of the pier, some thirty feet out. The figure faced out toward the water, contemplative and alone.

Mackenzie walked down the dock, her still-dusty sneakers causing the old planks to creak as she moved. The silhouetted figure turned to face Mackenzie as she arrived.

For a moment the two of them stood in the darkness, staring at each other. Then the figure spoke.

"It's over?" Eleanor Eden's voice broke the stillness of the night.

"It's over," Mackenzie said.

"Stanley Yoo?"

"Alive."

"Kovalev?"

"Not."

Eleanor blinked at Mackenzie, features tense. "I think they got Roger."

Mackenzie nodded. "Boarding a jet to Moscow."

Eleanor took a deep breath. "And us?"

"We're clear." Mackenzie could barely believe the words as she said them.

"Nothing?"

"Nothing." Mackenzie shook her head. "I have to give an official statement. But it's just a formality."

Eleanor stared at her in the dark. She smiled. "It's really over."

Mackenzie returned the smile. "I think it really is."

Eleanor made a strange, gasping sound, somewhere between a laugh and a cry. Then she stepped forward and engulfed Mackenzie in a bear hug.

Mackenzie froze for an instant, surprised. But then she laughed and returned Eleanor's embrace.

"Are you laughing," Mackenzie asked, "or crying?"

"I don't fucking know," Eleanor said. And then she made the sound again.

The two women stood together in the night, laughing and crying with relief. And the water of Lake Tahoe lapped quietly around them, deep and ancient and full of secrets.

CHAPTER 42

Two months before Trevor Canon's death

"Nice place," Mackenzie said. "When did you close?"

"Couple weeks ago," Eleanor said. "Come on in."

Mackenzie stepped into the house. It was an old Tahoe cabin, one of thousands like it that dotted the shores of the lake. The inside looked just how Mackenzie had imagined: exposed timbers, over-sized stone fireplace, wooden floors. There was no furniture.

A slight breeze drifted through—Eleanor had opened a set of glass patio doors to let in the summer air. Mackenzie looked through them and saw a backyard lawn and the outline of a dock, both bathed in moonlight.

Eleanor led Mackenzie through a doorway. "We'll talk in the kitchen."

The kitchen was new but already dated. There were light wooden cabinets, a giant range, a farmhouse sink. A trapezoidal island had been squeezed into a space that wasn't big enough for one.

Like the rest of the house the kitchen was empty, save for a bottle of white wine on one of the massive granite countertops. A sleeve of red Solo cups sat next to it, top torn open.

Eleanor gestured to the wine. "Want a glass?"

"Sure."

Eleanor's motions were hurried, her features flat and drawn. Her shoulders were hunched, as though carrying an unseen weight. It took Mackenzie a moment to recognize the emotion, because she'd never seen it from Eleanor before.

Nerves.

She's anxious, Mackenzie thought. Whatever she wants, it's not small.

Eleanor withdrew two red cups, twisted open the screw-top bottle, and poured tall portions of wine. She handed one to Mackenzie and then moved to the far side of the island.

"No chairs yet," Eleanor said. "Afraid we'll have to stand."

"Eleanor, it's me." Mackenzie smiled across the kitchen. "You know I don't care."

"I know." Eleanor looked away, eyes falling to the floor.

Mackenzie took a sip of wine and rested the cup on the island. She found the refrigerator door behind her and leaned against it.

"Okay," Mackenzie said. "Mystery text, I drive three and a half hours, and you're clearly not yourself. What's going on?"

Eleanor took a deep breath, as though preparing a long speech.

"For as long as we've known each other, you've said you want to do something big. Build your own table. Control your own destiny." Eleanor looked up at Mackenzie, meeting her eyes. "I need to know if you were serious about all that."

"If I was serious?"

Eleanor's features were etched with tension. "Yes."

"Of course I was serious," Mackenzie said. "Don't you know that?"

"Yes," Eleanor said again. "But I need to hear you say it. Again."

"Why?"

"I'll explain in a minute."

Mackenzie scoffed. "Isn't that the entire basis of our friendship? No bullshit. No personas. Our real selves."

"Yes," Eleanor said. Her expression was still flat.

"So why do I need to confirm it?"

Eleanor just stared at her, saying nothing.

Mackenzie sighed. "Yes. I want to build my own table, control my own destiny. I want to do something big. You already know that." Mackenzie flipped her palms. "I mean, *shit*, Eleanor. I discovered that Roger built his firm on blood money—and I didn't turn him in. I leveraged it."

Eleanor nodded. "I know. And why did you do that?"

"Why? You already know."

"Humor me."

"I did it because you were right," Mackenzie said. "It was an opportunity. A chance to level up into a better position."

"A chance to get closer to your goal," Eleanor said. "Closer to controlling your own destiny."

"Yes."

"And how has that gone?"

Mackenzie paused. "You mean, how has being Roger's investigator gone?"

"Yes. It's been over four years since you took the position."

"We talk about it all the time."

"Not the nuts and bolts," Eleanor said. "Big picture. Think about the decision you made: leveraging the information instead of turning Roger in. Do you regret it?"

Mackenzie didn't hesitate. "Never."

"You still feel like it was the right move?"

Mackenzie smiled. "The right move isn't always the smart move."

"Touché." Eleanor smiled back. "But I'm serious. Would you do it again?"

"One hundred percent." Mackenzie shifted her stance. "I still spend a lot of time doing bullshit. Chasing down founders who're misbehaving, looking for dirt on rival executives. And there have been . . . other consequences." Mackenzie flexed her right wrist. "But I've gotten personal access to Roger. We've established a relationship."

"Does he trust you?"

"Roger?"

"Yes, Roger Hammersmith. Does he trust you?"

"Yes," Mackenzie said.

"How much?"

Mackenzie shrugged. "Nobody else knows where his money comes from."

Eleanor's eyes lit with intrigue. "Really?"

"Not even his wife," Mackenzie said. "He doesn't have any option but to trust me. It's why he keeps me close."

Eleanor moved off the island. She began pacing in the kitchen.

"Have you ever considered," she said, "that one day Hammersmith might decide the trouble isn't worth it anymore? That trusting you isn't worth the risk? A man of his stature, with that much to lose . . ."

"We're talking about what I think we're talking about."

"Yes."

Mackenzie raised her right arm, hand facing Eleanor. "Did you forget?" she asked.

Mackenzie's wrist had healed in the years since Kovalev's visit, but on occasion her hand still ached with a deep, distinctive soreness, as though the bones and ligaments carried the memory of their trauma.

"Of course not," Eleanor said.

"Then you know I've considered it," Mackenzie said. "I consider it every day."

"You're trapped."

Mackenzie nodded. "I can't leave the job. They'd never let me."

"So let's say you got another opportunity. A much bigger one. The kind that would leverage your relationship with Hammersmith, but also provide you an escape from it. The kind that would set you up— not just for the next few years, but for life."

"The kind I've *really* been waiting for?" Mackenzie asked. "The big one?"

"Yes," Eleanor said. She stopped pacing and looked at Mackenzie. "If you got that opportunity, what would you be willing to do to seize it?"

Mackenzie stared back across the empty kitchen. "You know the answer to that."

"I need to hear you say it. What would you be willing to do?"

It was a question Mackenzie had pondered countless times. And she'd always known the answer, ever since she was a teenager staring up at the bright, tawdry lights of the Christmas tree in downtown Reno.

"Whatever it takes," Mackenzie said.

Eleanor released a long exhale. She reached for her wine and took a big gulp.

"Eleanor," Mackenzie said, "you need to tell me what the hell is going on."

Eleanor kept her cup in her hand. She leaned casually against the island, tension easing from her shoulders. Her anxiety had settled. A course had been chosen.

"Trevor Canon is fucking me over," Eleanor said matter-of-factly. "He's fucking a lot of people over. The entire company. Your boss. Basically everyone but himself."

"How?"

Eleanor paused. "I'm sure you've read about Journy's work on autonomous vehicles."

"Of course," Mackenzie said. "Roger talks about it all the time. It's Journy's next big thing."

Eleanor smirked. "So everyone thinks. In reality the only thing it's been is a money pit."

Eleanor put her cup back on the island. She reclined against the countertop behind her, crossing her arms.

"Trevor's been obsessed with AV since I joined. He's poured billions into AV projects with nothing to show for it. A few years ago I convinced him to bring in Hugo Chamberlain, give AV to him. I thought maybe that would turn things around. But anytime Hugo makes progress, Trevor says it's not big enough. He has a hissy fit and lights the whole thing on fire."

"Sounds like Trevor."

"AV is a marathon, not a sprint. Trevor doesn't have the patience to make it through the first mile."

"Okay," Mackenzie said. "But that can't be surprising. You knew how Trevor was when you took the job."

"I did."

"So what's changed?"

"What's changed is the consequences. He's been so busy immolating cash on AV that he's ignored everything else. Everything important, everything that actually made Journy the rocket ship it was. Our core product, features, the code base, dealing with competitors—all of it. I've tried to keep the trains running on time, but Trevor keeps blowing up the tracks."

Eleanor shook her head, blood rising in her cheeks. "Do you know *how many times* Trevor's completely fucked something up, right after I told him not to? The pattern is always the same. Something comes up. I counsel Trevor on how to deal with it like an adult. He pretends to listen to me, then does the exact opposite of what I advised. Invariably, he makes the situation ten times worse. Then, for the coup de grâce, he sends me out in front of *Blender* to clean up after *his* mistakes. It's *endless.*"

"I know it's been rough," Mackenzie said. "But again—it's been that way for a while. Something's happened, I can tell. What is it?"

Eleanor calmed, closing her eyes. She raised a hand to her forehead. "Eighteen months ago, Journy's numbers flattened out. A year ago, they started to go the wrong direction."

"What do you mean?"

"Growth has stagnated. We're hemorrhaging users."

Mackenzie's mouth dropped open with shock. "What?"

"Our competitors are closing the gap—fast. Especially in our biggest markets."

"But . . ." Mackenzie laughed, incredulous. "That's not possible. Journy's *the* rocket ship. The next Spyder, or StoryBoard."

"Not anymore," Eleanor said. "We're spiraling."

"Jesus Christ." Mackenzie shook her head, struggling to process the ramifications. "But what about the Journy Fund? The five billion from Roger?"

"Trevor blew it."

"What about the seventy-billion valuation?"

"Long gone."

"What about the offices, all the press, the IPO?"

"It's all bullshit. That's what I'm telling you, Mackenzie." Eleanor stared at her, expression somewhere between sad and furious. "Trevor Canon built the golden goose. And then he killed it."

"Holy shit." Mackenzie took a beat, reaching for her cup of wine. She took another long taste, her mind racing. "So what does this mean?"

"I'm getting there next," Eleanor said. "Have you ever heard the name Stanley Yoo?"

Mackenzie frowned. "He's at Journy, right? CTO?"

"In name only," Eleanor said. "He couldn't manage a hamster. But he's the smartest technical mind I've ever met."

"Okay."

"A few years ago we had an executive summit about autonomous vehicles. Big meeting. Budget reset. We were going nowhere, as usual. So I suggested something to Trevor. I told him that we were already behind on AV, so we should skip a level. Take all our resources and pour them into the next thing. The even bigger thing."

"Artificial intelligence," Mackenzie said.

"Yes." Eleanor straightened, took another sip from her glass. "Trevor ignored the idea, of course. But after the meeting, Stanley Yoo approached me. He showed me a side project he'd been working on: an artificial intelligence that he called M1ND."

"Mind?"

"Spelled M-One-N-D. Stanley's work was rough, but it was incredibly promising. Siri and Alexa had come out recently. M1ND far outpaced both of them. It was much more than a digital assistant. It was . . ." Eleanor looked up at the ceiling. "It was one of those moments where I saw something and I just *knew*. This was it. Stanley was onto something even bigger than Journy."

"AI is a big swing. I know Roger's been sniffing around it for the past few years."

"He knows what everyone else knows. AI will be a step-change technology—even bigger than the internet."

"So what happened?"

"Stanley and I joined forces. We worked together for months, fine-tuning M1ND. Then we presented it to Trevor. Our pitch was that M1ND should replace Journy's entire autonomous vehicle program. We'd lost the race for AV, but we could win the race for AI. If developed further, M1ND could power the future of the company."

Eleanor's eyes narrowed, her features falling. "But Trevor dismissed us. He was furious that we'd spent so much time working on M1ND instead of Journy's existing AV program. He called us names. Shut the whole idea down."

"When was this?" Mackenzie asked.

"Six months ago. At the time I was surprised. I've said plenty about Trevor—but he's not stupid. I thought he'd see the obvious potential in M1ND. But I didn't have much choice. Stanley and I parked the idea. With Journy doing so poorly, I had plenty of other fires to put out. But then, a few months ago, Trevor started acting strangely."

"Doesn't he always act strangely?"

Eleanor smiled. "This was different. He grew incredibly paranoid. He began disappearing for long stretches, stopped showing up for meetings. When he was in the office, he withdrew into his little penthouse sanctuary—unusual, for him. And he lost all interest in our autonomous vehicles program. After years of obsession, suddenly Trevor didn't care about it. For me, that was the biggest signal. I began to suspect that something was off. And a few weeks ago, I started to dig around."

Mackenzie leaned against the fridge. "What do you mean by 'dig around'?"

"I hacked Trevor," Eleanor said simply.

Mackenzie raised her eyebrows. "Hacked him?"

"Yes."

"How?"

Eleanor gave a thin smile. "Since joining Journy, I've spent more time with Trevor than any other human being on earth. Much more time than I spent with my ex-wife." Eleanor set her red cup back on the island, recrossing her arms. "I've known Trevor's password for years. He uses the same juvenile one for everything: seventeen."

Mackenzie furrowed her brow. "Like the number?"

"Seventeen is the number of investors that passed on Journy, back when Trevor was first pitching the idea."

"Jesus."

"Trevor holds grudges." Eleanor shrugged. "I started with his Journy account, then his personal email. It didn't take long to unravel what he's been up to." Eleanor's eyes grew cold. "And it's worse than I thought."

Mackenzie felt like an audience watching a play unfold. She stood upright in the center of the kitchen, riveted. "What is it?"

Eleanor's voice sharpened. "Trevor didn't *actually* dismiss the idea for M1ND. He didn't *really* think it was a waste of resources. In fact, he immediately recognized M1ND's potential when we presented it to him. He just didn't want to share it."

Mackenzie felt the pieces falling together. "No."

"Trevor and Stanley have been developing M1ND in secret, on their own. Trevor's decided that Journy is a sinking ship. So he's bailing on it and building a new ship, bigger and better—and just for himself."

"He cut you out of your own idea."

"Yes." Eleanor nodded. "But not just me. The entirety of Journy. All the people who've spent years working for him, catering to his every capricious demand. He's fucking everyone over. The company's already headed in the wrong direction. Once Trevor ditches it and announces his new venture, Journy will be dead in the water."

Mackenzie's mind reeled. She thought of Hammersmith Venture's massive investment into Trevor Canon. She thought of where the money came from.

"If Trevor does this," Mackenzie said, "he won't just fuck over the people who work for him. He'll fuck over his investors, too."

"Very much so."

"Does Roger have a clue about this?"

Eleanor shook her head. "Trevor and Stanley have been very careful. Far as I can tell, nobody's figured out what they're up to. Except for me . . . and Indira Soti."

Mackenzie felt her eyes widen. "Soti?"

"He's bankrolling them. He's funding M1ND."

Mackenzie almost laughed. "Roger is going to absolutely lose his mind."

"I'm banking on it," Eleanor said. "I've wasted *years*, Mackenzie. I've dedicated my entire life to Journy. I've protected the rocket ship and kept it on its trajectory. And now, after ignoring my guidance, sending me out to clean up his messes, dismissing my ideas for saving the company, Trevor's blowing up the whole fucking thing. Not only that, but he has the gall to take *my* idea and use it as an escape hatch, leaving me behind. That's what really pisses me off."

Mackenzie studied her across the kitchen, letting the quiet hang in the air. "So what are you going to do?" Mackenzie let her mind spin. "You could sue Trevor."

"I could."

"Or you could go to the press—publicize what he's been working on."

"I've thought about that, too."

"Or," Mackenzie said, "you could take everything you have on M1ND and give it all to a competitor. Like Spyder."

"I've considered all of those options. But I'm not choosing any of them."

"Then what are you going to do?"

Eleanor's eyes didn't move. She stood rigid as a statue in the kitchen, unblinking, staring at Mackenzie.

"I'm going to kill Trevor," Eleanor said. "And I need your help."

CHAPTER 43

One year after Trevor Canon's death

Senior Special Agent Osiris Jameson Danner, Jr., exited the elevator and moved into the modest lobby. Windows provided a fourteenth-floor view of downtown Chicago and the rolling summer blue of Lake Michigan beyond.

Danner walked to a broad white reception counter. A tall man sat behind it, staring at a monitor. The floors were oak, walls white, furniture bland and contemporary. The lobby could've been anywhere.

Past the counter lay a set of imposing steel doors. The only indicator of the vast riches waiting behind them was a word painted on a nearby wall, the letters thick and off-white.

M1ND

The man behind the desk looked up. "Jameson Danner?" Danner nodded. "Your clearance just came through. Miss Clyde will be out shortly." The man's affect was ex-military. "Have a seat anywhere you like."

Danner chose to stand. He looked up to the ceiling, where security cameras rested in each corner.

Mackenzie watched Danner from a monitor in her office, two hundred and fifty feet away.

Danner looked the same. He wore a dark suit, dark tie, white shirt. His features looked as clean-shaven and angular as ever. Mackenzie even spotted a hint of the Patek Philippe under a sleeve.

Better get this over with, she thought.

Two minutes later she emerged through the steel doors, standing at the lobby threshold. She gave Danner a small smile.

"Agent Danner. Long time no see."

Danner returned the half-smile. "Hello, Mackenzie."

Mackenzie led Danner back into M1ND's headquarters.

The exterior walls were lined with private offices, ten-by-ten cubes with privacy glass walls and clean white furniture. Open standing desks lay throughout the space, surfaces full of Apple gear. Floating staircases led up and down to other floors.

The office was busy but uncrowded. People in T-shirts and jeans moved between conference rooms, huddled over cups of coffee, smiled and said hello to Mackenzie as they passed. Windows were everywhere, suffusing M1ND's headquarters with the bright Chicago morning.

Everything was clean and sedate. No ping-pong tables. No ball pit. No designer sofas in odd shapes. The entire space felt sober, adult.

"Doesn't look much like a tech company," Danner said.

"Thanks," said Mackenzie.

Mackenzie led them to a bank of offices on the far side of the building. Several had unassuming nameplates beside their doors.

"Congratulations, by the way," Danner said. "On the funding."

"Thanks," Mackenzie said again.

"I saw the valuation. Guess it makes you a billionaire."

Mackenzie shrugged. "Guess so."

"I bet Indira Soti wasn't happy."

"His agreement was with Trevor, not Stan. Wasn't anything he could do."

They passed a darkened office, privacy glass clouding its contents. The nameplate read STANLEY YOO, CTO. Mackenzie kept walking.

"Is Yoo here?" Danner asked.

"He's probably in the lab," Mackenzie said. "It's a few floors down."

"How many floors do you have?"

"All of them."

"All of them?"

Mackenzie nodded. "We own the whole tower."

They passed another office, this one occupied. Eleanor Eden sat at a desk, iPhone to her ear. She waved as they passed; Mackenzie returned it. Danner spied the nameplate: ELEANOR EDEN, CO-FOUNDER.

The next office was Mackenzie's. It was a carbon copy of Eleanor's. Plain, modestly furnished. The nameplate contained the same title: MACKENZIE CLYDE, CO-FOUNDER.

Mackenzie closed the door behind Danner, then gestured to two white leather chairs that faced her desk. Danner took a seat.

Mackenzie sat behind her desk. She leaned back in her chair, crossing one leg over the other. She placed her hands in her lap.

Endgame, she thought.

Mackenzie opened. "Congratulations on your promotion."

"Thank you," Danner said. "They gave me my own task force."

Mackenzie and Danner assessed each other. A trickle of tension sparked in the air, settling over the office with a distinctive frisson.

"I hear Roger might not go to trial," Mackenzie said.

"Looks that way. Are you giving a deposition?"

"If they need me."

Danner nodded, as aloof as the day she'd met him. Mackenzie continued. "But the DOJ folks tell me they've got plenty, with or without me."

"They do," Danner said. "Hammersmith's going to prison. Probably for the rest of his life."

Mackenzie stayed quiet.

Danner shifted in his chair. "It's funny, though. Hammersmith's been adamant about one thing: He says he never told Kovalev to kill Canon. He never gave him a badge."

Mackenzie shrugged. "So? Roger's lying."

"He's eating a lot of other charges. Why would he only lie about this one?"

"Because it's murder." Mackenzie smirked. "Roger spent a decade hiding his blood money. He knows how to hide a lie."

"Maybe." Danner waited a beat. "But Hammersmith's denials got me thinking. I began to find other loose ends. Nothing that's going to keep Hammersmith out of prison. But stray threads, here and there."

Mackenzie remained still. "Like what?"

"The neighbor," Danner said. "Who called in to Belvedere police, said she saw a man dumping something on Hammersmith's dock."

"I remember. The laptop and the gun."

"The neighbor's name was Laura Glenellen. She gave local cops her number. Fernandez called it and she confirmed her account over the phone."

"So what's the problem?"

"A few months later, DOJ lawyers went to Glenellen's home to formalize the testimony. When they showed up, Glenellen had no idea what they were talking about."

"What do you mean?"

Danner's eyes were cold. "Glenellen never called Belvedere police. She's never been associated with the phone number Fernandez had for her. And she has no idea who talked to the FBI about Hammersmith's dock."

"Huh." Mackenzie kept her features as impassive as Danner's. Two sphinxes in a staring contest.

"Someone wanted us to search Hammersmith's marina," Danner said. "They used a burner phone to call the local police, impersonating his neighbor. They knew the complaint would go up the chain to the FBI."

"Sounds pretty complicated."

"I agree. It required a lot of forethought."

"Wouldn't this fake tipster know their impersonation would fall apart? Eventually the FBI would talk to the real neighbor."

"They didn't care," Danner said. "By then we'd found the gun and laptop. And we had probable cause to search Hammersmith's property either way, so it's still admissible."

Mackenzie shrugged. "Then I guess it doesn't really matter where the tip came from."

"No," Danner agreed. "But it was another loose end. And then I started thinking about something else."

"What's that?"

"You," Danner said.

"Me?"

"You reported directly to Roger Hammersmith for years." Danner edged forward, eyes steady. "How does someone go from relative anonymity to directly reporting to Hammersmith—and that quickly?"

"I went over that during the investigation."

"You gave me a vague story, ambiguous enough to avoid any details." Danner sniffed. "When the Canon investigation started, I worried you'd be an amateur. But you weren't. You had good instincts. You put together AI and the warehouse. Stanley Yoo and Burning Man."

"I'll take that as a compliment," Mackenzie said.

"Then I remembered something from your background check. Your mother went to prison. Fraud and embezzlement."

"So?"

"The experience must've given you some familiarity with financial crimes. On top of your legal education. And your natural cynicism."

"I'll take that as a compliment, too."

Danner ignored her. "You played it perfectly. When we saw Kovalev on the footage, you gave us the link to Hammersmith right away. And then when Whitaker and I told you about Hammersmith's connections to organized crime, you reacted as I expected. You were shocked. Like it was a stunning revelation."

"It was."

Danner blinked. "I don't think so."

"What are you saying?"

"I think you already knew. I think you knew all along where Hammersmith's money came from. Given everything I just outlined, how could you not? And then I thought about something else: the break-in at your apartment."

Mackenzie remained calm. Danner was gaining steam, unfurling a series of epiphanies that he'd clearly rehearsed.

"The note," Danner said, "left on your window. At the time, I didn't think much about it. I was more focused on the break-in itself. But the note itself was very strange."

Danner lifted a hand, spelling the words in the air. "'We are watching.' *Who* is watching? It implies that whoever left the note was familiar to you. They were confident you'd know who they were."

Danner's eyes sparkled with self-satisfaction. "Then it all came together. You *knew* that Hammersmith's money was dirty. You knew where it came from. And *they knew that you knew*. Kovalev and the Ten weren't just following you to get to Stanley Yoo. They wanted to make sure you didn't get squirrelly and flip to the FBI's side. And they gave you a message to that effect: 'We are watching.'"

Mackenzie said nothing. She locked her eyes onto Danner's, waiting for him to continue.

"Things unraveled from there," Danner said. "You knew Hammersmith was under pressure from the Ten. You knew he needed to salvage the five billion that Trevor Canon wasted. You knew he'd be apoplectic when he learned about M1ND and Indira Soti. You knew Hammersmith would want M1ND for himself. And you knew exactly why he was attaching you to the investigation: to make sure he got to Stanley Yoo before we did."

Danner continued, momentum building. "But during the investigation, you played dumb. Acted like Hammersmith's unwitting pawn. Pretended to be overwhelmed by a murder case, stunned by M1ND and the revelations about your boss. But you knew *all of it*. You played me. You played me, and Whitaker, the entire damn time."

"How could I have possibly known about M1ND, or the warehouse, or Journy's internal numbers?" Mackenzie asked.

"That's the second half of the equation," Danner said. "You weren't the only one acting. You had a co-star. Eleanor Eden."

Danner shifted in his seat. "At the start of the investigation, I was sure that Kovalev killed Canon. But I still had to prove that none of the execs could've done it."

"Their alibis were airtight."

Danner nodded. "So I thought. But thanks to you, there was one alibi that *seemed* stronger than it actually was. Eden's."

"She was at the *Fortune* gala," Mackenzie said. "You saw the photos yourself."

"She was at the gala," Danner said. "But not for the *entire* night. There's a gap where Eden doesn't appear in any photos: 11:09 P.M. to 11:34 P.M. Then I realized: *You* filled that gap. You said you bumped into her in the bathroom line. You obliquely said it was right before last call—letting me put the timing together for myself. Your supposed 'bump-in' with Eleanor was conveniently aligned with the time of Canon's murder. *You* covered the gap in her alibi."

"This is all getting a bit confusing."

Danner leaned forward. "Then let me simplify it. Eden found out about M1ND. She knew about Journy's numbers. She knew Trevor was bailing on Journy to start something new. You, meanwhile, knew about Hammersmith's blood money. You knew about the pressure he was under, how he'd react when he learned about M1ND. So you and Eleanor Eden joined forces. Combined your knowledge and hatched a plan."

Mackenzie tilted her head. "A plan? To do what?"

"You never saw Eden in the bathroom line. Just after 11:09 P.M., Eleanor left the gala. She took a Buggy to Journy HQ, badged in, took the elevator to Canon's office. She shot him, took his laptop, exited the way she came. She drove back to the gala, and returned to the party in time to get photographed at 11:34 P.M."

Mackenzie made a face. "I hope you know how preposterous that sounds."

"It's logical. Eden knew Journy's offices better than anyone. The W Hotel was only a few blocks away. She had a badge and access to Canon's office."

"The gala was in *her* honor."

"It was a big event," Danner said. "Plenty of drinking. People coming and going. By the time anyone noticed, Eden was back."

"She sent you her Journy history. A phantom Buggy ride would've been on there."

Danner smirked. "Eleanor ran the company for years. If anyone could delete their own Journy history, it'd be her."

"You said whoever killed Canon was an expert marksman. It was a perfect shot."

Danner nodded. "Eden mentioned her aunt was a cop. Someone

taught her how to shoot. I did some digging; Eden used to be a regular at a shooting range near San Jose."

Mackenzie maintained a front of complete composure. "Sounds like you've been very busy, Agent Danner."

"I've had plenty of time to think about it."

"Do you realize the gravity of your accusations here?" Mackenzie's voice was calm, her gaze level. "Eleanor's one of the most prominent leaders in corporate America. A bestselling author."

"Exactly," Danner said. "She played me, just like you did. The soccer mom image, the minivan, it's all bullshit. It's cover. The two of you were working together from the very beginning. Before all of this."

Danner gave a wry shake of the head. "You two even *admitted* that you knew each other. It was under my nose the entire time. But you never actually dated—did you?"

Mackenzie answered only in her mind. No.

The fake dating history had been Eleanor's idea. They'd both known it was possible someone would uncover their pre-existing connection. Eleanor had suggested inventing a fling to distract from the truth.

"Believe me," Eleanor had said. "Once we say we dated, no straight man is going to ask for more details. They'll be too uncomfortable to push on it."

"But *I'm* straight," Mackenzie said.

Eleanor blinked at her. "Yeah. So?"

"So I don't like leveraging your sexuality in that way."

"In what way?"

"As the basis of a lie. It feels gross. Exploitative."

Eleanor had laughed aloud. "Mackenzie, in the entire history of civilization, do you think any man, *ever*, has thought twice about leveraging his sexuality?"

And that had been that.

Agent Danner pressed on.

"Eden killed Canon while you filled the hole in her alibi. She took Canon's laptop. She opened it near Yoo's loft, knowing it'd engage the tracking. Then she dumped it with the gun at Hammersmith's marina."

Mackenzie raised her eyebrows in disbelief. "You think Eleanor snuck onto Hammersmith's property?"

Danner shook his head. "She dumped it off a boat. Eden and her ex-wife sailed. It was in her book." Danner placed his hands together in his lap. "Eden dumped the toolbox. Searched online for one of Hammersmith's neighbors. Used the name and address to call in the complaint to Belvedere PD. And led us right to the gun and laptop."

"This sounds awfully complicated."

"It was," Danner said. "It was masterfully planned. Everything accounted for."

"Not everything," Mackenzie said. "Your little theory is still missing something."

"What's that?"

"Motive," Mackenzie said. "Why the hell would Eleanor, or I, go to all the trouble you just outlined? Why would we ever take those kinds of risks?"

"We're sitting in the answer to that." Danner smiled, rotating his head as he opened his palms. "You wanted M1ND for yourselves, just like Hammersmith. And you saw the opportunity to take it."

Danner's eyes hardened. "Kill Canon, and pin it on Hammersmith. He's the perfect fall guy: tons of motive, secret criminal ties. To kick things in motion, you and Eden make sure that Hammersmith learns about Canon's secret side project."

Mackenzie interjected. "You think *we* told Roger about M1ND?"

"You knew exactly how furious he and the Ten would be. So you leak him the info. Hammersmith and the Ten find out, and off you go.

"Now you have cover," Danner continued. "Canon's dead. The dead money clause is great for you: It creates even more distraction to hide behind. You and Eden don't care about the shares—all you need to take M1ND for yourself is Stanley Yoo. Eden encourages the FBI to take jurisdiction and offers herself as liaison."

Danner's voice was growing more animated as he spoke. "Now you and Eden are in perfect position. Your role was the naïve amateur, in over her head." Danner pressed his lips together. "And I'll admit, you played it well. You knew we wouldn't trust you. So you reported the break-in at your apartment. Then said you recognized

Kovalev. You never actually saw him at Hammersmith's offices, did you?"

No, Mackenzie thought, flexing her fingers in her lap. Not at the offices.

Danner continued. "Meanwhile Eden continues with her soccer mom act. You both pretend to be shocked as the investigation uncovers all the things you already knew. And you watch as Hammersmith and the Ten fall into our crosshairs."

Mackenzie kept her eyes fixed on Danner. She breathed deeply through her nostrils, cooling her blood.

One wrong word—just one—could be death.

"I risked my life," Mackenzie said. "At Burning Man. I put *myself* in the crosshairs, trying to get Stanley Yoo out of there."

"Yes," Danner said. "Because you needed Stanley Yoo. He was your key to M1ND. Without him, killing Canon would've been worthless. And, just as important, you needed Kovalev to die. You were waiting for us to kill him, because he was your fall guy as the triggerman on Trevor Canon. If he stayed alive, denied everything, even gave an alibi . . . Your whole plan would've unraveled.

"But with Kovalev dead," Danner continued, "everything fell into place. He gets pinned with the murder. Hammersmith goes down for the conspiracy. And you and Eden are free to combine forces with Stanley Yoo, taking M1ND for yourselves."

Danner smoothed his tie, aping Whitaker. The Patek glinted under a cuff. "Are you familiar with matryoshka dolls?"

"The wooden nesting dolls? One figure inside the other?"

Danner nodded. "They're Russian, appropriately. From the start, this case has been a series of nesting dolls."

Danner cupped his hands, as though holding a basketball. "On the outside is the biggest doll. Trevor Canon, CEO of the hottest startup in the world, is murdered. One of his own executives killed him, not knowing about the dead money clause in his will. Everyone has an alibi except Stanley Yoo—and he's disappeared."

Danner moved his hands sideways, tightening them. "But the investigation reveals another layer—a smaller doll hidden inside the first one. Journy is going down the tubes. Roger Hammersmith is crooked. He and his criminal funders are pissed that Canon's built a life raft with Indira Soti. They kill Canon, then plan to capture Stanley Yoo and take the tech for themselves. And Hammersmith attaches his own investigator to make sure it all goes as planned. That's the doll with the DOJ right now."

Danner moved his hands sideways again, tightening them further. He kept his eyes on Mackenzie. "But there was still a third layer to the case: you and Eden. Combined, you know everything. Hammersmith's blood money, the real state of Journy, M1ND. You use the other dolls to hide yours. You kill Canon, pin it on Hammersmith. You make sure Yoo survives and Kovalev doesn't. You take M1ND. And now, one year later, here you are: billionaires."

Danner leaned back in his seat, pursing his lips. His voice adopted a reflective tone. "You and Eden have manipulated this entire thing from the very start. It's been the two of you, all along. You used me. You used the FBI. And you did it right under our nose."

Mackenzie didn't reply. She stared at Danner and waited, letting a thick silence build between them. She let it grow until it became obvious, lingering in the air. Seconds turned to a minute; she said nothing. She sat in her chair, features calm. She waited for Danner to squirm in his chair.

Then she spoke.

"Are you done?" Mackenzie said.

"Am I done?" Danner replied.

"Is that it?"

"What do you mean, is that it?"

"Is that all you've got?"

Danner frowned. "I just laid out the entire case. You and Eden killed Trevor Canon. You heard me."

Mackenzie leaned forward, shaking her head. "That's not what I heard," she said. "I heard the ravings of a disturbed FBI agent. He's conjuring up accusations and smearing the reputations of two women who survived a harrowing ordeal. That's what I heard."

The placid, frozen lake of Danner's features began to crack. "You're bluffing."

"Are you here to charge me with anything?" Mackenzie asked. "Are you going to read me my rights, cuff me, walk me out the door?"

Danner hesitated. He began to speak, then stopped.

"That's what I thought." Mackenzie paused, looking up at the ceiling. "What did Whitaker say, during one of his little lectures?" She dropped her eyes. "You don't deal in suspicions, he said. You deal in evidence. Proof. And as entertaining as your little story was, you can't prove a fucking word of it. So that's all it is: a story."

"I'm right," Danner said. "About all of it. You know it and I know it."

"I'll tell you what I know," Mackenzie said. "You and Whitaker used *me*—not the other way around. The day we met, you treated me like I was radioactive. Then the very next day you went all warm and fuzzy. You even apologized. Why? Because you and your bosses realized that I wasn't a pain in the ass—I was an opportunity. You *used* me as a conduit to Hammersmith. It's why you kept asking me about him. It's why when Hammersmith called, you encouraged me to answer—in front of you. Meanwhile, you told me nothing about what was really going on."

"We didn't trust you," Danner said. "And we were right not to."

"Bullshit," Mackenzie said. "It wasn't about trust. It was about your case. You used me as *bait*. I heard you and Whitaker at Roger's marina. To get Roger, you needed to flush him and Kovalev out of the shadows. Catch them in the act. So you kept me in the dark.

"Agent Eagerly wasn't protecting me. You just wanted him there in case Roger or Kovalev made a move on me. I was bait. And you wanted to know the *instant* you had a fish on the reel."

Danner curled a lip. "I know what you're doing. It's not going to work."

Mackenzie ignored him. "Then you used me as bait one more time. You saved the best for last: Burning Man."

"*You* chose to go to Burning Man," Danner said. "Going in alone was *your* plan."

Mackenzie shook her head. "I figured out Stan was at Burning Man. I knew I could find him there. But everything from that point forward was *your* plan. And it made zero fucking sense.

"You didn't need to engineer a shoot-out with Kovalev. You had plenty to arrest him for Canon's murder. You could've just grabbed Stanley, used his testimony. But you wanted Hammersmith. Whitaker even said it himself: 'We need a direct link between Hammer-smith and the violence.'"

Danner, for once, remained silent.

"You wanted proof of conspiracy. So you used me, and Stan, as the bait. I text Hammersmith a location, Kovalev shows up right after. In the *Hammer Angel,* no less. Boom: conspiracy."

Mackenzie smirked. "But that wasn't enough for you. You wanted to catch Kovalev in the act of a violent crime. So you watched him chase Yoo across the Playa, leaving bodies in his wake. You saw it all unfold. You sat there, and you *waited.*"

"I didn't have a—" Danner's voice cracked, mid-lie. "I didn't have a clean shot."

"Bullshit," Mackenzie said again. "You were just waiting. You needed Kovalev to use his gun, show full intent to kill. Once he aimed at me, *then,* finally, your case was made. Roger to Kovalev to violence. Everything your heart desired." Mackenzie stared daggers at Danner across the desk. "You want me to thank you for shooting the shark? *You* put me between his jaws."

"That's not fair."

Mackenzie made a face. "Whitaker said it himself: You weren't looking to arrest Roger. You wanted to take him down. But before all this, what did you actually have on him? Financial crimes. Paper-work. Bank records."

Mackenzie scoffed, leaning back in her chair. "There's not a single U.S. attorney who'd touch that case. You'd have a jury full of glazed eyes. Roger would bring in a battleship of Manhattan lawyers and they'd suffocate you with motions. At most, he'd serve eighteen months in a federal summer camp."

Mackenzie raised a finger in the air. "But a *shoot-out?* Guns, bod-ies, blood, *and* tons of witnesses? Now *that's* a case. That gets a jury's attention. And for a guy with Hammersmith's resources, that's what you needed to take him down."

Danner's lips were tight, shoulders tensed in his chair. "You and Eleanor Eden killed Trevor Canon. I know the truth. We both do."

Mackenzie straightened in her chair. "Here's what really pisses me off, Danner. You never cared about the truth. You weren't motivated by justice. You wanted to take down Hammersmith because you wanted the *prize*. You wanted a big old buck to mount on your wall so you can show everyone at the DOJ that you're more than just Ozzie Danner's son." Mackenzie leaned forward, placing her hands on her desk. "You wanted to get out of your daddy's shadow—and you didn't care if I had to die in the process."

Mackenzie pushed her chair back and stood, unfolding to the full measure of her height.

"As I see it, you've got three options. One, try to charge me with something, in which case I'll call my lawyer. Two, sit there and keep spewing bullshit, in which case I'll call security. Or three, you can stand up and get the hell out of here."

The moment hung in the air. Danner took his time, wishing to conserve his last measure of pride. But he did what Mackenzie knew he'd do: He stood. He smoothed his tie, re-buttoned his jacket, and tucked the Patek Philippe under his sleeve.

Mackenzie moved around the desk and opened the door. Danner's eyes followed her, burning with frustration. She moved into the hallway and held out an arm, beckoning Danner to follow.

She walked him out the way they came in. They paced in silence, each staring straight ahead, jaws shut.

Mackenzie pushed through the steel doors and led Danner across the lobby to the elevator. She pressed the call button. The doors opened.

Danner stepped into the elevator car, then turned to face her. The anger had fled his eyes, replaced by the cold, familiar reptilian flatness. They faced each other across the threshold.

"You don't really think you're going to get away with this," Danner said.

Mackenzie smiled. "This is America, Agent Danner. People get away with murder every day."

The doors closed. Mackenzie turned and walked away, the smile still traced on her lips.

In her experience, there were exactly three ways of dealing with a rich asshole.

The first way?

Flattery.
The second way?
Verbal blunt force trauma.
The third way?
Kill 'em.

ACKNOWLEDGMENTS

Stephen King once wrote, "Life isn't a support system for art. It's the other way around." I needed no reminder of this while writing *Dead Money*—I began the process when my wife and I had two children under the age of two. Meghan, this book simply wouldn't exist without your endless support, encouragement, and patience. Thank you for always indulging my long-winded rambles and for helping me create the space to finish *Dead Money*. Most of all, thank you for believing in me. I couldn't have written a single word without you. I love you. And Teddy and Sam—please don't read *Dead Money* until at least the year 2036.

My heartfelt thanks go to Liz Parker, Noah Ballard, Jake Dillman, Emma Kapson, and the peerless agents at Verve Talent. Special thanks to Liz, my literary agent: You were the first to see something in my writing that I wasn't always sure I could see myself. Thank you for your advocacy, your keen eye, and your faith in my work. Noah and Jake, thank you for your guidance as I navigated a new world.

On the publishing side, I am deeply appreciative of Julian Pavia, Caroline Weishuhn, and the entire team at Ballantine Bantam Dell and Penguin Random House. Julian, you understood *Dead Money* with a level of precision and depth that I found both astonishing and incredibly gratifying. Your candor, incisiveness, and levity has made *Dead Money* the best book it could be. Thank you. My thanks also go to Ted Allen for being our production editor and to Madeline Hopkins for the diligent copy edits; Will Staehle and Carlos Beltran for our beautiful cover and Alexis Flynn for the interior design; Kathleen Quinlan and Katie Horne for their hard work on the marketing and publicity front; and of course to Kara Cesare, Jennifer Hershey, Kim Hovey, and Kara Welsh for their all-around publishing prowess.

I owe a great debt to all my earliest readers. The Ten Mile Book Club: Christopher Rivers, Jenny Holland, Jeanne Messmer, Mary Lou Lee. The T.O.B.: Beth Hoggard, Lauren Yauch, Sarah Cantrell. Marc McCabe and Aoife Anderson, who compelled me to get back to the page when I was dragging my feet. Maggie Carr, who has impeccable taste. The BN readers: Kyle Pickering and Dave O'Neill. Joanna Powell, Sarah Campbell, and Ashley Maliken, who tore through *Dead Money* at an alarming (and flattering) speed. The Portland Originals: Jon Murray, Frank Ford, Sally Ford. Garrett Parks, who (wardrobe notwithstanding) isn't as stuffy as the Big Law firm I named for him. Jennifer Williams and especially Justin Cheung, who has always been among my biggest champions. Ryan and Hanna Nordvik, who somehow managed to provide excellent feedback while raising twins, and Colin Isler, who carved out time to read while raising three young daughters. Eric Weitz and Taylor Sbicca, who by this point have suffered through nearly half a million of my words. My old Seattle crew, including Amanda Raphael, Aaron Booy, Noel Pelland, Ryan Leaman, and Liz Faulkner. And my Comms Bombers, including Nick Papas, Kim Rubey, and Courtney O'Donnell: My inbox is now a happier (but arguably less interesting) place.

Thank you to the other writers and creative folks who have provided me with wise counsel, including Bonnie Garmus, Annie Hartnett, Anna Winger, Laurie Gelman, Eli Saslow, and Marc Adelman.

A special thank-you to John Newman, who was among the first to encourage me to write a novel and to take inspiration from my own life experience.

To my family. Two people who I wish could be here to read *Dead Money:* Doug Davis, still among the funniest people I've ever met; and Marianne Dworkin, still among the cleverest people I've ever met. To Marian Kerr, for a lifetime of grammatical corrections that (hopefully) made their way into my prose, and to Bill Kerr, for maintaining that the overlong sci-fi epic I once wrote is actually not that terrible. My sister, Ariel, for her own creative spark and shared sense of humor. And Nancy and Paul Rivers, for their grace, their steadfast support, and the many mountains they move on behalf of our family.

And, finally, to my parents, Lisa and Bruce, who have read everything I've ever written. You've always nurtured my attempts at creativity, and you allowed me to spend my childhood with my face buried in a succession of chapter books—even while dining out at restaurants or on family vacations. The act of writing a novel can be painful; it is easy to become overwhelmed by self-doubt and insecurity. Your lifetime of love and support gave me the courage to overcome those hurdles and put pen to page. Thank you.

ABOUT THE AUTHOR

JAKOB KERR is a lawyer and communications executive in the tech industry. He was one of the first employees at Airbnb and spent a decade shepherding the company from tiny startup to global phenomenon. Jakob has also been a bartender, sportswriter, and—for one disastrous afternoon—the driver of an ice-cream truck. After fifteen years in San Francisco, he recently returned to his native Pacific Northwest, where he now lives with his wife and children. *Dead Money* is his first novel.

jakobkerr.com